SHINGLE
STREET

SHINGLE STREET

a novel by
James Hayward

CD41 PUBLISHING

This edition first published in 2002 by CD41 Publishing

CD41 Publishing Ltd
1 Spinney Close
Beetley
Dereham
Norfolk NR20 4TB
United Kingdom

jnice@ltmpub.freeserve.co.uk
www.ltmpub.freeserve.co.uk/cd41home.html

A CIP record for this book is available from the British Library

ISBN 0-9540549-1-1

Typeset in Times New Roman
Printed in Great Britain by Barnwell's of Aylsham
CD41 logo by Just Wizard

Cover photography by Paul Lewis Isemonger
Thanks to the Second Battle Group and
Vickers Machine Gun Society

JUNE 1940

ONE

Jack Brinkley, auxiliary coastguard, arthritic at fifty-two, had never much cared for gardening. Now, in wartime, by starlight, he cared for it even less.

As he stood upright Brinkley flinched at a stab of pain in his back, then squinted at his small back garden in the thin silver light. So far his amateur contribution to the Grow More Food campaign had yielded disappointing results. Where once his wife's bedding plants had filled the borders, beetroot and parsnips now grew, but with little of the urgency demanded by total war. Brinkley thought about lighting up a cigarette, but then remembered that he had none left. Then he swore beneath his breath. Now that he thought about it, he was certain he had sowed several rows twice over during the past hour, some with different seeds.

Still, unlike the other villagers, he had at least been able to lift his most recent crop, and keep an eye on his cottage. For already looting had started: three tame rabbits gone from his hutches, seven and a half pounds of unrationed meat snatched from his larder in one fell swoop. And windows had been broken, and locks forced on the fisherman's cottage next door.

The village of Shingle Street stood in the middle of Hollesley Bay, on the Suffolk coast a dozen miles east of Woodbridge. Five days previously every man, woman and child - fifty or so people, all told - had been ordered to evacuate their homes on forty-eight hours' notice. It was, according to a bowler-hatted lackey of the Regional Commissioner, their civic duty to relocate for the duration of the national emergency. With only one lorry to assist in the hurried exodus, many of his neighbours had been forced to leave with little more than they could carry, leaving behind a profusion of odd chattels and furniture. But now only the four coastguards were allowed to return to the empty fishing village to complete long watches. And the army, of course. *Three rabbits, they'd had away...*

In truth, the abrupt departure had not upset Brinkley unduly. For there was now an abundance of beach mines beyond the straggling line of shacks and bungalows, and a powerful demolition charge hidden beneath the bridge on the single road that lead inland to Hollesley. True, he didn't think much of the six shillings a week he paid as rent for his new lodgings. But following Dunkirk and the collapse of France, Hitler's jack-booted bullyboys were expected any day, straining to tear through East Anglia to London like a pack of mad dogs. And John Brinkley did not care to see his wife and child caught in their jaws.

'Digging for victory, mate?'

Brinkley started, and raised his garden fork like a pikestaff. The voice was jeering, cockney-tinged. Although its owner was hidden behind the privy shed, he knew the voice belonged to one of the soldiers who patrolled the beach nightly from Shingle Street to Bawdsey, two miles to the south. Several dozen from a battalion of untrained Territorials were housed under canvas on the heath inland, and comprised, so it seemed, of nothing but spivs, townies and Brylcreem Boys. Not, as he was forced to admit, it had been much different in his day.

'I'd have a squint through my telescope if I were you, mate,' the voice continued. 'The Bismark could slip past while you're topping turnips back here.'

The joke roused an obsequious chuckle from a second invisible squaddie. Despite himself, Brinkley felt his temper stir.

'I tend my garden in my own time.'

'You should get out more. Chase up some nuns and Quislings with the Look, Duck and Vanish brigade.'

'Shut it, Ward.'

Brinkley guessed it was a sergeant. But his bark sounded tired, and lacked conviction.

'All I meant was, it takes more than a pound of carrots to stop a panzer in its tracks.'

'I said, shut it.'

The patrol was moving away now, the sound of their hobnailed boots heavy on the hard ground parched by the indian summer.

7

'Sack 'o bastards,' Brinkley muttered below his breath. For all he cared the whole lot of them might tread on a mine and be blown to kingdom come. *Three good rabbits, those buggers had away.* For a moment he remembered the taste of the pig his platoon had shot on the road up to the Scarpe in 1918. Then, wincing at another sharp twinge in his back, Jack Brinkley returned his fork to the stubborn soil and turned another sod.

A mile to the south, the sentry listened as the tide worried the shingle and shivered in the feint sea breeze. Corporal Peter Weidenmann glanced at the illuminated dial on his rubberised watch: two-seventeen. The section had been ashore for just over an hour. According to the technician who had briefed them twelve hours earlier, the target, a decimeter telegraphy station, was capable of tracking aircraft by means of electronic echoes and radio waves. Lieutenant Wagner and the others must certainly have scouted it by now, and begun their return journey. Assuming, of course, they had not come unstuck.

Weidenmann swallowed hard at the thought of capture. Like the rest of the eight men who made up the reconnaissance party, he wore British issue khaki battledress, British pattern webbing and a round steel 'battle bowler', as the Tommies called their helmets. Yet his uniform bore no rank or unit insignia, while his weapon was unknown in any British armoury, an Erma sub-machine gun fitted with a stout silencer. For Weidenmann belonged to Bau-Lehr Battalion zbV 800, and had sworn allegiance not to the King but to Adolf Hitler. And like every other member of the elite special operations unit known as Brandenburg, he knew full well that capture by the enemy meant swift and certain execution as a spy.

Weidenmann glanced at his watch once more. Soon the tide would be turning. With or without Leutnant Wagner, in less than thirty minutes he and Schrek would have to haul the rubber boats back down to the shill salt water and slip quietly away. He cursed impatiently beneath his breath, then returned his eyes to the crude night-vision scope, which bathed the raised shore ridge between his position and Shingle Street in sickly green luminescence.

Empty since April, the windows of the old Lifeboat Inn had been boarded over, and the seaward veranda purloined for firewood. On the door a hastily-painted sign announced to no-one in particular: CLOSED FOR THE DURATION. Beyond the pub could be discerned the squat outline of a Martello Tower, built to repel Napoleon's armies more than a century before.

It was here that the Territorial patrol paused before pressing on to Bawdsey. In between the two points there was nothing but two unbroken miles of silence and darkness, and the shimmering, silver-black vastness of the cold North Sea, at constant odds with the banked pebble shore. With the exception of Sergeant King, for each of the men it was their first night patrol, and although none cared to admit it, the experience was profoundly unsettling. Invasion, whether by sea or by air, was expected during the hours of darkness, and as possibility turned to probability the period had become one of increasing tension.

'Do you reckon he'll come, sarge?' The speaker was Ramsey, a callow and impressionable youth of eighteen.

Sergeant Leslie King inhaled sagely as he marshalled an answer. King had served through the Great War in the trenches of Flanders, and fondly imagined that the likes of Ramsey, at least, held him in no little awe.

Private Bernard Ward beat him to it. 'If Jerry kicks off round here, mate, he'll be shit through a goose. Do you know what those blue-jobs up at the Manor have got to protect their secret bloody wireless station? Five revolvers, two dozen rifles and a slit trench. Oh, and as of today an antique naval gun that Nelson would've laughed at.'

'Give your tongue a rest,' growled King.

Ward ignored him. 'Those Liverpool Scottish lads on the beach are no better off.'

King released a hacking cough. 'That's right, son, poison their minds with alarm and despondency. I'll wager the minute Jerry lands you'll be down here hawking bloody bath-towels and maps.'

'Not until they've lifted them mines,' Ward snorted. 'Bleedin' lethal, they are. Ask those poor sods from the Royal Engineers who's laying 'em. Another one rolled a seven yesterday. His mates are still picking up the pieces.'

Recognising his cue, Private Hollis offered an obsequious laugh.

King squared on Ward in the dim moonlight. 'You're a nasty bit of work, lad. I don't mind saying it - I hope you cop one when the brown stuff hits the fan.'

'What's that, sarge? A shitzkreig?'

'Very bloody funny, I'm sure. You'll be laughing on the other side of your face at the enquiry tomorrow. Don't go thinking the boss doesn't know who took off with the battalion cash box.'

'Now, now,' Ward replied, a cool edge to his insubordination now. 'That's slander. Best not say anything you might regret. Like you said, loose talk can cost a man dear.'

'I'll give you bloody slander, boy. If Archie Fowler loses his stripes because of your petty thieving, you'll rue the day you were born.'

'I don't know nothing about it,' Ward replied evenly. 'Fifth Columnists, if you ask me.'

'Yeah,' snickered Hollis. 'Dressed up as nuns.'

'It's the colonel who'll be doing all the asking tomorrow. Mark my words, Ward - you reap what you sow.'

Ward spat on the ground at the sergeant's feet. Despite the privilege of rank, King did not rise to the challenge. Bernard Ward might be little more than a Medway razor-boy, but no thanks to the Colonel he wielded considerable power within the battalion. No bloody thanks at all.

'Permission to smoke, Sergeant?' Ward asked facetiously.

'Piss off,' hissed King.

A moment later the match flared, and flickered for perhaps three seconds. Three seconds in which the distant pinprick of light bloomed bright green in Feldwebel Weidenmann's scope a mile to the south.

Several minutes later, Weidenmann was able to pick out the Wessex patrol on the shore ridge. Four men, moving slowly. In another ten they would be on top of his position. Even if the Tommies were blind, and missed both of the Brandenburg sentries, and their rubber boats, there was every chance they would run into Wagner's group on their way back from the DeTe station. True, in the night all cats were grey, and each one of the men with Wagner spoke English well enough to stand an even chance of passing a challenge. It was, after all, their principal qualification for service in Brandenburg.

But the risk was too great. Schrek, his partner, was keeping watch towards Bawdsey. Weidenmann kicked lightly at his heel, then rolled aside to allow Schrek a view through the scope. Following a whispered counsel of war, the two men slid part way down the bank below the ridge and readied their weapons.

Long minutes crawled by on all fours, silent only for the faint wash of the shingle, and, for each man, the din of his own heartbeat and breathing.

A harsh, hacking cough cut through the quiet. Then four figures in dim silhouette against the night sky.

At a distance of three metres the two Brandenburg men opened fire, moving the muzzles of their weapons in a narrow arc. The soft hiss of the silenced bullets as they cut through the air was drowned by the rapid hammering of the steel bolt and the impact of the rounds. Amidst this eerie sound two of the four Wessex men, King and Ramsey, died instantly, uttering harsh sighs as they fell to the ground in a dull clatter of equipment. Mortally wounded, Hollis expired several moments later when Weidenmann scrambled up onto the path and fired a single round into the centre of his face, before moving on to deliver the same coup de grace to each of the prone figures.

They were, Weidenmann reflected, easier to kill than Polacks. He had raised his Erma above the fourth and final Tommy and squeezed the trigger when the gun chose to jam. Beneath him Ward groaned pitifully, his right shoulderblade shattered, a gaping hole punched through his thigh. Weidenmann cleared his weapon methodically and again took aim, then started angrily as a hand slapped the muzzle aside.

'Spare him. He's more use alive, if the poor bastard survives.'

The voice belonged to Lieutenant Wagner. Unheard and unseen, his party had returned.

'Bad habit, smoking,' mused Weidenmann.

'Come again?'

'Private joke, Herr Leutnant.'

Ward groaned again, this time louder. Wagner stepped forward and wrenched off his steel helmet, then struck the wounded Tommy hard across the temple.

Once more silence fell.

In the cramped downstairs kitchen of the coastguard station, by flickering candlelight, John Brinkley poured two large mugs of strong tea. To his own he added a generous measure of condensed milk, already a rare treat with the advent of rationing. As he climbed the stairs to take over the watch, Brinkley wrestled with the idea of cultivating other idle gardens in the village, for all were beginning to run wild. Or would that weasel from the Commissioner's office have him up before the magistrate on a charge of trespass? No, that would not do. And yet, if he asked permission of his erstwhile neighbours, they were sure to demand a portion of the fruits of his toil.

In the unlit observation room on the upper floor Dick Hinsley sat facing the dark expanse of the sea, a pair of powerful naval binoculars on the broad sill before him. Brinkley set down the mug beside them.

'Much of anything?' he asked.

'Some flares over the Ness,' the other replied, yawning extravagantly. 'Elseways quiet as.'

Although the war was not yet a year old, it was already standard operational procedure within Brandenburg to name each detachment after the officer commanding a particular mission. At two-forty the last of the ten-man reconnaissance team known as Gruppe Wagner clambered into their rubber boats and paddled silently away from the enemy coast. A quarter-hour later, half a mile from the shore, they fired the baffled engines and pulled away towards their rendezvous with the motor torpedo boat that would return them to the Dutch port of Den Helder.

Following standing orders, Gruppe Wagner left no trace behind them. The three corpses would go over the side halfway to Holland. The wounded man too, unless by some small miracle he continued to breathe.

TWO

The twin barrels of the twelve-bore shotgun hovered two feet from his temple. Captain John Goodman had served with the BEF in France, and had almost lost a leg for his trouble. Now he found a perverse irony in the fact that death might take him on a glorious summer day on the main street of a sleepy Suffolk village.

There had already been reports in the papers of motorists shot dead by zealous Local Defence Volunteers at similar roadblocks. The one protecting Bromeswell from spies and saboteurs was fashioned from a haycart drawn across the middle of the road, with a large Suffolk Punch harnessed patiently in its traps. Two of the three home guards who manned the barricade were rustic-looking specimens in caps and gaiters, and between them boasted the twelve-bore and a rook-rifle. The third, a gangly teenager in wellington boots, sported a sickle stuck into his belt, pirate-fashion, and clutched a brown paper bag tied with string. With an uncomfortable mixture of alarm and disbelief, Goodman realised that the youth, who was no more than a schoolboy, hoped to see off the Nazi horde with a bag of pepper. His best hope, Goodman reflected, was that the enemy would die laughing.

One of the elderly LDVs poured over Goodman's papers in an elaborate display of feigned expertise. 'Military Police, you say?'

'That's right,' replied Goodman, trying to avoid focusing on the business end of the shotgun. 'Look, I know you're simply doing your duty. But I'd be a lot more appreciative if you did it with the safety catch on.'

The gunman ignored him.

'I thought you lot was supposed to wear a red band on your caps,' the other continued, glancing back at his comrade-in-arms and drawing a sage nod of approval.

'And you've noticed green covers on ours.'

'S'roight.'

In four years at the Bar, Goodman had encountered his share of stubborn, ignorant old men, most of them judges. He was glad now that his patience was a deep well. 'We're Field Security Police. It's a separate unit. No doubt you've concluded that this is just the sort of elementary error a pair of enemy parachutists masquerading as British military policemen would make.'

'S'roight,' the man repeated. 'Just like I'm wondering what you two's doing with a civilian vehicle.'

'There's a war on, chum,' snapped Goodman's driver, Sergeant Kydd.'Not enough tanks to go around.'

The old man held Kydd's gaze as a mutual hostility took root.

'Look,' tried Goodman, 'we've driven up from London, and lost our way. Colonel Millward-Oliver of the Wessex Regiment is expecting us at Iken Hall. You could telephone him to confirm our credentials.'

'I might at that,' replied the man, refolding Goodman's papers leisurely, but not returning them. 'But it so happens the only telephone round here's up at the post office.'

'I'm sure one of you could risk it.'

The man shook his head.

'Look,' Goodman said impatiently. 'I'll even stand you the change.'

'Early closing today. The post office shut at half past twelve.'

Now the man with the shotgun joined in. 'Odd thing I reckon, an officer not knowing that.'

In a tree nearby a rook cawed, as if in mockery. For Goodman and Kydd the morning had been taxing to the power of ten. Following the harvesting of every signpost and milestone between Land's End and John O'Groats, the journey through Suffolk had been damn near impossible. Then there was the small matter of the decrepit, gear-stripped Austin issued to his section by the depot a fortnight before. The smirk worn by the pool officer had betrayed that the car was in some small way a revenge on his intellectual cousins in Field Security, who prior to Dunkirk had enjoyed, and frequently abused, first call on the best equipment issued to the Corps of Military Police.

His patience already worn perilously thin, Goodman considered drawing the revolver resting on his hip. A moment later, however, what promised to become an ugly situation was diffused by the arrival of a rotund figure on a motorcycle, whose askew tuning and blue exhaust belied a tank full of paraffin and mothballs. As the rider braked to a halt beside the car, the three LDVs lowered their weapons and stood respectfully aside.

After removing his leather flying helmet, a manoeuvre which involved no little theatre, the rider introduced himself. 'Major Bullingdon, commander of the local LDV. Retired, of course. I dare say you're thinking I've trained my men too well.'

'Something like that,' Goodman replied coolly.

The major glanced at Goodman's papers, then returned them, and gestured at his men to stand back. 'Stout fellows,' he whispered conspiratorially, 'but of rustic mind. Where are you headed?'

'Iken Hall.'

'Called in the professionals, have they? This business about the missing cash box, I presume.'

'You know more than I do.'

As he spoke, Goodman felt his anger subside. It could hardly be worse than his last field investigation, after all, wherein a vicar's daughter had reported as suspicious a young lieutenant who habitually failed to flush the lavatory at his genteel rectory billet. Only a German could conceive such an outrage, so reckoned the girl.

'Need an escort? You won't find the Hall on your own.'

'That would be kind.'

The major gunned his engine and produced a cloud of noxious blue smoke. Scowling darkly still, the LDVs coaxed the old horse forward to clear the road.

They drove for ten minutes. Iken Hall was a handsome eighteenth century house built in red brick, situated amidst formerly pristine lawns now scarred with air-raid trenches and khaki tentage. Since the first week in June the Hall had been home to the 1st/4th Wessex, a Territorial infantry battalion raised largely in East Kent. Outside the octagonal gatehouse, lately commandeered as a luxury guardroom, a sentry hurriedly concealed a cigarette as Major Bullingdon lead Kydd into the sweeping drive, pleasingly lined with flowering rhododendron bushes. As they approached the Hall itself Goodman spied an unusually large number of civilian cars parked on the forecourt, together with two buses. The latter, resplendent in bright red paint, still bore the gold leaf livery of the Foreland Omnibus Company, and for a brief, ridiculous moment Goodman wondered if the unit was holding an open day.

'Nice target for a Heinkel,' sniffed Kydd. 'Bloody liberty, really. Two hundred miles for a lousy cash box.'

'I should have thought petty larceny was right up your street, being an experienced Yard detective.'

Kydd tutted reprovingly as he applied the brakes. 'Hardly, sir. On the robbery squad we never pulled on our boots for anything less than a safe. Makes me wonder what you've done to upset Colonel Luther this time.'

'Nothing I know of. Apparently Millward-Oliver and the Devil go back to Wipers together.'

In truth, Goodman wondered himself. As security liaison officer at GHQ, he was almost important. Even within the boundaries of W6 his duties hardly included petty inquisitions and running down garden-variety deserters, let alone in the wilds of Suffolk. At their highest these were matters for the Special Investigation Branch.

The ailing Austin stalled before they reached a halt. Bullingdon lead them through the main entrance of the house to the duty office, where an elderly adjutant informed Goodman without ceremony that the court of inquiry had been cancelled. Tea was offered in place of an explanation, which arrived after a wait of fifteen minutes in chipped Naffi mugs, lukewarm and undrinkable. Bullingdon remained with them, chatting amiably about extemporised methods for beating the invader. At length Goodman and Kydd were escorted deeper into the house to the seat of power. As they walked the adjutant eyed Goodman's limp, which gave the impression of a small stone lodged in his left shoe. Prior to Dunkirk the reaction engendered had usually been one of suspicion, as though Goodman were a sick-note, and a waste of a uniform. Now it might as well have been a ribbon for the Military Cross.

At the rear of the Hall they were ushered into the spacious oak-panelled study in which the battalion commander had installed himself. With the exception of the blast tape on the windows, a

16

large wall-mounted map was the sole visible concession to military activity in the comfortable room. Colonel Millward-Oliver stood by a french window, overlooking what had formerly been a croquet lawn, and waited several moments before turning to greet his visitors. He was a tall man, aged around fifty-five, with steely-grey hair and a spare moustache. In his well-tailored tunic and Sam Browne belt bulled to perfection he looked every inch the distinguished field officer. Which, in 1917, he had been.

Goodman saluted smartly. 'Captain Goodman, sir. Field Security Police. This is my assistant, Sergeant Kydd.'

'Captain Goodman. Sergeant.' The colonel's tone was clipped, and barely polite. 'I hear old man Bullingdon guided you in.'

'Yes, sir.'

'That fellow demands more of my time than the War Office. On the scrounge, is he?'

'I'd say petrol, judging from the condition of the motorcycle.'

Millward-Oliver fixed Goodman keenly for a long moment, then sat down heavily behind his desk. Although there were several other chairs in the room, he did not invite his guests to follow suit. 'I suppose you're some sort of lawyer.'

'Once upon a time, sir. Now I'm security liaison officer at St Paul's.'

Millward-Oliver frowned. 'GHQ?'

Goodman nodded, but did not trouble to add that in chambers he had specialised in matrimonial matters, with some contentious probate outside the mating season. Besides which, Millward-Oliver was not listening, and appeared oddly flustered by the possibility that Goodman had the ear of the Commander-in-Chief Home Forces.

'Dear God - all I did was call in a favour with Dickie Luther at Mytchett.'

'I gather from your adjutant that our journey this morning has been wasted.'

The inference that Goodman was no longer needed brought the colonel around. 'Yes, had to call the inquiry off, I'm afraid. My prime suspect has disappeared.'

Goodman frowned. 'Deserted?'

'That's right. Cut and run, jumped his bail.'

'This morning?'

'No, last night. A private, name of Hollis, one of the bad two per cent. Record as long as your arm in civvie street. I've alerted the local Redcaps.'

But not us, Goodman thought. Not that he was in any particular hurry to return to his mundane routine at GHQ. He decided to tell a half truth.

'Sir, I will need to put something in my report to Colonel Luther.'

Millward-Oliver regarded Goodman closely and seemed about to bawl him out, then decided otherwise. 'Very well. Three nights ago a cash box was removed from a safe concealed in this room. It contained forty-eight pounds, six shillings and sixpence, to be precise.' He paused, evidently expecting that Goodman would note down this important detail. 'Quite cleaned out the battalion petty cash. Hence the inquiry.

'Would that be the safe behind the oil painting?' ventured Kydd.

'Yes. How the blazes did you know?'

'Just a wild guess, sir.'

Goodman followed Kydd's gaze across the study. On the far wall hung a vulgar portrait of a large red-headed woman attended by two King Charles spaniels. Dark square patches on the panelled walls betrayed where other paintings had hung, before being removed by the owners of the Hall on the eve of the arrival of the military. Even to the untrained eye, the position of the concealed safe could hardly have been more obvious.

'I suppose you'll want to inspect the interior?' demanded Millward-Oliver curtly. 'I know you lawyers are sticklers for detail.'

It was wholly unnecessary, but Goodman replied in the affirmative, for the colonel possessed a talent to annoy. Wearily Millward-Oliver rose to his feet and crossed the room, then removed the red-head from the wall and delved in his pocket for the key. Despite his best efforts the key steadfastly refused to turn in the lock, and the more exasperated the colonel grew, the more intractable the problem became. After half a minute he turned around to announce loudly: 'Whoever picked this lock has buggered it. We can add malicious damage to the charge sheet when the swine is brought to book.'

After much muttered cursing the lock finally yielded. Goodman stepped forward. The interior of the safe was small and remarkably empty, containing a service revolver, a box of home-made dum-dum bullets and two bottles of quality Scottish malt. No standing orders, or disposition plans, or much of anything that Goodman would have expected to find lodged there.

Goodman changed tack. 'Did this man Hollis go missing from here, at the Hall?'

'No, from Hollesley.'

'Which is where?'

'About six miles away. Far side of Rendlesham Forest.'

'Could I see a map?'

'If you must.' Millward-Oliver locked the safe and returned the key to his pocket, then strode impatiently across the polished floorboards. The large map mounted on the wall was dated 1901, and covered the coastline between Cromer and Clacton-on-Sea: eighty miles of open coast on which the enemy were expected to land any day now. Curiously, only those stop-lines and vulnerable points relevant to the battalion were flagged, as though the 1st/4th Wessex alone stood between Hitler and the conquest of the British Isles.

The colonel stabbed a finger at the southernmost flank of his sector. 'There - Hollesley. I've two platoons under canvas. I had Ward put on night patrol by way of punishment.'

'Ward?' queried Kydd.

'I meant Hollis.'

'What about the others?' asked Goodman. 'Didn't anyone try to stop him?'

The colonel paused. 'They were complicit. All three of them. Rotten to the core.'

'Meaning they turned a blind eye?'

'Meaning, the other three took off as well. Due to some slackness on the part of a junior officer, their absence was not noticed until the Stand To at dawn.'

Goodman and Kydd exchanged glances. Millward-Oliver's evident discomfort was akin to watching an elephant trying to hide behind a lamp stand.

'Nothing out of the ordinary in that,' the colonel added hastily. 'Some of these schoolboys run back to their mothers twice a week.'

'All four of them were in on the theft then, were they? And took to their heels for a quarter share of fifty quid?'

Kydd made no attempt to hide his sceptical tone. The sergeant was an experienced Scotland Yard detective, and one of the best recruits Field Security had so far received. Yet he was apt to forget that he no longer exercised power over all other mortals, regardless of class or rank. Before Goodman could intervene, the colonel detonated.

'Good God, you two insolent bastards are worse than Gestapo. Talk about tails wagging dogs! It's all very well for you Whitehall warriors - the closest you'll come to the front line is directing traffic towards it. I, however, find myself at the sharp end. No dainty little limp for me to hide behind.'

'I was wounded in France, as a matter of fact,' Goodman replied evenly.

'Blighty wound, was it?'

It was a Great War term, used to describe a self-inflicted injury that removed a man from the frightfulness of the trenches. Had the crude insult not been so patently absurd Goodman might have been offended. Instead he said: 'The bullet was entirely hostile, I can assure you.'

A tense silence settled over the room. Goodman held the colonel's stare until the older man cleared his throat and said quietly: 'I'm sorry I said that, captain. It was foolish of me. The truth of it is that half my command are so green they can barely put a shine to their boots. I've seven miles of coast to protect, and two Bren guns to get the job done. For the rest, it's Enfield rifles and cold steel. Frankly I might as well shoot them myself when the balloon goes up.'

Confronted with his own futility, Millward-Oliver seemed suddenly to have shrunk inside his uniform. In his mind's eye Goodman glimpsed the two red buses, filled with raw Territorials heading towards a beach swarming with liquid courage and certain death. Here, at the last ditch, the nation teetered on the edge of the abyss. A line from the classroom crossed his mind: *the angel of death has been abroad throughout the land - you may almost hear the beating of his wings.*

Goodman broke from his reverie. 'Would you excuse us a moment, sir.' He gestured Kydd to follow him into the middle of the room, and there whispered conspiratorially. 'This is beginning to smell.'

'Just a bit, sir. I reckon we should visit the scene of the crime.'

Goodman nodded, then turned back to the colonel. 'I think we'll have a dig round at Hollesley on our way back to town.'

'As you wish.' The colonel had already returned to his desk, and began to shuffle papers in an elaborate charade of urgency and action. 'On your way out, please be good enough to tell Bullingdon that I'm unable to spare him any time today.'

'Could I borrow one of your men as a guide?'

'Use Bullingdon.' Already the colonel's humility had evaporated.

'Is he familiar with the area?'

Millward-Oliver cursed beneath his breath, then snatched the telephone from its cradle and dialled a single digit. 'Kimpton? Has Lieutenant Leadbetter left for Hollesley yet? Good. Round him up and hand him over to these Gestapo johnnies from GHQ. No, he hasn't done anything. Just bloody well winkle him out PDQ.'

THREE

The labyrinth of narrow lanes wound first between lush waving fields of corn and barley, then through long, green tunnels of foliage after the car entered Rendlesham Forest. Iken Hall was about eight miles distant from Hollesley. At the crossroads in the centre of the village Kydd turned down towards the beach at Shingle Street, where another world was revealed, of waving green marshland, open sky and wild shore.

At Dumb Boy Sluice, with the sea in sight, a narrow humpbacked bridge crossed the tidal creek, recently widened to form a tank trap. Beside the bridge stood a small round pillbox of Great War origin, from which two bored looking Wessex privates emerged to wave them through. In the middle distance lay the hamlet of Shingle Street, deserted and exposed to the east wind atop a great bank of pebbles. Kydd drove the Austin towards the straggle of huts and bungalows at a snail's pace, for the unmetalled track was worn and rutted, and the car's suspension shot. As they passed by the handful of empty, boarded dwellings Leadbetter pointed out the coastguard barracks, the Mission Hall and, at the furthest end, the squat Martello Tower and the Lifeboat Inn.

The only boat to be seen in the once-thriving fishing hamlet was a lone dinghy, whose owner had neglected to move it inland. Now it sported a gaping hole in its hull.

'Our chaps handiwork, I shouldn't wonder,' explained Leadbetter from the cramped back seat. 'All in all they're pretty good at breaking things and wearing them out.'

'And going absent without leave, it would seem.'

Leadbetter shifted uncomfortably. 'Actually the old man was hoping they'd fallen asleep in one of the shacks.'

Although bright and talkative, Second Lieutenant Leadbetter

inspired little faith as an infantry officer. Barely twenty years old, his appearance was deeply unsoldierly. Strands of unruly fair hair poked from beneath his cap, his buttons were dull, and his battledress looked to have been applied with a shovel.

'Is that par for the course?' asked Goodman.

'Well, it's been a pretty exhausting regime since Dunkirk. The ranks spend the whole day digging trenches and filling sandbags, and then from dusk to dawn we Stand To. It takes some getting used to, I can tell you.'

Kydd parked beside the Inn, an ugly structure fronted with corrugated tin and surrounded by a bewildering multitude of sheds and outhouses. A crudely-executed sign on the door read CLOSED FOR THE DURATION. Another, much neater, and positioned a dozen yards nearer the sea, warned: DANGER - MINES.

'The Sappers are laying them all the way to Bawdsey,' said Leadbetter. 'Trouble is, the shingle keeps moving all the time. All it needs is one good storm to fling the whole lot back in our faces.'

Goodman stepped forward and scanned the long, gentle crescent of Hollesley Bay. The tilted shore formed a sounding-board for the boom and rasp of the cold, reverberating sea, and was devoid of features save the countless millions of smooth pebbles, and a further brace of derelict Martello Towers. Due south, beyond Bawdsey village, four tall steel masts stood in line, piercing the clear blue sky. Several weeks earlier, Goodman had seen something similar on top of the cliffs at Dover; now his curiosity was aroused again.

'What's that - the BBC?'

Leadbetter followed his gaze. 'Bawdsey Manor. Air Ministry Experimental Station in RAF lingo. It's connected with long-range telegraphy in some mysterious way. Most of the locals insist it's a death-ray.'

'Where was the patrol last seen?'

'That would be the checkpoint at East Lane. Third Martello along.'

'So they made it to Bawdsey.'

'Oh yes. The Liverpool Scottish chaps checked them through sometime after two this morning.'

'How far is it?'

'Two miles, more or less. Nice stroll on a day like this, so long as you stick to the ridge and steer clear of the mines.'

Goodman considered the idea. After several long and uneventful weeks at GHQ, and the tense half hour with Millward-Oliver, he concluded that had earned the fillip. Besides, it meant he could wriggle out of meeting his wife that evening.

'Mind if I smoke?' asked Leadbetter, as they set off.

Goodman nodded, but declined a cigarette from the packet the junior officer offered. Leadbetter lit his cigarette clumsily, as though he were new to the habit, then inhaled heavily and fought back a cough.

'That's Bawdsey village to the right of the masts. Pretty little place. You can just see the church tower above the trees. Twelfth century, lovely lych-gate.'

'You're an enthusiast?'

'It's in the blood. My father's a clergyman. Until a few weeks ago I was reading classics and theology at Christ Church. Are you an Oxford or a Cambridge man?'

'Oxford,' Goodman replied shortly. Now that the conversation had strayed into the personal he knew that his limp would come next, as surely as night follows day.

'Cop that in France, sir?'

'Yes,' Goodman replied. 'Well, on the Belgian border.'

'What was it - strafing from the air, or a bit of hand-to-hand?'

'Neither. I was shot from afar by a man I never saw.'

'Bad bit of luck,' Leadbetter commiserated.

'Yes and no,' Goodman replied. 'My sergeant took a bullet through the head.'

Leadbetter looked at Kydd aghast. 'Crikey. You look well on it.'

A moment later the young officer realised his error and flushed crimson, then fell stony silent. Out to sea a lone Avro Anson reconnaissance aircraft droned slowly across the horizon, following the coastline on its regular patrol, vigilant against signs of invasion. Its appearance returned Goodman's thoughts from smalltalk to the job in hand.

'Is he popular, this man Hollis?'

'Not at all,' the lieutenant replied. 'But people take care not to cross him, seeing how he's one of Ward's acolytes.'

'Did Ward tell Hollis to steal the cash box?'

'He may have done. But I should have thought that Ward was

the only one capable of picking the lock.'

'Yet Ward wasn't up on a charge today.'

'Heavens, no.'

'Any particular reason?'

'Well, he's battalion QM. Ward can procure pretty much anything, what with his black market contacts. Petrol mainly, but spirits and cigarettes too. He's indispensable really, what with half the officers still having to rely on their own cars.'

Goodman frowned. 'Do you mean to say he's usurped the War Office as your main supplier of fuel?'

'That's about the size of it. Purely for the war effort, of course. We've a big sector to cover here. Five or six gallons a month on private ration doesn't stretch nearly far enough. There's only so much paraffin you can add before the carburettor clogs.'

'And this is with the blessing of Millward-Oliver?'

Something of the truth was beginning to emerge. Now Leadbetter's ingenuous expression clouded with worry. 'Crikey - I assumed the old man had already been in the confessional. Have I stuck my head in a noose?'

'More like your arse in a sling,' Kydd observed blandly

Leadbetter's gloom deepened visibly. 'Look, the old warhorse is scared stiff he'll be put out to pasture. He's been buying extra fuel out of his own pocket so the battalion can tear about like the Light Brigade, and best every other unit in the Division. Without Ward it just wouldn't be possible.'

'Were the other two men involved as well?'

'Oh no. Ramsey's a perfectly decent young lad, and Sergeant King's straight as a die.'

'You surprise me. Your colonel was adamant all four of them were hardened thieves.'

'He told you that? Well, it's nonsense. And anyway, there's bad blood between King and Ward.'

'Why's that?'

'King thinks the battalion has gone to the dogs. The cash box business is just the icing on the cake. The old man is gunning for the corporal in charge of the guard detail. I should think Ward and Hollis probably ducked off into the forest somewhere. Left the others tied to a tree, I shouldn't wonder.'

'Is that likely?'

'Anything's possible with a type like Ward.'

Goodman rubbed his chin pensively. 'Lieutenant, would you mind walking on ahead while I talk to Sergeant Kydd.'

'Gladly,' Leadbetter replied, and struck out rapidly along the path, smoking furiously.

'So, what does the Yard make of all this?' Goodman asked once the lieutenant was out of earshot.

'Like you said, it stinks badly. Very badly indeed. I smell blackmail. If you ask me the old fool set himself up for it.'

'Over petrol?'

'Over all sorts. He probably pays Ward in his office, and didn't try to hide the safe. We've only the colonel's word for it that nothing else went missing. What does he keep in there anyway?'

'His private bar. No doubt stocked by you-know-who.'

'No paperwork? Sealed orders?'

'None I could see.'

'Like I said, sir, it stinks very badly. There has to be more to it than fifty quid.'

'But why put one of Ward's stooges on a charge?'

Kydd shrugged his shoulders. 'Keeping up appearances, maybe. Perhaps he was trying to stop the rot.'

Goodman shook his head. 'It doesn't add up. And why trek three miles to Bawdsey? Ward and Hollis could have slipped away hours before, as soon as it got dark.'

'I can't answer that.'

'Nor me. Which leaves us where?'

'Trying to catch smoke in a bottle, sir.'

Goodman weighed the evidence for a moment, then said: 'I think I'd better call the Devil.'

No sooner had he spoken than Goodman was distracted by Leadbetter, who was now scrambling clumsily down the bank behind the shore ridge fifty yards ahead. The pair hastened forward to where the lieutenant was picking around in the long coarse grass.

'Lost something?' asked Goodman.

'Quite the opposite,' said Leadbetter, squatting down on his haunches at the bottom of the slope. 'Somebody will get a rare rocket for this. There must be a dozen empty cases down here.'

Leadbetter stood upright and tossed a single short brass

cartridge case through the air. Goodman caught it neatly in one hand. That the round was rimless and of nine millimetre calibre indicated that it was of foreign origin. The engraving around the closed end put it beyond all doubt that it was German.

'Sergeant,' he said slowly, passing the spent case to Kydd, 'I think this investigation has just passed out of our hands.'

FOUR

In June 1940, even with the war almost a year old, few in the German military establishment knew of the existence of Special Purpose Training Unit 800. The fact that the Brandenburg battalion fell under the aegis of the Abwehr, Germany's labyrinthine counter-intelligence service, was sufficient to deflect any awkward questions about the sudden appearance on the battlefield of small squads of men who seemed not to appear on any regular establishment. Which was fortunate, in view of the fact that Gruppe Wagner were still dressed in British uniforms when they disembarked at the Dutch port of Den Helder as dawn broke on the morning of the 27th.

Brandenburg had originally been formed in company strength in October 1939 under the command of Captain von Hippel, a former colonial soldier in East Africa eager to raise a combat unit for clandestine commando and sabotage operations behind enemy lines. The recruiters favoured volksdeutsche, ethnic Germans who had lived in expatriate or Germanic communities beyond the borders of the Reich, and who possessed a good working knowledge of foreign languages, customs and cultures. The first detachments formed and trained at the depot which gave them their name, Brandenburg-Havel. Some, such as those from Alsace, the Sudetenland and the Polish border region, were scarcely strangers to the new Reich. But others had undertaken a far longer journey home, many from the far flung mineral mines, timber mills and rubber plantations of South America and Africa. In the years following 1918, and again during the great depression, thousands of families had emigrated to escape the economic slump that crippled all Europe. After Hitler came to power in 1933, or so it seemed from half a world away, Germany had been reborn, and countless thousands of exiles had returned to the Fatherland.

Even amongst the cosmopolitan ranks of Brandenburg, Leutnant Paul Wagner was unique. For Wagner had returned to Germany on an American passport, and had lived in New York City for eighteen of his twenty-six years. Indeed his family resided there still, having left Koblenz to cross the Atlantic in 1920. Furthermore Wagner had not returned to a homeland he barely remembered through any political conviction, or for reasons of economy. Rather, in 1938 he had switched continents and enroled in the rapidly expanding German army much in the same way that the French Foreign Legion attracted romantics and fugitives. In short, he had joined to forget.

On gaining his commission, Wagner had been transferred to Brandenburg too late to take part in its modest contribution to the Polish campaign. Instead, his first experience of combat had come late in May 1940. Disguised in Belgian uniforms, a twelve-man squad had seized the Nieuport-Ostend road bridge, in order to deny the retreating British Expeditionary Force the opportunity to open the Yser sluices and flood the surrounding countryside. On two occasions during the week that followed, Wagner, now in British uniform and adopting Canadian guise, had breached the shallow British perimeter around the beaches at Dunkirk. From there he had radioed back target information, upon which the Luftwaffe had acted fitfully and to little effect.

On the same fateful day on which the signing of the Armistice concluded the Battle of France, OKW had abruptly instructed the Abwehr to inaugurate an intensive military intelligence assault against the British Isles. The random codename assigned to this project was Hummer, or Lobster. It was as an adjunct to Hummer that Gruppe Wagner had landed in Hollesley Bay, scouted the radar station at Bawdsey Manor for the benefit of Luftwaffe technical intelligence, and eliminated four clumsy Tommies.

At Den Helder, on a secluded quayside cordoned off by military police, they were met by Colonel Erwin von Lahousen, the tall, aristocratic Austrian who ran the department known simply as Abwehr II. Following a short drive to a secluded villa, and a detailed debriefing, the men retired to their bunks, and waited for the benzedrine pills which had carried them through the long night to subside. Lahousen's department was already the largest and most active Abwehr bureau, charged with sabotage and special duties, a nebulous agenda which embraced a dazzling range of operations. The safe return of Gruppe Wagner, the first enemy raiding party to set foot on British soil since the French debacle at Fishguard in 1797, ranked as its greatest coup yet.

At noon, as the Brandenburg men slept, and as Captain John Goodman placed the call to GHQ which was to trigger a major invasion alert along the entire east coast of England between the Thames and the Wash, Colonel Lahousen payed a visit to the Dutch naval hospital. There he was informed by a hostile doctor that the condition of Bernard Ward was grave, and that the Englishman was not expected to survive. Afterwards Lahousen returned to the villa to compose and telex his preliminary report. Finally, as afternoon slipped into evening, the Colonel roused Wagner for the drive to Hamburg.

FIVE

Before his journey to Suffolk, the closest Goodman had come to facing down the invasion threat had been his turn on the duty roster at GHQ Home Forces. His shift, when it came around, which was all too often, involved fighting off sleep in a cubicle equipped with an unsavoury camp bed and a lone white telephone. According to standing orders, the telephone would ring in the event of an enemy landing anywhere in the United Kingdom. Since the fall of France, Goodman had spent countless long nights recumbent on the unmade bed, re-reading paperbacks and magazines, waiting for the telephone to ring with a guilty sense of hope, wondering whether he might hear Churchill's low growl on the line. Instead, however, the invasion hotline had remained obstinately silent. Except for one notable occasion, when Goodman had sat bolt upright and snatched up the receiver, only to hear a drunken voice request a taxi.

His call to GHQ half an hour earlier could hardly have been less galvanising. Faced with the prelude to an enemy landing in force, Goodman had found little difficulty in deciding that his duty lay in London rather than Suffolk. However, the directions given by Leadbetter for Woodbridge had proved to be inadequate, and now once more he and Sergeant Kydd found themselves lost in an unfamiliar landscape devoid of signposts and milestones, in which even the tall steel masts at Bawdsey were soon lost to view. When, two short miles beyond Hollesley, they reached the umpteenth unmarked junction in yet another anonymous village, Kydd laid down a hurricane barrage of profanity and braked to a halt. Then, as he prepared to worry door-knockers, a figure hove into view on a bicycle.

Goodman watched through the windscreen as the cyclist drew nearer. The rider was female, and wore the blue-grey uniform of the Womens' Auxiliary Air Force. Her pace was neither leisurely nor urgent, and he sensed from the uneven movement of her feet that the gears were slipping. Probably she was from the wireless station at Bawdsey; probably she knew the way to Woodbridge. Goodman clambered out of the car, crossed the dusty road, and raised his hand to hail her.

The elderly machine's rusted brakes protested loudly as the WAAF slowed to a gentle halt and swung nimbly from the saddle. She was young and very attractive, her slender frame made no less pleasing by thick lisle stockings and black regulation oxfords. Her dark hair was gathered up beneath her uniform cap, which framed a small pale face dominated by a pair of bright, sparkling eyes. The insignia on her shoulder, bolts of lightning gathered in a fist, denoted a wireless operator. No more than twenty-two, her smile was bright and her fingers bore no rings. Goodman wholeheartedly approved.

'Hello, captain,' she said, glancing at the pips on his epaulettes. 'I don't think I've seen the Irish Guards round here before.'

'Irish Guards?' Goodman said, mystified.

'The green cover on your cap?'

Hardly a day passed without some new misunderstanding of his nebulous duties arising. Most were in some way insulting, but now Goodman smiled. 'Good Lord, no. Field Security Police.'

'Crikey - am I in some sort of trouble?'

'Not if you can point me towards Woodbridge. It keeps moving.'

The WAAF smiled. 'You're in luck. I'm heading that way myself.'

'Is it far?'

'About six miles.' She raised her cap slightly, then produced a handkerchief from her tunic pocket and dabbed at her brow. 'We can be there in fifteen minutes. Got a spare wheel on your wagon?'

'Yes, but it's flat.'

Her expression exposed his words as the wettest remark in the history of the world. 'I mean, you can hitch my bike to the back of your car. Then we can go all the way together, if you'll pardon the expression.'

Her smile carried with it the beginnings of a pout. The pretty WAAF had not saluted once, and apparently cared nothing for Goodman's rank. He found it pleased him. As he ushered her towards the Austin Kydd shone him a coarse grin from across the bonnet, as though the pair of them were cruising a dancehall. Goodman ignored it, and at the back of the car hung the ancient bicycle upside-down over the spoked spare wheel. Then he walked around the car to the open passenger door and pushed forward the seat. As the WAAF climbed into the cramped interior Goodman caught a faint whiff of good perfume, and noticed the gentle curve of her hips. He sensed a faint stirring within. It had been more than a year since he had even so much as touched a woman.

'This is the best lift I've had since I got here,' she announced, as Kydd turned the key in the ignition and manfully wrestled the gears into first.

Goodman turned round to face her. 'Poor you.'

'You wouldn't believe some of the things we thumb lifts in. Coal lorries, hearses, horse and cart.'

'You're from Bawdsey, I take it?'

'I couldn't possibly say,' she replied, not missing a beat. 'Name, rank and number, that's all you get.'

'Well, it's a start.'

'647759 Sophie Gold, Aircraftswoman First Class.'

'Been in the mob long?'

'Just finished my probationary period.'

As they spoke Kydd picked up speed. Although the alarming discovery at Shingle Street demanded that they return to London as quickly as possible, inwardly Goodman willed his sergeant to slow down. For he found himself much attracted to their passenger.

'Top secret business in Woodbridge too?'

'Oh, terribly hush-hush,' she replied, mock-serious. 'Actually Nivea. One of the riggers said that Boots have got some in stock. You can't get it for love nor money these days, so I hopped on the station bike as fast as I could.' She paused for a moment, frowned, then continued. 'God, I hope George wasn't having me on.'

'Be sure to let me know. I can have him shot at dawn.'

'Is that what the Field Security Police do?'

'Oh, I couldn't possibly say.'

Sophie laughed. 'I walked straight into that one, didn't I.'

'Slap bang.'

'So what do you two do?'

'Let's say we don't waste our time pulling padlocks.'

Kydd delivered his line with an air of fatuous mystery. A second later, as they rounded a blind bend, he was obliged to swerve violently to avoid colliding with a convoy of Bedford three-tonners. Packed full of stony-faced infantry, the trucks were hurtling towards the coast at impressive speed, part of a mobile reserve formation ordered in to reinforce the sector following Goodman's doomsday call. The rapidity of the response surprised even Goodman. Then again, for all anybody knew the enemy armada was already half way across the North Sea.

'Someone's in a hurry,' muttered Kydd.

Oblivious to the underlying danger, Sophie Gold leaned back on the rear seat and stretched an arm across the back. 'Intriguing, isn't it, all these secrets. So what shall we talk about, seeing as work is off limits? We're still ten minutes from Woodbridge.'

Kydd wrestled with the steering wheel as he coaxed the car from the verge to the road. 'Can't be much to talk about, being stuck out here in the middle of nowhere.'

'Oh, we don't do too badly. We've got a ballroom on the station, and our own five-piece band. Do you have a ballroom where you are, sergeant?

'One or two,' Kydd replied, 'seeing how our billet's in Hammersmith.'

'Lucky you,' she said, without any hint of envy. 'As a matter of fact I'm going up to town this weekend. Wangled myself a seventy-two hour pass. Anything I can't afford to miss?'

'I saw The Tempest at the Old Vic last week,' Goodman said, as though he only dimly remembered. 'But I doubt you'll find a ticket.'

'Any good?'

'Very. There's John Gielgud, Alec Guiness, and Peggy Ashcroft too.' Goodman paused. 'It's fashionable to say just now that London is full of theatres, but no theatre, what with the war. But I think that's taking it too far.'

Goodman hoped he was not boring Sophie. He was conscious that he was trying hard to sound interesting, that with his rank and driver and posting all London belonged to him. He did not add that his visit to the theatre had been his first social foray in how many months, or that the ticket had cost him a steep six shillings, or that he had gone only because an ATS girl from the signals pool had blown out Toby Porter at short notice. In truth, his life formed a vacuum. His FS section was supposed to be responsible for securing GHQ from incursions by enemy agents who might try to pry out its secrets, or subvert its personnel. This gave Kydd and the rest of his men licence to do almost anything, and go almost anywhere. If they went drinking in public bars or visited cinemas, it was to watch out for suspicious characters. If they chatted up girls, it was to probe their intentions in frequenting the locality. Goodman, however, derived no pleasure from these excursions. More usually, he lost at chess to a devoutly catholic lance-corporal named Bray. Or waited in the malodorous cubicle for the white telephone to ring.

'My father has tickets for Rebecca on Saturday evening,' declared Sophie. 'Have you seen it?'

'No,' Goodman replied quickly, feeling suddenly uncomfortable. 'But I read in the paper today that Alfred Hitchcock has directed a promising film version in America.'

'I'll make do with the play. After all, there's only so much jealousy and melodrama one can enjoy on a three day pass.'

Kydd furrowed his brow, as though the subject troubled him. 'Rebecca? Would that be at the Queen's?'

'Yes, I believe it is,' she replied.

He paused, then turned to Goodman and said deliberately: 'Isn't your wife in that particular show, sir?'

Goodman fixed Kydd with a gimlet stare, but the other man kept his eyes on the road. For several rancorous moments Goodman wished he'd allowed Millward-Oliver to tear a strip off his wilful NCO. He did not recall even discussing his marriage with Kydd, let alone the fact that his wife was an actress who was almost well-known, or that their relationship had failed miserably. Yet it seemed that already the tale was current amongst his section, and one from which Kydd now saw fit to fashion a joke at his expense.

Were it not for presence of their passenger Goodman might have said something terse and unpleasant. Instead he said: 'Quite so, sergeant. Does this sudden interest in more subtle forms of stage entertainment mean that you've finally tired of the nudes at the Windmill?'

A faint smile played across Kydd's lips. 'I've only ever attended in a purely professional capacity, sir.'

'Professional possibly, pure I doubt.'

Goodman's annoyance subsided quickly, replaced by a vague sense of irritation that he continued to forgive so readily. He did not turn to look at Sophie Gold. Probably she was enjoying his discomfort, and a whiff of scandal involving a rising actress. Besides, mention of his wife brought with it a sudden realisation of how futile was his instinctive attraction. He an army captain based in south London, she a WAAF on to a secret base two counties distant. Less than an hour before he had uncovered certain proof of an enemy landing, and yet here he was indulging himself in mild fantasy about an unavailable stranger. It was, he knew, a pinnacle of the ridiculous.

The silence which settled over the occupants of the car endured until the spires and rooftops of Woodbridge rose from the landscape. They dropped Sophie Gold outside Boots on the Thoroughfare, just in time to see the counter assistant reverse the OPEN sign which hung inside the door. Sophie's uniform gained her entry, although as Goodman unhooked her bike the look of rage that crossed her face inside confirmed that George the rigger possessed a cruel sense of humour.

SIX

Although the central headquarters of the Abwehr were located in a large townhouse on the elegant Tirpitzufer in Berlin, the bulk of its work was conducted by various sub-stations spread throughout Germany's military districts. The Hamburg Stelle, known simply as X, was amongst the largest and best established, and for this reason had been assigned the greater part of Operation Hummer. It was in a spartan conference room at X, after a drive conducted at often terrifying speeds, that Paul Wagner, now back in the uniform of a Brandenburg lieutenant, was introduced for the first time to Adolf Hitler's chief of intelligence.

Admiral Wilhelm Canaris was not quite as the American had expected. Although his worn uniform tunic was adorned with the Iron Cross First Class, his bearing could hardly have been less martial. He was a small man, perhaps five feet four inches tall and round-shouldered, with snow-white hair and bushy eyebrows. Despite a sailor's ruddy complexion, he wore an air of fatigue, and with his bowed head and stooped shoulders seemed almost frail. More like a theatrical agent, Wagner determined, than a senior German officer, and very far from the forceful and uncompromising spymaster he had anticipated.

'I believe congratulations are in order, leutnant,' Canaris began, offering his hand. 'The successful completion of our first operation against the English mainland is surely worthy of an Iron Cross.'

The voice was diffident, and the handshake weak. Good Lord, wondered Wagner, the man even lisped.

'Thank you, Herr Admiral.'

'Who knows, perhaps the factory can be persuaded to weave the stars and stripes into the ribbon.'

The exchange was ironic twice over. So far more than half of the Brandenburg establishment of six hundred men had received the Iron Cross. It was one of the very few aspects of his private army which gave Canaris any pleasure. Yet Wagner was not among its holders, his own Dunkirk exploit having fallen foul of the Fuhrer's desire to bring about peace by sparing the BEF from bloody annihilation.

'Tell me, was your voyage worthwhile? I should imagine the Suffolk coast is most pleasant at this time of year.'

'Most rewarding, Admiral.'

'So Lahousen tells me. Not only did you breach their defences, but you bring back four defenders too. One of them even alive.' The admiral's expression betrayed the merest hint of distaste. It was, after all, little more than a year since he had rejected the concept of Brandenburg as morally unsound. 'I assume it was necessary to eliminate these men?'

'Absolutely, sir. They would have discovered our boats and raised the alarm.'

'Of course,' Canaris nodded. 'You understand, leutnant, I don't mean to question your operational judgement. It is simply that awkward questions may be asked in higher places.'

'As a matter of fact,' ventured Wagner, 'we learned more from the patrol than anything we saw inside the perimeter of Bawdsey Manor.'

Canaris arched his eyebrows. 'How so?'

'They're guarding DeTe stations with old men and schoolboys. And each man was carrying only twenty-five rounds.'

'Meaning?'

Wagner sensed that Canaris knew the answer already. 'British webbing equipment can accommodate one hundred and fifty rounds. The troops around Bawdsey had no automatic weapons, and no radio equipment either.'

'Are you certain these men were regular troops? Not part of this so-called broomstick army?'

Wagner reached inside his tunic and produced a khaki forage cap, then placed it on the desk, the dull brass cap badge facing upwards. Canaris took it up and frowned.

'The insignia denotes the Wessex Regiment,' offered Lahousen. 'Reservists probably, but certainly not home guard.'

Canaris turned the cap over in his hand, then pushed it back towards Wagner. 'Rather a macabre souvenir.'

'I thought their uniforms might prove useful.'

'For German moths perhaps,' smiled Lahousen. 'At Dunkirk they left us more stores and clothing than we can catalogue or move. I'll wager we can field a better-equipped British army than Churchill.'

Canaris hesitated, then said to Wagner: 'So your impression of the state of their defences was negative?'

The ease with which his team had completed their mission had preoccupied Wagner throughout the return crossing. He needed no second bidding. 'An American word describes them best.'

'Cockermamie?' Canaris anticipated, negotiating the word with no little difficultly.

'Actually, I had in mind crackerjack. If you discount the older stone towers, the only blockhouses date from the First War. They're already marked on your maps.'

'"Your" maps?'

'Ours, sir.'

The admiral nodded. 'Mines?'

'Nothing you can't pick your way through. The DeTe station itself is surrounded by wire and fencing, but we had no trouble getting inside.'

'You weren't challenged?'

'Not once. But we were lucky. I doubt we could fool anyone for long, at least not until we can come up with a better cover than masquerading as Poles.'

'What about the injured man? Will he live?'

Lahousen replied for Wagner. 'They intend to move him to a military hospital in Antwerp as soon as he has recovered sufficiently.'

'And are his guards reliable?'

The colonel looked puzzled. 'In what way reliable, Admiral?'

'Meaning, no word of this operation must be allowed to leak out. Especially to the Propagandakompagnie - they're bound to want photographs of Gruppe Wagner plastered across the cover of Signal magazine. And I don't want Feldgendarmerie watching over the wounded man either. Get the Amsterdam Stelle on the case. And see to it that the Red Cross hear nothing, at least for now.'

'Yes, Herr Admiral.'

'Have the dead men been buried yet?'

'They're still in the morgue in Den Helder.'

'Get it done, quickly and quietly. Tell whoever needs to know they were merchant sailors, fished out of the North Sea by a trawler crew.'

As Lahousen nodded his assent Canaris stood and crossed to the window. The chief of intelligence was, Wagner decided, a difficult man to fathom. His shabby uniform, unguarded jokes and casual manner gave first impressions of a fool, or a burnt-out case. Now, however, as the admiral turned to address him once more, Wagner glimpsed one of the sharpest analytical minds in Germany.

Canaris allowed a brief silence to settle on the room before he continued. 'Leutnant, now that the Fuhrer has conquered Europe as far as the Spanish frontier, he has set his sights upon humbling England. Henceforth all Abwehr operations against the British Isles are to be conducted on what is termed an "emergency" basis. Never mind that we were once prohibited from placing agents there - OKH demands that we now produce a detailed blueprint of the enemy order of battle, like a rabbit from a hat.'

'Give me a desk and a typewriter and I can prepare my report immediately,' offered Wagner.

Canaris waved his hand dismissively. 'Not on my account, please. The tonnage of paper already exceeds that of lead in this conflict.'

'Will there be an invasion?'

'Perhaps. As a naval officer, I reserve my opinion on the wisdom of attempting a seaborne assault on an emergency basis. Lahousen, however, will no doubt side with the Fuhrer.'

'Admiral?' Lahousen frowned.

Canaris smiled without warmth. 'Surely, Colonel, all Austrians are terrified of salt water?'

Lahousen gave an uneasy laugh. Wagner, too, smiled only thinly, and sought to bring the briefing back on track. 'Churchill will sue for peace. A naval blockade and bombing from the air will convince the Brits enough is enough.'

Canaris shrugged. 'Presently the Fuhrer thinks otherwise. The coming struggle will be their finest hour! The great WC himself has told the world on the BBC. Only a fool could believe differently.'

An uneasy silence settled over the room. On the far wall hung the obligatory portrait of Adolph Hitler, whose eyes seemed suddenly everywhere in the room. Whatever the admiral's purpose in testing his political reflexes, Wagner refused to be drawn.

'I guess London will capitulate,' he said flatly.

'An interesting opinion,' Canaris replied. 'Yours is, after all, an essentially American mind.'

'I can't deny that. But Stateside the press reckons Britain will tough it out.'

'It's true that the Fuhrer has few friends amongst North American editors. London has agents of influence working on them from California to New Hampshire even as we speak. Oh yes, we have much work to do in America. As in England, our organisation barely exists.' Canaris lifted his head and fixed Wagner with a cool stare. 'You could be of great value to us, Paul.'

'I thought I already was.'

'So you are. But there are many ways to wage war.'

Wagner shook his head. 'I prefer to go to work in a uniform, sir. I'm a simple man. My father is a baker. He didn't rub shoulders with press barons and congressmen back in New York. Nor did I. And I won't fight Americans.'

'Who said anything about fighting?'

'You did. Something about there being many ways to wage war. I came back to Germany to join the army, not to spy.'

'Would you not agree that wearing British uniforms is a form of espionage?'

'Maybe. But Germany's at war with Britain, not Uncle Sam and the FBI.'

'Some might say it's just a matter of time.'

'I won't spy for you, Admiral,' Wagner repeated with as much force as the yawning chasm between their ranks allowed. 'One way or another, if I got caught it'd be a whole world of hurt for my family. Besides, America was good to me.'

'Then why leave?'

Wagner paused. 'I believe it's on my file.'

'As I said before, leutnant, I'm not one for documents. I'd like to hear it from you.'

'I left on impulse,' Wagner said quietly. 'Following a broken engagement. As simple as that.'

He had anticipated derision. Instead Canaris nodded slowly, as though he approved of such shameless sentimentalism. Wagner dropped his gaze to his lap. On this occasion, at least, he had avoided a return trip to the land of the free. Next time, he knew, it would not be so easy.

Now the chief of intelligence cleared his throat. 'As of today all Brandenburg leave is cancelled. I have my doubts as to whether a landing in England will take place. However, I'm charging you with the task of assembling our best English speakers for future operations against the English mainland. Do you accept this assignment?'

'Of course, Herr Admiral.'

'Excellent,' Canaris replied, but without obvious enthusiasm. 'Report directly to Lahousen. Gruppe Wagner will have full priority. Draft men from any of the other three companies if you need them, and be prepared to move at minimum notice. I have a feeling, leutnant, that you will be very busy over the next few weeks.'

SEVEN

Goodman had visited Wormwood Scrubs twice before, as a pupil barrister assisting a criminal silk in a murder trial. Now, five years later, and under the management of MI5, the procedure for gaining entry to the sprawling prison compound was unchanged. At the turreted gate Goodman's papers were checked by an indifferent civilian warder, who directed him through the small judas door towards the dark, imposing block still referred to as A Wing.

Goodman was surprised to find the temporary headquarters of the security service alive with women. On the lawn outside the chapel, neatly tended despite the national emergency, two registry girls sat smoking and plotting, their jackets unbuttoned, enjoying the warmth of the sun. Goodman's green cap and lame leg aroused only fleeting interest, for after all, intrigue was scarcely at a premium within the hush-hush departments referred to by envious outsiders as secret shows. Inside A Wing his credentials were once more examined, this time by a striking young woman with sharp blue eyes and a page-boy bob. She wore civilian clothes, as did most of the personnel Goodman passed and observed as a second, similarly attractive girl walked him to his appointment. The individual offices at the Scrubs were situated in cells off each of the five landings. These were reached by a narrow spiral staircase, made hazardous by a mass of telephone cables channelled untidily down the worn cast iron steps. The registry girl drew, and enjoyed, appreciative looks and comments from several rakish males as she escorted Goodman the length of the gallery. Indeed with its proliferation of debutantes and rowing blues, at ten-seventeen in the morning on the day invasion might fall, the jail seemed imbued with an incongruous party atmosphere.

Women had occupied Goodman's thoughts throughout the long

and sleepless night. On his return from Suffolk, he had collected several messages from the section office, one of which was from his wife, requesting his presence in her dressing room at the Queen's Theatre before her performance in Rebecca on Saturday evening. Another was from Colonel Maxwell Luther, the fearsome commandant of the Field Security Police, instructing Goodman to deliver a written report to MI5 by hand the following morning. Of the two, the prospect of seeing Elizabeth worried Goodman more. Nonetheless, he had bashed out a summary of his findings at Iken Hall and Hollesley Bay on his old Olympus, conscious that the invasion might be in progress even as he typed. For it was no secret that the General Staff expected the attack to come through East Anglia, which offered better tank country than the South Downs. After two hours he had retired to bed, alone, save for a glass of Pimms and a mind alive with sticky endings.

And Elizabeth.

And Sophie Gold.

On the topmost landing of A Wing Goodman was ushered into a small, dingy cell in which two bunk beds were still fixed to the grey brick wall. The only other items of furniture in the spartan room were a trestle table, a filing cabinet, a small safe, and three folding chairs. On one of these sat Colonel Luther. On another, beneath a small grimy window, a second officer, whose office it was, wore the uniform of a major in the Brigade of Guards.

As she departed the girl carefully pulled the heavy cell door closed, but only halfway, for all the doors in the building locked automatically when shut, and had no interior handles.

The major smiled briefly at his visitor. 'Captain Goodman? Thank you for dropping by this morning. My name is Morley. Do take a seat.'

Goodman sat down on the subordinate side of the desk. He guessed that Major Morley was somewhere in his early forties, although his dark hair and lean build made him seem ten years younger. His Old Etonian accent and sophisticated air identified him as Mayfair rather than military, although a clipped moustache relocated him to some equidistant limbo. On his desk lay a half-smoked packet of Player's Passing Cloud. These, and three telephones, one of them red, offered a clear indication that Morley was a man of some importance.

Colonel Luther offered Goodman no greeting. His expression, as was customary, betrayed no great liking for his Field Security subordinates. He was a tall, lean man of forty-eight with steely grey hair and sharp, unforgiving eyes. A professional soldier since 1911, Luther lived for the destruction of the King's enemies, specifically German, following the death of his twin brother in a phosgene attack at Ypres. Too old for a field command, yet too great an asset to be cashiered, he now commanded the FSP without pride or enthusiasm.

'I believe you have a report for me, Goodman,' Morley began. 'More than a few of us here at the office are very keen to see it.'

Goodman unfastened his briefcase and produced both the original and carbon of the brief resume. It occupied a single side of foolscap and covered the burglary, the black market fuel, the supposed desertion, and the German ammunition. He also produced a brown paper bag.

Morley scanned the documents for barely fifteen seconds, then set them carefully to one side. 'Well, the spent cases would seem to nail the desertion theory. I take it you didn't leave any in situ.'

Goodman pushed the paper bag across the desk. Morley shook it open and spilled a puddle of brass cartridge cases noisily across the table.

'We collected thirty-two in all,' Goodman explained, not that the statistic seemed to matter. 'I presume they're from an automatic weapon.'

'Could they have come from an aircraft?'

Goodman shook his head. 'They would have been more spread out, over a large area of ground.'

'Calibre's too small,' snapped Luther bluntly.

Morley took one up between his finger and thumb and squinted at the markings around the percussion cap. The cases were short, fired from weapons which had almost certainly left the four Wessex men dead. 'Bound to happen sooner or later,' he pronounced with a sigh. 'We've been anticipating probes of this kind since the end of May. It might not even be the first.'

He offered the case to Luther for inspection, but the other's fierce gaze remained fixed on the pile of cases, as though they had robbed the lives of men under his own command.

'I take it your sergeant can be trusted to keep his mouth shut?' said Morley.

'Of course,' Luther answered testily, not waiting for Goodman to reply. 'I can say the same of every one of my men.'

Morley ignored him. 'What about this fellow Leadbetter?'

'I told him to keep quiet about the German rounds,' Goodman replied. 'Anyway, he's already terrified that Millward-Oliver will carpet him for spilling the beans about the petrol.'

'Not very likely. Colonel Millward-Oliver shot himself at six-thirty this morning.'

Goodman blinked, recalling the Webley in the safe, and stole a glance at Luther. The colonel appeared unmoved. Goodman experienced a sudden pang of guilt, as though he had jaywalked and tipped over a cyclist, only to learn that they had inexplicably succumbed to a bruise.

'Rather fortunate in some respects,' Morley continued blandly.

'In what way?' Goodman asked.

'The late colonel was considerate enough to leave a farewell note. Your hunch about blackmail was bang on target. Three maps were removed, all insignificant battalion stuff, or so he says. I suppose Jerry might have them, but I doubt this chap Ward would have carried around incriminating evidence in his back pocket for four days.'

'I'd hardly call that fortunate.'

'We need to raise a smokescreen, Captain Goodman. If the truth leaks out and about the least of our problems will be trigger-happy defenders. Black market and blackmail are grist to the rumour mill. Ditto the fact that the checkpoint at Bawdsey reported that the patrol passed through safely.'

'So they did.'

Morley shook his head. 'I sent the RSLO over from Cambridge to dig a little deeper. They counted five men through at East Lane, not four.'

'Meaning?'

'Apparently that German troops in British uniforms can wander around Suffolk at will. Never mind nuns and postmen. Anyway, it looks as if we can pass the whole thing off as an exercise.'

'Does it signal the invasion?'

'Perhaps,' Morley replied. 'But you can rest assured the Wessex

Regiment are being replaced with something a little more battle ready even as we speak.'

'Pack them off somewhere remote,' added Luther, 'with fewer ears for wagging tongues.'

Morley scooped the spent cases back into the paper bag, then rose to his feet and deposited them in the safe, together with both copies of the report. Goodman glimpsed there a bottle of sherry, and a copy of The Field.

'Colonel Luther informs me that you were a barrister in civilian life,' he said, turning back to Goodman.

'Yes. I was called to the bar in thirty-four.'

'Which Inn of Court?'

'Grays, sir.'

The major frowned. 'You're not Welsh, are you?'

'No, I followed my father.'

'Any particular specialism?'

'Divorce mainly, some probate. When things were slow I did some pro bono work for the Bentham Committee - my bit to assist the poor and needy.' Goodman did not mention that he had prosecuted several cases for the National Council for Civil Liberties following fascist disturbances in the East End, and assaults on jewish refugees. Here, at the heart of MI5, it did not seem appropriate.

Morley hesitated, drumming his fingers on the desk. 'Perhaps you'll accept a brief from me. Deserters have to be pursued, and we've got to make some pretence of going after these four. I don't want this dealt with by the ordinary military police, most of them are nothing but Automobile Association patrolmen in a different uniform. I'd like you to take on the case, Goodman. Search their houses, lean on their nearest and dearest a little, that sort of thing.'

'Put a bit of stick about,' added Luther. 'Just like you did with Tommy Millward-Oliver.'

Goodman considered the proposal for a moment, the said evenly: 'Is this an invitation, or an order?'

'I didn't think a barrister could turn down a brief,' muttered Luther with undisguised contempt.

'This is hardly a brief, Colonel. It just so happens that I took pride in going to court with clean hands. You're asking me to deceive widows and tell lies. It's dirty work, Major. Will you be stopping their pay?'

Morley nodded. 'No choice.'

'It seems rather harsh on their dependents.'

'Rather harsh!' Luther barked. 'Shall I tell you something, Goodman? The state of our defences is such that the Hun could take a penny steamer from Calais to the coast, and stroll up to London before sunset. It will be a bloody sight harsher if Hitler holds a victory parade in Whitehall.'

Goodman held Luther's flinty stare. Morley looked between them and allowed the silence to drag, then asked quietly: 'What, if anything, do you know about the RAF installation at Bawdsey?'

Goodman recalled, and dismissed, Leadbetter's tale of a death ray. 'Eavesdropping on the enemy?'

'Not quite,' Morley replied, apparently satisfied with the Goodman's ignorance. 'It's a radio direction finding station, RDF for short. We have a string of twenty-one between the Shetlands and the Isle of Wight, known as Chain Home. In layman's terms it's a kind of electronic eye which warns of the approach of hostile aircraft by means of radio echoes. I'm told RDF has an inaccuracy factor of about three hundred per cent. Still, it gives an approximate idea of numbers, height and heading up to a range of one hundred and fifty miles.'

'Electronic early warning,' Goodman said, thinking aloud. Although he had no bent for science, the information was fascinating, the equal of anything plucked from the pages of HG Wells.

'Some such witchcraft,' said Morley. 'The aim being that Fighter Command can direct our chaps onto the Hun and knock the buggers down. Until last September Bawdsey was the Air Ministry's main research station. The Germans have had more than an inkling about it for a few years now, judging from the number of Lufthansa aircraft that flew over in peacetime. They even floated the Graf Zeppelin over the east coast a couple of times trying to pick up signals.'

'I remember,' Goodman said. 'It made the front pages.'

'As soon as war broke out the boffins were removed to a less exposed location. Whether Jerry suspects as much is anybody's guess. Meanwhile Bawdsey remains a key operational CH station, and a Category A risk for seaborne attack. They may try a smash-

and-grab raid on Bawdsey to glean technical intelligence, or else to knock a hole in the chain.'

Luther glowered at Goodman from across the desk. 'Perhaps now you understand why a few white lies about dead Territorials is hardly the end of civilization. If it gets out that the Hun are paying house-calls in mufti, Home Forces will end up skirmishing like Roundheads and Cavaliers.'

Goodman thought about protesting further, but he knew it would make for a feeble show. Nothing but blanks fired into the air. He said quietly: 'You seem to have me on the hook.'

'Good,' Morley said. 'Of course, everything connected with this little sideshow must remain most secret. If any complications in respect of the families arise, they speak only to you. Involve your sergeant if you need to. I'm sure he knows the drill.'

'Be unsubtle,' said Luther scathingly. 'It's not too difficult if you set your mind to it.'

As the colonel spoke one of Morley's telephones began to ring, sounding very loud within the confines of the cell. Morley took up the receiver, listened, rolled his eyes, then announced to the caller: 'Five minutes.' As he replaced the handset, he said to Luther: 'Well, Colonel, I need detain you no longer.'

The MI5 man might have been dismissing a butler. Luther looked first at Morley, then at Goodman, fuse smouldering. Then he stood and crossed briskly to the steel door, which he swung open, stepped through, and slammed heavily behind him. The click of the lock was clearly audible above the echoing din.

'Buggeration,' Morley sighed. He took a cigarette from the packet on the desk, then lit it with an ornate lighter.

'Interesting life at St Paul's, Goodman?'

'It has its moments.'

'Tiny Ironside a bit of a tyrant, perhaps?'

'I rarely see him,' Goodman lied. 'He has his own private lair in the headmaster's quarters.'

'Really? How very apposite.'

'Indeed,' Goodman agreed. For the hierarchy and geography at GHQ were completely in tune. Four majors to each small classroom, a brace of colonels in the larger ones, and a single brigadier for each master's study.

'What about Field Security? The prefects' common room?'

'I've a billet nearby.'

'Comfortable?'

'Moderately so.'

The major leaned back in his chair. 'Unlike Tuesdays and Saturdays.'

Goodman stiffened. 'Sorry?'

'Oh come on, Captain. The nights you spend spying on General Ironside. I'm in military intelligence, remember? It's not a total contradiction in terms.'

'I'm not at liberty to discuss that assignment with anyone other than Colonel McGillivray,' Goodman said carefully.

'Ten days ago Jack McGillivray handed you a piece of paper reporting on how the car of the commander-in-chief is frequently seen parked outside a certain address in Holland Park, some of whose occupants are thought to enjoy dubious political associations. Am I right so far?'

'Ask Colonel McGillivray.'

'No need. As a matter of fact, I gave him the note he passed on to you.'

Goodman felt as though he were treading on the floorboards of an unsafe building. First a false manhunt for dead men, now this. 'Then ask McGillivray yourself.'

Morley drew heavily on his cigarette. 'Not as easy at that, I'm afraid. Relations between the security service and the War Office are never straightforward at the best of times. If it got out that we were sniffing around Tiny Ironside, things might get a little heated.'

'So my hand was guided towards the flame instead.'

'It's nothing personal, Goodman. Have you formed an opinion on Ironside yet?

'Not yet. Sitting in a car across the street in the blackout hardly lends itself to revelation.'

'But you'll let me know as soon as you do?'

'As long as Colonel McGillivray consents. Although I expect he'll want to tell you directly.'

'Tell me yourself, and tell me first. Look, you'll be doing yourself a favour. Field Security may be a cushy number now, but it won't last forever. There's already talk of a new intelligence corps. If that comes off you chaps will be swallowed whole, green caps and all.'

Goodman felt his arm being twisted - but towards what? The promise of a transfer to MI5, or a swift kick downstairs to the Department of Army Legal Services? To Goodman, neither much appealed.

Morley proffering a small printed card. 'My number. I fear the service will be shut inside this awful place for a few weeks yet.'

As he unbuttoned his breast pocket Goodman glanced at the card. Morley, it transpired, in addition to the Guards, was a timber merchant named Bowles. Or, more likely, he was neither.

Now Morley dialled a single digit on a telephone. 'Jane? Would you perform a small kindness and escort Captain Goodman to the gatehouse. And while you're at it, bring up the keys to my cell door.'

EIGHT

In the downstairs bar of the Queen's Theatre, Goodman sought solace in a whisky soda. That his meeting with Elizabeth had been as brief as it was unpleasant was only the half of it. Now, in his mind's eye, he wrung the neck of the day gone by with a sense of vicious satisfaction, then flung its corpse on the dung-heap.

That morning, in company with Sergeant Kydd, he had driven to a small terraced house in Dartford, and there conducted a contemptible search of four small rooms and an outside lavatory. Or rather, Kydd had searched, while Goodman pushed questions on a confused and tearful old woman, he unable to meet her eye, his gaze instead drawn to a mantelpiece cluttered with medals, mementos and photographs of Sergeant Leslie King. For fifteen long minutes, and at regular intervals in the hours since, Goodman had felt that he was no more contributing to the survival of the free world than if he were giving elocution lessons to Lord Haw Haw.

Assailed from all sides by shards of regret, Goodman drained his glass and rose to leave. The long night watch on General Ironside in Holland Park seemed almost appealing. But as he stopped forward to pick up his cap a finger tapped lightly on his shoulder, and on turning he found himself face to face with Sophie Gold.

'Well, well,' she began, flashing him a knowing smile. 'Fancy meeting you here.'

What with Elizabeth and Dartford, Goodman had quite forgotten his half-formed plan to engineer a meeting in the foyer with the pretty WAAF from Suffolk. Now he felt vaguely embarrassed, and managed only an inadequate: 'Hello.'

Sophie nodded at his glass. 'Drowning your sorrows?'

'Something like that. Actually I was just about to leave.'

'Oh,' she said flatly, her grin giving way to a frown.

Standing beside her, Goodman felt his desire to leave ebb quickly away. If Sophie Gold had seemed attractive in her blue uniform two days before, in civilian dress she was quite stunning. Her face looked less childish than he remembered, and her eyes darker still. Like many women she wore her dark hair over her shoulders in the style of Veronica Lake; unlike many women, it suited her perfectly. Her fragrance, too filled his nostrils and lifted his soul. L'heure Bleu perhaps? Evening in Paris? Or were those brands beneath her station? Goodman rued the fact that he had no relevant knowledge. He was certain, however, that her dove grey suit, elegant and expensive, was unobtainable in wartime. Indeed for the first time Goodman felt vaguely embarrassed in his own somewhat crumpled khaki serge.

'Sorry,' he apologised. 'That was rude of me. You look wonderful.'

'Thank you. Until today I'd almost forgotten what it's like to wear comfortable clothes.'

Goodman shuffled his feet. 'Did you come up to town today?'

'This morning, by train.' Sophie grimaced at the memory of the journey. 'Four of us squeezed onto a bench made for two. Too matey for my taste.'

At that moment the bell rang for the first act, and the throng around him began to finish their drinks and move toward the doors of the auditorium. Goodman had no desire to end their encounter, but said anyway: 'You'll miss the beginning.'

She glanced back across her shoulder briefly. 'It's a pity you're not staying. I've got a spare ticket.'

'Oh? I thought your father was coming.'

'So did he. But at sixty you don't argue with migraine.'

'How unfortunate,' he lied.

'It needn't be. That is, if you're free tonight.'

Goodman thought quickly. Kydd was perfectly capable of keeping tabs on Ironside alone. To hell. 'I suppose I could risk leaving the defence of the realm in the hands of my sergeant for an hour or two.'

'Splendid. But there is a condition.'

'Which is?'

'You tell me your name. I can't call you captain, and I won't call you sir.'

'No secret about that. It's Goodman. John Goodman.'

She smiled mysteriously. 'Just like Benny.'

'Sorry?' said Goodman, nonplussed.

However Sophie Gold offered no reply, and instead took his arm and lead him towards the auditorium.

No sooner had they entered and started down the aisle than the houselights dimmed, so that the final stage of the journey to their seats was accompanied by much knocking of knees and hostile muttering. By the time they were seated, the curtain had risen on a set depicting the lounge of a smart continental hotel. As Maxim de Winter folded his newspaper and summoned the waiter, a terse whisper in Goodman's ear demanded that he remove his cap. He did so, then settled into the hard theatre seat as best he could, the fierce aroma of a good cigar filling the air from somewhere close by.

A moment later, and all too soon, Elizabeth took centre stage. As the second Mrs de Winter she was cast as the pure young heroine, eager of heart and free of guile. How sweet the irony, Goodman mused, and how complete. After Dartford, his brief meeting with his wife had come as a blow on a bruise. Goodman had knocked on the door of her dressing room with high hopes that Elizabeth might consent to a divorce. Instead she had asked for the kind of money that he had seldom earned even as a barrister in peacetime, let alone as a captain in Field Security. Even the stage she now trod served as yet another bittersweet reminder. Two years before, The Ghost Train had been the first West End role in which Elizabeth's name had appeared in the programme. She had left him for the producer a fortnight later. A serial heartbreaker, within another fortnight she had left the producer also.

Goodman glanced sideways at Sophie, but she appeared absorbed in the actors on stage, her expression critical. It occurred to Goodman suddenly that she might have offered him the ticket as some sort of cruel amusement, to be shared with the rest of her billet, and afterwards relayed in letters to distant friends. No sooner had Goodman cast this uncharitable thought from his mind, however, than Elizabeth approached the footlights at the front of the stage, working towards a moment of high drama. Goodman became acutely aware that the seats they occupied were very close to the front of the stalls, and that being one of the few people in the audience in uniform, Elizabeth might conceivably spy him out. She might notice Sophie too, and store the information away, to be used against him at a later date. Or would she imagine that the cuckolded lawyer was still besotted with his wayward actress wife, and had resorted to nursing his bleeding heart in the cheap seats? The possibility that Elizabeth might suspect he held a torch for her still annoyed Goodman intensely. For at bottom it was true.

Goodman's discomfort persisted for sixty minutes more, until the curtain descended on the first act, and the audience adjourned for interval drinks. Goodman lead Sophie through to the bar, where he ordered a gin sling and another whisky soda from the lone septuagenarian barman, grateful that his uniform carried him to the front of the scrum, for the man had only one good arm and fetched the drinks as quickly as a cloud crosses the horizon on a windless day.

As Goodman handed Sophie her glass she raised it level with his own. 'We should drink to something.'

'Migraine perhaps?'

She nodded. 'Here's to spare tickets and chance meetings.'

As their glasses touched, Goodman trawled is mind for an apt conversational gambit. As far as courting went he felt out of condition, as stiff as a rusty old bicycle.

'I hope you got even with that rigger. You know, the Nivea hoaxer.'

'Oh, he got his alright. Fell off one of the TX masts and broke his leg.'

'There's a pun about come-uppances in there somewhere.'

Sophie pulled a face.

'Sorry. So, how goes the WAAF?'

'It goes.'

'Been in long?'

'Four months. I signed up on my twenty-second birthday. I've probably aged years already.'

'Hardly,' said Goodman, and meant it.

'I only waited as long as I did to join up because I was worried how father would react.'

'He's protective?'

'I'm his only daughter. Father is a merchant banker, mother died when I was six. We lived in New York for two years, came back here in thirty-eight.'

'Sounds exciting.'

'Some and some.' Sophie paused, and took a thoughtful sip at her drink. 'Anyway, that's enough about yours truly. Tell me about John Goodman.'

'I was a barrister in peacetime.'

'Prosecution or defence?'

'Well, neither. Divorce mainly, and some contentious probate outside the mating season. Always monotonous, usually sordid.'

'Oh dear. So the war saved you too.'

'Terrible thing to admit, isn't it. Truth is, the flea of the Bar never bit me very hard.'

'Something else did?'

Goodman thought about lying, but decided to tell the truth, albeit laced with an apology. 'I'd like to write, I'm afraid.'

'No need to apologise. Any success?'

'I had a couple of things in Purpose last year. All things considered 1939 wasn't the best time to kick off a literary career.'

'Doesn't Victor Cazelet run an anti-aircraft battery full of writers and artists?'

'And actors and dancers,' nodded Goodman. 'Silk pajamas in barracks and dried flowers sent down from the CO's greenhouse isn't quite my thing.' He sipped at his scotch, and wondered if the label was wholly honest. 'Who's Benny?' he asked, suddenly remembering. 'Boyfriend?'

'Hardly,' she grinned. 'Benny Goodman, the American clarinet player - the King of Swing. I adore him. Do you like jazz?'

'We were never formally introduced. Jack Hylton possibly? I might have heard him on the BBC.'

Sophie pulled a face. 'Too square for my taste.'

'Actually I'm not terribly musical.'

'It's a passion with me,' she continued, unperturbed. 'Mind you, nowadays the pickings are pretty slim on this side of the pond. In New York we were spoiled for choice.'

Goodman sensed the conversation moving out of his depth. For him jazz was a dark continent, to be explored by braver souls in the disreputable cellar clubs of Soho and Leicester Square. In an attempt to make light of it he said: 'I suppose all the musicians are digging slit trenches. Or is jazz a reserved occupation?'

'Very droll. As a matter of fact, I did hear of a place in Hammersmith. Isn't that your stamping ground?'

'It is, but I don't know of any jazz clubs.'

'We could try to find it, if you like. They call it Pee Wee's Place.'

Goodman frowned. 'Tonight?'

'Why not?'

Because the law according to Sod and Murphy dictated that he would run into a member of his section there, for one. Then there was the small matter of a lame leg and two left feet. 'What about Rebecca?' he said uncertainly. 'By the time it's over your club might be closed.'

'Not if we leave now. Besides, as soon as your wife stepped on stage you looked as though you'd rather be somewhere else. Have you still got that little car?'

As Sophie put her question the bell rang for the second act, daring him to refuse her invitation. The prospect of throwing shapes to jazz in a smoky cellar, in battledress and with a revolver swinging from his hip, touched at Goodman's stomach like a cold finger of fear.

'Alright,' he agreed, despite himself. 'I'm parked at Lincoln's Inn. God only knows where we'll find a taxi.'

'Let's walk,' Sophie smiled. 'It's a lovely evening.'

And getting better with every moment that passed. Goodman downed the rest of his scotch, straightened his tie, and dived into the river.

Outside the theatre, as the sun sank toward the rooftops over Piccadilly Circus, the evening air was warm, and the West End streets were busy with jostling crowds determined to enjoy freedom while it endured. Although no bombs had yet fallen on the capital, even phoney war had changed London immeasurably. Bands of bright white paint marked every kerb and lamp post, while the pillar boxes were daubed with squares of a bilious yellow formulation which changed colour in the presence of gas. Despite the fact that the air war was still restricted to the English Channel, the sky above the capital was cluttered by a thousand barrage balloons, silver and elephantine. The display windows of the big department stores were latticed with tape against blast, and some boarded over so that browsers were obliged to squint at the displays within, as if at a peepshow. Petrol rationing had further transformed the urban landscape, leaving the buses and taxis fewer in number and more crowded than ever before.

So far Sophie had made all the running. In a belated attempt to take the initiative Goodman took her arm, and was gratified to find that she gave it gladly. They set out along Shaftesbury Avenue toward the Charing Cross Road, he drawing occasional salutes from other ranks, she turning heads with every step. The throng of nationalities through which they were moving was dizzying: French, Dutch, Norwegian, Polish, Czech - the debris of half a dozen broken continental armies. Goodman again experienced the curious sensation of swimming in the full tide of history. In Soho they passed an empty Italian restaurant, its frontage boarded over with plywood sheets. Following Mussolini's declaration of war on Britain a fortnight before a mob had rioted, propelling rocks through the windows of cafes and ice cream parlours, and hurling blows and abuse at perceived aliens. Lately a pungent wave of xenophobia had swept through the capital, as senseless almost as the cruelties visited upon dachshunds in 1914. Goodman had even seen innocent refugees - women and children - jeered in the streets.

'Are you alright walking? asked Sophie. 'I should have asked.'

'I'm fine.'

'That limp of yours looks terribly brave. Were you over in France?'

'Only for the Sitzkreig. My unit spent most of its time drinking and digging.'

'No heroics, then.'

'None at all. We turned a stream into an anti-tank ditch and built a road. The first hard frost put paid to that.'

'At least you had your ditch.'

'Don't remind me. The only way to keep your clothes dry was to take them off. Two chaps got frostbite. Lord Gort turned up one day for a snap inspection. I don't think we impressed him much, saluting a Field Marshall in gumboots and underpants.'

'So what happened to your leg? Don't tell me you fell off a barstool.'

'Oh, it's a war wound alright. I copped it in Belgium.' Goodman decided to share another guilty secret. 'Actually, the bullet was Belgian too.'

'I thought they were our allies.'

'They were, after the roof fell in. But until the Hun crossed the frontier in May the Belgians treated us as hostile too. One night in January a balloon went up. My patrol strayed too close to the border, and some rustic Walloon opened fire.'

'How dreadful.'

'Yes and no. My unit ended up in the rearguard at Dunkirk. But for that Belgian I'd either be dead, or kicking my heels in a German camp.' Goodman paused, in his own mind still unable to determine whether his being shot six months earlier had marked a beginning or an end. 'Anyway, after that little escapade I kicked around in hospital for a month. Then they punished me with an extra pip on each shoulder and a posting to Field Security.'

'It sounds to me as though you owe that Belgian a drink.'

'Perhaps. Something with a good kick to it.'

'We had firearms training last month. Five rounds on the range with a Lee Enfield.'

'Did you shred the bullseye?'

'According to the instructor, I couldn't hit a cow on the backside with a shovel. But I can strip and load as fast as the next man.'

Sophie shone him a mischievous grin, and nudged him softly in the ribs. Meeting her bright dark eyes, Goodman sensed an invisible current beginning to flow between them.

NINE

The coming of war had despoiled the clean architectural lines of Lincoln's Inn only slightly. A large static water tank, recently constructed in the middle of the central green, all but hid the fountain, while bright red arrows marked the route to the air raid shelters. In this tranquil urban acre Goodman's tired Austin Seven also struck an incongruous note, its camouflaged paint scheme seeming all the more ridiculous below the ornate south window of the Great Hall.

They reached New Square as the chapel bell began to toll the curfew. Suffolk Chambers stood hard by the gatehouse on the north-western corner of New Square. It was from a cramped attic office on the topmost floor that Goodman had practised law for three years prior to the outbreak of war, and his father for thirty before him. Goodman lead Sophie up the narrow staircase to the neat, orderly third floor office occupied by Tom Ashworth. It contained both a telephone and a bottle of good sherry, from which he and Goodman had drunk earlier that evening while discussing the small mountain of cases Tom was handling on behalf of his absent brothers in law. Ashworth was a highly capable Cambridge man, too asthmatic even the most sedentary military service, killing time in chancery work before his inevitable appointment to the bench.

Goodman checked in with Kydd at the section office, while Sophie removed her coat and poured two glasses from the decanter on the desk. As she passed one to him in the falling twilight she looked very beautiful.

'Not too bad,' she pronounced after he had rung off, exercising her palette.

'It's oloroso. There's some brandy tucked away if you prefer.'

Sophie shook her head, then cast her eyes around Ashworth's neat, orderly room lined with law reports and satirical prints. 'I like it here. Are there many women barristers?'

'None that I've seen before a judge. It would be pretty hard for a woman to find a vacancy in chambers. On the whole solicitors don't like to instruct the fairer sex.'

Sophie studied him gravely a moment. 'Good enough to face off the Luftwaffe, good enough to argue a case, I'd say. I suppose you went to Oxford or Cambridge.'

'Oxford, briefly. I read English at Magdalen.'

'But you didn't finish?'

'I was sent down.'

She nodded approvingly. 'Under a cloud, or run out of town?'

Goodman downed half his sherry in a single draft. 'During my second term one of the porters discovered a woman in my room. The Dean determined that an example should be made, pour encourager les autres. After that, my father as good as ordered me to study for the Bar examination. I joined the Inns of Court Terriers after Munich, and spent the next twelve months trying to kid myself I didn't want a war with Germany.'

'Was Elizabeth the girl the porter found?'

'Lord, no.'

'So where did you meet?'

'At a party.'

'I've met plenty of men at parties. I've never been tempted to marry any of them.'

Goodman emptied his glass. 'There was a shotgun involved.'

'Oh,' she said quietly.

'But no children. She miscarried.'

'I'm sorry. Is this getting too personal?'

'Not really,' he said, without inner conviction. 'It was never much of a marriage. She only wanted to see me this evening because of a leaking roof.'

'Can't she find a builder?'

'It's not that simple. All the tenants in the block have been served with notice of a hefty premium. And she wants me to pay.'

'But surely if it's her flat-'

Goodman shook his head. 'When we married we took a flat in Hampstead. A year ago the landlord baled out to South Africa. The

61

tenants formed a management company, and our shares were registered in my name.' Goodman chose not to mention that he had agreed to accept the shares during their last attempt at reconciliation, which had lasted just twelve days, and which, he now suspected, had merely been a ruse by Elizabeth to obtain his signature on the stock transfer form. 'Thanks to the war the block is a third empty, so the calls are even steeper. Marvellous, isn't it? I pay for rent and repairs on a flat I've slept in once since August 1939.'

'Why should you pay?' Sophie frowned, sipping modestly at her drink. 'After all, Elizabeth Easterbrook is halfway to Hollywood.'

'My wife has expensive friends.'

'You could always petition for divorce.'

'Oh, I put in my pitch this evening.'

'And she refused?'

Goodman nodded. 'Publicity. Now she's landed her first leading role, her agent believes divorce proceedings would attract the wrong sort of press. His considered advice is to wait until after the invasion, when a celebrity decree won't cause such a splash.'

'After the invasion?' Sophie's face clouded with anger. 'Sweet Jesus! To think I'm ruining my eyesight and sharing a grubby dorm with eleven women to protect people like... like that.' She looked away briefly, then regained her composure. 'Sorry. My family's Jewish, you see.'

'I understand,' said Goodman.

'Sorry, but I don't see how you can.'

'I've half an idea. When I wasn't dividing families and challenging wills I took a few briefs for the National Council for Civil Liberties, and the Board of Jewish Deputies. You know, Brick Lane, blackshirt razor boys, that sort of thing.'

Sophie regarded him closely for a long moment. 'Good for you,' she said quietly. 'Look, I'm sorry I made you sit through that silly play.'

'Not to worry,' he said quickly. 'Anyway, my back pages are pretty tedious reading. Tell me about New York.'

'Where would you like to begin?' She moved into the room and set her glass on the tray, then settled on the end of Ashworth's cluttered desk, as though riding side-saddle. 'I'm wearing one of my best memories from Bloomingdales. When snow falls the view of Central Park from the Dakota Building is inspirational to the power of ten. There's magic in the air in Greenwich Village, and on Broadway. And sometimes love.'

Goodman raised an eyebrow.

'Well, once. At a Benny Goodman concert, when he played to raise funds to fight Franco. Granollers had just been bombed, worse than Guernica. I gave fifty dollars to an impossibly handsome man on the door collecting money in a fire bucket. Paul turned my head a hundred degrees, much to father's disapproval.'

'Because he was a jazz aficionado?'

'Because he was German. Oh, Paul was as American as Kansas, more interested in learning to play the saxophone than politics. We were very happy together. But his family were immigrants, and as good as Nazis as far as father was concerned. So Paul was strictly off-limits.'

'Did you obey?'

'Did I hell. We met in secret for a year. It was all very Romeo and Juliet - dancing in the aisles at the Paramount Theatre, stomping at the Savoy. But then father received an anonymous letter, and within a fortnight we were on the clipper back to Southampton.'

'Bad bit of business,' offered Goodman inadequately.

Sophie shrugged her shoulders. 'Doors close, doors open. Besides, I would have come home anyway to fight the good fight. And now I'm in uniform I can do as I please.'

'Do you love him still?'

'My father, you mean?'

'No, this chap Paul.'

Sophie paused, then said: 'Probably not. But I haven't loved anyone else since.'

A silence fell down on the darkened room. Goodman glanced briefly at the clock on the wall. Ten thirty-five. By the time they reached Hammersmith the club would be closing, if ever they found it. He experienced a sudden and overwhelming desire to kiss Sophie. They stood mere feet apart, she little more than a silhouette in the darkness. Goodman wanted to take her in his arms, to feel her body against his, to bury his face in her hair. He was certain that the attraction was mutual, yet to make the first move seemed too blunt, too presumptuous. Futile even, with war so close at hand. They remained just so for several moments, amongst the books and shadows and uncertainty.

'It's getting late,' Sophie said at length. 'Would you drive me home?'

'Of course.' Goodman felt at once relieved that she had eased the tension, and disappointed that the moment had passed.

Rising from the desk, Sophie stepped towards him and touched a hand to his shoulder. 'I'd like you to kiss me first.'

Her scent. Her waist. Her slender frame. As their lips met, Goodman glimpsed again a world that had for too long been lost to him.

TEN

Two minutes' walk from the Grand Place, his contact had assured him. Follow the Rue de la Tete d'Or past the police headquarters, then cross into the Rue du Marche. Paul Wagner wiped his brow with a handkerchief already sodden with perspiration. The heat was close and oppressive, and made worse by the stifling air, which seemed to hang motionless over the centre of the Belgian capital like an invisible fog.

Six short weeks after the occupation of Brussels an uneasy truce persisted between victor and vanquished. Idle German servicemen loitered on the boulevards, crowded tourist attractions, and infested every cafe terrace. Most were eager to invade England, and indulged in keen speculation on their chances of being chosen for the first wave of the assault. Some studied English in their spare time, and read up on cathedrals and historic spots they might visit - provided, of course, these sites had survived the campaign. Others, taking advantage of the forced exchange rate, lavished occupation marks with liberal abandon on cameras, watches and jewellery. So freely did they spend, indeed, that the eastward flow of valuables back to the fatherland had lately reached a volume unseen since the Franco-Prussian war of 1870.

In seeking out an innocuous shop in a quiet Brussels side street, Paul Wagner pursued a very different purpose. Acting on information received the previous evening, the Brandenburg lieutenant harboured high hopes of uncovering a treasure trove of superior English and American jazz shellacs.

Within the context of the thousand year Reich jazz music enjoyed a peculiarly anomalous status. Although officially decried by race hygienists as atonal negro-Jewish noise, and by self-serving journalists as a treason against civilized culture, such dictates were punctured by compromise and accommodation. True, the importation of unlicensed foreign sheet music had been forbidden since December 1937, and Goebbels had since issued a decree prohibiting the sale of all recorded material by non-Aryan artists. Yet the fact remained that a large cross-section of the population rejoiced in modern dance band music, and maintained a demand for real jazz and swing which ersatz concoctions - so-called Neue Deutsche Tanzmusik, and the ridiculous marschfoxtrot - had signally failed to displace.

In the newly-occupied territories, if not at home, pragmatic considerations obliged the architects of the New European Order to turn a blind eye to such deviancy. The first was purely circumstantial, in that the speed of the fall of the West had left little or no time to set the apparatus of proscription in place. A second was economic, since the gap in the market left by now-unobtainable English imports could be filled by state-sanctioned recordings, and substantial profits channelled back into the coffers of the Reich. Above all else, there was the necessity to court the tastes of the armed services in order to maintain morale. Among the appetites traditionally cherished by soldiers on pacified alien ground, uninhibited music ranked second only to the company of uninhibited women, and for this reason was tolerated. In this way, both native jazz ensembles and touring Truppenbetreuung service groups were able to cross the fine line dividing acceptable rhythms from raw swing without fear of reprisal.

With the Dutch, Belgian and French currencies now devalued five hundred per cent against the German mark, avid collectors like Wagner had lately enjoyed rich pickings. Against a background of uncertain legality, however, he had determined to take no risks in seeking out further rare sides. Therefore Wagner made his way through the busy streets of the Belgian capital in mufti, his wallet thick not with occupation marks but native francs, intending to mine this new seam quietly, and without fanfare.

The store was situated halfway along the Rue du Marche. Melodie was a small outlet which, unusually, sold no musical instruments, its small display window stocked instead with label catalogues, free-standing disc advertisements and assorted printed ephemera, a stack of imported American books taking pride of place. As Wagner entered the shop a bell sounded incongruously -

a momentary, discordant reminder of the general store on Rosemont and Ninth, two thousand miles away. He was relieved to find there were no other customers inside. The largest wall was taken up by racks of sheet music, and another with colourful pre-war promotional flyers and signed photographs. On a table an expensive-looking Phillips phonograph delivered Django Reinhardt through an old fashioned conical horn.

Behind the counter a stout middle-aged man sipped from a coffee cup while perusing a copy of Down Beat, months out of date. He glanced up briefly as Wagner crossed the floor, scowled, then returned to his reading. At close quarters the coffee cup appeared absurdly small beside his impressive bulk.

'Je voudrais voir quelque de votre disques,' Wagner announced in poor French.

'You are German?' the shopkeeper answered coldly, his eyes still fixed on the journal. Like many Lowlanders he chose to address presumed enemies in English, a form of passive resistance to which Wagner had already grown accustomed.

'American,' he replied, responding in kind. 'I'm a foreign correspondent with Associated Press.'

At this the man became animated, his coffee and magazine forgotten in a trice. Grinning broadly, he extended a fat hand across the counter. 'Hey - I heard the Cotton Club closed a few weeks ago. I spent the best night of my life there in thirty-seven. What's the story?'

'Search me,' Wagner replied flatly. 'I've been stranded here in Europe since March.'

'You are looking for scoops to take back to the Big Apple?'

The adoption of argot by non-Americans never failed to irritate Wagner. He shook his head. 'No scoops. Just indulging a personal interest.'

'Let me guess,' the Belgian continued, his enthusiasm undimmed despite Wagner's best efforts. 'Be-bop?'

Wagner thought fast. Be-bop was a new elaboration of the jazz language, rumoured to be exploding from the black clubs in Harlem. He knew next to nothing about it, save that which he had gleaned from a few dismissive paragraphs in the International Herald Tribune. Clearly the Belgian was equally intrigued, assuming that the visiting American journalist knew the musical route, and might add to his own meagre store of knowledge.

'Mainly swing, as a matter of fact,' Wagner replied, feigning casual disinterest. 'I haven't had time to take the latest temperatures.'

Crestfallen, the man bent down and produced a bundle of catalogues from behind the counter. 'Of course, not everything is in stock,' he explained. 'The master race, you see. They buy up all the jazz they can lay their hands on, at double-price too, for in Germany swing is forbidden.' He passed his finger across his throat and grinned broadly. 'Hey - that would make an interesting story for your readers in America.'

'It might,' Wagner said absently, reluctant to encourage the conversation. He leafed briskly through a dozen or so catalogues: Brunswick, Odeon, Decca, RCA Victor, Vocalion - all the usual suspects. Most of the listings he had poured over a week before, in a better store in the Hague.

'A few of the Nazis are serious,' the Belgian continued, his tone contemptuous. 'But most are fools. Imagine - I even sold some Henry Hall. I mean, they might as well spend their money at home on the rubbish Hitler permits.'

'If rubbish is all you have then I guess I'm wasting my time.'

'Oh no,' he replied hurriedly, raising his hands defensively. 'Selling good sides to Nazis is collaboration. I keep the hot wax aside for regular customers - and friendly powers, of course.'

'Of course,' Wagner repeated. 'What have you got?'

'No be-bop, for sure. You want Basie maybe? Ellington? Or are you looking for European swing to take home to America?'

'Not right now. Do you have any Gene Krupa?'

The man hesitated. 'Kind of. Three discs, two with Roy Aldridge and Anita O'Day. But it's a customer order, very expensive.'

'Is he a regular?'

'He was. I haven't seen him since May.'

'I'll double whatever he offered you,' Wagner said quickly, without thinking further. He wanted the discs, and badly, regardless of cost. The prospect of obtaining the desirable trio of sides instilled in him a temporary insanity, a willing and delicious loss of self-control, as though the very proximity of the records released some powerful intoxicant into the air. There was no greater joy than the din produced by a steel needle in a tight spiral groove, and no other use for his service pay. Retrieving his wallet from his pocket, Wagner allowed the man to glimpse the generous fold of currency.

The Belgian frowned, still uncertain whether to allow the coveted discs to leave the premises beneath a stranger's arm. Then, slowly, he stepped into the back of the shop, and returned with a neat brown paper parcel. Wagner opened it carefully and examined the trio of heavy shellac discs. They were in mint condition, all but unobtainable in Europe. He would have to paste dummy labels over the originals, of course, just in case some stooge came snooping around his billet; something strident by Wagner or Bach.

'How much?' Wagner asked eagerly.

'Five hundred francs.'

'For the three?'

The Belgian shook his head. 'Each record.'

Far too much, Wagner thought, as he counted the notes from his wallet. Not that it mattered.

'I also have some Fletcher Henderson,' the man continued hopefully.

'Not so interesting,' Wagner replied. As he spoke the bell sounded behind him, and a second customer entered the shop. Wagner glanced across his shoulder and saw a bespectacled Luftwaffe corporal in full uniform. He felt uneasy now, and, taking up the package carefully, turned to leave. 'I guess I'll leave it with these.'

Wagner was halfway to the door when the storekeeper spoke again. 'Perhaps I'll see you at the Beursschouwberg tonight.'

He turned on his heel impatiently. 'Say what?'

The man nodded toward a poster on the wall listing forthcoming attractions at a local venue. Tonight was the turn of Fud Candix. Wagner knew the name vaguely: Candix led a band that played up-to-date arrangements of standards in the style of Count Basie. Wagner had not seen a big band show in more than eight months. Had the shopkeeper not struck up the unwanted conversation he might have considered attending, for faux swing was better than no swing at all.

But instead Wagner replied: 'Not my scene. Besides, I'm just passing through.'

ELEVEN

Blackstock Road comprised two anonymous terraces, crouched and shabby, and sufficiently far removed from the Margate seafront to allow any households who wished to remain in residence to stay. Few had. On the opposite side of the street one of the houses had been gutted by fire, its blackened shell now serving as a playground for a riot of truanting schoolboys, engaged in noisy pursuit of a nominate Hitler from room to room.

As Sergeant Kydd pulled up outside number twenty-two Goodman steeled himself to ransack his fourth home in two days, and fork through the domestic minutiae of further undeserving strangers. Today was the turn of Bernard Ward's family. Goodman had elected to visit the ringleader's household last of all, not because he savoured the prospect, but because Major Morley had suggested they rendezvous later in the afternoon on the coast nearby. Something about burning the sea, the surreal message had read, leaving Goodman certain that the facts had been scrambled.

The front door opened directly onto the pavement. From behind it the sound of a wireless was audible.

'Hardly a robber's palace,' Kydd observed sniffily, before pounding on the knocker.

Footsteps approached, after which the letter box snapped open and closed like a judas. A female voice demanded: 'Who is it?'

Goodman cleared his throat. 'Field Security Police. Private Bernard George Ward is presently absent without leave. I wish to conduct a search of the house and grounds.'

Beneath the stern tone Goodman felt inwardly ridiculous: he wished. The grounds. The task ahead of him was hardly eased by pomposity.

Moments later the door was opened by an attractive bottled

blonde in her early twenties. She was smoking a cigarette, and eyed the uniformed strangers with cool hostility.

'Don't tell me,' she anticipated wearily. 'Bernie done a runner?'

'That's right,' replied Goodman. 'Are you his wife?'

The woman nodded. 'That's me, Dorothy Ward. You won't find him here.'

'In that case you won't mind us having a look around,' Kydd said bluntly, stepping across the threshold.

Dorothy Ward stood her ground and blocked his way, then blew an insolent plume of cigarette smoke into his face. The enmity between the pair was immediate and powerful, like opposite magnetic poles.

'Got a warrant?' she demanded.

'There's a war on, love,' Kydd replied scornfully. 'My warrant's the Emergency Powers Defence Act 1939.'

She hesitated, then stepped aside and allowed both the military men to pass into the hallway. Unaffected by any finer sentiment, Kydd strode straight through to the back of the house, killing the music from the wireless somewhere between the kitchen and the back yard.

If Goodman had half expected to uncover a hoard of contraband goods in the Margate backstreet, he had scarcely anticipated finding the house crammed floor to ceiling with furniture, much of it little more than firewood. There were bundles of clothes also, wrapped up in bedsheets, and boxes of books and toys, ornaments, and pots and pans. Edging into the crowded sitting room Goodman fancied he had entered a Pickford's warehouse, or a bailiff's sale, and looked about in vain for something accessible to search or examine.

'It's from over the road,' Dorothy Ward explained from the doorway, nodding at the sticks of furniture. 'They got burned out two weeks ago. Upset candle in the blackout.'

'Very charitable of you to give it house room.'

'Charity don't come into it. I'm charging four shillings a week.'

Goodman made a show of running through a sideboard, and found his fingers blackened with soot from the blaze. She watched him keenly, arms folded.

'He's not in there.'

There and then Goodman elected to leave the bedroom to Kydd.

71

Straightening up, he cast around the room for something else to check. A gaudy silver frame on the mantelpiece housed a bromide portrait of a young man, handsome enough but for a lantern jaw. Though his records had not yet reached his desk, Goodman guessed it was Bernard Ward.

'Is that your husband?'

'Correct,' she answered flatly, splitting the word into two distinct syllables. She drew heavily on her cigarette. 'So when did he make off?'

'Three days ago.'

'I'd check the West End if I were you. Girls and gambling, that's more to his liking than Margate now.'

The brittle edge to her voice told Goodman that Dorothy Ward was telling the truth. She extinguished her cigarette and lit up another immediately.

'I don't like my husband,' she continued, suddenly anxious to speak her mind. 'He's a bastard, frankly. I'm as sorry as you are that he's deserted if it means he'll turn up here. That mugshot sits there to keep his mother sweet, not me.'

Goodman might have offered some sympathetic reply, had Kydd not that same moment returned from his reconnaissance of the back of the house. 'There's no alley to slip away down,' he reported cheerfully. 'And he's not holed up in the khazi.'

'Check in the cistern, did you?'

Kydd regarded Dorothy Ward with studied contempt for a long moment, then demanded: 'Can I see your gas mask?'

Goodman knew the direction in which his sergeant was heading. Rationed petrol supplied for commercial use was coloured a distinctive red. It was a matter of common knowledge that the tell-tale dye could be removed by running the fuel through an ordinary gas mask filter. Bernard Ward had dealt in black market fuel. But now Ward was dead, and Kydd meant merely to humiliate his widow.

'That won't be necessary,' he said.

'Very good, sir,' Kydd replied, with a trace of annoyance. 'Check upstairs?'

Now Dorothy's hostility gave way to a heartfelt plea. 'Do you have to? Only his mother's up there. She's as good as bedridden, and senile with it. I have to cope with the old cow on my own. If

72

you so much as look round the door I won't hear the end of it for days.'

'I'm sorry,' replied Goodman, 'but we've a job to do.'

She gave a resigned shrug. 'Don't say I didn't warn you, that's all.'

Kydd lead the way upstairs. They entered Dorothy's bedroom first. Goodman stood by as Kydd rifled through various draws and sniffed each side of the pillows for the scent of hair-oil, much enjoying the charade. Goodman's gaze alighted on a gramophone set atop the dresser, and thought immediately of Sophie Gold. They had met again yesterday, all too briefly, when he had driven her to Liverpool Street, a journey broken by a walk through the rose garden in Regent's Park and afternoon tea at the Cafe Anglais. On the platform Sophie had presented him with a record, It Had to be You by Benny Goodman. Back in Hammersmith he had requisitioned the portable player owned by Lance-Corporal Bray and lugged the heavy machine round to his own billet. The gentle melody fascinated him, as did Sophie Gold, so much so that he had spun the disc several times over. Goodman was acutely aware that he had allowed himself to fall in love with a woman whom he could neither telephone nor see, and could write to only via a guardroom. He was, he knew, a fool to himself.

In the small back bedroom Goodman and Kydd were confronted with a silver-haired wreck of a woman propped up on a mountain of pillows. From the bed rose the unmistakable stench of urine.

'Oh God, not again,' sighed Dorothy.

Behind her Goodman recoiled. As Kydd approached the large iron bedstead the old creature spat at him fiercely. Although he made his examination of the bedside table untypically brief, she managed two more direct hits before he was able to retreat out of range. Afterwards the air turned blue with a torrent of obscenities, which continued unabated even after they had retreated from the room and closed the door, her harsh, broken croak sounding for all the world like some hideous caged bird.

'I warned you,' Dorothy repeated, with evident satisfaction.

'Drop that over Berlin and it'll be over by Christmas,' Kydd joked stonily, wiping the spittle from his sleeve with his cuff. Well-used to the art of the search, he now glanced up at the narrow hatch

73

which lead to the loft.

'Got a ladder?'

'No.'

'Chair?'

'In my room.'

Dorothy Ward reached into her pocket for yet another cigarette. Goodman alone noticed that her hand trembled slightly as she spun the flint on her lighter, and sensed that something above their heads was amiss.

'I'll shin up there, sergeant,' he said quickly. 'Can't have you hogging the limelight.'

'I reckon you've deserved it,' Kydd replied, turning to fetch a chair from the empty bedroom.

Kydd returned with a rickety stool. With no little clatter Goodman knocked back the hatch and hauled himself up into the dark, musty space. After Kydd passed up the torch he stood upright and played the beam around the loft. It fell immediately upon two large cardboard cartons stencilled with a familiar acronym: NAAFI. Stepping carefully across the creaking joists he found the first box empty, and the second almost full with packets of Player's Weights. There were five thousand cigarettes, at a guess, all purloined from service stores. No wonder Dorothy Ward was able to indulge in chain smoking.

Below Goodman could hear Kydd reciting a litany of stock warnings as to the penalty for sheltering deserters, and withholding information as to their whereabouts. He knew full well that he should report the find. Yet Ward's wife clearly lead a miserable enough existence as it was. Besides which, Goodman doubted that stolen cigarettes would be of great concern to the mandarins of MI5. He decided to turn a blind eye, and returned to the hatch.

'Anything tasty, sir?' Kydd enquired hopefully, as Goodman descended.

'Nice as ninepence, Sergeant. Sorry to say.'

TWELVE

The two Field Security men had barely commenced the second leg of their drive through Kent when Goodman noticed a distant pall of black smoke. It rose and billowed in the sky above the rooftops of Thanet, and at first Goodman fancied that an aircraft had crashed on the airfield at Manston. Ten minutes later, however, as they left Broadstairs and entered the charmless suburb of Dumpton, he realised they were heading directly toward its source.

Dumpton Gap was a small cove formed by a natural cleft in the white foreland cliffs. Although the smoke had thinned out by the time they arrived, the acrid, choking stench of burning petrol hung heavy on the air. A sunken lane lead down to the shore which formed a steep defile, blocked by an Auxiliary Fire Service tender. Beyond it Goodman saw what appeared to be a burned-out lorry chassis, on which the hoses of the firemen were trained. The surface of the road was blackened also, and the trees and vegetation on the banks either side of the defile scorched and wilted. Here and there a few patches still smouldered desultorily. Kydd was flagged down by a brace of military police motorcyclists, who examined their passes with exaggerated care. Without exception regular CMP personnel looked askance at the disparate collection of men who had volunteered for FS duties. In the view of the more literate Red Cap, the sundry schoolmasters, journalists and encyclopedia salesmen were nothing but a troupe of displaced New Statesman readers, and of no more utility.

'Has there been an accident?' Goodman enquired.

'Your guess is as good as mine, sir. The sappers flood the road with petrol, torch it, then the fire brigade damp it down. Then it starts all over again.'

'Has a Major Morley arrived yet?'

'Couldn't say, sir. There's more brass up there this afternoon than at the War Office.'

The sergeant waved the Austin off to the right, where a rough track lead up onto a grass field on top of the cliff. Two dozen vehicles were scattered around the perimeter, chiefly staff cars and polished ministry Daimlers. Their owners, forty or so all told, were huddled in small groups along the edge of the defile, some holding handkerchiefs and scarves across their faces. Midway between them stood an army fuel bowser, from which several fuel lines lead across the field to the sunken lane.

Goodman left Kydd with the car and walked toward the crowd, which comprised civilians and officers from all three services. Among them he recognised several faces from GHQ, as well as Lord Maurice Hankey, cabinet member and Minister Without Portfolio, and the petroleum secretary, Geoffrey Lloyd. He found Morley in conversation with a junior naval officer, whose bleary eyes betrayed a severe hang-over.

'Captain Goodman - what a pleasure. You've missed the firework display, I'm afraid, but we are promised a sea-fire spectacle.'

'What on earth is going on?' Goodman asked.

'The AGM of the Heath Robinson Appreciation Society,' muttered the navy man tartly.

Morley ignored him. 'A colonel from the Petroleum Division is demonstrating how to burn the Hun back into the sea with surplus petrol stocks. So far they've exploded several barrels of oil, and destroyed an enemy tank which was unwise enough to advance along the lane.'

'Bloody useless it looks too,' declared the senior service man, rubbing at his brow.

'Fleming is upset because he can't smoke. But I have to agree that so far it doesn't seem too hopeful. Unless the War Office has in mind to persuade Hitler that England is populated by ungovernable lunatics.'

'We followed the smoke from Margate,' said Goodman. 'As secret weapons go, it's hardly-'

'Secret?' Morley anticipated. 'Oh, I doubt they intend it to be.'

Their attention was diverted by the petroleum colonel, who now mounted a wooden ammunition box and clapped his hands to summon the attention of the observers.

'Gentlemen,' he began, 'presently our greatest enemy is time. In locations where time precludes the installation of a permanent flame trap, we have at our disposal a limited number of bowsers. Each sector command can form a mobile column of tankers, to operate oil fire ambushes at points where the enemy has to pass.'

A sparse murmur of approval rose from the crowd, as if the deliverance of the kingdom were at hand. A small man in a trenchcoat declared authoritatively: 'The Hun doesn't stand up well to flame. Saw that for myself in 1917.'

Against a background of like mutterings the colonel pressed on. From his briefing Goodman gleaned that the mechanics of disabling armour with blazing oil was not to fire the vehicle itself, but to starve both the engine and crew of oxygen. Based upon enemy types encountered in France, it was calculated that a tank might be stopped in six seconds flat. Having responded with further vague signs of approval, the crowd made their way toward the seaward edge of the cliff, where the destruction of a tank would be demonstrated as it emerged from the sea.

As they walked Morley steered Goodman to one side. 'Anything to report?'

'On the Territorials, or Ironside?'

'Why not start with the former.'

'We've searched the houses. There's no indication that any of the men have returned home.'

'Were the families suspicious?'

'King's widow, perhaps.'

'Which fellow was he?' Morley might have been speaking of a batsman who had hit consecutive sixes.

'The sergeant. They were married for more than twenty years. She might smell a rat, if ever she stops weeping.'

'You should have told her he'd been seeing another woman. Or gone mad.'

Goodman let it pass. 'Has anything kicked off at Bawdsey?'

'Not as yet,' Morley replied blandly.

Goodman cursed inwardly. The previous day, as Sophie boarded her train, Goodman had offered up an unspeakable prayer:

that the station at Bawdsey had been attacked and levelled in her absence. Now the fear that she was sitting pretty on a ticking bomb tugged at his stomach with renewed urgency.

From the observation point on the edge of the cliff they watched as the colonel dashed to and fro on the sandy beach, endlessly checking and tweaking his mysterious equipment. The breeze was freshening, and the view from the cliff revealed a bank of menacing clouds above the Goodwins which threatened rain. As the weather and the tide began to turn, and after several false starts, the crowd's mounting impatience was hardly assuaged when the extemporised anti-tank weapon was finally unveiled: a rusting Singer Junior car crammed with explosives and cans of petrol. What followed was farce. Represented again by a lorry chassis, the tank emerged from the water towed by a Bedford four-tonner at the top of the beach. As the wreck slowly cleared the breakers, a sapper coaxed the Singer into life and gingerly started forward across the sand. With thirty yards to go the driver took his hands from the wheel and leapt clear, rolling heroically away, leaving the little car to trundle bravely on toward the advancing enemy.

Left to its own devices, the vehicle veered to the right and curved gently away, coming to stop in a foot of water and detonating twenty yards clear of the intended target. Unscathed, the dummy tank continued its stately progress up the beach towards London.

The spectacular blaze produced further clouds of thick, pungent smoke which caused the spectators to retreat with undignified haste. To his left, Goodman spied Morley's naval acquaintance being violently sick.

Presently, after the smoke had cleared and the coughing had subsided, the colonel returned to his box looking somewhat flustered. 'I can't deny,' he began, 'that the trial has not produced quite the result we had hoped for.'

The confession drew a ripple of mild laughter. Goodman turned to Morley. 'Will you need a report?'

The major shook his head. 'What about Tiny Ironside? Still making housecalls in Holland Park?'

'Oh yes, regular as clockwork.'

'Found out what he's up to?'

'Still too early to say. It's none too easy. His driver waits outside, and there's a blackout curtain behind the door.'

'Are there other visitors?'

'None that coincide.'

Morley paused. 'It sounds like a woman to me.'

'Is that good or bad?' asked Goodman.

'That rather depends on the woman.'

The petroleum colonel waited for quiet to settle before he resumed his briefing.

'The final demonstration will, I'm sure, offer proof of the value of petroleum defence. If oil can be used on the sea itself, a minimum of men will be required to defend the beaches, and the bulk held in reserve. The idea is to distribute a film of petrol on the surface of the water. As the barges approach, the fuel is ignited by means of tracer bullets or a signal flare.'

A voice spoke up. 'Are you saying that the sea can actually be set on fire?' The speaker's sceptical tone reflected the mood of the majority of the audience.

'Exactly,' the colonel replied, rallying a little. 'We have two schemes in mind. The first is an underwater pipeline running a suitable distance offshore. The second - and this is my favourite conception - is a controlled minefield of submerged drums, fired by an electrical charge or tracer rounds. It may be possible to render beaches unapproachable over prolonged periods, or to inflict decisive casualties upon the enemy if caught at a propitious moment.'

Morley turned to Goodman and raised his eyebrows. Goodman recalled the young home guard and his bag of pepper at Bromeswell four days earlier. Now it was intended that the army would confront the invader with boiling oil. What next, he wondered? Breastplates and halberds released from the Tower of London?

Once more the onlookers on the cliff were directed to look down to the beach. On the foreshore a sapper crouched over a detonating box, from which a length of cordtex ran into the surf, then thirty yards further out to sea on a string of floats. On the sea bed, invisible to the naked eye, sat three five-gallon drums charged with volatile fuel oil. To each was attached a small watertight gelignite charge, joined by cordtex to a float on the surface, which in turn carried an electronic detonator.

From his box the colonel bellowed: 'When you're ready, men.'

On command, the sapper cranked the handle on his boxes, then plunged down the handle. For several moments it seemed that nothing would happen. Then, but slowly, three dark pools of oil appeared on the surface of the water, much calmer than the sea surrounding them. When they had spread the sapper depressed the plunger again, whereupon three sharp reports sounded from the floating detonators. Thus encouraged, two of the oil pools began to burn, almost imperceptibly at first, but quickly producing a fierce orange flame and further billowing clouds of pungent black smoke.

The pools burned only briefly before the action of the surf dispersed the oil. Yet in that short space of time a series of dramatic episodes followed one after another like falling dominos. First, from a point somewhere inland, an air-raid siren began to emit its banshee wail. Moments later the deep hum of aero-engines reached the ears of the crowd gathered on the cliff, as a formation of twin-engined enemy aircraft emerged from the advancing cloudbank, flying south to strike at shipping in the Dover Strait.

Attracted by the smoke from the flame barrage, one of the raiders peeled away from the ragged formation and dived down towards Dumpton Gap.

A voice yelled: 'Air raid!'

Another: 'Take cover!'

As one, the spectators took to their heels and fled back across the field towards the scatter of vehicles. In turn, their drivers dived from the vehicles and sprinted into the fields beyond. Goodman found himself racing a red-tabbed staff general toward the nearest cover at a pace he scarcely thought possible. Both crashed to the ground in unison, and rolled under the chassis from opposite sides.

As the roar of the diving aircraft grew louder a Bofors anti-aircraft gun opened fire from somewhere nearby. Now the roar of the radial engines became deafening. Goodman closed his eyes and waited for the whistle and crunch of bombs, or the staccato crackle of machine gun fire. None came, however, and as the seconds stretched he heard instead the sound of pistol shots above the din of the bomber and the Bofors.

A moment later, the roar of the aircraft had passed and quickly receded. Very slowly, Goodman crawled out from under the car.

Some two dozen figures were scattered across the grass in the immediate vicinity, some stirring and picking themselves up, but most still hugging the earth. From somewhere a voice was complaining loudly of a broken ankle.

Through the midst of this irregular scene Morley strode like King Harry at Agincourt. With no little astonishment, Goodman realised that the shots had been the major firing at the enemy bomber with his service revolver.

As he drew closer, Morley returned the weapon to the holster on his hip and grinned broadly. 'Damned tricky bird to hit, Goodman. But I fancy I winged the bugger.'

JULY

THIRTEEN

The central office of German military intelligence in Berlin lay beyond the drab portals of 72-76 Tirpitzufer, a shabby apartment building which stood beside the Landwehr Canal. On account of its labyrinthine passages, innumerable doors and cramped, gloomy offices, occupants and visitors alike had come to know the building as the Fox Hole. By 1940 the property had become unsuitable for an organisation as large as the Abwehr had grown, yet Admiral Wilhelm Canaris, the chief of intelligence, obstinately resisted either a move or modernisation.

His own offices were situated on the topmost floor, four stories above the street. Colonel Erwin von Lahousen rode there from his own suite on the second in the decrepit elevator, on which a mechanic had only just completed the latest in an unending round of repairs. Beneath his arm the head of Section II carried a slim, yellowing dossier which the registry had taken the best part of a day to locate. At the top of the shaft he negotiated the folding metal grille, and at the furthest end of a dimly-lit corridor entered a small outer office. There, following the customary exchange of pleasantries with a female secretary and a senior aide, Lahousen was ushered into the inner sanctum.

For those unacquainted with the manner and habits of the Chief of Intelligence, the first impression conveyed by his modest quarters was disconcerting. No other military operations centre in Berlin gave less impression of power or style, and indeed on occasion braver subordinates had voiced concern at its unmilitary appearance. The furnishings were plain, and included a leather couch, some mismatched chairs, a conference table, numerous books, and the inevitable camp bedstead. On the scarred, brass-bound desk sat a model of the light cruiser Dresden, together with a trio of bronze monkeys symbolising the cardinal virtues of the secret service: see all, hear all, say nothing. Three picture frames ranged around the walls housed portraits of Colonel Nicolai, the Kaiser's espionage chief, a large photograph of General Franco, replete with a lengthy personal dedication, and a representation of a grimacing dragon, a gift of the Japanese Ambassador. The worn Persian carpet on the floor added further to the curiously oriental feel. In thirty years of soldiering Canaris was by some distance the most difficult superior Lahousen had encountered: contradictory in his instructions, prone to whims, often mysterious, and not always fair. Yet although he impressed more as a philosopher than as a man of action, Canaris was not a man to cross, or underestimate.

The admiral stood at the window, beyond which his balcony overlooked the still waters of the canal. At his feet the pallet which belonged to his favourite wire-haired dachshund lay empty. The spoiled little dog arrived daily in the black Mercedes which conveyed its master to the Tirpitzufer from his home at Schlachtensee. Unusually, today the pampered hound was absent.

'Seppel will not be joining us this morning, Herr Admiral?' Lahousen inquired with good humour.

'The poor fellow has developed a cold,' Canaris replied gravely, turning into the room. 'Naturally, my concern is that he'll infect Sabine. She's been off her food for several days. The veterinary, as usual, is of no assistance at all.'

'My prayers are with them,' Lahousen commiserated.

Canaris sat down at his desk, and invited Lahousen to take a chair. As Lahousen placed his thin file on the desk, Canaris eyed it closely, his expression betraying mild surprise.

'Is this all we have on petroleum warfare?'

'So it would seem, Admiral.'

'Well, you'd better brief me on what little we know.'

Lahousen opened the file and read aloud. 'In January 1928 the Times reported on an enquiry by the London Port Authority into the containment of oil fires, spurred by the rupture of a tanker at Liverpool. The panel was chaired by a Professor from the Royal Naval College. Experiments involved the ignition of fuel on static and flowing water, as well as analysis of evaporation times and the flashpoints of different fuels.'

'Their conclusions?'

'That a blaze on open water does not readily spread, and is difficult to ignite or sustain. After due consideration permission was granted for tankers to navigate the Thames as far as Purfleet.'

Canaris frowned. The clipping was a typical piece of overt intelligence. Like the bulk of data amassed by intelligence agencies the world over, it had been gleaned not by agents in the field, but from freely-available newspapers and books. The exigencies of Operation Hummer were more demanding.

'What about agent reports?' he asked.

'We've a little more to go on there. In April 1937 agent BANK reported rumours that some form of flame-throwing apparatus had been tested on the Essex coast, near Felixstowe. The following year Krafft reported that a detachment of Royal Engineers were burning oil on water in the vicinity of Christchurch, in Dorset.'

'Sussex,' Canaris corrected. He leaned forward and again examined the photographs taken over Dumpton Gap ten days earlier. The Luftwaffe's air interpretation section had taken more than a week to reach an impasse on whether the three blurred prints depicted anything more extraordinary than a spillage of oil. Now the technicians required a second opinion.

'As evidence of a coastal defence system, it's inconclusive,' Lahousen anticipated.

Canaris looked up. 'But surely, my dear colonel, there's no smoke without fire?'

Lahousen smiled thinly. It was the admiral's habit to respond to one query with another, a trait which annoyed the Austrian intensely. He said: 'Do you really think the English would attempt such a desperate measure? They might as well re-commission HMS Victory.'

Canaris sniffed and produced a handkerchief from his tunic pocket. 'At the Falkland Islands in 1914 I myself witnessed fire on the surface of the sea. An extremely unpleasant spectacle, I can assure you.'

'But as a weapon of war in 1940? It seems positively medieval.'

Canaris pushed a print across the desk. 'Tell me, what do you make of this scene on the high ground?'

The print was the third and final frame in the sequence supplied by the Luftwaffe, taken as the Dornier had passed directly over the cliff. Lahousen studied it closely for several moments. 'A good deal of smoke... figures fleeing toward vehicles.'

'A great many figures,' agreed Canaris. 'And, to the right, just in shot, what appears to be a fuel tanker near the edge of the cliff. Does this not suggest to you a group of observers watching a demonstration of some kind? Perhaps the same weapon tested at Christchurch two years ago?'

'Perhaps,' Lahousen allowed cautiously, unwilling to commit himself. 'Herr Admiral, in every neutral territory the press report that the final German attack upon England is expected any day now. Thousands of barges and vessels are said to be standing by on the Channel and Atlantic coasts. Why should the English test a secret weapon in full view of the enemy? It smells of black propaganda.'

'Propaganda perhaps,' nodded Canaris. 'But not black. I take it you've digested the latest directive from Keitel at OKW?'

'I skimmed it.'

Canaris took up a copy of the signal from his desk and read from it several sentences he had already underlined in red ink. '"The Fuhrer and Supreme Commander has decided that a landing in England is possible... all preparations to begin immediately... landings on a broad front... supported by parachute assault... devise plans to transport a maximum number of troops with minimum shipping and aircraft capacity..."' With no little theatre, he allowed the paper to float back down the desktop. 'You know, in his wisdom I think the Fuhrer sees the English Channel merely as an inconvenient river. Are you aware of the extent of his sea legs?'

'No,' Lahousen confessed.

'Our supreme commander's experience of salt water is limited to a few hours on board his yacht, in crass mimicry of the Kaiser, and one brief, inglorious voyage to Memel. Even on the tideless waters of the Baltic, the Fuhrer's lunch was swiftly sacrificed to Neptune.'

Canaris smiled at the memory. In each government office it had long been mandatory to display a photograph of the Fuhrer. With subtle irony, Canaris had chosen one of Hitler boarding the battleship Schlesien, which hung behind his desk, so that he sat with his back turned to it.

'In my opinion there will be no invasion,' Lahousen ventured.

'Hohenlohe-Langenberg is talking to the British ambassador in Berne. Britain may be willing to come to terms. Add to that the current discord between Churchill and Halifax.'

The admiral's good humour seemed suddenly to fade. 'The English will never come to terms! Their national character prevents them from entertaining any thought of rational settlement. Hohenlohe's contact is playing for time, and succeeding famously. Besides, the great W.C. actively enjoys the waging of war. In his philosophy, only dead men cannot fight.'

Lahousen adopted a placatory tone. 'Herr Admiral, like you, I consider invasion should be attempted only in the last resort.'

'An improvised landing would be a suicidal undertaking,' Canaris continued, his bile still rising. 'Yet already the sycophants at the Chancellery talk of taking tea in Claridges before the end of August. In London they are fortunate to have a true statesman to lead them. Here we have only a guttersnipe who bawls across the Channel.'

'Churchill commits the greater error in refusing to sue for peace,' offered Lahousen. 'For all his unconditional hatred of our regime, he fails to discern a far worse system in the Soviet Union.'

'I very much doubt that the great W.C. has overlooked the threat posed to the Reich by Stalin,' Canaris snapped, as though Lahousen had slighted a personal friend. He paused, and let his temper subside. 'You understand my abhorrence of this invasion idea, colonel. The pre-requisites are nothing less than complete air superiority, and the creation of a mine-free corridor at sea. It will not be the same as Norway. The Wehrmacht is untrained in the art of invading across water, let alone in the teeth of overwhelming English naval superiority.'

Lahousen nodded, but held his tongue. His superior possessed remarkable intellectual and human qualities, all too rare in an automaton regime dominated by totalitarian ideology and fanatical crusades. Since the collapse of France it has become abundantly clear that the Fuhrer had no long-term strategy beyond the victories already achieved. Now, even if ultimately successful, any attempt at the sea borne invasion of England would leave the Channel white with German dead. Unlike his superior, however, Lahousen shrank from such frank expression. Within the Third Reich the Abwehr boasted enemies without number. The

Sicherheitsdienst, Himmler's SS intelligence organisation, had long been waging a sub rosa campaign to devour and absorb the Abwehr. Lahousen knew for certain that the SD had already tapped external Abwehr offices and telephone lines. So far the Tirpitzufer remained secure. But he was not a man to take unnecessary risks.

'It seems we have travelled some distance from these troublesome photographs,' Lahousen ventured diplomatically, anxious to divert the direction their conversation had taken.

'Perhaps not so far,' Canaris replied thoughtfully. 'The English will stop at nothing to defend their island. Add the possibility of English coastal petroleum defences to your next OKW summary. If nothing else, it might keep Foreign Armies West from our throats for a few days.'

Lahousen nodded. 'Word has it Liss intends to circulate a damaging report condemning the quality of our intelligence. In his opinion, the Abwehr is neglecting its duties over England.'

Canaris waved his hand dismissively. 'Have we any other new scraps to cast before that damnable man?'

'Tomorrow, perhaps. Gruppe Wagner undertake their second reconnaissance tonight.'

Canaris crowned. 'Tonight? Where?'

'St Margaret's Bay, east of Dover.'

'I thought that mission was not due for another two days.'

'Moon and tide,' Lahousen replied. 'The navy insisted we move forward, or row our own boat.'

'His Iron Cross is still under consideration, by the way,' Canaris observed blandly. 'I'll wager that the tin will reach his tunic, perhaps even from the Fuhrer himself. Such delicious irony!'

Canaris sniffed loudly again, and slid open a draw from which he produced a bottle of pills. An inveterate hypochondriac, the Admiral nursed an almost morbid fear of illness. He poured a glass of water from the carafe on the desk, then tossed back his head with well-practised ease as he swallowed the pill.

'Good God,' he complained, 'can I have caught Seppel's cold too?'

'I should have thought that most unlikely,' Lahousen assured his commander. As unlikely, he meditated, as the safe return of the Brandenburg unit from the Kentish shore.

FOURTEEN

Goodman checked his wristwatch: ten twenty-four. For the first time in a month General Edmund Ironside was late.

The routine adopted by the Commander-in-Chief Home Forces for his nocturnal rendezvous in Holland Park was immutable. Each Tuesday and Saturday at ten pm sharp Ironside left GHQ for a smart address in Jordan Crescent, which he entered discretely, the door shrouded by a heavy black-out curtain. Thus far it had been impossible to determine who received him, or who bade him farewell after his customary hour inside. No other visitors came or went, scotching Kydd's suspicion that the house was a brothel. Ironside travelled from Hammersmith not by staff car, but in his own vehicle, where his driver remained while Ironside conducted his mysterious business behind closed doors.

The Austin's distinctive camouflaged scheme further hampered close observation, so that Kydd had to park the laughing stock of GHQ fifty yards distant along the street, while, as now, Goodman was obliged to lurk furtively behind walls and trees. The net result was that in two weeks Goodman had made no progress with the investigation.

He checked his watch again. Two minutes had crawled by. Had Ironside's car been involved in an accident in the black-out? It was common enough these days, after all. Or had another absent-minded vicar rung his church bells, triggering another false invasion scare? Goodman glanced up and down Jordan Crescent one last time, then extricated himself quietly from the shrubbery opposite and returned to the car.

On opening the passenger door he was immediately assailed by the pungent odour of camphor. With the idea of moving Ironside's driver on, Kydd was dressed in a long-mothballed, blue uniform of a Metropolitan Police constable. The former detective added to the fug by smoking a thin, bitter-smelling cigar.

'Shown up, has he?'

'Not as yet,' replied Goodman, lowering the passenger window with a sense of urgency.

'Law according to sod and murphy, sir. Dig out your best whistle, then your date blows you out.'

'Look on the bright side. If Ironside's not here he can't have you arrested for personating a police officer.'

'There is that. Mind you, can't say I like the feel of being back in a tall hat.'

Goodman peered through the windscreen into the darkness. Still there was no sign of Ironside's car.

'Maybe his driver rumbled us last time,' Kydd anticipated, drawing heavily on his cigar.

Goodman grimaced as the sergeant exhaled a thick plume of smoke. 'Where on earth did you get those foul sticks of weed?'

'Colleague down at Surrey Docks took charge of a haul of black market goodies a month ago.'

'And despite exhaustive enquiries the rightful owners cannot be traced, I suppose.'

'Something like that.'

'What are they?'

'Partagas, sir. Naturally I prefer Henry Clays.'

'Naturally,' Goodman repeated, waving his hand to clear the air. 'By the way, did your contact on the vice squad turned up anything useful.'

'There isn't a brothel within half a mile. If it is a woman, she's either the lady of the house, or else he's installed his own floozy. Frankly I can't see why McGillivray is so interested.'

'It isn't the colonel that wants to know. It's MI5.'

'I'm impressed. Who do they think lives here - Mata Hari's daughter?'

'The house has some connection with a fascist group which used to operate under cover of an anti-vivisection society.'

'I thought they'd rounded up Mosley's rabble two months ago under Regulation 18b.'

'I'm as much in the dark as you are, sergeant.'

Kydd ran his finger round the inside of the rough stand-up collar of his tunic. 'It doesn't smell right. If MI5 are pulling strings at GHQ then Special Branch should be doing the spade work, not us.'

'Pawns in the game, sergeant.'

'I never did care for chess,' said Kydd with a trace of annoyance. He stubbed out his cigar on the wing of the car and peered into the night. Then he asked seriously: 'Are you being measured up for a cloak and dagger, sir?'

'I doubt it,' Goodman lied.

'It's just that the lads in the section are worried. Word on the grapevine is that Field Security is going to be disbanded.'

Goodman considered his response, and decided there could be no harm in sharing what little he already knew. 'Apparently there's a proposal for a new intelligence corps. But I've no idea how many of us they might spit out.'

Kydd took the news in his stride. 'I dare say we can rely on you to put in a good word on our behalf, sir. Can't say I fancy the idea of being stuck with a rifle and pack.'

Goodman let his thoughts push forward. Try as he might to prevent his mind from straying toward the possibility, Goodman nursed a guilty desire to be transferred to a secret show. Guilty, because he found the false manhunt distasteful, and because a transfer to MI5 would severely proscribe his freedom to see Sophie Gold. Unless the invasion kicked off in his absence, the nebulous scope of his duties at GHQ were such that Goodman could vanish for twenty-four hours without fear of discovery. But how likely would that be under Morley? Or in the new intelligence corps, if the wind of change blew less favourably? A letter had arrived at his billet from Suffolk that morning, pleasantly scented, her fourth in a fortnight. In four days' time, she said, they could meet in Felixstowe, as long as that her watch roster remained unchanged. Felixstowe! Goodman had not previously thought it possible that a cheerless East Anglian port could seem so wildly appealing; now it held the lustre of Paris in the spring.

Goodman's ambivalent reverie was broken by the sharp impact of a set of knuckles across his temple. Starting violently, he reached upwards and grabbed hold of the ghostly hand, forcefully pulling its owner towards the open window.

'What the bloody hell-' he demanded angrily.

A face loomed in the darkness. Goodman raised his torch and

switched it on, the beam diffused by several sheets of blue tissue paper taped behind the lens. Expecting to confront an officious air raid warden, he instead found himself nose to nose with Major Morley.

'Terribly sorry,' Morley apologised jovially. He was dressed in a dinner suit, and his breath was suggestive of drink. 'Meant to rap on the window. You've got the blighter down.'

'Keep your voice down,' Goodman hissed. 'Sir.'

'Sorry again.'

'What are you doing here anyway?'

'I should've thought that was obvious. Is the old man here yet?'

'He's more than half an hour overdue. We were just about to chuck in the towel and go back to GHQ.'

'Well stay put. The general left St Paul's fifteen minutes ago.'

Again Goodman felt a twinge of irritation. Not only that the major had turned up at all, and tight with it, but that Morley's resources seemed always to render his own labours superfluous.

'Look here,' demanded Morley, 'are you going to let me into your miserable little car? Or do I have to commandeer it?'

Reluctantly Goodman swung open the door and stepped out onto the pavement, then held the seat forward as the major clambered onto the back seat. Morley sat down heavily, and immediately barked with discomfort.

'Christ! I'm sitting on a commode. You have a commode in your car, Goodman.'

'My tin helmet, sir,' Kydd replied. 'Begging your pardon.'

'It says POLICE on it,' Morley continued, his tone accusing. 'And what on earth is that fearful stink?'

'My sergeant,' Goodman replied, settling himself back into the passenger seat. 'I asked him to dust off his old uniform with a view to-'

Goodman was cut short as Kydd raised his hand and snapped his fingers. All three strained to listen as the sound of an approaching vehicle grew louder in the darkness. A moment later the narrow slit of light thrown out by a shuttered offside headlight became visible, drifting gently to the right as Ironside's car pulled into the curb, fifty yards ahead. As the engine cut and the headlight died a door slammed heavily, followed by the sound of footsteps as the driver walked around the car to release his passenger. Then a second set of footsteps sounded, moving slowly, as Ironside crossed the pavement and ascended the steps. A brittle knocking followed, as though he were tapping on the wood with a cane. Then nothing: not even the slightest chink of light as the door was opened, and the elderly warrior disappeared inside.

The driver returned to his seat and lit a cigarette, the tip of which glowed orange as he inhaled.

Morley craned forward. 'Is that it?' he whispered, with evident displeasure.

'I'm afraid so,' confirmed Goodman. With practised silence he and Kydd raised their own windows, the better to converse. 'It's impossible to get any closer without alerting his driver.'

'Most annoying,' rued Morley. 'Anyway, about your sergeant's malodorous garb.'

'Just an idea, sir. Ironside rarely stays inside longer than an hour. I thought that Kydd could move his driver on just before the general is due to leave. That way we might see whether his host wears jackboots or a negligee.'

'Not bad, but I have a better idea. Does Ironside know you by sight?'

'I doubt it. We've not spoken face to face.'

'Good. I say we bluff our way inside the house.'

'Sir?' Goodman wondered whether Morley was serious, or merely drunk.

'It's simple enough, captain. I'll borrow your sergeant's uniform and become a policeman. You will change into my clothing and assume the role of a man who's spent a very pleasurable evening at White's. But with your gun in your pocket. Sergeant Kydd will remain with the car while we effect our entry. I pass you off as a concerned neighbour who spotted a light at a window. Naturally, you telephoned the police. Happens all the time, eh sergeant?'

'All the time, sir.'

'There you are. So our neighbour, setting self aside, agrees to assist the constable in pinpointing the source of the infraction. Once inside the house he becomes disorientated, and thus the constable - yours truly - is obliged to investigate every front-facing room. Which gives me a fighting chance of sniffing out whether the old man is sleeping with the enemy.'

Goodman recalled Morley's death wish on the cliff at Dumpton

94

Gap. Now, in a state of uncertain sobriety, he wished to masquerade as a police officer and embark on an adventure which might end in all three of them digging latrines for the rest of the war. Not for the first time, he sensed that the major was directing him down a path he did not care to follow.

'Well?' Morley demanded. 'Are you game?'

'Isn't it all a bit tawdry? Smacks of photographers in closets, and cheap boarding houses in Brighton.'

Morley groaned despairingly. 'By God, I'm beginning to think that Luther was right about you after all, Goodman. Let me tell you something about Tiny Ironside. There are four hundred miles of open coast between the Wash and Southampton. Presently we have a single armoured division at full strength, and not the faintest idea where the first blow will fall.'

'I know all that. It's just that I fail to see the connection with Ironside.'

'Tiny isn't fit to take charge of a Home Guard bicycle section, let alone formulate an effective strategy for home defence. All he's done since Dunkirk is dig ditches and erect jerry-built blockhouses, half of which face the wrong way.' Morley produced a hip flask from his pocket and swallowed a short draft. 'If the Hun invades tomorrow he'll find penetrating our land defences no more difficult than brushing a way through cobwebs.'

'So we stab him in the back.'

'Does it matter? I can't even see you losing any sleep over a gang of muddle-headed Empire loyalists and Right Club types. For God's sakes, we're talking about people whose purpose is to persuade senior establishment figures that war with Germany is a misguided crusade to save the European jews. Ironside attended one of their cosy soirees at this very address as recently as April.'

A silence fell down on the car. Goodman watched the rise and fall of the driver's glowing cigarette as the weight of Morley's words sank in. Finally he asked: 'Why not just sack him?'

'Politics, captain, and friends in high office. But if we can catch him with his trousers down he's more likely to do the decent thing and resign.'

It was, Goodman knew, a foregone conclusion. In a nearby house occupied by two elderly spinsters, the three men exchanged their clothes in a gaslit drawing room, then returned to the Stygian darkness of the black-out. Although a pale moon was visible in the night sky, the world beneath it lay cloaked in inky blackness, producing a sensation akin to falling through a trap door. The trio were obliged to help one another descend the steps of the house in the manner of mountaineers, then remained together on the pavement for several minutes until their eyes re-adjusted to the darkness. As they made their way back along Jordan Crescent, Goodman winced as Morley's too-small shoes pinched his feet.

When he crossed the road with Morley, Goodman expected the driver to emerge from his car and issue a challenge. However, the moment Morley's blue torch became visible he turned over the ignition, and drove hurriedly away. Approaching the front door of the house, Morley stumbled noisily as he climbed the steps, then felt blindly around the door until his fingers found the bell-pull. A muffled ringing sounded from deep within the house, followed immediately by the barking of a dog closer to hand - a very large dog, so it seemed.

After several moments the door was opened halfway without inquiry, and a disembodied head emerged from behind the black-out curtain, the hallway behind illuminated by dim blue light.

'Police,' snapped Morley, stepping forward. 'A light has been reported.'

'Wrong house.' The voice was female, and hostile. 'Try next door.'

Morley stepped forward and barged open the door with his shoulder. The woman uttered a short cry and stumbled backwards into the hallway, her heels loud on the tiled floor. Brushing aside the sateen black-out curtain, Morley stepped inside and switched on the torch. Across his shoulder Goodman looked on as the major played the beam on a young woman in a dressing gown, somewhat plump and sour-faced. From behind one of the doors which opened on to the passage the barking of the dog grew more intense, as it scratched and clawed at the woodwork.

'This gentleman was passing by,' Morley continued. 'He saw a light from the street.'

'Rubbish,' the woman snapped, raising a hand to shield her eyes from the beam. 'Which floor?'

'I couldn't be sure,' Goodman improvised. 'Certainly above ground level.'

'Where are the stairs?' Morley demanded bullishly. 'I'll check your windows.'

The woman glanced at the door beside her, evidently weighing the pros and cons of releasing the dog. Morley brushed her aside and hastened along the passage into the body of the house. Before the woman could gather her wits Goodman followed, hurrying through the hallway and up the staircase to join Morley on the first floor landing. Four doors opened onto it, the nearest of which was ajar and spilled out a tall shaft of yellow light. Morley gestured Goodman forward, then tried the handle on one of the front-facing rooms. Finding the door unlocked he disappeared inside.

Goodman pushed open the door and stepped into the room, squinting in the bright electric light. The room was some sort of office, the longest wall lined with untidy shelving overloaded with books and box files. There was a desk also, equipped with an ancient typewriter and an empty in-tray. Bizarrely, given the indian summer, the remains of a fire burned in the grate. But by far the most striking feature was the large black banner which hung from the other long wall. The axe and bundle of sticks which formed its centre were a blatant imitation of the symbols and flag of Mussolini's Italian fascisti, its homespun air contriving to combine the sinister with the ridiculous. Goodman took in the banner for several moments. It was a veteran, quite probably, of Cable Street, of the Albert Hall rally, and a hundred other festivals of bigotry and hatred. Mere ownership of such an article now invited imprisonment without trial; its owner, in his right mind, would have buried such incriminating evidence. Or burned it.

Goodman considered tearing the flag from the wall and casting it onto the remains of the fire, but was distracted by a rapid pounding on the staircase. The sour-faced woman, he assumed, but realised his mistake as a low shape flashed past the open doorway. It was a large black dog - the same dog, he assumed, previously contained in the room downstairs, and now unleashed like a canine torpedo. A moment later a fierce bark presaged a clatter and thud, and a sharp cry from Morley.

'Jesus Christ! Goodman!'

He hastened through the doorway, and in the shadows at the end of the landing saw Morley writhing on the floor, his calf clamped in the jaws of an enormous German shepherd. The animal snarled viciously as it shook its head from side to side, oblivious to Morley's desperate attempts to slap and punch it aside.

'The damned thing is devouring me alive!'

'Use your helmet,' Goodman offered, unwilling to approach in case the dog turned on him.

'Use your gun!' Morley countered angrily, an edge of panic to his voice.

A snort of derision sounded behind Goodman. Turning, he found the sour-faced woman standing at the head of the stairs, hands on her hips, smiling broadly.

'Call that creature off or I'll shoot it,' he demanded smartly.

'So they're arming passers-by, are they?'

Morley let slip a strangled scream, then yelled above the dog's carnivorous snarlings: 'For God's sake, Goodman - kill this bloody animal!'

Goodman reached into his right pocket and withdrew his revolver, then walked several paces toward Morley, cocking the weapon as he moved. He was far from being a crack shot with the heavy Webley, and to fire from any distance ran the risk of hitting Morley. Stealing himself, Goodman crouched down and held the gun level with the dog's hindquarters, jabbing the barrel into the well-groomed hair like a bayonet. The dog ignored the intrusion, and continued to snarl fiercely as Morley gasped and swore.

Goodman pulled the trigger. In the narrow confines of the passage the report was deafening, and as its hindquarters slumped to the floor the dog released an awful scream, high-pitched like that of a distressed child. Dropping Morley's leg, it jerked its head back toward Goodman, the whites of its eyes forming two desperate crescents in the dim light. Goodman felt a sharp stab of disgust and pity - emotions which evaporated as soon as the animal began snarling with renewed vigour, and painfully set about hauling its crippled body and operative jaws towards him.

Goodman stumbled backwards and almost dropped the revolver, then raised it, aimed, closed his eyes, and shot the dog through the head.

Sickened and shaken, he scrambled to his feet, unable to bring himself look at the carnage below - and then collapsed unconscious across it, as a thrown china vase met the back of his head and smashed into a thousand pieces.

FIFTEEN

Within the Greater German Reich political policing was the exclusive responsibility of the Reich Central Security Office, or RSHA. An amalgamation of the criminal police, Gestapo, and the SS security service, by July 1940 its plans for the occupation of Great Britain were already well advanced.

All able-bodied males aged between seventeen and forty-five, a total of some eleven million men, would be transported to the continent as forced labour. An SS Standartenfuhrer, Dr Franz Six, formerly dean of the economics faculty of Berlin University, would establish his headquarters in suitably opulent premises in London, and had already pegged the rate of exchange at nine and a half Reichsmarks to the pound sterling. His lengthy sonderfahndungsliste, a special arrest list of subversive elements, was substantially complete, the detainees ranging from obvious personalities, such as Churchill and de Gaulle, to more innocuous figures such as HG Wells, Noel Coward and Virginia Woolf. Elsewhere, the RSHA foreign intelligence section, SD-Amt IV, was largely preoccupied with the preparation of a small handbook for German service personnel, Informationsheft Gross Britannien. The pamphlet provided basic information on key political, administrative and economic institutions in Great Britain, and would also contain instructions - not yet complete - on the measures to be taken when occupying the Foreign, Home and War Offices, and various departments of the Secret Service and Special Branch.

The chief of Amt IV was SS Sturmbannfuhrer Walter Schellenberg. The son of a bankrupt piano manufacturer from Bonn, Schellenberg had studied medicine and then law before enlisting in the SS, a move prompted less by transcendent political creed than shrewd pragmatism. His rise within the ranks of the Fuhrer's black guard had been swift and dazzling. Conspicuous initially due to his gift for languages, Schellenberg was headhunted directly for the SD by its leader, Reinhard Heydrich, and during three years as a senior aide his protege had authored a series of brilliant coups, including the kidnapping of two senior British MI6 officers from the Dutch frontier post at Venlo in November 1939. Three months later, Walter Schellenberg had been appointed head of Amt IV. The SS Sturmbannfuhrer and Major-General of Police was just thirty years old.

For the better part of five months Schellenberg had worked tirelessly, juggling a root and branch re-organisation of his bureau with a constant stream of special assignments, only one of which was the preparation of Informationsheft GB. Another, which had landed on his desk only that morning, was a scheme to kidnap the Duke of Windsor from Spain, where the former English monarch had fled following the fall of France. For this reason Schellenberg had assigned a junior officer to undertake a thorough analysis of the invasion plan now code-named Operation Sealion. Hauptsturmfuhrer Eichner was a bright young officer who had served with distinction in Poland. He now sat in Schellenberg's office on Wilhelmstrasse, his file open before him.

'In essence,' Eichner explained with characteristic precision, 'OKW plan a surprise crossing on a broad front, extending from Ramsgate to a point west of the Isle of Wight. The Luftwaffe will act as artillery, and the navy as engineers. Preparations are to be completed by the middle of August.'

Schellenberg frowned. 'Is that possible?'

'I doubt it, Sturmbannfuhrer. Rounding up a fleet sufficient to lift forty divisions will take more than four weeks.'

'And what of the wisdom behind the proposal in Paragraph 1 for...' Schellenberg glanced briefly at the text of Directive 16, issued from Fuhrer Headquarters the previous day. '"A preliminary occupation of the Isle of Wight or the Duchy of Cornwall"?'

'Wisdom is not a word I would readily attach to either scheme,' Eichner replied coolly.

'My sentiments entirely. What do our colleagues at the Fox Hole have to say?'

Schellenberg's tone made light of a deadly serious matter. In the field of foreign intelligence Amt IV and the Abwehr were sworn rivals, and while Amt IV might be smaller in size, it did not lack equivalent influence. Indeed in Himmler and Heydrich, the two most powerful men in the SS state, the Abwehr possessed unwavering enemies. Each viewed Canaris and his organisation as objects of disfavour and suspicion, and overlooked no opportunity to denigrate both. Yet while fate had cast Schellenberg and Canaris in the role of arch rivals, the two intelligence chiefs enjoyed a professional relationship of guarded cordiality. Indeed on occasion the pair exercised their horses together during early morning gallops between the trees of the Tiergarten.

'As usual,' Eichner began, 'the left arm is wrestling with the right. According to the navy, on land the English are as weak as a kitten. Their entire defence will depend on the Royal Navy and the RAF.'

Schellenberg nodded as his aide leafed forward through several pages, then continued. 'Yet the Abwehr beg to differ. In their opinion, on landing in England our forces will face a well-prepared and utterly determined enemy, totalling thirty divisions. A construction programme of fixed defences in coastal areas is stated to have been in progress in England for the best part of a decade, and is even said to include a network of flame-throwing and marine petroleum devices, extending from Weymouth to Felixstowe.'

Schellenberg frowned 'Boiling oil? I thought that went out with the Middle Ages.'

'Perhaps not. As recently as July third, one such device was fired at Ramsgate. The Luftwaffe took several photographs.'

'Show me.' Schellenberg stretched his hand across the desk. Eicher passed across the same three prints that Canaris and Lahousen had deliberated over three days earlier. Schellenberg scrutinized them equally closely, and, without taking his eye from the third, opened a draw in his desk and withdrew a magnifying glass. When finally he looked up from the blurred image he wore a frown. 'The smoke could be anything - an oil spill, or a burning boat.'

'The summary delivered to OKW earlier this month includes additional evidence.'

'One could be forgiven, Eichner, for thinking that some amongst our colleagues on the Tirpitzufer do not welcome the prospect of invasion.'

'Perhaps,' Eichner agreed cautiously. 'Although word has it that the Abwehr have already conducted several operations against England.'

'Agent drops?'

Eichner shook his head. 'Two landings on the coast by a small armed force. I'm guessing Brandenburg.'

Schellenberg stiffened visibly. 'You mean Canaris has placed German troops on English soil?'

'It would seem so.'

Schellenberg paused. Brandenburg probes against the enemy coast were an admirable military achievement, certainly. Just the kind of coup, in fact, that Amt IV itself should be fielding.

'Well, that is something,' he said quietly, allowing himself a wry smile. 'Perhaps that will explain why the old bastard has been riding so well lately. Tell me more.'

'Unfortunately there's little to tell. From what I can gather, late in June two Brandenburg men - an officer and an NCO - were interviewed by Luftwaffe technicians at Rechlin on the subject of a wireless station on the east coast on England.'

'Which station?'

Eichner searched his memory for a second. 'Near the port of Felixstowe, I believe.'

Schellenberg nodded slowly. 'Bawdsey Manor,' he said, albeit in a pronunciation unrecognisable to any native of Suffolk. 'The principal British research centre for decimeter telegraphy, if memory serves me correctly.'

Eichner shrugged. 'They say Goring considers DeTe little more than a gimmick. Nothing that a few foolhardy fellows in Stukas cannot deal with.'

'Goring is living in the past. You said two probes.'

'Three days ago a party of British soldiers, fully armed, were observed boarding a fishing trawler at Boulogne. They returned six hours later, apparently with prisoners.'

'Brandenburg,' nodded Schellenberg. 'And to think some in Berlin still fear they are nothing more than Canaris's way of protecting his own cunning hide.'

'It occurs to me,' offered Eichner, 'that the Bawdsey probe might have concerned Knickebein.'

'I'm sorry?' Schellenberg was miles away. The Abwehr's feat-of-arms would not please Himmler at all.

'Knickebein is a beam-bombing technique based on the Lorenz blind-landing system. It allows aircraft to locate their target by means of radio waves. Two beams, one consisting of dots, and the other of dashes, are directed towards England, and positioned to intersect over the target desired. A receiver in the aircraft follows the first beam until it meets the second, and the bombs are then dropped on target.'

'And the connection with Bawdsey.'

Eichner rose and walked across to the large scale map of Northern Europe fixed to the wall. 'The Luftwaffe think the English are trying to jam the beams.' He took up a long wooden ruler and positioned it on a line bearing south-west from Northern Germany. 'If a line is drawn between the Knickebein transmitter at Stollberg, and the city of London, you will see that it passes directly over Bawdsey.'

'It's plausible, I'll grant you that,' nodded Schellenberg. Look into it further, Eichner.'

'DeTe, or Knickebein jamming?'

'Neither.' Schellenberg snapped shut the slim dossier before him. 'Concentrate your efforts on this Brandenburg unit, captain. Where they've been, what they've seen, where they're going. Find out who leads them, too. Amt IV can't afford to lose track of good men.'

SIXTEEN

At the Scrubs Goodman found A Wing all but deserted. Gone were the well-groomed Registry girls, and the bright young men recruited from Hambros and Slaughter and May, and gone too was the frivolous atmosphere. Apart from a handful of secretaries, and two elderly removal men, Morley alone remained, like a captain determined to go down with his ship. For several days envious rumours had circulated at GHQ that the Security Service were to relocate to Blenheim Palace. Already it seemed that the move to Oxfordshire was close to completion.

As Goodman stepped around the cell door Morley glanced up and took in the bright white bandage his visitor sported beneath his cap. The swelling it concealed was still the size of a small egg, and Goodman's splitting headache had now endured for twenty-four hours.

'If I didn't know better, I'd say you'd done something heroic.'

'If I didn't know better, I'd think I had. Are you following your colleagues to Blenheim, or have you become thoroughly institutionalised?'

'It's chaos up country. I refuse to budge until Jane has arranged for a south facing office.' Morley gestured at a folded newspaper on his desk. 'Seen the Thunderer this morning?'

'I picked up a copy of the Standard yesterday evening.'

Morley took up the paper and flicked to an inside page. 'They're so damnably polite, these ministry men. Past masters of the euphemism. "It is considered essential to place our Home Forces in the hands of a commander with immediate experience of command on France and Belgium." Twaddle, of course.'

'So we really did for Ironside.'

'More or less. Still, they've made him up to Field Marshal, and he's certain to be elevated to the peerage. The appointment of Alan Brooke as his successor is a vast improvement on any showing.'

'How's the leg?'

'On the mend.' The major sniffed. 'I assume Sergeant Kydd sketched in the detail after you were biffed by that ugly little creature.'

'Oh, ad nauseam. His heroic charge through the door, the two of us embarrassed on the landing, a dead dog. Two women, one half naked, and General Ironside in a silk kimono.'

'Is she being dealt with?' Goodman asked, deriving satisfaction from a vision of a Holloway cell.

'In a manner of speaking. Actually she's one of ours, from the counter-subversion wing, B5(b). They operate independently. It seems that one or two wires were crossed between here and Dolphin Square.'

As he digested the revelation Goodman experienced a sinking feeling. For the second time since the outbreak of war he had been injured in the line of duty, and for the second time the wound had been inflicted by a friend, not a foe. Now, farcically, he almost longed to be shot by a genuine, honest-to-God German.

'She tried to kill me,' he said pithily.

Morley shrugged his shoulders. 'Maxwell Knight's boys and girls are very dedicated.'

'Luther called me this morning. You were right - Field Security is being disbanded at the end of the month. They're putting him out to pasture.'

'Which leaves you where?'

'At GHQ, until further notice.'

'And where would you like to be?'

Goodman thought he recognised his cue. 'Blenheim, I suppose.'

Morley frowned. 'You surprise me, Goodman. I thought you found our work distasteful, lacking in moral propriety.'

'Perhaps I've become open to corruption.'

'That I doubt. The thing of it is, you're more use at GHQ than you would be in Five. I have given it some thought, Goodman. It's not that you've failed in any way, simply that we need people who don't need to think twice before taking the gloves off, or slipping a horseshoe inside.'

Goodman supposed it was a compliment, but said nothing. He

had flunked the audition, and wished now that he had allowed the dog to chew on Morley's ankle a little longer before dispatching it.

'Consider yourself lucky,' Morley continued. 'If we lose the next round, no-one in military intelligence is likely to be interned at the Dorchester. It'll be meat-hooks and piano wire all round. Best sit tight at St Paul's and wait for fate to show it's hand.'

Fate. Or the War Office. Or Hitler. Without waiting for Morley to dismiss him Goodman turned to leave, nettled that he had allowed his principles to be compromised so easily, and yet regretting his own sense of decency.

Not, he knew, for the first time. Or for the last.

SEVENTEEN

From the foot of the steps Paul Wagner cast a disparagingly eye around the hot, crowded cellar that housed the Rififi Club. In Antwerp, as in the clandestine jazz dives of Hamburg and Berlin, youthful swings were parading in custom-tailored suits, expensive crepe-soled shoes and white silk scarves. Some even wore trench coats in high summer, and sunglasses after dark. Piss carnations, according to German argot, and although Wagner failed to discern any meaning behind the contemptuous phrase, he could not have agreed more.

In their short skirts and silk stockings, lipstick and lacquer, Wagner found the female of the species infinitely more pleasing. However he had negotiated the tarts and black marketeers in the sidestreet behind the station not for the sake of the opposite sex, but a rare date by Scandinavian swing ace Arne Hulphers. As a Swede, and thus a neutral, Hulphers had immediate access to new material denied to most other European band leaders, and his repertoire, which consisted exclusively of original American swing numbers, was performed without compromise and no little verve. Two years earlier Wagner would scarcely have crossed the street for such an ersatz gig; now, in the New Europe, in which real jazz was condemned as an affront to occidental culture, the thirsty drank wherever they could.

The band were resting between sets, and Wagner edged his way towards the bar. His cropped hair and conservative suit announced his nationality as surely as a swastika flag, and drew a hostile look from the bartender. The accent was one hundred per cent Brooklyn, however, and secured Wagner his bourbon in double quick time. As he drank Wagner again surveyed the room above the rim of his glass. As well as the usual complement of Swing

Heinis and older, straighter jazz aficionados, there was a smattering of furtive German servicemen, each of whom stuck out like a sore thumb. Himself included, Wagner reflected.

His reverie was interrupted as his elbow was knocked sharply aside. The sudden blow deposited the rest of his drink down the front of his shirt, causing the flesh wound sustained in Kent six days earlier to smart fiercely. Wagner turned, ready to confront the culprit, and found himself face to face with a young woman, intent on forcing a passage to the bar.

'I didn't plan on finishing it anyway,' he said in English, waving his empty glass in her face.

The girl ignored him, and tried instead to catch the eye of the barman. She was perhaps nineteen years old and not tall, but nonetheless pretty, with short blonde hair and vivacious eyes. Wagner noticed also that she wore a small union jack pin in her lapel.

'You think I'm a Nazi?' Wagner continued.

'All Germans are Nazis,' she replied curtly, not missing a beat.

'You might just have a point there. But it so happens I'm American.'

The girl scrutinized him closely. 'Then why dress like a German?'

'Because not every journalist can swing a fat contract with Columbia Broadcasting, or the New York Times.'

The girl looked crestfallen. 'I suppose I should offer to buy you another drink.'

Wagner shook his head. 'There's no need.'

She rallied a little. 'Good, because I've scarcely enough money for my own.'

'Allow me. God knows, you're not having much success in getting served.'

'He knows I only order mineral water.'

'That's your poison?'

She thought for a moment. 'No. You ca make mine an Americano tonight.'

'If that's meant to be a joke, I rate it as poor.'

'Actually it's Campari and red Cinzano mixed with lemon and soda.'

Wagner flinched. Had he ordered such a mongrel cocktail in any self-respecting New York bar he risked being kicked out onto the sidewalk. Nevertheless, he turned and caught the attention of the barman, ordering for himself another bourbon. The Americano arrived in a tall glass, and did not come cheap.

'To freedom,' she announced gaily, tapping her glass against his.

'Freedom,' he rejoined, as their eyes met. Already he was beginning to feel uncomfortable with the roleplay. A better man would confess all to the girl: yes, that he was a New Yorker, via Brandenburg-Havel and the comfortable villa given over to Gruppe Wagner at De Panne. Yet something about her touched him. Her small act of defiance gracing her lapel, perhaps, or her smile. A smile which reminded him too much of Sophie Gold.

She sipped at her drink cautiously, as though she had not tasted the concoction before. 'You're from New York?'

'That's right.'

'Are you reporting on the war?'

'When I can. Now that the Germans have sealed off the coast, there's not much to see to write up.'

The girl looked incredulous. 'Are you blind? Every barge in the country is being requisitioned, and more and more soldiers are arriving every day. It's obvious that the Nazis will invade England.'

'If you say so. I only got here today. I've been in Luxemburg.'

'Listen,' she pressed urgently, 'my father is a jeweller. Only yesterday a German officer spent ten minutes haggling over the best price for a diamond ring. Finally he decided he could do better in England. There's a story for your paper.'

Wagner shook his head. 'It wouldn't get past the censor.'

Sensing an impasse, she changed tack. 'Are you here for a story, or because you like jazz?'

'A little of both, I guess.'

'How do you rate the band?'

'Not too shabby,' he shrugged. 'How about you?'

'Pretty hot. A little like Het Ramblers. Have you heard them?'

'Can't say I have.'

'I suppose you get to see all the greats back in New York City,' she said enviously.

'Pretty much.' As he spoke Wagner realised that these were the first true words he had uttered.

'Who's your favourite artist?'

'Benny Goodman, I guess.'

'Were you at the Carnegie Hall concert?'

'Sure was. You like him too?'

'He's okay,' she replied with exaggerated nonchalance. 'I like Ellington better. These days I find Goodman a little tame.'

The conversation lapsed momentarily. Not wanting her to drift away, Wagner asked: 'How about you tell me your name?'

'Her name is Klaartje.'

The voice, male and belligerent, came from across his shoulder. Wagner turned and found himself face to face with a full-blown peacock in a glen-check suit and patent leather shoes. He sported slickee boy hair and a thin moustache, and an unlit cigarette in an ivory holder. Wagner disliked him instantly.

'This the boyfriend?'

'My big brother, Willem,' Klaartje blushed. 'He probably thinks you're a Nazi too.'

'Can he prove otherwise?' the other said accusingly.

'He's an American journalist.'

'Let him prove it.' Willem turned to Wagner. 'Show me your passport.'

Wagner bristled. 'Not that it's any business of yours, but I don't have it with me.'

Willem snorted. 'A neutral wouldn't risk it. The police or Gestapo can hold you for hours - days even. You could easily be Gestapo yourself, spying on all the other Nazis in here tonight.'

Wagner glanced at Klaartje, and saw that her eyes too now betrayed an element of doubt. He was sorely tempted to tell her brother to perform some sort of anatomical impossibility, but instead said: 'Look, friend, I'm just a hack who happens to like jazz.'

Willem raised his eyebrows, and said cryptically: '"There'll be some changes made."'

Wagner frowned. 'Come again?'

'"There'll Be Some Changes Made." If you're really hep to jazz then tell me who waxed that side.'

'Eddie Condon.'

'And?'

110

'And his Chicagoans, I guess.'

Willem looked disappointed. 'Okay - when?'

'Last year.'

'What about the title on the flipside?'

'I don't know,' Wagner snapped irritably. 'Look, I'm not a Condon disciple, and I don't memorise the contents of every label catalogue. Besides, I'll bet you every German in here tonight can tell you everything you need to know.'

Willem fixed him closely, his expression a portrait of suspicion, then turned back to his sister. 'Come back to the table Klara, or you'll lose your chair.'

'I'm staying put,' Klaartje replied defiantly. 'Frank and Luc bore me tonight. The company's more interesting over here.'

Her brother released another snort of derision, then turned on his heel and retraced his steps through the crowd.

'Nice guy,' Wagner said.

'I'm sorry,' she apologised. 'Willem means well, but I'm big enough to look after myself.'

'You being Klaartje, right?'

'Yes. But friends call me Klara. What do friends call you?'

'Paul. Paul Wagner.'

Klara smiled. 'Pleased to meet you, Paul Wagner.'

With the intermission over, the band now returned to the postage-stamp stage. Above, or rather below, the hum of conversation the deep thrum of a double bass sounded as its player tuned a string. The saxophone player cradled a Selmer, just like the horn Wagner had thrown into the East River two years before. *A Mark Three, New York assembled, loose springs and worn lacquer, sounding just like the city itself...*

Wagner deliberately shifted his focus to the a statuesque blonde in blue velvet, who now took centre stage to chorus of appreciative whistles from the floor.

'Greta Wassberg,' Klara informed Wagner. 'She's not bad, but not as close to Billie Holiday as she'd like to think. And not as pretty either.'

'Dare I disagree?'

Klara did not answer, and instead listened intently as the band slipped into a slow-burning torch song. As the dancefloor began to fill, she asked him: 'Will you dance?'

The request caught Wagner by surprise, but he nodded assent, and followed Klara through the crowd to a spot close by the lip of the stage. There they began to move slowly - a little awkwardly at first, for she was much shorter than him, and initially took hold of his arm over the spot where a stray British bullet had carved a hole the size of a fat cigar. Quickly they found their own rhythm, however, and in Klara's arms Wagner rediscovered a place in his heart left abandoned since his departure from America.

Soon Paul Wagner was quite unaware of the room, of the people around them - and of the Amt-IV operative in the shadows at the back at the bar, who had eavesdropped on their entire conversation.

EIGHTEEN

While Sophie busied herself in the bathroom along the hallway, Goodman sat on the end of the rickety single bed and wished their tryst could have been staged in surroundings more salubrious than the Peninsula Guest House. It was not an inspiring venue: two solid Victorian houses knocked into one, with broken stone steps leading up to a forbidding front door, and peeling white paint. Room 4B offered grimy windows, unwashed curtains and a damp mattress. Every slammed door raised eyebrows, while the merest hint of laughter drew disapproving comments. At least, Goodman reflected, the sheets on the bed were his own. Except in the largest urban hotels, guests who stayed for more than a night or two were now expected to provide their own bedding and toiletries. At the Peninsula, the sole guest house in Felixstowe to which civilians were still admitted, this much at least was a blessing in disguise.

True, the afternoon had been as close to perfect as the national emergency allowed: a leisurely walk through the coils of barbed wire on the promenade, then tea in a dying tearoom, and a display of colourful flares out to sea after dark. Back at the Peninsula the magic had all but evaporated, however, and having booked a single room Goodman had even been obliged to spirit Sophie inside. Now he rose to his feet as she returned from the bathroom at a furtive trot.

'I'm sorry,' he began, 'all this seems so...'

'Seedy? It's not so bad, John. On the station I have to share an attic dorm with twelve other women and God knows how many mice.'

Sophie stood before the dressing table and began combing her hair. Still Goodman felt a need to apologise. 'My digs in

Hammersmith are no palace. The old dragon who owns the house declared the geyser out of bounds, so the Service Corps major in the next room is using camp equipment.'

'Because of the hot water?'

'That, and the fact he can now claim a field allowance.'

Satisfied with her hair, Sophie turned to face him. In her blue serge uniform she looked every bit as delicious as in London three weeks before.

'Did you bring any emergency ration cards?' she asked.

'No.'

'It's just that the breakfast here is minuscule. Two tiny chipolatas and half a slice of bread.

'Have you done this before?' he asked, only half joking.

Sophie rehearsed her best how-dare-you look. 'What a terrible suggestion. I'm a good girl who just happens to know one or two bad ones.'

'Tell me more.'

'Are you always so prurient?'

'Always.'

'Just so long as I know. Most of the girls string along chaps from the station, or the ack-ack guns. That way you never have to polish your own shoes.'

'Anyone polishing yours?'

'I'm still waiting to meet the right shoe-shine boy. Besides, we're supposed to be rotated around different stations every three months. It's here today, gone tomorrow as far as romance goes.'

'So there's virtue in dirty footwear.'

'That rather depends on your point of view. Besides, look at Elizabeth.'

'I don't follow.'

'I should have thought her shoes were worn through with all the buffing.'

Goodman managed only the thinnest of smiles.

'Did that silly roof business resolve itself?'

'In a manner of speaking. It cost me £75 and ten shillings.'

'Golly.'

He sought to make light of it. 'It was the ten shillings that killed me. Actually, I borrowed most of it from my father.'

'You should have asked me.'

Goodman saw that she was serious. 'I thought you detested Elizabeth.'

'As should you.'

Elizabeth had intruded upon their day, and her presence was unwelcome. 'Can we change the subject?' he said. 'What with one thing and another I'm not having a very good war at the moment.'

'Anything to do with that lump on your head?'

Goodman hesitated. Despite Morley's several warnings, confiding in Sophie seemed suddenly very necessary. 'A woman threw a vase at me.'

'I hope you weren't buffing her shoes.'

'Hardly. I suppose you know that General Ironside was replaced yesterday.'

'I may have heard something in the NAAFI.'

'Well, I had a hand in it. Three weeks ago I was instructed to put the C-in-C under surveillance. He'd taken to visiting a house owned by fascists. On Monday night we practically kicked down the door, only to discover that the old man was visiting a mistress. Two days later they chopped off his head.'

'Was it his mistress who threw the vase?'

Goodman shook his head. 'Some mystery woman, who turned out to be in MI5.'

'I don't follow.'

'You and me both.'

Sophie considered this a moment, her expression moving from light to serious. 'Some of Mosley's rabble wear a little badge, you know, depicting an eagle killing a viper. The snake represents the Jews and the communists. I certainly shouldn't feel bad about unseating Ironside if he keeps that sort of company.'

'I don't, really. But Field Security is going to be disbanded at the end of the month, which means no more freedom to come and go as I please.'

'Where will they send you?'

'Haven't the foggiest. MI5 don't want me, that's for sure.'

'I should have thought they prized intelligence.'

'Apparently I'm too decent. Marvellous, isn't it - I get shot in the leg by a Belgian, and written off as u/s for a fighting unit. Then when opportunity knocks for a secret show I shoot myself square in the foot.'

'You're too hard on yourself. Besides, I don't want you in the front line. They throw far more than vases.'

'I shouldn't have told you about Ironside,' Goodman said ruefully.

Sophie crossed to the end of the bed and sat down, dropping her voice to a conspiratorial whisper. 'We could trade secrets, be as bad as one another.'

'I already know what you do.'

'Really?'

'You're an RDF plotter.'

She fixed him disapprovingly. '*Operator,* thank you. Plotters are those pretty little creatures who crowd around the map table at Fighter Command. RDF operators are hand picked, the creme de la creme.'

Goodman lay back on the bed and crossed his hands behind his head. 'And what exactly is it that you superwomen operate?'

'A cathode ray tube.'

'You've lost me already.'

Sophie paused. 'You know, we're told never to breathe a word about our work on pain of death. Now you've persuaded me to break my vow I'm not even sure I know how to.'

'Pretend I'm a Nazi spy.'

'I can try. Where to begin?'

'How were you selected?'

'I was a maths swott at school. They said they wanted girls like me for some sort of hush-hush signalling work.'

'Who were they?'

'Lady someone-or-other at the WAAF selection board. She treated me to lunch.'

'At the Dorchester?'

'I wish. A mountain of potatoes in a sea of mushy peas at the NAAFI canteen.'

Goodman waved his hand dismissively. 'That's low grade intelligence. Blind me with science.'

Sophie took a deep breath. 'Chain Home stations have two sets of aerials. The transmitters send out radio waves, which bounce back to the receivers if they hit an object. Given a good line of shoot, at fifteen thousand feet, any aircraft within a hundred miles will show up as a blip on the tube. On a good day we can determine numbers, height, range and heading - but you pick up birds and boats too, so there's an art to it.'

'And you man this... ray tube?'

Sophie nodded. 'It's something like a television set, if you've seen one. Murder on the eyes, though. And if you look away or nod off it's a court-martial offence. We're on a three-watch system at Bawdsey. That means six five hour shifts in seventy-two hours, with no proper sleep or regular meals. It's pretty sapping.'

Sophie allowed herself a satisfied smile. Guiltily Goodman thought of his long nights spent in the cubicle at GHQ, waiting for the white telephone to ring. There his so-called duties extended no further than reading, writing and listening to the Home Service, and on more than one occasion he had dozed off.

'After an hour on the tube you have an hour off, then an hour on the plotting table, then another telling, and another recording. The six of us move down the console as the watch progresses. It's like a game of musical chairs, except locked inside a concrete bunker with iron doors and rifles at the ready, in case the enemy attack.'

Goodman frowned. 'And you volunteered for this?'

'Oh, like a shot. There's nothing else technical you men trust to the fairer sex. Besides, the top secret stuff sounded far more intriguing than Balloon Command.'

Goodman nodded approvingly. 'Of course, you realise this is strictly forbidden. Me, an officer, consorting with other ranks.'

'I'll turn myself in at the guard room.' Sophie rose from the bed. 'Shall I turn this ghastly light off? This room might look better by moonlight.'

Without waiting for his reply, Sophie killed the light, then drew back the curtains with a theatrical flourish.

'We should keep them closed, you know,' Goodman said, wincing even as he spoke.

She clicked her tongue. 'There's not an ounce of romance in you.'

Goodman was tempted to tell Sophie to wait and see. Instead he rose from the bed and joined Sophie at the window, then followed her gaze out over the moonlit town beyond the window pane. He unfastened the catch and lifted the sash to allow in the faint sea breeze. In the street below a loud clatter was followed by cursing as a pedestrian collided with a carelessly parked bicycle. Then nothing.

'Not much of a place, is it,' Goodman thought aloud.

'It's here. That's about all you can say.'

'I suppose there can't be much by way of entertainment across the river. Besides shining shoes, that is.'

'It could be worse. One of the army gunners is a terribly good violinist, and there's a medical orderly with a beautiful voice. They've mined the beach, of course, but the tennis courts are still serviceable.'

'Sorry to drag you away.'

'I like it here better.'

Goodman snaked his arm around her waist. She took his hand and squeezed it tightly. Now a certain frisson settled over the room, delicious and too long unfamiliar to him, which increased tenfold as Sophie broke away, crossed to the chair, and opened up her overnight bag.

'Warm that bed up, John,' she said quietly.

Goodman settled himself on the bed and watched as Sophie began to undress. She removed her skirt and blouse first, then placed a foot on the chair to unroll her grey lisle stockings, one after the other. Turning half away, she unfastened her coarse, cotton service bra, its straps the width of a man's belt. Then, almost before her underwear was on the chair, she wrapped her tunic around her shoulders, and stepped over to the cracked washbasin to clean her teeth.

Goodman stood, and attempted to hum an easy tune as he undressed. He sensed more than heard Sophie shrug off her jacket and slip quickly between the sheets, then turned, and met her smile, and slipped into her arms.

NINETEEN

Wherever his wanderlust took him, no distance was too great to prevent Admiral Wilhelm Canaris from telephoning Berlin daily for news of his beloved dachshunds. Indeed legend had it that the director of the Spanish secret police, who monitored Canaris' telephone conversations during his frequent visits to Spain, had been deeply puzzled as to why the chief of intelligence was so intimately concerned by the bowel movements of two Abwehr agents named Seppel and Sabine.

Even Canaris found humour in the anecdote. However, for this reason he no longer placed calls from the comfortable private address of Herr Helm, the Abwehr III officer with whom he lodged when in Madrid, and instead he and Colonel Lahousen had installed themselves in a secure office within the Madrid Stelle. The Iberian station operated behind a front organisation, the Excelsior Import and Export Company, which in turn maintained sub-stations in Morocco, Algeria and Libya, together employing more than six hundred informers. The bureau was also furnished with information by Spanish diplomats worldwide, and could even boast moles within the Spanish government.

For the past two days the two men had been touring Gibraltar and the surrounding locality on Argentine passports. OKW had lately proposed Operation Felix, a combined attack with the Spanish on the rock of Gibraltar, in order to close the Mediterranean to the Royal Navy, thereby cutting Britain's oil supplies from the Middle East. From the outset Canaris had viewed the scheme with unbridled enthusiasm - not least, Lahousen suspected, because the plan deflected attention from the invasion of the British Isles.

Although it was early evening the heat was still oppressive and

Lahousen wiped his brow with his handkerchief. After Canaris had concluded a protracted and often unmilitary exchange with his aide in Berlin, he replaced the receiver and turned to Lahousen, his expression one of bemusement.

'The Duke of Windsor is currently in Lisbon, waiting to leave for the Bahamas. The Great W.C. wishes to appoint him governor, but the Duchess is upset because troublemakers have been throwing stones at the windows of their villa. Can you guess who?'

'Naujocks?'

'Walter Schellenberg. The Fuhrer has charged him with the task of kidnapping the Duke and Wallace Simpson.'

Lahousen uttered a snort of derision. 'Why? So that Edward can lead the invasion from the front, like Henry in Richard the Third? "God and Saint George! Richmond and victory!"'

Canaris laughed. 'According to Ribbentrop, the once and future king has declared himself to be against Churchill, and is ready to collaborate in the establishment of "better relations" between England and Germany. Five million Swiss francs have also been mentioned.'

'Schellenberg as kingmaker - a novel concept. But why throw stones?'

The admiral shrugged. 'Who can tell what excites the minds of our colleagues on Wilhelmstrasse. Have you seen their arrest list? Noel Coward and Virginia Woolf! As if the first wave will be thrown back into the sea by bad art.'

'What news of Sealion?' Lahousen asked, serious now.

'The usual nonsense. Jodl strongly disagrees with your estimates on the strength of the enemy defences.'

Lahousen sipped at his glass of ten-year-old Calvados, but said nothing. Like his superior he had little time for Jodl, but on this issue he tended to agree.

'Foreign Armies West have also voiced alarm at our minute on flame defences,' Canaris continued, with evident satisfaction. 'Now OKW have asked us to instruct one of our legion of agents in England to take dig deeper.'

Lahousen savoured the irony. Until 1939 the Abwehr had concentrated exclusively on France as the future enemy in the west, Britain having been purposefully neglected by express order of the Fuhrer. True, they possessed a handful of agents in England, but few were nationals, and were for the most part conspicuous. The counter-espionage expertise of the British secret service only served to compound the problem.

'Is there anyone we can use?' inquired Canaris.

An uncomfortable realisation dawned on Lahousen that Canaris was serious. He swallowed a generous draft from his glass. The admiral was an impossible man to predict, certainly, but his desire to satisfy this particular whim seemed especially perverse.

'Can we be sure it would justify expending the necessary resources, Herr Admiral?'

'Never more so, colonel.'

Lahousen thought for a moment. Somewhat reluctantly, he decided to tell the truth. 'Wichmann has two agents in training for an air-drop.'

'The Danes, yes?'

Lahousen nodded. 'Schmidt and Bjornson. But neither is ready to go into the field.'

'What about the Welsh ring?'

Lahousen shifted uncomfortably in his chair. 'Wichmann and Ritter would fight it tooth and nail. It runs contrary to policy to risk valuable agents on speculative assignments.'

'Come, come - what is the point of the Abwehr if not to benefit wider military strategy? Besides, I can think of no better way of re-establishing JOHNNY's credentials after that nonsense in May.'

Here Canaris had a point. JOHNNY was a Welshman named Arthur Owens, whose small espionage network formed the linchpin of the entire Abwehr organisation in England. By profession Owens was an electrical engineer. His firm, the Owens Battery Company, manufactured accumulators, and included the Royal Navy among its customers. Pre-war business trips to the Continent had taken Owens to several shipyards in Northern Germany, where, in 1936, for money, he had been recruited to spy for Germany. Codenamed JOHNNY, his case officer at the Hamburg Stelle was Major Nikolaus Ritter, alias Dr Rantzau. By the end of 1939 Owens' network boasted half a dozen agents, predominantly Welsh Nationalists. Chief among them was A.3551, a retired Swansea police Inspector intent on contaminating reservoirs which served the industrial Midlands. A further agent,

A.3725, a photographer, assisted in the despatch of JOHNNY's lengthy reports to Germany by reducing them onto microfilm. Lately, however, clouds had appeared on the horizon. In May Owens had arranged a rendezvous with a U-boat at a position south of the Dogger Bank, where he was to have met Ritter, and hand over a new recruit for training in Germany. Owens and his trawler failed to appear, and although JOHNNY continued to report by wireless, some within the Abwehr now doubted his loyalties.

With trepidation Lahousen now wondered what his contrary superior had in mind for the Welsh Ring. Like all networks on foreign soil it needed to be nurtured gradually, like a delicate cutting, and allowed to take root. He was not about to allow Canaris to jeopardize its very existence in pursuit of some private intrigue.

'Herr Admiral, before May it was relatively easy for agents to enter England by posing as refugees. Since the fall of France infiltration has only been possible through Sweden and Portugal, which has created a dangerous bottleneck. For now we're reliant on parachute or submarine.'

'Spare me the lecture,' Canaris snapped impatiently. 'Come to the point.'

Lahousen pressed his case as forcefully as he dared. 'We are entirely reliant upon the Welsh Ring to provide us with background information for false identity papers. To risk any one of them is to jeopardize our entire war organisation in the United Kingdom.'

'How, then, should we implement OKH's request?'

'Time is against us,' Lahousen replied, at a loss to provide a more persuasive answer. 'Even if we had a suitable agent available - and we don't - they'd need three months of intensive training. Sealion is timetabled to take place in two. Rush a job like this and you guarantee failure.'

'Could we not send an Englishman?'

'The English have yet to form a queue at the door.'

'What about prisoners-of-war? Surely one or two captured in France have expressed interest in Abwehr service?'

'A pair of Glasgow Irishmen captured in skirmishes around the Maginot Line came forward last year, claiming IRA connections.'

'Hardly a reliable qualification.'

'They wished to secure a ticket home, nothing more.'

'Civilians, then?'

Lahousen shook his head. 'Their faces are mostly too well-known. The same goes for politically-motivated military prisoners.'

'Leutnant Wagner?'

'Out of the question,' Lahousen replied, without hesitation. 'Besides, he was wounded during the raid at St Margaret's Bay.'

Canaris cast his eyes upwards, as if appealing to some higher authority. 'Can the Abwehr not produce a single expendable individual whom we can send to England, if only to convince Liss and the General Staff that we are doing our utmost to implement this ridiculous invasion charade?'

Lahousen considered his superior's demand. The placation of Foreign Armies West seemed to him a slender motive for condemning a man to certain death. However, experience told the colonel that he would have to play along with this new scheme until it was forgotten.

'Ritter did mention an Englishman,' he began slowly. 'A petty criminal who fled to France before war broke out. He was picked up by the French police for some minor offence and got trapped in June. He's made it known to the camp commandant that he's willing to work for Germany, provided the price is right.'

The admiral's expression registered keen interest. 'There's no political motive?'

'Apparently not. But he's certainly known to the English police.'

'We're concerned with the secret service, not ordinary British bobbies.'

'With respect, admiral, such a man is unsuitable agent material. To bundle amateurs into boats, or out of aircraft, is to invite certain death.'

'On the contrary, he may be perfect for a one-off mission. After all, the man has escaped from England once already. Where is he now?'

'St Denis, I presume, along with the rest of the British internees.'

Canaris clapped his hands. 'Splendid. Call Ritter in Hamburg and have him meet you in Paris tomorrow. Interview this Englishman personally and take his temperature.'

Lahousen nodded his assent, then finished his Calvados. Among the enduring faults of the chief of intelligence was his propensity to issue irrational and contradictory instructions at the drop of a hat. That these might ride roughshod over the wishes of his subordinates mattered to him not at all. Canaris plainly detested Sealion, but having concluded that the cartography of the Rock ruled out Felix, he now sought other ways to scuttle the assault on England. Even, it seemed, a suicide mission.

TWENTY

On his arrival from in Paris Colonel Erwin Lahousen traced Johnson not to the British civilian internment camp at St Denis, but to the prison fort at Romainville, a near suburb of the capital, where the authorities had concentrated perceived troublemakers.

Lahousen knew that Romainville was only the latest in a long line of jails in which Harry Johnson had cooled his heels. The first, following his third absence-without-leave, had been the military prison at Colchester. On his release in 1936, Johnson possessed three pounds in cash, a civilian suit, a jail crop, and an army testimonial which declared simply that his services were no longer required. He travelled to London, and for a time held down menial jobs in the West End, gambling and pilfering all the while, and drifting towards the rapids of serious crime. Within a year of leaving the glasshouse Johnson was back behind bars, having bungled a raid on a jewellers in Conduit Street by stalling his getaway car. Towards the end of a nine month stretch in Lewes jail he fell in with a certain Tommy Collyer, a safe-breaker. On the outside the pair formed a partnership, and prospered quickly after Johnson lit upon the simple expedient of blowing safes with gelignite. This unusual method fascinated both Fleet Street and Scotland Yard, who honoured the pair with the formation of a special gelignite squad.

And so, for a time, life was sweet for 'Flash' Harry Johnson. He had money, women, a car and a comfortable flat in Gerrard Street. The nightclubs of Soho - the Nest, El Gaucho and Shim Sham - came to know him well.

While the detection of serious crime in London was an imperfect science, by the spring of 1939 word reached Johnson and Collyer that the Yard were closing fast. While Collyer opted to take his chances in London, Johnson contacted a Maltese who specialised in spiriting wanted criminals to Costa Rica, from where there was no extradition, via Marseilles. Two days later Johnson flew from Croydon to Paris, where he booked into the Hotel Quatre Vents, intending to enjoy a last hurrah in the City of Light before heading south. But Flash Harry Johnson was unable to resist the temptation of burgling the hotel safe, and was caught. Preferring jail to the Foreign Legion, he received a two year sentence, and broke stones at Sceaux as the German Blitzkrieg swept first through Poland, then Norway, and finally France.

Thus far the summer of 1940 had proved to be unusually hot and breathless, and everywhere across Europe grass withered, rivers shrank and wells ran dry. Behind the thick stone walls at Romainville Fort the heat was particularly unbearable, and the discomfort heightened tenfold by the stench of sweat, urine and rotting vegetables. As Ritter and Lahousen were ushered inside the cramped and malodorous cell, the seven French prisoners with whom Johnson shared leapt smartly from their palliasses. At Romainville hardly a day passed without fresh rumours of summary executions, and in their wide-brimmed hats and dark civilian clothes the Abwehr men passed easily for Gestapo. Indeed Ritter had cause to employ the ruse on a regular basis.

Johnson rose to his feet only after the guard had hustled his cellmates away to the exercise yard. Lahousen took in the English safe-breaker. He was a man of average height, in his middle thirties, who had been stocky before prison thinned him. The same regime had begun to grey his hair, although his cheeks were ruddy still. His outstanding feature, Lahousen decided, was the sharp, untrustworthy glint in his eye.

'My name is Doctor Rantzau, Mr Johnson,' Ritter began amiably. His English was perfect, and bore traces of the ten years he had spent in the United States. 'This is Herr Brandt. How do you find the conditions here?'

'It's no hotel,' Johnson replied casually, is manner self-assured, if not quite insolent.

'Not like the Quatre Vents.'

'Not exactly.'

'Although the two are quite intimately connected, I think.' Ritter turned around in a slow half-circle, inspecting the shabby

126

cell. 'And the cuisine? The commandant tells me that you can look forward to more dried vegetables today.'

'I've known worse.'

'Then in life you've been truly unfortunate.'

Ritter withdrew his cigarette case from his pocket and offered it to the Englishman. Johnson took one and waited for Ritter to light it. The Abwehr man did so with a Zippo lighter.

'Personally speaking,' Ritter continued, 'this place strikes me as a boil on the arsehole of the world.'

Johnson gave no reply, and drew deeply on the cigarette, savouring the smoke in his lungs before he exhaled. Lahousen stepped across the cell and peered out through the small barred window, through which the sun shone brightly. Beyond the prison wall tiny figures went about their business, and in the distance could be seen the Sacre Couer, ablaze with light, and the Eiffel Tower.

'Herr Johnson,' Ritter asked suddenly, 'you are interested in working for Germany?'

'That's right. Talent like mine needs gainful employment.'

'And precisely what talents do you imagine are required of an espionage operative?'

Johnson considered the question. 'Guts I reckon, and patience. Skill with a miniature camera, that sort of thing.'

Ritter laughed loudly. 'I see we're dealing with an expert!'

'On the contrary,' countered Lahousen, turning back into the room. 'Herr Johnson has forgotten the secret passwords and invisible ink. Not to mention the glamorous Russian Countess in the hotel bar.'

Ritter turned back to Johnson. 'Are you fluent in any language besides English?'

'I've picked up a bit of French.'

'So little? You surprise me.'

'They had the silent system in force at Sceaux. I've only been in this hole a month.'

'What is your religious denomination?'

'Church of England, I suppose.'

'Have you ever been a member of any political party?'

'No.'

'You have never been a member of any trade union, or the

Communist Party?'

'No. Politics don't interest me in the slightest.'

Lahousen joined in the conversation. 'So is it for money, or through hatred of the English authorities that you wish to work against them?'

'Just the money,' Johnson replied evenly, before adding, as if reading from a prepared script: 'But I do dislike Britain, mainly on account of the prisons and the police.'

'I take it you're still a wanted man?'

'I'll cop at least fifteen years if they catch up with me. Which they won't.'

Lahousen noted the evident pride in the Englishman's voice, then produced from his pocket a sheet of paper, which he unfolded and handed to Johnson. It was a partial copy of the Treachery Act 1940, the opening section of which read: *If, with intent to help the enemy, any person does, or attempts or conspires with any other person to do, any act which is designed or likely to give assistance to the naval, military or air operations of the enemy, to impede such operations of His Majesty's forces, or to endanger life, shall be guilty of felony and shall on conviction suffer death.*

Lahousen allowed the Englishman time to digest the full implication of the text. Then he said: 'Let there be no misunderstanding, Herr Johnson. If you are caught you will pay the ultimate penalty.'

Johnson shrugged his shoulders and handed the extract back. 'Like I said, they won't catch me. They haven't yet, have they?'

'No. Unlike the French.'

Johnson raised his hand. 'That was different. In foreign climes, wasn't I? Back home I know the ropes.'

'Assuming you were to get home,' continued Ritter, 'would you be prepared to carry out acts of sabotage?'

'Easy as pie. I'm a dab hand with explosives.'

'So I read. But could you kill a fellow countryman?'

'I could kill a copper.'

'But an innocent person? A child who witnessed your arrival, for example. Or the landlady who finds some incriminating item in your room.'

'Yeah, if I had to, I reckon I could. Can I have another cigarette?'

As Ritter obliged, Lahousen studied the Englishman with a jaundiced eye. Thus far, Johnson's replies had carried not one wit of conviction. Even in his present frame of mind, Canaris would surely blanche at recruiting such a transparent opportunist. He caught and held the Englishman's gaze.

'Herr Johnson, so far you've given us no reason to trust a word you've spoken. Let me disabuse you of the notion that your services would be unique. Since the chaotic evacuation of the British Army from France we have received more than two hundred similar offers from disgruntled prisoners-of-war. Some are sincere, but others believe that they can fool us into assisting their return to England.'

'Not me.'

'Why so? And before you answer, please spare me the version by which, being a wanted criminal, you couldn't possibly surrender the moment you arrive.'

Johnson sniffed. 'Look, on the level, I could turn King's evidence and tell your opposite number everything I'd learned about your firm. But it seems to me that your side is going to win this war, so then where would I be? Besides, I doubt old man Churchill would be willing to pay me as well as your boss. Like I told you, I'm just interested in the money.'

Lahousen nodded. 'And what might your price be?'

Johnson took a thoughtful pull on his cigarette. 'I reckon £500 a month would suffice. To begin with, anyway.'

Major Ritter uttered a short, theatrical laugh. 'Forty-five thousand Reichsmarks? You value yourself highly.'

'Sin of pride, mate. Never did me no harm.'

'You confuse pride with avarice, Herr Johnson,' Lahousen replied. 'We have men who'll work for nothing.'

'Take my advice, chum - they'll be worth what you pay them.'

Lahousen glanced at Ritter, signalling that the interrogation was at an end. As the guard unlocked the door and the Abwehr men made to leave, Lahousen half expected the Englishman to hastily retract and lower his price. But he remained silent, watching his visitors carefully from behind a plume of grey tobacco smoke, leaving Lahousen with the uncomfortable hunch that Abwehr II had not heard the last of Harry Johnson.

AUGUST

TWENTY-ONE

The Director of B Division, Guy Liddell, occupied a converted bedroom in the east wing of Blenheim Palace, the opulent if overcrowded new home of MI5. Two visitors sat before him: Colonel Tar Robertson, the head of B1(a), the section which ran double-cross agents, and Major Morley. Liddell was studying the gloomy post-mortem on the flame warfare trial held at Dumpton Gap at the beginning of July, six weeks earlier. When Morley was satisfied that the Director had digested the document, he rose from an exquisite Queen Anne chair to deliver his pitch.

'Sir, the various test programmes have now been unified under the Petroleum Warfare Department. That's a grand name for a handful of sappers and Post Office electricians. As you read in my brief, so far only the static flame trap shows much promise.'

'I gather the Prime Minister is keen on the idea of fire-ships,' said Robertson. 'Old tankers packed with fuel and explosives, steered into enemy ports like torpedoes. Worked well enough at Zeebrugge in 1918.'

'Did it? Besides, I hear quite the opposite from Hankey,' the Director replied quietly. 'Apparently Winston favours choking the enemy with clouds of poison gas.'

'There's a complication,' continued Morley, in an effort to steer the dialogue back on track. 'The Ministry of Supply are carrying out their own flame trials, and are keen to preserve their autonomy. Now the navy have teamed up with the PWD, and the RAF with the Ministry. An OTU squadron at Boscombe Down has been playing around with some kind of bulk oil bomb, but the RAF isn't letting much on.'

Liddell already looked bored. 'I suggest you isolate what little of it you wish to leak to the other side, and submit it to the Wireless

Board for approval.'

'There's more to it than that, sir. Dumpton was a shambles, but it just so happens that the Luftwaffe were stooging around. Now our friends in Hamburg have asked JOHNNY for more information on British petroleum defences.'

'JOHNNY?'

'SNOW, sir,' said Robertson. 'The Welshman, Arthur Owens.'

'You're still running him from Wandsworth, I take it.'

Robertson nodded. 'Two nights ago Hamburg informed JOHNNY that they intend to send over an agent with the same end in mind. If Rantzau is willing to take such a risk the German High Command must be worried sick about flame.'

'It's a gift horse,' added Morley. 'We can write up the potential of our flame capability, and at the same time hand the Germans some prime chicken-feed.'

Liddell cleared his throat. A shy and mysterious man, it was his habit to gaze into the middle-distance when addressing his subordinates. 'If I understand you correctly, gentlemen, your proposal is not that we allow SNOW to transmit the information by wireless, but to permit an enemy agent to enter this country, poke around at will, and relay details of a secret defence programme back to Germany.'

'Not quite, sir. If the PWD can oblige us with a burn at a prepared site, we can kill two birds with one stone. We feed the Germans advance warning of a hopeless weapon, long before it can be put into service, and reassure the Abwehr they're running an effective network.'

'Why not use CHARLIE? He is, after all, an experienced photographer.'

Robertson shook his head. 'I've already made it quite clear to Morley that I'm not willing to endanger a single member of the SNOW ring.'

'I'm not sure, Morley. We don't want another Venlo.'

'Venlo was an SIS operation,' Morley replied curtly. At Venlo, in November 1939, Walter Schellenberg had snatched two MI6 officers from a Dutch border post, a sting which had triggered seismic repercussions within the British intelligence community. Among them was a mortal fear of launching bold offensive strokes which might conceivably backfire.

'If our double-agents continue to transmit nothing but banalities the enemy will lose interest,' joined Robertson.

Still the Director looked dubious. 'Might you not be handing Goebbels a prize propaganda opportunity? As far as I'm aware, to deliberately attack a man with fire runs contrary to the Geneva Protocol.'

Morley nodded. 'We call his bluff. Jerry's hardly likely to shout that loud about a weapon intended to undermine morale amongst their invasion troops. Besides, they used flamethrowers themselves against Eban Emael in May.'

'That was a fortress, an inanimate object. The Protocol allows for that. This PWD nonsense is designed to burn German soldiers alive. Advertise that to the world at large and you risk the worst kind of Nazi terror reprisal - aerial bombardment of London, even poison gas.'

'Dumpton was six weeks ago,' countered Morley. 'Their propaganda people have had ample time to concoct a lurid story for the neutral territories. So far they've done nothing. The ultimate purpose of BI(a) is to decide what information can safely be passed to the enemy, and to ensure that the flow of information is consistent. We assess the probable gain in divulging each piece of intelligence against probable loss. Since the enemy are already aware of our work in progress, that loss would be minimal. Whereas the gain could be immense.'

Liddell began to pluck pensively at his thinning head of hair. This, Morley knew, was a bad omen.

'Sir, we're running out of time. Two days ago the German air force pressed home its first concerted attack on mainland targets. Four Chain Home radio-location stations were hit, and Ventnor is still off air. The Fighter Command forward fields at Manston, Hawkinge and Lympne also took a pasting.'

Robertson nodded gravely. 'The volume of signal intelligence is increasing daily. They're gathering barges, fitting engines, pooling transport aircraft. The Wehrmacht is moving up to the coast in ever greater numbers.'

Liddell considered this. 'Since you're so well informed, Tar, you must also be aware that the German High Command have done nothing but bicker for the last few weeks. The army want to land on a broad front between Margate and Weymouth, while the navy insists on a narrow one. The whole plan betrays nothing but haste and confusion.'

'Haste and confusion didn't stop us lifting three hundred thousand men off the beaches at Dunkirk in six days.'

'I don't see how you can ensure this man will complete his mission successfully. We can't simply pick him up, chauffeur him to a pre-arranged trial site, then pack him off in a submarine. That would tax even German credulity.'

'He'd be chaperoned,' replied Morley.

'By who? You've already told me the SNOW network can't be directly involved.'

'SNOW has apparently convinced the Abwehr that he's running a cell comprised of fanatical Welsh nationalists. Some of these sub-agents are notional, with fictional identities. Our man could pass himself off as one of them.'

The Director paused, deep in thought, his eyes now fixed on the Vermeer on the facing wall. At length he said: 'Certain conditions would have to be satisfied. The agent must be captured immediately on landing. He must not under any circumstances he allowed to communicate with his control. And his capture must involve the barest minimum of trustworthy people on our side. If he's caught in circumstances which are in any way public he'll be useless to us.'

'Obviously, we don't want it to end on the scaffold,' agreed Robertson. 'Dead agents are no use at all.'

Liddell turned to Morley. 'You'll need a safehouse, and a reliable escort.'

'I've someone in mind, sir,' Morley replied, much relieved that round one of the battle had been won.

'Background?'

'Lawyer.'

'Expendable?'

'Completely.'

TWENTY-TWO

Ritter and Lahousen watched as Harry Johnson arduously climbed the rungs of a ladder propped against a tall tree, braced himself, jumped, and fell heavily onto the lawn. In Berlin, Lahousen received daily reports on the Englishman's progress. In the fortnight that the self-styled master criminal had spent at the training school near Wiesbaden, not one instructor had discerned in him a solitary praiseworthy trait. Johnson displayed enthusiasm only for food and fornication, the latter pastime in a plush brothel on the Lindlarstrasse reserved for officers. Despite the fact that his pay had been back-dated to the beginning of July he had already run up a sizeable tab.

Johnson's expression as he picked himself up from the lawn betrayed a degree of physical discomfort in which his controller and the head of Abwehr II found no little pleasure. Ritter moved from the window to the door of the hut and called out to the Luftwaffe instructor, then sat down beside Lahousen and waited for Johnson to enter. In the room next door the voice of another agent in training was faintly audible, persevering in an unequal struggle with the English language. Lahousen opened his case and produced a sheaf of neat-looking papers which he set on the table, together with a fountain pen.

Johnson greeted his Abwehr masters with a cocksure smirk. 'Dr Rantzau, Colonel Brandt. Not entirely an unexpected pleasure.'

'How so?' Lahousen asked.

'Now you've got me practising for a parachute jump, I reckon you'll be chucking me out of a plane before too long. This my final briefing?'

'Not quite. How long have you been landing and rolling?'

'Four days.'

136

'Thirty jumps a day, until he's used to a drop of eight feet,' confirmed Ritter.

'By the time you lot finish with me I'll be two foot shorter.' Johnson nodded at the sheaf of documents on the table. 'This my will?'

Lahousen pushed the papers forward. 'Your contract with the German government.'

Johnson picked up a copy of the agreement and scanned it briefly. 'It's in German.'

'You have my word that it accurately reflects the terms we agreed. I'll be happy to provide a verbal translation, should you wish.'

'And what court do I appeal to if you welsh on the deal?'

Lahousen smiled. 'I can recommend several excellent lawyers in Berlin.'

'Just run through the financial arrangements.'

Lahousen recited the terms from memory. 'In return for your services you will receive the sum of one hundred thousand Reichsmarks, or, if you prefer, the equivalent in foreign exchange. During your absence a salary of four hundred thousand marks per month will continue to be paid. If, as a result of your espionage activities, you are captured and jailed, a sum of five hundred thousand marks per month will be paid onto a German account in your name.'

'Until they hang me,' Johnson said.

Ritter shrugged his shoulders. 'If you are tried in camera and hanged in secret we may never know. Do you have any dependents?

Johnson hesitated. 'No, there's no-one. Anything else in the small print I need worry about?'

'You must not reveal that you are an employee of the German government, or divulge the names of any personnel. In the event of your disclosing such information to the British authorities, or your betraying the German Reich, the penalty imposed shall be death.'

'Fair enough. What about expenses?'

'You will receive a further £500 in sterling. Any other expenses will be reimbursed on your return to Germany.'

Johnson nodded approvingly. 'It's good money, I can't deny

that. What does the Fatherland wants in return?'

'The success of your mission will be established if you return with still or moving pictures of certain British coastal defences.'

'Where?'

'Kent, most probably.'

'There's a lot of coast in Kent. I hope you don't expect me to cover every sand dune and beach hut.'

'One location only, possibly two. Your contact will brief you more fully when you arrive. He has also requested £1000, which you will deliver.'

'In addition you are to note troop movements, unit insignia on military vehicles, and so forth,' added Ritter.

'I've got eyes. When do I go?'

'Tomorrow night.'

Johnson paled visibly. 'Jesus Christ! What about a practice jump? From an aircraft, not a tree.'

Ritter shook his head. 'No time. Besides, you'll be jumping at low level on a static line. Nothing could be simpler. Just close your eyes and think of England.'

'And avoid hitting it too hard,' Lahousen added for good measure.

'Bloody marvellous,' muttered Johnson. 'A night jump for starters.'

'We've settled on your code-name.'

Johnson raised his hand. 'No need - I've already thought of one.'

The Abwehr men exchanged dubious glances. 'Go on,' said Lahousen.

'RAFFLES.'

Ritter was nonplussed.

'The gentleman thief,' explained Lahousen. 'An English fictional character. Herr Johnson, why not leave the planning to us?'

'What's wrong with RAFFLES?'

'Connections might be made to your past. Besides, it's too late. Your contact is already expecting CRACKER.'

'As in he who cracks safes? Sounds like a circular argument to me. What about a wireless?'

'All communication with your home station will be routed

through your contact in England.'

'We might get separated.'

Lahousen hesitated. It was a fair point, after all. Indeed he knew that Johnson had already complained that his training was irregular. From another of the trainees he encountered at meal times, a German named Petter, Johnson had learned that the standard Abwehr programme consisted of a minimum of three months of intensive instruction in sabotage, languages, morse and wireless telegraphy. True, he would be returning to his native land, and therefore needed no instruction in his mother tongue. However, his own crash course had consisted chiefly of still and cine photography; ten solid days of aperture, film speed and zoom. According to Petter, Johnson asked more questions of his fellow trainees than of his instructors.

So far as Lahousen was concerned the mission was already scratched. Flash Harry Johnson was nothing more than an incorrigible con. In less than thirty-six hours the Englishman would be on home ground, seeking out MI6 and a royal pardon. Today he had swindled the Reich out of a few hundred thousand marks. Tomorrow, if he were lucky, British justice might too be cheated.

The colonel said slowly: 'Herr Johnson, you represent a high risk investment for our organisation. We have no guarantee that you will not surrender as soon as you land, and reveal everything you know of the innermost workings of the German secret service.'

'When the two of you looked me up in Paris, there was a lot of talk about sabotage and killing. Other people here are trained to concoct thermites and dynamites from household materials. Why not me?'

'You sold yourself to us as an explosives expert.'

'I am - with finished product, from quarries. Mixing stuff up in a bathtub is another matter.'

'You will not be required to carry out acts of sabotage on your mission. Or do any killing.'

'But what if some hero tries to kill me? All you've given me is two sessions with a peashooter.'

'I'll see to it that you get another hour on the range before you leave.'

'How long will I be in the field?'

'A week, no more.'

'And how do I get back?'

'Your contact will brief you more fully,' Ritter repeated.

'Have you done this before?'

'Often enough,' Lahousen lied smoothly.

'One hundred thousand Reichsmarks,' reminded Ritter.

Johnson held their stares for a long moment. 'Fair do's. Where do I sign?'

'At the bottom of the last page, next to the pencilled cross. All six copies.' Lahousen turned to Ritter. 'We need two witnesses. Preferably not regular staff. Is there anyone suitable?'

'Only Drugge. He's with Dierks next door.'

'Very well. Call them in.'

As Ritter rose and crossed to the door, Lahousen watched as Johnson took up the pen and set about adding his untidy signature to the documents. As he wrote, the same knowing smile returned to play upon his colourless lips.

Against all sensible logic, and in pursuit of his own mysterious designs, Canaris had decreed that the Englishman be dispatched without further delay. It was not the first occasion on which Erwin Lahousen had sent forth a man to certain death. For the first time in his career, however, the colonel realised that he cared not whether one of his own operatives lived or died.

TWENTY-THREE

With an impatient flourish Goodman drew a bold line through the half page of scribbled lines, tore the sheet from the pad, and screwed it into a ball. He thought about blaming the rough utility paper, which caused his nib to splinter and splay over undigested lumps of wood and cotton waste, but knew full well that the prose was bad for very different reasons. What was it that pundit had recently opined in the New Statesman? That since the invention of the novel, there had been no moment when fewer people wished the read them. Ordinarily, Goodman might have assumed that a thousand literary masterpieces would germinate from the bloody debris of total war. Yet the few evacuation novels he had skimmed had been distinctly middle-class, and mostly pejorative of the masses. The fall of France had panicked the reading public, and their literary curiosity - always a fairweather emotion, dependent upon a background of security and order - had vanished overnight.

Gone too, so it seemed, was his own inspiration. Everything he knew was either secret, or mundane, or simply irrelevant. There was Elizabeth of course, and Sophie too. *Love and hate, hate and love*. Yet as a writer he aspired to scale higher ground than romance and escapism... Or was the lowbrow what war demanded of fiction?

Goodman's reverie was broken suddenly by a knock on the door. Before he could respond, Sergeant Kydd's head was inside the room.

'Visitor, sir.'

'Who is it?' The section office received few callers, most of them in error.

'That queer bird Morley.'

Kydd arched his eyebrows. Goodman flipped over his notebook

and dropped it into his empty in-tray. 'You'd better show him up.'

Morley entered a half minute later, dressed once more as a major in the Brigade of Guards. He cast a critical eye around the upstairs room which served as Goodman's office. 'Not much, is it. D'you know, I've got an Adam bureau in my room at Blenheim.'

'You'll forgive my disinterest. I'm being transferred to the Judge Advocate-General's department.'

'So I hear. Up your street, I should have thought.'

'Except that my new street is in Plymouth.'

'Ah.' Leisurely Morley charged his cigarette holder with a Passing Cloud. 'What do you know about spies, Goodman?'

'That we hang them.'

'Yes, although in that respect the Treachery Act is rather unhandy.' The major touched a match to his cigarette. 'Anything else?'

'Only what I read in John Buchan.'

'I see. So what would you say to looking after a real spy for a couple of days?'

Goodman experienced a flash of deja vu. No doubt it was another task too menial for one of their own. 'I suppose you want me to keep tabs on some displaced Dutchman.'

'Not quite,' replied Morley, turning to push the door closed. 'Two days from now a German agent codenamed CRACKER will arrive in this country. His mission is to see whether our coastline is protected by a flame barrier. You were at Dumpton in July so you know what I'm yapping on about.'

Goodman digested the information. As given, the facts seemed back to front. 'How on earth can you know that?'

Morley thumbed his nose. 'Need to know, old man. Anyway, don't be fooled by that Dumpton fiasco. With the benefit of experience the petroleum warfare people reckon they can put on a far better show. Our job is to ensure that our visitor captures the whole thing on film, and returns the evidence to Germany.'

'And you think this scheme might prevent an invasion?'

'Probably not. But we might waste a little of their energy and time. How's your Welsh accent?'

'I really have no idea.' Goodman paused, then continued in character: 'Not very good, I imagine. Never been further west than Bristol, see.'

142

'That sounded more Delhi than Cardiff.'

'I doubt a German would notice.'

'Assuming, of course, that our friend is a Hun.' Morley paused, manoeuvring his cigarette holder between his fingers. 'Look, before I say anything more I need to know if you're willing to give it a go.'

Goodman weighed the question with a feeling of unease, remembering the fiasco with Ironside a month before. 'How dangerous will it be?'

'Not very. Spies make for a pretty pitiable breed, as a rule.'

'And I don't have to take him back to Germany myself?'

'Good Lord, no.'

'For a couple of days, you say.'

'Well, perhaps seven.'

Goodman breathed deep. Seven days, starting in two. He was due to meet in Sophie at the weekend, this time in London, and had thought of little else since the date and the hotel had been arranged. Then on Monday, the disbandment of his section, a slow train to Plymouth, and the JAG, with its staple diet of brawls, absents and boredom. And no more Sophie. Even demob would have been preferable.

'Why me? I thought I'd flunked the exam.'

'It's not a matter of grades,' Morley replied stiffly. 'Are you interested or not?'

'You know I am.'

'Good. I need your blower. Is it scrambled?'

'No.'

'Not so good.'

Goodman sat in silence as the MI5 man dialled a number. The conversation was brief and to the point. Yes, Goodman had accepted the job. Yes, he was a reliable sort. A barrister, Grays Inn. No, he would deal with JAG and the Petroleum Warfare Department himself. Yes, Tar should contact Hamburg right away.

The exchange lasted no more than twenty seconds, after which Morley rang off and returned his attention to Goodman. 'Right, brass tacks. Your character is a Welsh Nationalist. You reside in Swansea and have homosexual tendencies. In 1937 you were convicted for indecency at Bow Street, and following a humiliating stretch in Wandsworth decided to betray the bastard

English to Germany in return for the promise of an independent Wales. You were recruited by a man known to you as GW. Your codename within his espionage ring is TYRO. Major Robertson will sketch in the fine detail tomorrow.'

'On the Welsh free state, or homosexuality?'

'You can research the nancy boy angle in your own time,' Morley answered drily. 'If our visitor tries to delve any deeper into your personal affairs, tell him to mind his own business.'

'Is he coming by air?'

'We don't know as yet. There's a safe house in London, where the pair of you can stay until the flame barrage trial. I'm trying to swing that for the eighteenth.'

'You want a nanny.'

'Of a sort,' Morley nodded. 'At no time allow him out of your sight or earshot. With luck he'll bring over a wireless set, which should be left behind. On no account let him use it. In fact, if you get the chance then damage it slightly. It'll be one less thing to worry about.'

'So how does he contact the other side?'

'Through me. I'll explain ways and means later. If CRACKER gets restless, tell him all traffic is relayed through GW and nobody else.'

'GW being an agent you already have in custody?'

'Something like that. Anyway, after CRACKER has seen the burn on the coast he's got to be delivered back into German hands. Given the apparent urgency of his mission it's just possible that they will risk a seaplane or a submarine for the return journey. Again, as far as CRACKER is concerned, all arrangements will be made through GW.'

Goodman frowned. The avalanche of facts seem too fantastical. 'Major, has MI5 attempted this type of operation before?'

'No, as a matter of fact.'

'You don't think this chap might see through the whole charade as soon as he lands?'

'He might,' Morley allowed. 'But if the German secret service know as much about us as we know about them, then I doubt it. It's something of a rush job, I'll grant you, but it'll all fall together in the next forty-eight hours.'

'I take it this grand scheme has a cover name?'

'Operation Twenty. Written in Roman numerals, the figure twenty is represented by a pair of X's, which-'

'Form a double-cross,' Goodman anticipated.

'Quite so,' Morley said, with a hint of annoyance. Then, quite calmly, the major stood back and withdrew his revolver, thumbed back the hammer, and took aim between Goodman's eyes from a distance of four feet.

'Captain Goodman,' he began evenly. 'Every last detail of this operation must remain Most Secret. Should you divulge any part of it to any unauthorized person at any time, regardless of circumstance, I shall personally shoot you dead in the name of the King.'

Goodman eyed Morley coolly. The tableau struck him as ridiculous beyond words, yet the major's expression was stony and deadly serious. Finally he said: 'Isn't all this a trifle theatrical?'

'Utterly,' Morley replied, lowering the pistol, his manner affable once more. 'But I know of no better way to make my point.'

TWENTY-FOUR

The once flourishing French summer resort of Le Touquet had been selected as the venue for an extensive landing exercise, carried out under the watchful gaze of the head of the army high command, Field Marshal von Brauchitsch, and his general staff. The dress rehearsal involved infantry, mountain guns, artillery tractors, horses, and even crude amphibious tanks equipped with floats and pontoons.

From his vantage point on the roof of the Hotel Splendide Walter Schellenberg raised his field glasses to focus on a party of assault pioneers. The men had gingerly embarked on a number of small launches which retreated a short distance from the shore, then put in again to allow the troops to stumble on to the beach, knee-deep in cold salt water, and clear the dunes and empty cafe terraces of imaginary defenders. It was impressive, to a point, although to Schellenberg the motley invasion flotilla of pleasure steamers and coal barges bobbing and weaving further offshore seemed somehow to debase six weeks of exacting work on his invasion handbook, Informationsheft GB.

Eichner, his intelligence officer, explained the seaward manoeuvres with an uneasy mixture of mirth and disgust. 'Every serviceable canal and river barge in France, Germany and the Low Countries has been requisitioned. Two thousand so far, plus a third of the entire German merchant fleet. According to Amt II the effect on our Baltic trade will be catastrophic.'

'How many troops will make up the first wave?'

'125,000 men and four panzer battalions.'

'Can the navy lift that many?'

'Over three days, with calm weather. Each barge can lift about one hundred and fifty men. The yards are cutting off the bows and lining the holds with concrete as protection against mines.'

Schellenberg lowered his glasses. 'Which hardly makes for speed.'

'Most are tows. The irony is that our invasion fleet will cross the Channel at a speed somewhat slower than Caesar's legions two thousand years ago.'

'Can it succeed?'

'On a narrow front, conceivably. But the navy are insisting on a crossing in broad daylight.'

'The barges will be sitting ducks.'

'Quite probably. Added to which the enemy will be able to estimate our strength and landing zones, and gain a clear day to prepare their defences.'

'Raeder has gone mad.'

'He prefers daylight for marshalling purposes. And he can turn back with fewer losses if the Royal Navy break through.'

'Is that likely?'

'Their Home Fleet alone comprises five battleships and eleven cruisers. If they intercept our barges during the first few days it hardly bears contemplation.

Schellenberg raised his glasses once more. Further along the exclusive Paris Plage a group of mountain troops stood and gaped at the water's edge, marvelling at the rise and fall of the tide. As yet none had even been issued with lifejackets. So far the armed Waffen SS units had been frozen out of the Sealion planning. On today's showing, mused Schellenberg, it was probably as well.

'What about Brandenburg?' he asked Eichner.

'Most detachments are training with motorcycles in a conventional military role. Some are earmarked to take out gun batteries on Beachy Head and the Dover Heights. Others will neutralize strongpoints along the Royal Military Canal.'

'It would be better to land troops by glider, surely.'

'All suitable landing areas have been obstructed.'

'And the mysterious Leutnant Wagner?'

'His section got shot up on the Kent coast last time out, but by all accounts he's a very capable field officer. Iron Cross first class last week. Pinned on by the Fuhrer himself at the Chancellory.

'What is he? Patriot or rogue?'

'A dark horse, for sure. Not a Party member. Here's a thing. He's been frequenting a jazz club in Antwerp, claiming to be an American journalist to charm a pretty little Belgian girl. Seen her twice since, too.'

'Brandenburg men are nothing if not resourceful.'

'She's a Jewess, the daughter of a diamond merchant.'

Schellenberg considered this. 'Well, well,' he said slowly, 'jazz and jews. A dangerous combination for a German officer.'

'And a race hygienist's dream come true.'

'Spare me the pseudo-science, Eichner. What else has reached your ears from the Tirpitzufer? Now that the Duke of York has been spirited away to the Bahamas I'm feeling starved of intrigue.'

'Something and nothing. There is a certain bordello in Wiesbaden, on the Lindlarstrasse.'

'I know of it. We have a female informant there, as I recall.'

Eichner nodded. 'She called Hesse this morning. Apparently some sort of riot broke out last night. The artillery officer she was entertaining was convinced the building was being attacked by enemy paratroops. It turned out to be a row over payment between a girl and a client. An English client - very drunk, very talkative.'

'She's absolutely sure?'

'Claims to have serviced the same man herself three times in the past week. Says his name is Harry.'

'He could be an American. Like Wagner.'

'She says not. Anyway, within ten minutes the whole neighbourhood was ablaze with the news that the troublemaker was a secret agent whose mission would take him to England tonight.'

'Tonight?'

Eichner nodded. 'And there's more. The car that took him away came from the pool at the Abwehr training school.'

TWENTY-FIVE

For four long hours Goodman had struggled to immerse himself in a dense espionage novel by Compton Mackenzie, Water on the Brain. It was a work he would have found a steep hill at the best of times, let alone now, hunched on the back seat of a Humber Snipe, forcing his eyes from line to line with the aid of a masked flashlight. The well-thumbed paperback had been pressed on him by Major Robertson of B1(a), with instructions to digest as much of the text as he could before the nocturnal rendezvous with CRACKER. Now he felt a thick headache coming on.

For the umpteenth time Goodman set the book aside and released an extravagant yawn, then manoeuvred his head through the open window.

'Any sign?' he asked, without great hope.

'Neither hide nor hair.' Gilmour stood on the road a dozen yards away, his neck craned skyward. 'Fifty minutes overdue. No bloody sense of occasion.'

In peacetime, Goodman had known Gilmour as an unprincipled private client solicitor, whose unctuous manner had survived a transfer to MI5 as a Regional Security Liaison Officer. Now he began to pace slowly back along the moonlit country lane toward the ugly concrete telephone box which served as their ad hoc communications centre, whistling softly but badly. Goodman sank back into the car and willed himself to return to the book, but in no time at all found the words bouncing off his brain like hail off a tin roof.

The past thirty-six hours had already merged into an exhausted blur, in the midst of which he had been obliged to cast aside his past and present, and to assume in their place a wholly alien identity. The process had begun immediately after his meeting

149

with Morley at the section office. The major had driven him at high speed to an address behind Kensington High Street, where he was briefed on the unique features of the MI5 safe-house in which he and CRACKER would co-habit until Operation Twenty was concluded. Following a sleepless night he had been flown to Swansea in an army Lysander, where he was met by Major B.A. Robertson, the MI5 case officer who controlled the notional Welsh Ring. Their whistle-stop tour of the city included dockyards, the main post office, a power station, several military installations, a cinema, a residential street and the central police station. Robertson justified the flying visit in terms of verisimilitude: no lie, he instructed Goodman, would convince an opponent unless it rested on a firm foundation of truth. To be tripped on a single half-learned biographical detail was to invite a bullet. There ended the lesson.

Afterwards they had continued on to Bristol, where Goodman took delivery of the Austin saloon in which he would drive CRACKER to London. He had rendezvoused with Gilmour just after seven in the evening, and had now been waiting in the quiet country lane near Upottery for six bottomless hours.

He felt at once drained by the hours of ceaselessly novel activity, and overloaded by an equivalent period absorbing spy craft and spurious personal history. Above all Goodman felt isolated, a lone messenger dispatched down a long, dark alley. And now, as the tense wait stretched ever further into the wee small hours, his sense of unease increased by the minute. So far the promised false papers had failed to arrive. He felt ill-briefed and unarmed, and the skin of his feigned persona seemed no better a fit than the brown pinstriped suit borrowed in haste from Sergeant Kydd.

He wished that he had found sufficient courage to turn Morley down, that some other willing expendable had been cast in the role of TYRO. Instead of waiting on an enemy spy, the night should have been spent in the soft embrace of Sophie Gold. Goodman cursed beneath his breath. Had his letter reached her before she left Bawdsey for London? Or was she waiting at the Dorchester now, sick with worry or - more probably - cursing his eyes?

Damn it. Damn Morley, damn CRACKER. Damn it all.

His bitter reverie was broken by the sound of an engine. He sat bolt upright, imagining for a moment that it belonged to an aircraft. Then a dispatch rider hove into view on the moonlit road, and after a breach exchange with Gilmour by the kiosk coasted downhill towards the Humber.

Goodman left the car and took from the Don R a leather satchel. Unbuckling the straps he was relieved to find that it contained two sets of false documents, as well as an antiquated naval Luger pistol with a long, ungainly barrel.

The rider look on, clearly intrigued. The tension made Goodman ill-tempered.

'Need a signature, do you?'

The rider shook his head.

'Then push off. Round here we shoot messengers.'

He regretted the outburst immediately. However the rider remained mute as he opened his throttle and vanished noisily into the night.

Back in the Humber Goodman examined the papers more closely. His own were made out to Geraint Thomas and had been artfully aged. The second set, for one Paul Horowitz, a French refugee, was incomplete: supposedly CRACKER would arrive with a forged identity card in the same name, replete with photograph.

Still whistling, Gilmour strolled over and glanced impatiently at the luminous dial on his wristwatch. 'Two-fifteen, if you please. We should have heard something by now.'

As if in answer, the telephone rang loud and clear in the cool night air. Gilmour doubled back to the kiosk, and returned a half minute later, lowering his head level with the window of the Humber.

'That was Ashburton. The RDF station at West Prawle picked up a trace two minutes ago. If it's our boy, his ETA is five minutes.'

Goodman nodded, and set about gathering his wits.

TWENTY-SIX

The matt black Heinkel 111 bomber bore no markings and flew low as it crossed the French coast above Cap Frehel, almost invisible against the night sky. As the smell of the dark sea water below shot up through the gap between the bomb-doors Harry Johnson felt his stomach heave. The bomber had been in the air barely ten minutes, yet already he bitterly regretted the extravagant farewell meal he had enjoyed with Doctor Rantzau in Rennes two hours earlier.

The crew of the aircraft scudding low over the Channel towards the south coast of England at two hundred and fifty miles an hour belonged to KG200, the elite Luftwaffe formation which carried out covert operations. Their landfall would take them over Sidmouth, thereby taking advantage of a gap in the British radar chain over Lyme Bay, after which the navigator was confident of locating the drop-zone by dead reckoning alone. Although reserved for special operations, the aircraft had not been adapted for parachute drops, and Johnson would be leaving it through the bomb-doors. This in turn meant completing the journey on his stomach with forty pounds of parachute strapped to his back. Coupled with the stench of rubber from his oxygen mask, and the continual slipping and swerving of the aircraft, his steerage class berth did little to soothe the parlous state of Johnson's stomach.

It was cold, too. Beneath his dark jump overalls Johnson wore a civilian suit, three shirts, and four pairs of woollen underpants and socks. His uncomfortable posture made it hard to maintain adequate circulation, or even to rub his legs together to rid them of cramp. Now his teeth began to chatter. Johnson bit his lip, and had progressed to worrying about frostbite by the time a triumphant war cry from the cockpit crackled in his earphones: 'Wir sind jetzt uber England!'

A split second later the pilot threw the bomber into a steep climb to three thousand feet. As the aircraft rose through the air Johnson felt as if he was travelling in an extremely fast elevator. Then his stomach gave up the unequal struggle, giving him barely enough time to tear off his oxygen mask before the vomit rose in his throat. Some of the spray fell towards the gap between the bomb-doors, and was propelled back into his face by the velocity of the airflow. Oddly, it felt cool and refreshing.

Once the aircraft had returned to level flight the wireless operator appeared at the edge of the bomb bay and patted his hand on his head. Recognizing his cue, Johnson removed his gloves, unfastened his oxygen mask, and donned a padded canvas jump helmet. The airman's next signal was unclear, and seemed to indicate that the Englishman should pick something up, followed by an elaborate and increasingly frantic pantomime of tying a knot.

Suddenly Johnson understood: the static line on his parachute had become detached from the aircraft. He felt his heart skip several beats, and began to sweat profusely despite the biting cold. A few moments more and he would have plunged to his death. With his mind now almost as numb as his fingers Johnson managed to fasten the nylon line to a stout bolt jutting from an ammunition feed. Then he waited, wide eyes fixed on the wireless operator crouched three feet in front of him. The hand of the other man rested on a small lever, awaiting the command from the cockpit. When it came, the bomb doors beneath Johnson would fall open and release him into the night.

Flash Harry Johnson experienced a sudden and urgent nostalgia for his flyblown cell back in Romainville Fort. Without further warning, the airman wrenched back the lever, then waved a gloved hand as the terrified Englishman dropped headlong into empty space.

In the teeth of a howling wind Johnson felt his breath dragged forcibly from him. Then, as the tail of the bomber streaked overhead, he heard a thunderous crack above the roar of the engines, followed by his own hoarse scream. His parachute opened almost instantaneously, threatening to wrench his limbs from their

153

sockets and knocking the breath from his body. Then, as the din of the engines died away in the distance, Johnson found himself floating beneath a brilliant moon and a shimmering galaxy of stars, quite without any sensation of falling, his parachute swaying gently in the dark sky like the pendulum of a vast clock.

In the clear summer night the countryside was spread out below him. Peacefully, quietly, from out of the sky, Harry Johnson was coming home.

Below him the weight of the case housing the wireless transmitter pulled the harness tight across his groin. The sensation was acutely painful, and for a moment Johnson thought about cutting it loose. But the set was his policy of insurance, and the ground was fast approaching. He caught a glimpse of a clump of trees, above which he seemed to be hovering, and plucking a half-remembered instruction from the back of his mind he kicked his legs furiously in an effort to steer away. Now a fortuitous breath of wind caught in the canopy and carried him beyond the copse towards a large slate rooftop. At this Johnson panicked. Sailing over the house towards a patch of open ground, his training deserted him, and flailing wildly he hit the ground hard, his chin and knee connecting with a sickening crack.

Johnson sank backwards, enveloped in a canopy of camouflaged silk and searing pain, dimly aware that he had lost several teeth. Too winded to move, he lay flat on his back for ten minutes or more, staring up at the moon through the dark fabric, listening to its silent laughter, and spitting blood and splinters of tooth.

At least, he consoled himself, he was in England.

Or was he? Suddenly the possibility dawned that the drop had been a dummy run, a trick by Rantzau to test his resolve. Johnson recalled the German's broad grin as he had watched his protegee climb aboard the Heinkel. For all he knew, the bomber had dropped him over France, or even Germany. No glimmer of light disturbed the blacked-out landscape. There was no telling where he was.

In the gloom and the pain and confusion, every waving shadow held menace. Deferring his original plan - to evade his contact, and surrender as quickly as possible - Johnson elected to follow instructions to the letter until he could be certain where he was.

Rising unsteadily to his feet he struggled out of his parachute harness, wincing at a pain in his left wrist as he did so, and wondering if it were fractured. Then he stepped out of his overalls, and changed his boots for the pair of smart leather brogues stowed in his pocket.

The field in which he had landed was pasture and followed a gentle slope. The only visible feature was the house at the top of the meadow. Leaving the heavy wireless case where it had hit the ground, he clumsily parcelled up the parachute canopy and carried the bundle downhill, away from the house. At the bottom of the field he discovered a thick hedge, beneath which he concealed his jump equipment, overalls and boots as best he could.

He had been in the ground for perhaps twenty minutes, but still there was no sign of his contact. Was he in England? Surely even Devon was not such a wilderness...

Somewhere close by the hedgerow rustled. Johnson started, then began back across the meadow to collect the dead weight of the transmitter.

TWENTY-SEVEN

Goodman parked the car two dozen yards from the farmhouse that Gilmour had commandeered earlier in the day, and closed his fingers around the grip of the Luger in his pocket. He left the shuttered headlight on, in the vague hope that the man code-named CRACKER would be drawn towards the feeble beam like a moth to a candle. A second later Goodman started as the door of the farmhouse creaked open and a tall figure emerged into the moonlight.

CRACKER? No. With a profound sense of relief Goodman recognised Sergeant Kydd. At least in this small, dark corner of Devon he was not entirely alone. At the three points of a triangle three miles square there were stationed teams of Field Security Police, whose job was to spot CRACKER if he drifted wide of the drop zone. Ten minutes earlier Kydd had called Gilmour in the telephone box, to report that the agent had landed just outside the northernmost point of the triangle, one hundred yards from the farmhouse. In the inky blackness on country roads it had taken Goodman ten minutes to cover the mile and a half.

'Is he still here?' Goodman asked in a low whisper.

'Been playing silly buggers in the meadow behind since he landed. The rest of the squad have cordoned off the area.'

'Where is he now?'

'Looks like he's after cutting towards the road further down. There's a gate in the hedge about a quarter of a mile ahead. I reckon your best bet is to catch him there.'

Goodman nodded, and turned back towards the car.

'Best go on foot,' Kydd suggested. 'The motor might scare him away.'

Goodman hesitated. But Kydd was right.

156

'Good luck, sir.'

'Thanks.'

'Stand you a pint in the Star next time, sir. My shout.'

'I'll hold you to that, sergeant.'

Goodman set off in the direction of the gate, aware that his footsteps now seemed deafeningly loud on the surface of the road. Glad of the moonlight he glanced constantly back and forth across his shoulder, feeling highly exposed, and foolish too after he was startled by two enormous black and white bulls which noiselessly poked their great heads over the hedgerow to peer at him in meditative fashion. Despite his anxiety Goodman still found himself yawning continuously, and wondered if Morley and Robertson had appreciated that he was likely to have to survive for several days without sleep.

On reaching the gate he leaned over it and strained his eyes, but detected no movement in the field. He wondered whether to whistle, or hail CRACKER by his codename, but abandoned thoughts of either and instead continued along the lane. He had barely covered thirty more yards when he became aware of a second set of footsteps above his own. Someone was ahead of him, walking slowly, with a heavy tread.

The moment had arrived. Goodman stood still and cleared his throat loudly, then said: 'Happy landings'.

The unseen stranger stopped walking, and a dead silence settled over the lane. A cautious voice answered, somewhat awkwardly: 'Who goes there?'

'TYRO.' Goodman took a step forward.

A single gunshot rang out. As the flame bloomed in the darkness ahead a bullet whizzed past Goodman's cheek, so close that he felt the rush of air. He dropped heavily to the ground and rolled towards the hedge at the side of the road, his mind racing. For an instant he was transported back to the ditch into which he had tumbled nine months earlier, after a Belgian rifle bullet had torn a hole in his thigh. Then Goodman shook his head clear and scrambled upright. Although nothing was visible in the gloom ahead the sound of running feet was clearly audible, receding quickly. Instinctively Goodman found his feet and sprinted after CRACKER.

Despite his leg, Goodman still moved faster than his quarry, and a dozen seconds later brought him down with an inelegant but effective flying tackle. The pair sprawled hard across the road, Goodman recoiling off Johnson and grazing his palms. A brief scuffle ensued, during which Goodman managed to pin the other man down and land a right hook on his chin. Then he wrestled the Luger from his pocket and tugged at the slide until the unfamiliar weapon cocked itself.

'You bloody fool!' he spat breathlessly.

The pain in Johnson's mouth was excruciating, and for a moment he offered no reply. On hearing TYRO's challenge he had panicked, in doing so breaking the golden rule to which he had adhered rigidly throughout his career as a professional criminal. Now, having dropped his own gun, and staring down the barrel of another, Johnson began to think rationally. There was no doubting now that he was in England, nor that the Abwehr operative would shrink from shooting him dead if he guessed his true purpose.

Unless, Johnson decided, he could kill TYRO first.

'Well?' snapped Goodman. 'You speak English, I take it.'

'Lost my head, didn't I,' Johnson answered thickly. 'I'm a novice at this spy game.'

Goodman frowned. Robertson and Morley had primed him for any number of opening scenarios, but CRACKER trying to shoot him had not been one of them. Nor had he expected the Abwehr man to be English. Dutch or Belgian perhaps, or a quisling from Norway, but not a cockney. However the more pressing issue was that Kydd's squad must surely have heard the gunshot, and would now come running.

Goodman opened his mouth to appraise CRACKER of this when a series of shouts from the direction of the farmhouse saved his breath. He froze. Should he stay in the road and hand CRACKER in, and in doing so scratch Operation Twenty before it was properly begun? It seemed madness to proceed, all things considered. If he meant to maintain credibility then retrieving the Austin in the midst of a manhunt was out of the question.

Goodman made a snap decision. Hauling CRACKER to his feet, he waved the Luger at the suitcase.

'Pick that up and get over the hedge.'

'It's too heavy.'

'Just do it.'

Johnson did as he was ordered, and launched himself into the thick thorn hedgerow. As they began to run across the field on the far side a voice sounded on the road behind them.

'Come on - the bastard can't have got far.'

The hunt was on.

TWENTY-EIGHT

Hot, bothered and parched after a tortuous six mile march across the Devon countryside, in Honiton TYRO and CRACKER found temporary refuge in an empty church. Goodman had approached the building warily, but Johnson simply abandoned the transmitter suitcase in the middle of the aisle and hastened to the font, from which he proceeded to drink noisily. Goodman looked on with mild distaste, minded of a dog.

'Did you bring the money?'

Johnson raised his face from the water and wiped his mouth on his sleeve. 'In the suitcase.'

'The full £1000?'

'No, £400. What with the invasion coming up Hamburg is running short of currency.'

'I was told you'd bring £1000.'

'And I was told to tell you that in six weeks' time you'll be liberated by the German army.'

Goodman knew full well that CRACKER was lying, just as surely as he had feigned sleep in the wood where they had hidden during the night. He let it pass, however, and retrieved from his briefcase the false papers delivered by the Don R what seemed like an eternity before.

'Did you bring your identity card?'

Johnson rummaged in his pocket. The document was convincingly creased and bore CRACKER's false name, as well as an address at 27 Sussex Gardens W2, and a National Registration number. To Goodman's untrained eye the forgery looked perfect, but for two telling slips: the seven had been crossed in the continental style, and the surname spelled as Horowitcz.

'They've spelt your surname wrong.'

Johnson shrugged. 'Don't reckon there's much we can do about that.'

Goodman supposed not. 'Anyway, seeing how you've cost me my car, you can hand over that £400. We'll need tickets for the London train.'

With great deliberation Johnson retraced his steps along the aisle, then returned with the suitcase and laid it flat on the flagstones. He sprang the locks and lifted the lid to reveal the wireless transmitter, together with sundry booklets and papers, some Ordnance Survey maps, a small camera and a larger cine model, and several bundles of banknotes.

Goodman could scarcely believe his eyes. The paper seals in which the notes were wrapped were marked Deutsche Bank, and overstamped with a military serial number and a swastika.

'Is this somebody's idea of a joke?'

Johnson merely shrugged again, and made to close the suitcase. Goodman stopped him short.

'Strip off those wrappings. I'll need a match.'

At least, Goodman noted, CRACKER's matches were an English brand. He burned the incriminating seals on the stone floor, then ground the sooty ashes with his heel. Despite the show of anger, he found these German blunders perversely reassuring: if his Abwehr spymasters were as guileless as CRACKER himself, Operation Twenty still had an outside chance of success.

Now the other man dabbed hesitantly at his cheek with his fingertips, pulling quickly away as though his skin were burning. 'I need to see a doctor.'

Goodman stalled. 'Not until we reach London. After your performance last night we can't risk anyone local.'

'I could get lockjaw.'

'Here - let me have a look.'

With no little difficulty Johnson forced his mouth half-open. Goodman lowered his head and peered inside, remaining careful not to draw too close in case the other man tried to overpower him. CRACKER had lost two or three teeth, and another was broken and bleeding.

'Well?'

'It doesn't look too clever. But we can't risk you being reported.'

161

'What for? I ain't done nothing yet.'

'No. But you're still a traitor.'

'Not me, mate. I'm in this for the money, pure and simple. The way I look at it, this caper is no different from doing a post office.'

'They'll still hang you.'

'They'll hang you, chum. Me, I can turn King's Evidence.'

Goodman shook his head. 'If that's your plan you should have given yourself up as soon as you landed. For all the Special Branch know, you could have sent a dozen signals back to Germany by now.'

'I don't think so. That box of tricks is for your lot. I'm just a courier. I don't even know how to switch it on.'

'No court will believe you.'

'But a jury will. All I'll need is a good brief.'

'There's no trial by jury for spies. If they don't stretch your neck on an English rope, you'll dangle from a length of piano wire once the Germans have landed and taken control. I guarantee you, our network would see to it.'

Johnson stared hard at Goodman for several long seconds, a dark hatred smouldering behind his eyes, then spat deliberately on the flagstones and walked away down the aisle. Slowly Goodman reached for his gun, fearing that the other man might attempt to leave the church. However, Johnson merely sat down on the end of a pew and set about brushing and straightening his dusty clothes.

Goodman remained by the font for a minute, deep in thought. In the eight hours since CRACKER had landed he had distilled two explanations for the opening shot. The first was that CRACKER had indeed panicked, as he claimed. The second was that Operation Twenty had been betrayed to Morley's opposite numbers in Germany, and that the man with the broken teeth was merely an assassin, albeit of an inept sort. Weighing the alternatives as best he could, Goodman favoured the first, and wondered what conclusions Gilmour and Morley had drawn from the events of the night before. Had they aborted the scheme and thrown a security cordon around the area? Or would the absence of a body - his own body - lead them to assume that Twenty remained viable? For every question, however, there were a dozen answers, and for every answer a dozen further questions.

Goodman yawned deeply. If anything at all was certain, it was that sleep was a luxury he could ill afford. He might talk, or be dispatched with his own gun. Yet already he felt exhausted, and famished too. He thought about bathing his face in the font, but on checking found that CRACKER had streaked the water with blood.

When eventually the pair left the church they stepped into brilliant sunshine and struck out for the station. Although moderately busy, the long, straggling main street of Honiton was devoid of uniforms and roadblocks, and Goodman allowed himself a sigh of relief. Johnson evidently found the changed state of the nation disconcerting, and frowned uncertainly at the blast tape on the window panes, the daubs of yellow anti-gas paint on the pillarboxes, and the patient queue of women outside the butcher. Twice he ducked into shops without warning, first a newsagent, where he purchased a copy of the Daily Express, much slimmer now than when reporting his own exploits three years earlier, and afterwards a tobacconist, where he tried and failed to purchase a pack of Senior Service cigarettes. On both occasions Goodman feared his charge would try to slip the leash, or compromise either or both of them, but instead CRACKER merely made his purchases with few words, and ill-temper.

As they rounded the final corner and approached the station Goodman felt his heart sink like a falling elevator. Parked outside the entrance to the ticket hall was the khaki Humber Snipe in which he had spent the previous evening. Beside it, a Field Security corporal he did not recognise was checking the papers of a short man in a bowler hat. As they drew closer the FS corporal scrutinized the strangers closely, his eyes hidden beneath the slashed peak of his green service cap. Then, with two dozen yards to go, Gilmour emerged from the ticket hall. Goodman glanced briefly at Johnson, but met no reaction.

At the entrance the corporal raised his hand to bar their way. 'Papers please,' he demanded, his accent darkest Black Country.

'Of course.' Goodman's voice emerged as a croak, his throat suddenly bone dry. Tucking his briefcase under his arm he reached into his pocket for his wallet and found instead the bundle of banknotes. Digging deeper, he found his wallet and handed it over.

As the corporal ran his eyes over the fictional particulars of Geraint Thomas, Gilmour stepped closer and peered over his shoulder.

'A London man I see, Mr Thomas' he began, fixing Goodman keenly. 'Doing what, so far from home?'

'I'm a salesman,' Goodman replied.

'And your friend?'

'A salesmen as well.'

'Really?' Gilmour arched an eyebrow, like some repertory ham. 'Pray, what do you sell?'

'Second-hand books.'

Gilmour nodded, and glanced down at Johnson's suitcase. 'So the case is full of literature?'

Goodman tensed. If CRACKER was going to lose his nerve, it might as well be now. He said to Gilmour: 'That's right. I suppose you'll want to take a look?'

Gilmour shook his head. 'I don't think so, Mr Thomas. I never was a great reader.' He paused. 'Unless you've any Michael Arlen. The Green Hat, for instance.'

The pun would have been feeble enough at the best of times, but in the present circumstances it was simply foolhardy.

'I had a copy in last week,' Goodman replied tersely. 'But it went yesterday.'

Gilmour opened his mouth to say something more, but thought better of it. The corporal returned Goodman's papers, and afforded Johnson's identity card only a cursory glance before passing it on to Gilmour.

'I see that you are French, Monsieur Horowitz.'

Johnson nodded stiffly.

'Et vous et un marchand des livres, comme Monsieur Thomas?'

First Arlen, now this. In his mind's eye, Goodman drew the Luger and shot Gilmour dead on the spot. It was over, finished. He waited for CRACKER to raise his hands, or run. But instead the reluctant agent surprised him.

'Maintenant, chef. Mais avant la guerre je suis serrurier.'

Goodman suppressed a frown and stared at his shoes. Even the accent was good. Too good, in fact, for Gilmour, who turned smartly on his heel, leaving the corporal to wave the two book salesmen through.

According to CRACKER's yellowing copy of Bradshaw's Railway Timetable, dated 1933, the London train was due to depart in ten minutes' time. Now, in wartime, the two men found themselves with more than an hour to kill. After Goodman had purchased two second class singles from the ticket window they repaired to the station buffet. The room was small and smoky and short of chairs, but with a phone cabin, for the moment occupied by a loquacious woman in the uniform of the WVS, arguing passionately with some faraway opponent. Goodman directed Johnson to a bench on the far side of the room, then queued at the counter. For his pains he was rewarded with a single cup of tea. A shortage of cups, the woman explained, rendered a second impossible. A prohibition no less absolute applied to the half-dozen stale-looking potted meat sandwiches on display beneath a dusty glass dome. These, she informed him with evident disapproval, were reserved for servicemen alone.

'Is this what it's like all the time?' Johnson asked when Goodman returned with the tea, nodding in the direction of the ticket hall. 'Martial law?'

'Not quite.'

'Were they Redcaps?'

'Field Security Police', Goodman replied, lowering his voice. Although instinct urged him to give nothing away, Morley had warned against appearing entirely ignorant.

'I was in the army once myself,' Johnson offered without prompting. 'You reckon they were after us?'

'Possibly.'

'Surprising they didn't pull us in,' Johnson continued, though without overt suspicion.

'No more than your colleagues leaving those wraps on the banknotes.'

'What about the queues at the shops. Food on ration?'

'Some of it. Meat and dairy produce. Petrol too.'

'So the blockade's working, then. They say the U-boats have sealed off the Atlantic.'

'Nobody's starving,' Goodman replied shortly, adding by way of a hurried afterthought: 'More's the pity.'

Johnson shrugged and blew on his tea, then lapsed into silence. A moment later the WVS women slammed down the receiver on the telephone and stormed from the room. Quickly Goodman rose to his feet, anxious to reach the cabin before anybody else.

'I need to call someone,' he told Johnson.

'Who?'

'GW.'

'Is he a doctor?'

'No. But I can call him too.'

'You do that.'

The number Goodman requested was a direct line to Morley at Blenheim. His voice, when finally it came on the line, sounded infinitely distant.

'Hello?'

'This is TYRO.'

'Hello TYRO. Gilmour just called, I know where you are. What the hell is going on?'

'CRACKER tried to pot me last night.'

'So I heard. Are you injured?'

'No.'

'In danger?' Morley sounded almost hopeful.

'Not as long as I stay awake. Right now sleep's the main enemy.'

'Is he armed?'

'No, he lost his gun last night. Anyroad, he smashed some teeth on landing and needs a doctor, or a dentist. Is there anyone in London?'

Morley paused. 'I can send someone over to the safe-house. Probably one of the girls in the Registry used to be a nurse.'

'I've already told CRACKER it's a he.'

'Well, never mind. I'll sort something.'

'Make it around eight this evening. We should be back in town by then, unless the train runs very late.'

'It probably will. Did he bring the transmitter?'

'Yes.'

'And the money?'

'Some of it. £400. He's English by the way, a Londoner. Says he was in the army before.'

'Fascist? BUF?'

'Crook, I should say. Fluent French too, but he's no great conversationalist.'

'Probably left behind at Dunkirk. Is he suspicious?'

'Not yet, no thanks to Gilmour.'

'Good. If he's English we're in with a sporting chance of

fingering his identity.'

'Could you post someone at Paddington for when we get in? He might try to lose me in the crowd. Should be around four.'

'We'll be there. Now, you'd best ring off. Fill me in later, from Cheniston Crescent. You remember the drill, I take it?'

'How could I forget?'

'Right-oh.'

As Goodman replaced the receiver, he glanced through the window and saw Gilmour and the Field Security corporal climb into the Humber and drive away. Once more he felt very alone.

TWENTY-NINE

Twenty-two Cheniston Crescent stood at the centre of an unkempt Georgian terrace behind Kensington High Street. Standing five stories high, it had been partitioned into separate apartments two decades before, and the whole rented by MI5 for the duration from an officer posted overseas. At first glance the dowdy flat on the top floor was unremarkable, yet Number 22 was no ordinary apartment. In each of the four rooms was concealed a microphone which, while unsophisticated, was capable of picking up normal conversation. There was a still camera also, positioned in the lavatory where the sound of the cistern flush masked the noise of the shutter. The camera and microphones were connected to the floor below, in which were quartered an armed guard and a female telephonist-stenographer. Whenever the top-floor apartment was occupied it was her job to record in shorthand every syllable uttered within it. Where a more rapid or literal transcription was required a short sound recording could be made on a system of clumsy wax drums, although this apparatus had stood idle since its problematic installation by the BBC.

Goodman and Johnson's journey to the flat was both lengthy and fraught. For seven hours between Honiton and Paddington they were obliged to stand in the corridor of a packed train, each mile adding further to Johnson's discomfort. As his cheek swelled so his mood deteriorated in inverse proportion, and on the platform in London he had demanded immediate medical attention. Goodman kept hold of CRACKER only due to the dense press of bodies around them, and had to wait until they reached the safe-house for the situation improve. During the afternoon a prescient attendant had imported a bottle of brandy, which Johnson set about consuming with zeal. The spirit performed as a potent anaesthetic, and within thirty minutes the reluctant spy was comfortably numb.

While Johnson got cosy with the bottle Goodman wolfed down a loaf of stale bread, having eaten nothing in the past twenty-four hours save a bar of German chocolate and half a tin of sardines. Then, after checking that CRACKER was still oblivious, he set about a careful examination of the contents of the suitcase. As well as the cameras, transmitter and maps he found a novel assortment of espionage paraphernalia. The two circular cardboard discs fastened together with a brass split-pin he took to be a coding device. There were also sheets of graph paper bearing a number of place names, including Dumpton, Christchurch and Hastings, as well as five batteries of various sizes, two spare valves wrapped in corrugated paper, a voltmeter, headphones, and a morse tapping key. CRACKER had probably been telling the truth when he claimed to be unable to use the equipment. Nonetheless, Goodman disabled it just as Morley had said, tugging two exposed wires free of their connections.

Goodman then retired to the lavatory. Inside he held up the coding wheel, the graph paper and a printed questionnaire before the hidden camera lens, and was rewarded by a series of clicks. He followed this with a detailed and highly self-conscious situation report to Morley via the hidden microphone, and finally emptied a slow tumbler of water into the lavatory for added verisimilitude, in case CRACKER was eavesdropping.

At ten minutes past nine a knock sounded on the main stair door. The doctor, Goodman assumed. Hastily repacking the suitcase, he walked through to the hallway and opened the door. On the landing, however, he found himself face to face not with a medical man but with Morley, dressed in a dapper pinstripe suit and a black homburg.

'What the hell are you doing here?' he demanded, whispering harshly.

Morley raised aloft a small patent leather valise. 'For the next half hour you know me only as a Belgian veterinary surgeon, who treats humankind for hard cash.'

'Not a good idea. He speaks perfect French.'

'Ah. Well, show me the patient. And for God's sake keep a straight face.'

Goodman lead Morley through to the sitting room. Johnson was sprawled in an armchair, unconscious still, the empty brandy bottle cradled in his lap.

'This him?' Morley asked superfluously.

'Brandy on an empty stomach.'

'And his teeth are broken?'

'That's right. Two or three.' Goodman leaned forward and shook Johnson's shoulders until his eyes drifted open. 'Paul - the doctor's here.'

As the words sank in through the comfortable brandy haze Johnson sobered quickly, and initially shied away as Morley bent over him and reached toward his chin. 'Anaesthetic,' he hissed sharply, his jaw clenched tight. 'You ain't laying a finger on me without anaesthetic.'

'You've been drinking,' Morley offered solicitously. 'Volatile cocktail, alcohol and painkillers. You might go up like a firework.'

Johnson muttered an obscenity, then struck the arm of the chair with his fist and jutted forward his chin. Carefully Morley took hold of his swollen jaw, prized it open, and examined the interior of his mouth. Where the three teeth had been knocked out clean Johnson's gums were no longer bleeding. But the broken tooth remained bloody, and the gum inflamed.

Morley gently moved Johnson's jaw from side to side, then raised his head and clicked his tongue. 'Possible fracture too, it's difficult to tell. The molar's split down to the nerve. I'll have to pull it.'

'Are you sure?' Although Goodman had experienced a guilty pleasure at CRACKER's discomfort, amateur root canal surgery struck him as beyond the pale.

'You called me here,' Morley sniffed. 'If you don't want me to treat the patient, I'll gladly leave.'

Goodman glanced at Johnson. Johnson shook his head.

'Very well. Just don't expect me to watch.'

Morley shook his head. 'You'll have to lend a hand. Without a sedative his reaction... may lack a certain restraint.'

The following four minutes were easily the most sickening Goodman had experienced in his thirty-two years. Setting down his valise on the table, Morley withdrew a stainless-steel instrument which resembled a pair of pliers. Unable to look

Johnson in the eye, Goodman's stare settled instead on his knuckles, which glowed white as they gripped the chair. Still in character, Morley instructed Goodman to move behind Johnson and take a firm grip on his head. Cowed low in his seat, Johnson began to tremble like a leaf, his eyes darting wildly around the room, as though seeking an escape route, then shutting tight as Morley turned around, holding the pliers before him like a prayer book.

The sensation of cold metal inside his mouth caused Johnson to start bucking in the chair, and release a keening sound from the back of his throat. The whimper turned to an animal scream as Morley obtained a purchase on the broken molar and applied the pressure. Johnson writhed like a rabbit in a snare, so hard that Goodman feared he might tear off his ears. Mercifully, as the tooth worked free, Johnson passed out.

Goodman looked at Morley. Very pale now, the amateur dentist wiped the sweat from his brow with a handkerchief, then produced a syringe from his valise and filled it carefully from a small glass phial.

'Penicillin,' he explained. 'The new wonder drug, so they say. Roll back his sleeve, will you?'

The sight of the thick steel needle as it punctured Johnson's skin proved too much for Goodman. He began to flush hot and cold, and as his stomach began to heave he raced through the flat to the lavatory, upsetting a chair as he went.

Kneeling over the porcelain bowl, retching heavily, he was not amused to hear the shutter of the hidden camera click open and closed.

When he returned to the sitting room he found Morley by the window, examining the brandy bottle with conspicuous care. Although CRACKER was still unconscious, Goodman elected to continue his conversation with Morley in character.

'How much do I owe you, doctor?'

'£10 for my time, and £15 for the penicillin.'

Goodman reached into his pocket and separated three notes from the bundle that CRACKER had surrendered in Honiton. Morley dropped the money into his valise, then took up the empty brandy bottle once more and made to leave, stepping into the hallway. They paused at the front door.

'Why the bottle?' Goodman asked.

'Fingerprints. We might get lucky.' Morley handed Goodman a small cardboard pillbox. 'To keep you awake.'

'What are they?'

'Benzedrine. You'll have to grab some sleep at some point, mind. Push the table across the bedroom door if you feel there's any danger.'

Goodman pocketed the pills. 'What if he tries to make a break for it?'

'He won't get beyond the front door. Chap on the floor below will see to that.'

'I think you enjoyed that bit of amateur butchery.'

'Not particularly. But I spent two laborious hours this afternoon being lectured on the basics of dentistry. Unlike my patient, I came half prepared.'

'Do you think he's the genuine article?'

Morley rubbed his chin. 'Difficult to say. Could even be that he's on our side.'

'Sorry?' Goodman frowned.

'You said yourself he was a squaddie once upon a time. If he was captured in France, this might be his bid for freedom. In which case, he may well think that by bagging you he'll be performing King and country a sterling service.'

Goodman weighed the evidence. If true, Morley's hypothesis explained much: his nationality, the shooting, the basic mastery of French. Honourable as it might make CRACKER, however, it was the worst of all possible worlds for Goodman.

'If your guess is correct he may try to kill me again. And he's hardly likely to want to return to Germany.'

'True,' Morley conceded. 'But we can't risk telling him the truth.'

'You'll just have to stay on your guard. Now, I've rigged the flame-barrage trial for three-fifteen tomorrow afternoon at Shoeburyness. Leave your car behind the Black Buoy public house in Great Wakering and walk across the marshes. We've prepared a rough map of-'

'I don't have a car,' Goodman interrupted.

'Taken care of. There's a black Ford Eight parked in Warwick Gardens, registration plate EW2 671. You'll find the key in the ignition. The police have been warned not to move it.'

'Distributor arm?'

'Still in place, and the tank's full too. Got your coupons?'

Goodman nodded.

'Splendid.' Now Morley opened his valise and produced a sheaf of papers. 'You'll need this permit to enter the coastal defence area. Make sure you don't get to the barrage site before two o'clock. I've marked the best vantage point on the map. Any closer and CRACKER might tumble what we're up to.'

'Will we be tailed?'

Morley shook his head. 'Can't risk it. Look, if he cuts up rough you'll just have to shoot him.'

'Like that bloody big dog,' Goodman replied drily.

'Very droll.' Morley twisted the handle on the door. 'Well, must dash. Got to let the Hun know things are running smoothly.'

'One thing, sir.'

Goodman withdrew an envelope from his jacket pocket. He had written the letter two days before, but since then there had been no chance to even obtain a stamp, much less post it.

Morley took the envelope, arching an eyebrow as he scanned the address: Sophie Gold, Bawdsey Air Ministry Experimental Station, Suffolk.

'I really shouldn't, you know. Sloppy fieldcraft.'

'Very probably. But you will.'

THIRTY

As usual the Rififi Club was filled with noise, smoke and off-duty German servicemen. On the cramped stage at the far end of the heaving cellar Het Ramblers were blowing up a storm, underpinned by a flamboyant drummer who kept the irresistible rhythm to which Klara was dancing energetically with a girlfriend. Tonight, as usual, she was chaperoned closely by her peacock brother, Willem, and once more he had seized the opportunity to interrogate the American correspondent.

'Tell me something,' Willem began, leisurely exhaling a perfect smoke ring. 'We get American papers here. A month late, admittedly, but I never see your name on the reports from Belgium or Holland.'

'Nothing strange in that to me.'

'Why so?'

'I'm freelance,' replied Wagner. It was not the first time Willem had grilled him, and for this reason he had rehearsed his answers well. 'Like I told you already, I sell to agencies. And mostly the agencies sub-edit me to hell and stick their own name over the report. Oftentimes they label me "our correspondent" or "staff reporter", or "a reliable source". Plus I use different names. That way I can sell the same story ten times over.'

'Such integrity.'

'Integrity never put bread on the table. You got any idea how much a freelancer earns? Talk about peanuts - I live on shells.'

Willem nodded at Wagner's bourbon, his third in an hour. 'You don't seem to do so badly.'

'I get by, that's all.'

'So why stay in Europe?'

Wagner was tempted to tell his inquisitor: because I want your

174

sister. Instead he gave a nonchalant shrug. 'Maybe there's a book in all this.'

Willem snorted. 'Some book that will make. The inside track on every bar and hotel lounge between Ostend and Amsterdam.'

'Got anything better? I mean to say, hanging out in jazz dives with a rolled umbrella for company ain't exactly thrill-a-minute.'

'Yeah. Try this: the Nazis plan to land in Scotland.'

Wagner frowned. 'Oh really?'

'The city is swarming with Austrians and Bavarians. Mountain troops, you can tell them by their soft peaked caps. There are no mountains in the British Isles except in Scotland. Even a fool can work it out'

Only a fool, Wagner thought, but held back. 'Last time I had the pleasure of your company, you were sure there wouldn't be any invasion.'

'And there won't be.'

'I think the evidence is against you.'

'On the contrary. You know where the trouble started in Germany in 1918?'

Wagner wondered where this was leading. 'With the navy, as I recall.'

'Exactly. And it'll begin there now. They can't man all the barges without help from civilian rivermen and tugboat crews. Naturally, information leaks out.'

'Such as?'

Willem leaned forward conspiratorially. 'Triple barges, for instance. They lash three together at the bow and stern, then lay a concrete deck over the whole. Voila - a floating coffin. Last week two of them collided and sank off the coast, both fully loaded with troops. The sea was white with dead.'

Was it true? Wagner doubted so. The rumour mill had been running at full capacity since Dunkirk, producing a dozen new fictions each day. Now their conversation left him feeling uneasy, not least because Willem was obliged to raise his voice above the music, and walls had ears.

'Another thing,' Willem continued. 'The captain of a tugboat towed a barge full of Nazis far out into the North Sea, then cut the hawser and ran for England. I tell you, the day the Bosche invasion fleet sails they'll run straight back to Kiel.'

As the band finished Honeysuckle Rose the cellar erupted into fevered applause. With his sharp cream suit, union jack lapel pin and folded copy of the London Times, now six weeks old, Wagner had no time for Willem. His kind had been the first to run for the cellar when the tanks had crossed the border in May. And he professed to liking Cole Porter.

'Well?' Willem challenged.

'It's an interesting theory,' Wagner said blandly, raising his glass and tipping it towards Willem. 'Another three of these and I might even swallow it.'

Scowling, Willem leaned across the table once more. 'There is resistance, you know. Even here in Antwerp.'

Wagner raised his hand defensively. 'Is this the one about the shop-girl and the German officer? He asks to buy a bathing suit, she asks him if he's going swimming in the Channel? That one I heard already.'

Willem shook his head. 'Jazz is resistance.'

'Like hell it is. Half the German army digs jazz and swing. They press discs in Germany for export to countries like yours, and rake in a tidy little profit for their thousand year Reich.'

'Sabotage, then. Would that make the front page back home?'

'I guess it might.'

'And would they print your name above it?'

'They might. If I let them.'

'What do you mean?'

'I got no intention of being deported just yet. Or strapped to a chair by the Gestapo.'

'You could use a false name,' Willem pressed, 'disguise the location. Then you can sell your exclusive, and prove who you claim you are.'

Wagner raised his hand. 'Stop right there, little man. I don't need to prove a damn thing to you.'

'Maybe you do. See, I can make sure you never set eyes on Klara again. She's seventeen years old. All I have to do is tell our father that she's been keeping bad company - again - and she's grounded.'

'I'm bad company? In the middle of a German occupation?'

Willem nodded. 'Especially you. Even Klara thinks you're a spy. She thinks you work for London, but I put you nearer Berlin.'

Inside his head an alarm bell clamoured. Wagner knew that he should rise and walk through the door, there and then. God knows, he had already made up his mind to do just that, as near as dammit. Since he had first met Klara a month before they had met at the club on three occasions - never elsewhere, and never far from Willem's watchful gaze. True, she had kissed him last Thursday, and had allowed him to respond in kind. But there was no future, he knew, in his designs on Klara: no walks in the park, no weekends at the beach, probably not even a fling in a discrete hotel.

As he pondered this impasse the band slowed the tempo, and Klara returned to the booth.

'What's with you two?' she asked, still breathless. 'Did somebody die?'

'Paul wants a story. An act of resistance to stir up the fence-sitters back home.'

'That's bullshit,' Wagner countered sharply. Willem was steering him into a corner he was keen to avoid.

Now Klara sat down beside Wagner and took his hand. 'Then let's not disappoint him,' she said, fixing her brother defiantly.

'Maybe some other time,' Wagner evaded. 'We're not far off curfew.'

Klara turned to Wagner. 'There's no danger, Paul. We've done the same thing a dozen times already.'

'You mean you're in on this too?'

'Of course. I hate the Nazis. It's the least I can do.'

Wagner glanced sideways at Willem, who now cracked a self-satisfied smile and mouthed silently: 'Bad company.'

Had Klara not been holding his hand still, Wagner might have punched her brother into the following week. He should walk, he knew. Yet Willem was seeking to prove his point by gambling with his sister's freedom. And the worst of it was that the little piss carnation was right. That, and absurd desire to demonstrate to Klara that he was not what he was, and three bourbons, saw Wagner surrender to a shallow madness.

'So what is your thing, exactly?'

'Come and see for yourself.'

'Just so long as you don't plan on leaving any corpses behind. Ours included.'

Willem nodded, stubbed his cigarette, and rose to leave. Klara squeezed Wagner's hand and pecked his cheek. Wagner sensed already that he would pay dearly for the kiss.

Outside Willem paused on the pavement and glanced up and down the deserted street, then lead Klara and Wagner into the mouth of a narrow alleyway. The passage ran towards the rear of the club, the tall blank walls on either side forming a dark brick canyon. The three walked the length of it in silence, their footfalls loud on the cobbles in the cool night air. Wagner felt at once confined and exposed, and for a moment wondered if Willem had organised some sort of physical reception. He quickly discarded the idea, however. With Klara in tow, and on his arm, a beating was hardly on the cards.

At the end of the alley they entered a scruffy courtyard choked with moonlit shadows. After checking they were alone, Willem ducked over to an untidy clutter of refuse bins and beer crates stacked beside a flight of steps. Lifting the lid on the nearest bin he reached inside and retrieved two objects, which, on his return, Wagner recognised as tins of paint. Handing these to Klara, Willem reached inside his jacket and produced two brushes.

'You wait here,' he told Wagner. 'If you see anyone, whistle.'

Klara winked at Wagner, then followed her brother across the courtyard. They stopped in front of the furthest wall, on which a row of proclamations had been posted. The sheets, already commonplace across the occupied territories, were printed in German and Dutch and detailed matters such as curfew orders and air raid precautions, as well as lists of deportees and their transgressions.

A sudden burst of noise from inside the club caused the three of them to start, as Het Ramblers kicked into Tiger Rag. Then the pair set to work, each painting a dark border down the side of each notice, leaving a white stripe in the centre.

'Red, white and blue!' Willem whispered loudly. 'Long live Churchill and De Gaulle!'

Wagner allowed himself an ironic smile. Graffiti, rather than arson or assassination, was the act of selfless heroism he was supposed to immortalise from Seattle to Miami. Freedom fighters defacing outdated posters in a grubby private courtyard with the colours of foreign nations. Little wonder that Belgium had collapsed in a week.

Wagner might have slipped away there and then had a noise in the alley not wrested his attention. Cautiously he peered around the corner and squinted into the gloom. A figure was visible, treading softly towards them and hugging the wall. Wagner felt a twinge of fear. The stranger did not move like a civilian, or a drunk, but in the same manner as Wagner had been trained. Field police? Gestapo? Abwehr even? Cursing his stupidity, Wagner thought quickly. If they had been followed then the tail had probably been inside the club, and knew their faces already. Nothing more would be required to secure a summary conviction, even with his rank and decoration. For Willem and Klara, arrest would mean a ticket to some godforsaken camp in the east. Being Jews, it would be worse for them. Many, many times worse.

Wagner pursed his lips to whistle, but already the stranger was halfway to the mouth of the courtyard. Instead Wagner turned and doubled over to the stack of beer crates, where he selected a heavy bottle made of thick brown glass. Still engrossed in their work, Willem and Klara saw nothing. Silently retracing his steps, Wagner weighed the bottle in his hand, breathed deep, and turned into the alleyway.

Mere metres separated him from his unknown adversary. Wagner covered the distance in half a dozen rapid strides and brought the bottle down across the stranger's crown as he turned to flee. The bottle knocked the man sideways, and as he sank to his knees he began to yell blue murder. Grabbing hold of his collar Wagner dragged him upright, and drove his fist into his jaw. His head bounced hard off the wall and struck the cobbles as he fell backwards, one or other of the blows knocking him cold.

Wagner knew he should silence the man permanently. Indeed he might have done so, had not Willem and Klara appeared at his side and stood gaping at the prone figure. Willem, he noticed, had dropped his paint, which now covered the front of his suit. In the moonlight it looked like a spray of fresh blood.

For a long moment Wagner flashed on a saxophone hitting the cold waters of the East River. *Deja vu*. Once more it was time to cut and run.

179

THIRTY-ONE

Goodman swallowed the benzedrine half an hour before they left the safehouse at Cheniston Crescent. Thanks to CRACKER's agonies he had barely slept at all, but thanks to the tablet he now felt wired and alert, almost euphoric. Indeed as the two men shaped course for Warwick Gardens, intending to feign the theft of the car left by Morley the previous evening, his mind had raced ahead of his body, leaving CRACKER dawdling a half dozen paces behind both. Time enough, while Goodman strode briskly ahead, to rehearse a simple criminal skill and break into a Vauxhall Ten parked less than two hundred yards from the front door of the flat.

The first Goodman knew of it was Johnson's low whistle. Turning around, his heart sank. By rights the engine should have been disabled, or the tyres deflated by a vigilant policeman. But CRACKER was already behind the wheel, and as Goodman doubled back the engine shuddered into life, backfiring twice and shooting a cloud of blue smoke from the exhaust.

'What the hell are you doing?' Goodman hissed.

'Borrowing some wheels.'

'We're too close to the flat.'

'Bit late now, chum. All aboard.'

Goodman hesitated, but there was no way to make good the reverse without arousing CRACKER's suspicions. Quickly he doubled round to the passenger door, praying that they had not been seen, at least by anyone other than the MI5 personnel in the flat below, who might therefore alert Morley to the latest blunder.

As they drove away Johnson touched his hand to his jaw. 'That bastard last night nearly killed me.'

'What did you expect - Harley Street?'

'I didn't expect a maniac with a pair of plumber's pliers.'

'Actually he's a vet,' Goodman replied evenly, with a hint of satisfaction. 'He has to go where the work is, now that they've put half the dogs in London to sleep.'

Johnson shot him a dark look. They had passed St Paul's Cathedral before he spoke again. 'So where are we off to - Foulness?'

Goodman nodded. Despite the fact that the flame installation at Foulness was listed in CRACKER's Abwehr questionnaire, it still felt as though he were betraying a secret.

'I've got an old aunt in Southend. We could drop in for tea.'

'I don't think so.'

'Flame barrage thingy, is it?'

'That's right. So far as we can tell the whole of the south coast is ringed with them, from King's Lynn to Land's End.'

'Can't see it myself. Oil and water and all that.'

'You and me both,' Goodman lied. 'But we're hardly short of oil.'

Johnson considered this for a moment. 'So how come your firm know so much about it?'

'Contacts. There's plenty of Welsh patriots in uniform.'

'But how d'you know they'll fire up today?'

Goodman racked his brains for a credible answer, but was saved further effort as Johnson braked to a standstill outside Bank underground station. Two cars ahead the junction was blocked by a military police sergeant seated on a motorcycle. Behind him a convoy of heavy Bedford trucks rumbled slowly past, towing a battery of large 18/25 pounder field guns. The guns were of Great War vintage, lately fitted with new barrels at the Woolwich Arsenal, and pneumatic tyres in place of the old wooden wheels. Not, Goodman supposed, the kind of last ditch weaponry a German spy should see up close.

As Johnson lit his third cigarette of the journey and drummed his fingers impatiently on the wheel, Goodman idly surveyed the sandbagged facade of the Royal Exchange, and Chantrey's equestrian statue of the Duke of Wellington. When he glanced towards the junction once more, he noticed with no little alarm that the Redcap sergeant was staring intently in the direction of their car. Goodman's pulse quickened further as the sergeant climbed from the seat of his motorcycle and started towards them. What was it he could possibly know? Surely not that the car was stolen, or chock full of cameras and entry permits for the coastal defence zone.

The sergeant walked around the bonnet to the driver's window. 'Well, well - if it isn't Flash Harry Johnson. Last I heard you were banged up in France. What happened - Adolf grant you a pardon?'

Johnson turned to Goodman, his expression dead calm. Inside Goodman's mind, facts began to fall into place like lemons on a fruit machine. Gelignite, safes, the disappearance without trace, and a half dozen other details dimly remembered from tabloids two years before. Goodman knew perfectly well who Harry Johnson was. So too did the sergeant, and now Twenty was scuppered.

But Robertson had been adamant: maintain the pretence, come what may.

'Que est-ce qui ce passe?' Johnson asked.

'Il est un gendarme militaire,' Goodman managed, still struggling to conceal his astonishment. He turned to the sergeant. 'This gentleman is a French refugee. He is assisting me. I'm a commercial traveller, I deal in secondhand books.'

'And I wasn't born yesterday,' the sergeant countered. 'He's as French as my old mother. I was a constable at Bow Street when you were last hauled in, Harry. Turn off the engine.'

Johnson did as he was told. Still icy calm, he stubbed his cigarette out on the side of the car and dropped the butt at the sergeant's feet.

'I'm sorry, but you're mistaken,' Goodman persisted. 'You can check our papers.' He turned to Johnson. 'Votre papiers, Paul.'

As Johnson dug inside his jacket Goodman handed his own documents to the Redcap. The sergeant scrutinized them minutely.

'Geraint Thomas? You don't sound much like a Taff to me.'

'I'm a legitimate businessmen.' For a half-second Goodman was distracted by a vision of Wellington descending from his plinth on his charger, to lop off the sergeant's head with his sabre.

'Sure you are. Now you, Harry.'

Johnson surrendered his identity card, which the sergeant afforded only a cursory glance. 'Not bad. But I'd ask for your money back, what with that bar through the seven.'

'Que est-ce qui ce passe?' Johnson repeated.

'Stop lifting my leg,' the sergeant snapped curtly, serious now. 'Legitimate business? These papers are snide as sixpence.'

For a moment Goodman considered the merits of drawing his Luger. However, deliverance then came in the form of a loud metallic crash on the junction ahead. Turning into Threadneedle Street, the final gun in the convoy had sprung free of its towing hook, and yawed across the road to collide with the sergeant's motorcycle. Now the machine lay on the ground, its front wheel buckled and spinning, the runaway field gun scraping to a standstill with its business end trained on the Bank of England. Seemingly unaware of the mishap, the Bedford continued its stately progress towards Bishopsgate.

For several long moments the sergeant glanced back and forth between the retreating truck and the suspects in the car, torn like Buridan's ass between bales of hay. Finally he swore violently and started after the Bedford.

'You two stay there,' he yelled across his shoulder, hurdling the damaged motorcycle as he went.

Harry Johnson needed no second bidding. As the sergeant pounded away in the opposite direction he twisted the key in the ignition, ground the gears into reverse, and lurched hastily away.

THIRTY-TWO

Each of the ten Scammel bowser trucks parked out of sight behind the dyke was capable of delivering twelve tons of fuel an hour. Manned by chemical warfare troops on attachment from the Royal Engineers, the tanks were filled with a blend of fuel oil, diesel and petrol. This volatile mixture was to be pumped over the dyke and discharged into the sea by means of reinforced hoses, which were in turn rigged to anchors fixed below the high water mark.

At three-fifteen precisely the chief technical officer, Colonel Norton, poked his head above the sea wall, mindful of his strict instructions to remain out of sight. But for the light south easterly breeze, Norton was pleased to observe that the weather and tidal conditions were perfect. Turning back, he ordered the crews to open the valves, then watched and waited until a line of ten dark patches of oil formed thirty yards out and spread across the surface. The pools of oil were much calmer than the surrounding water, and expanded rapidly outward to form a continuous slick, fifty yards long and ten wide.

Satisfied, Norton cocked his Very pistol, aimed, and discharged a signal flare. It was a procedure which he had lately practised at some length, and he watched with satisfaction as the incandescent ball hissed across the water before settling dead centre in the slick, where it continued to burn fiercely.

But the oil stubbornly refused to ignite.

Although Norton had not been briefed on the reason for the secretive Foulness trial, he felt his blood run cold. In less than a week the Petroleum Warfare Department was due to stage an almost identical display on the shores of the Solent. Amongst the galaxy of spectators expected were three generals - Brooke, Alexander and Montgomery - as well as Professor Lindemann and

Lord Hankey. The last two in particular had the ear of the Prime Minister, who, it was whispered, had personally opposed the formation of the Department. Against this background a repeat performance of the unrehearsed fiasco at Dumpton Gap had to be avoided at all costs.

As Norton watched the flare fizz ineffectually on the surface of the oil a second figure clambered up the bank to join him. Topham, a chemist, was on loan from Shell-Mex and boasted a double first in pessimism. Following Norton's crestfallen stare, he shook his head slowly.

'Told you so. We should have used sodium pellets, or tracer.'

Norton grunted, acutely conscious that time was ticking away. If the oil spread too thinly it would never ignite.

Topham too recognised the danger. 'Shall I tell them to close the valves?'

'No,' replied Norton. 'I'll fetch Allbright and Wilson.'

Topham frowned. 'Who?'

Without answering, Norton slid down the bank and doubled back to his car. From the boot he removed a Lee Enfield rifle, and a small wooden crate.

When he returned Topham moved quickly aside. The crate was lined with straw and contained two stubby half-pint bottles. Alias the self-igniting phosphorus grenade, the A/W was a crude and notoriously unstable device charged with a fearsome blend of benzine, water and white phosphorus, with a measure of dissolved rubber to ensure that the mixture adhered to its target. Unlike those issued to the Home Guard, and following the salutary lesson of Dumpton, Norton had customised his own stock of bombs, which were wrapped in a jacket of buoyant foam rubber.

Standing unsteadily on the slope of the dyke, the colonel balanced the first of the grenades in his palm, judging its weight against the distance. Then he bit his lip and bowled it overarm across the brow of the dyke towards the still-expanding oil slick.

The bomb fell short. Quickly he took up the second and bowled again. It landed a yard inside the oil, dead centre in the slick. Swiftly Norton raised the Lee Enfield, aimed carefully, and squeezed off a round at the floating bottle. The bullet spattered into the oil several inches to the right.

Four shots later a violent yellow flame erupted.

A dozen seconds afterwards, as the first wisps of black smoke rose up from the sea, Harry Johnson flicked the lever on his cine camera and rolled the film. As if in response, the thin plume rapidly became a choking black cloud as the entire barrage ignited, and soon fearsome tongues of fire were shooting dozens of feet in the air from the boiling water.

'Bloody hellfire,' Johnson whispered quietly.

Goodman heaved a sigh of relief beside him, and gazed speechless as the blaze developed. As he exposed frame after frame with the Leica, the awesome spectacle of the burning sea put him in mind of Hades itself, the dual elements of fire and water combining to produce a sensation of instinctive, primal fear. At Dumpton Gap the very idea had seemed ridiculous, let alone the shambolic reality. Now Goodman imagined the barrage as seen through the eyes of an enemy approaching in an open boat, drawn by the waters of the Styx towards hell. In the midst of such an inferno, no human could survive for more than a dozen seconds.

At a range of two hundred metres, the observers remained oblivious to the practical flaws of the flame barrage as a weapon of war: cumbersome, immobile, vulnerable to air attack, unreliable in anything other than calm weather, and all-but useless without support from conventional forms of defence. Indeed the thick, billowing clouds of smoke were likely to provide the enemy with cover, and would blind the defenders in the face of a sea breeze.

As the minutes passed a black, velvet pall rose many thousands of feet into the clear blue sky, triggering the wail of air raid sirens on each side of the Thames Estuary. Quietly, unobtrusively, the two men made their way back across the marshes to the stolen car.

All that remained was to deliver Johnson and his precious film back to Germany. Sorting over the facts and possibilities laid bare by the Redcap sergeant at the Bank that morning, Goodman sensed the steepest slopes of Operation Twenty still lay ahead.

THIRTY-THREE

At ten o'clock on the night of August 18th, two uniformed men hastened to Cell 57 at Wandsworth Prison. The heavy steel door, guarded by an armed Special Branch officer, groaned open on its unoiled hinges. The first man to enter the cell was Major Tar Robertson, the BI(a) case officer who had for three years supervised the running of the Welsh double agent Arthur Owens, code-named SNOW. The other, a corporal, was a pre-war radio ham fluent in German. Over the past eleven months the operator had mastered every detail of Owens' wireless style, from his signature confusion of the letters R and S right down to the rhythm of his finger on the morse key. Under Robertson's watchful eye, the corporal switched on the five-watt transmitter supplied to SNOW eighteen months earlier, which under favourable conditions could achieve a range of four hundred miles, sufficient to reach Hamburg with ease.

Both men listened intently as the valves warmed and hummed, each of them conscious that tonight's signal was the most important chicken-feed yet delivered to their opposite numbers at Stelle X.

In March 1940, MI6 signals intelligence at Bletchley Park had succeeded in breaking several of the Abwehr's dedicated Enigma coding keys. In consequence it was possible to follow each fraudulent message transmitted by B1(a) through the German intelligence structure like a barium meal. The signal which flashed from Wandsworth through the ether above the North Sea was received first in an isolated field outside Hamburg, where a dozen monitoring stations were housed in concrete bunkers, installation intercepted telecommunications across the hemispheres as a matter of routine, from Moscow to Washington, London to Athens.

Some distance away, on a hill at Ulm, stood further transceivers which monitored radio traffic from London across all frequencies. Here too the signal transmitted from Cell 57 was recorded.

Upon reception, SNOW's signal was re-routed to the Stelle X on Sophienstrasse. There it was passed into the hands of his case officer, Major Nikolaus Ritter, alias Doctor Rantzau, who knew SNOW as JOHNNY. As Ritter scanned the teletyped words his pulse quickened. Scribbling down a reference copy, he immediately returned the slip to the signals room for onward transmission to Berlin in re-encrypted Enigma form.

There Bletchley Park lost the scent. Although Abwehr radio traffic was vulnerable to Ultra interception, landlines remained beyond the invisible reach of the SIS codebreakers. While a signal sent from Lisbon to Madrid might be monitored and read with comparative ease, the same message sent from Berlin, passing through a teletype link in Paris, remained wholly secure. It was therefore fortunate for Colonel Erwin Lahousen that on reaching his office in the Foxhole at six, and being handed a copy of the signal from Stelle X, he chose to contact Canaris by means of an ordinary telephone call.

He caught the chief of intelligence in Madrid with seconds to spare. Three days earlier the admiral had instructed Lahousen to accompany him on an unheralded trip to Paris, with no clearer purpose than to satisfy another of his periodic bouts of wanderlust. Having undertaken a snap inspection tour of Abwehr outstations in the occupied zone, Canaris had announced a snap decision to head south the Algeciras, leaving Lahousen to return to Berlin alone. The head of Abwehr II had come to his office on the Tirpitzufer direct from the train, feeling fatigued and forsaken.

'What is it?' Canaris snapped impatiently above the crackling line. 'I'm running late.'

'JOHNNY's been on air.' Lahousen raised the slip of paper and read aloud. '"CRACKER day trip to east coast. Many pictures - fine likeness. Ran into old friend. Essential return home by shortest route".'

'That quickly!' The admiral sounded genuinely astounded. 'Did he shoot film?'

'JOHNNY doesn't say, Admiral. It's a literal translation. The text is all there is.'

On the other end of the line Canaris paused. 'I take it you're aware that in our absence Liss has kicked up another stink? He's complaining our intelligence on England is the worst yet provided by Section II.'

'I've just this minute arrived at my desk, Admiral.'

'Then listen carefully. Liss is telling anyone who'll listen that we're twiddling our thumbs. I've been ordered to address OKW in person the day after tomorrow. I'll need all the ammunition you can lay your hands on.'

'You want a more detailed wireless report from CRACKER?'

'I want his film. How quickly can you get it back?'

'At the present time, Admiral, I think Lisbon-'

'Damn Lisbon! We've got two days, not two weeks. Can't you finesse OKM for a submarine?'

'At such short notice, I doubt it.'

'An S-boat, then?'

'Any attempt to collect CRACKER by sea would be unwise at the present time.'

'Unwise?' barked Canaris, his displeasure evident at a distance of two thousand miles. 'Permit me to tell you something about wisdom, Lahousen. In the next twelve months the Fuhrer demands that we seize not only Britain, but the entire Soviet Union as well. Add to that an invasion of French North-West Africa in support of Mussolini's debacle, and it should be obvious to anyone but a cretin that our leader has turned Germany onto a road down which disaster approaches, step by measured step.'

Lahousen visualized the admiral in the office on the Calle Castellena, his face flushed red with anger beneath his white hair. At the heart of the German military machine, Canaris alone sensed the scale and course of the world catastrophe which Hitler had precipitated. Yet here in Berlin the walls grew thinner with each passing day, and such outbursts, in anything other than the most private circumstances, caused Lahousen to fear for his own skin. Knowing full well that resistance was pointless, the colonel tried to deflect his superior one last time.

'Herr Admiral, activity along the British coast now would jeopardize Operation Lohengrin.'

'Perfect!' Canaris exclaimed, his mood reversed in an instant. 'Have the Englishman sent back with Gruppe Wagner. Is

CRACKER near the east coast?'

Lahousen could scarcely credit what he was hearing. 'Admiral, Lohengrin is of paramount-'

'*Do it!*' exploded Canaris, his voice so loud that Lahousen was obliged to hold the receiver away from his ear. 'Am I no longer in command of the Abwehr? I want CRACKER or his film in Berlin by tomorrow evening. Those are my orders. No buts, no further discussion.'

Without further ado the admiral severed the line. Deeply vexed, Lahousen stared at the receiver in his hand for several moments until his annoyance subsided. Briefly he considered disobeying the order, then summoned his aide.

'I need a flight,' he announced as Lamer entered. 'First thing tomorrow morning.'

The adjutant nodded. 'Short or long haul?'

'Den Helder. And not the Storch this time. That little gnat makes me airsick.'

THIRTY-FOUR

'English science is catching up fast. The station at Hopton is beginning to resemble a Wurzburg.'

'Sounds like something you shouldn't eat,' said Wagner, deadpan.

The civilian DeTe engineer that his men were to escort that night to the Suffolk coast that night was a short, plump, expendable civilian with greying hair, afflicted with a profound inability to explain any part of his expertise to a layman in comprehensible terms. He shot Wagner a disapproving look, then continued.

'Wurzburg is a short-range, medium wavelength ground apparatus, meant to replace Freya. If the English have achieved a comparable advance then our pilots will suffer more than a stomach ache.'

'Why, in words of one syllable?'

'On a good day Wurzburg is accurate enough to direct effective anti-aircraft fire against unseen aircraft. At night, for example, or through cloud cover. On two hundred megacycles at high frequency, with a pulse rate of-'

Kuhnke, the Abwehr Luftwaffentechnik liaison officer, interrupted him. 'From there it's a stone's throw to airborne interception equipment.'

Wagner digested the information. 'Why Hopton in particular?'

'See for yourself,' Kuhnke replied, pushing forward one of the enlargements. 'Two rotating aerial arrays - one mounted on a low gantry, the other on a mast. Over the last few months the masts have been springing up everywhere along the English coast like mushrooms. But the gantry array is new.'

'It looks pretty fragile. Can't you bomb them?'

191

'Our dive bombers have given the south coast stations a fair pounding, and put Ventnor and Poling off air. Then yesterday the Reichsmarshal decided to call off the dogs, and direct them instead against airfields.'

'Fat Hermann is living in the past,' the engineer declared confidently. 'He sees the air war purely in terms of shooting down enemy aircraft.

'You surprise me,' said Wagner. 'I thought our best scientific brains had concluded that the English DeTe configuration was a dud.'

The engineer shook his head wearily, as though Wagner were an imbecile. 'The English have at least twenty operational stations, whose beams form an unbroken electronic curtain. The technology is crude, but the application is more effective than ours.'

Kuhnke nodded in agreement. 'Make no mistake, Leutnant Wagner. DeTe will determine the outcome of the battle for England.'

Tired of hard science, Wagner checked his watch. 'The submarine skipper wants us on board within the hour. We'd better sort out a uniform for our fellow passenger.'

The engineer managed an uneasy smile. 'Excellent. I've often wondered what I'd look like in field grey.'

Wagner exchanged a knowing look with Kuhnke, but said nothing. The engineer would learn soon enough the difference between field grey and English khaki. In truth, however, the joke rang hollow. With each new visit to the enemy mainland Gruppe Wagner had found the defences stronger, and the defenders better prepared. The lingering stiffness in his left arm caused by the bullet he had taken at St Margaret's Bay served a constant reminder.

As they prepared to leave the briefing room a knock sounded on the door.

'Cold coffee, half an hour late,' tutted Kuhnke.

But it was Colonel Erwin Lahousen, rather than an orderly, who entered the room. Rising as one with Kuhnke, saluting smartly, Wagner felt the hairs bristle on the nape of his neck. In the few short days since he had brained the unknown tail in the alleyway behind the Rififi club he had felt like a walking corpse. It was only a matter of time, he knew, before the insane episode rebounded.

'Don't let me disturb you, gentlemen,' said Lahousen, crossing the floor and setting down his briefcase on the table.

'We were expecting coffee, sir,' Kuhnke said cautiously.

'Then I must disappoint you, Kuhnke. And I'm afraid what I have to say concerns Leutnant Wagner alone.'

Kuhnke began to gather his papers together, 'Of course, colonel. Our business is done. Unless you've any further questions, leutnant?'

'I know as much as I need to.' Wagner scanned the colonel's face for some clue, but gleaned nothing. It was scarcely reassuring. For all he knew the Feldgendarmerie were waiting in the corridor outside.

Lahousen waited until the other two had left the room before he spoke again. 'You won't like this, Wagner, and nor do I.'

Wagner steeled himself for the worst. 'Go on.'

'Canaris has ordered a change of plan. In addition to visiting the DeTe facility, you'll be picking up an agent.'

Wagner felt a great weight lift from his shoulders. 'Amen to that.'

Lahousen's expression betrayed surprise. 'Commendable enthusiasm, leutnant.'

Wagner's response had been involuntary, but now he checked himself. 'It could have been worse. Bringing back Churchill, rather than a V-Man.'

'You'd need a bigger boat.'

'There's that. Where do we find your secret agent?'

'Your choice. We can place him near to Hopton, but I'll need coordinates as soon as possible for our contact in England.'

Wagner digested this information, then asked: 'Do I get any background?'

'Not much. He's an Englishman, codenamed CRACKER, who has some rather valuable film.'

'Did you train him?'

Lahousen nodded. 'At Wiesbaden.'

'Because I don't want some brown-trousered amateur stumbling around and raising the alarm. Otherwise my men are dead in the water.'

'I've every sympathy, Wagner. But the order comes direct from Canaris.'

'Then I guess I don't have much choice in the matter.'

'None at all.'

Wagner turned to his map and scanned the topography of the border between Norfolk and Suffolk. It took him a dozen seconds to reach his decision. 'There's a railway bridge near the church, on Stirrup's Lane. If your man can reach it, we can rendezvous there.'

Lahousen studied the map critically. 'What about the church? It could be an observation post.'

Wagner shook his head. 'According to the legend it's a ruin.'

'Are there obstacles in place on the beach?'

'Not according to the latest obliques.'

'Taken when?'

'Eight days ago. If it's mined we'll just have to find a way through. I plan to put into shore about a half mile down from the DeTe site.'

'Might be too close.'

'It might,' Wagner agreed. 'But if we land further south we'll be knocking on doors in Corton village, and the north is too populated. Besides, the less distance we have to cover on land the better, after ten hours cooped up in a submarine.'

'How will you approach the station?'

Wagner pointed a finger at the map. 'The railway line between Lowestoft to Yarmouth passes within three hundred metres of the target. The guards and pickets will probably be less alert on the landward side. And, my men will have fewer problems locating your precious V-Man.'

'I'd like you to collect CRACKER yourself.'

'I've got an operation to lead,' Wagner replied shortly.

'As from now, he takes priority over DeTe.'

Wagner frowned. 'Too bad Canaris couldn't tell me himself. But I guess the old fox chasing other chickens, right?'

Lahousen smiled thinly. 'Something of the sort. Bring home this Englishman, or his film at least, and I'll wager the Admiral will add swords to your Iron Cross.'

Wagner too might have laughed. Two iron crosses. It would mean, perhaps, twenty years in Silesian coal mine, instead of a firing squad.

THIRTY-FIVE

The roadblock on the bridge above the railway bridge was manned by a picket of two Home Guards, armed with unwieldy Ross rifles imported from Canada and dressed in ill-fitting denim uniforms. Kydd found the unflattering garb particularly vexing, but at least the job offered respite from the crashing bore that was his lot in the regular military police, now that Captain Goodman's section had been broken up. The other bogus Home Guard was an FS corporal named Barnes, who had also been present when CRACKER had landed in Dorset four long days before.

Kydd had just touched a match to the last of his cigarettes when footsteps sounded, approaching through the darkness from the direction of the church. The sergeant was not unduly alarmed: of the half-dozen people they had stopped on the bridge since dusk, the most suspicious had been a war reserve constable on a rusty bicycle with flat tyres. For this reason Kydd did not trouble to extinguish his cigarette, or raise his rifle as he issued the time-honoured challenge.

'Who goes there? Friend or foe?'

'Friend,' replied a voice from the shadows, as the footsteps stopped dead.

'Advance and be recognised.'

As Kydd spoke Barnes shone a dampened torch through the darkness. The pale beam settled on three soldiers, the nearest an infantry lieutenant. At once both Field Security men snapped to attention, Kydd hurriedly discarding his cigarette across the parapet as he raised his hand.

'Smoking on duty,' the lieutenant admonished as he returned the salute. 'A little lax, wouldn't you say?'

'Sir,' Kydd apologised, judging from his accent that the officer was Canadian.

The lieutenant sucked in a lungfull of air. 'You men seen anything suspicious tonight?'

Kydd had opened his mouth to reply as the bullet smashed through his temple. He was dead before he hit the ground, as was Barnes after the silenced automatic wielded by Weidenmann coughed twice more. The torch clattered to the ground and came to rest with the beam focused on Kydd's face. The hole in the centre of his forehead, and his dead eyes below it, formed a grotesque tableau.

Wagner stepped forward and kicked the torch aside. 'Strip off the armbands,' he ordered, now speaking in German. 'Heave their bodies over the bridge, make sure they don't land across the tracks.'

Beneath the arch, twenty-five feet below, John Goodman held his breath. Despite the cool night air, and the last of the benzedrine, he was flagging badly for want of sleep. The coughing of the silenced pistol and the clatter of the bodies as they fell onto the road had confused him, but now the switch from transatlantic to German chilled his blood. His worst fears were confirmed when the two corpses thudded onto the embankment a dozen yards from the spot where he and Johnson had crouched in silence for six long hours.

As the second body struck the ground Johnson lost his nerve. Scrambling to his feet he struck his head on the masonry, then leapt out onto the railway line, hands clasped above his head.

'Don't shoot! Don't shoot! Ich bin kamerad!'

'Keep it down,' snapped a voice from above. 'Give me the password.'

'CRACKER!' blurted Johnson, stumbling backwards on a sleeper in the darkness.

Incorrect. Goodman raked his memory for the word on the note from Morley which had been pushed up through the kitchen floorboards at Cheniston Crescent. What was the sequence he had memorised? *Railway to Flying Scotsman, Flying Dutchman to Wagner. Lohengrin.* Quickly he yelled the word out loud.

After a moment's silence the voice ordered: 'Get yourself up here. Time is tight.'

Goodman scrambled up the embankment behind Johnson and climbed over the low wall onto the road, where he was immediately blinded by a powerful torch beam.

'I was only expecting one man,' the unseen American said. 'Which one of you is CRACKER?'

'That's me,' Johnson stammered.

'Got your films?'

Johnson nodded vigorously, holding forward his briefcase. 'They're in here.'

'Carry it yourself. We're your escort, not bell-hops.'

'Escort?' There was an edge of panic to Johnson's voice.

'Back with us. Some folks in Berlin want to pick your brains real urgent, so it seems.'

'But I need-'

'Not any more.' The American turned to Goodman, lowering his torch. Only now did Goodman see that the other three men were dressed in British uniforms, the American masquerading as an officer. 'Who are you?'

Johnson answered for him, the words stung with malice. 'A bloody Welsh Quisling, that's who.'

'Interesting hybrid,' the officer said. 'You work for the Abwehr?'

'Yes,' replied Goodman, as calmly as he was able.

'Good.' The officer gestured toward Weidenmann, who cradled the two Ross rifles beneath his arm. 'Take one each, and put on those armbands. If we run into anyone on route to the beach, you've just volunteered for the Home Guard.'

Goodman responded almost without thinking. 'Not me. Now you've got CRACKER I'd like to leave.'

'No way,' countered the American. 'Whoever you are, you don't leave the neighbourhood before we do. Take a rifle and start walking.'

Sensing that to argue would be to risk joining Charlie Kydd under the bridge, Goodman did as he was told.

They set off in silence, the German group glancing nervously to and fro in the darkness. Goodman watched Johnson closely. Only the prospect of a bullet prevented him from attempting one last bid for freedom. At bottom Goodman felt pity for the ill-starred villain, whose scheme to escape back to England had at once succeeded and failed so famously. Despite the fact that Johnson had tried to shoot him just days earlier, it was more for his sake than Morley's that Goodman hoped the film shot at Foulness was convincing, for otherwise tonight CRACKER might be returning to certain death. As for Morley, the floorboard note had promised that he would be somewhere close by the rail bridge at Hopton. Was he following them now? Or was he dead too? And what denouement lay in store at the beach?

With each step forward Goodman's feeling of dread increased tenfold. Then suddenly his train of thought was derailed as the American began to hum softly beneath his breath. He recognised the gentle, rising melody immediately: It Had to be You, Sophie Gold's favourite record. *Their record*. And Goodman knew then, beyond a shadow of a doubt, that the man walking beside him was Paul Wagner, her vanished New York lover, now the enemy of them both. Even in the divorce courts, he reflected, he had never before encountered anything so patently absurd. He wondered if his relationship with Sophie could accommodate the unwelcome secret with which he was now suddenly burdened. If indeed he even lived to see the dawn.

Clearly Harry Johnson had other ideas. By the time the church tower was visible against the night sky he had found the courage to try once more to prevent his return to occupied Europe.

'Listen,' he pitched earnestly, 'there's been a mistake.'

'I don't think so,' replied Wagner, breaking off from his humming.

'No, there has. My instructions were to take the pictures, then sit tight and wait for more.'

'More what?'

'Instructions.'

'And now you've got them. You're coming back with us.'

Johnson turned to Goodman. 'Tell him, for Christ's sake. We're all waiting for the invasion, aren't we?'

'You were recognised in London yesterday,' Goodman replied evenly.

Johnson dropped his voice to a whisper. 'Alright, so I lied when I landed. I did bring the thousand. There's seven hundred notes in my pocket right now. It's all yours if you can keep me on this side of the water.'

'Sorry - no can do.' In the circumstances it was the most honest answer Goodman could give.

'Then fuck you, chum.'

Johnson's curse sounded loud and clear in the still of the night. The next moment both barrels of a shotgun were discharged from the belfry of the church tower a dozen yard ahead. Instinctively the Brandenburg men dived for cover. Goodman and Johnson were too slow, however, and as he launched himself towards the verge Goodman felt shot pepper his back like hailstones, in the same instant catching a fleeting glimpse of Johnson as he sank down in the middle of the lane. Hugging the earth, Goodman was aware of a sharp stinging sensation across his shoulders, and - strangest of all - jeering laughter.

A split second later Weidenmann returned fire with his sub-machine gun, spattering the masonry with a long burst that left his magazine half empty. A moment later a blinding white flare arced gracefully up into the night sky from the tower, illuminating the surrounding area in an instant. Then the church bell began to toll dolefully.

'Scheisse!' cursed Weidenmann, turning his weapon towards Johnson's prone form.

'Nein,' barked Wagner, moving between the corporal and his target. After aiming a hard kick at the Englishman's backside, Wagner dragged Johnson to his feet and pushed him forward roughly, then stooped and shook Goodman's shoulder.

'You hit?'

'Not too badly,' Goodman replied, realising too late that a judicious lie might have ended his quandary there and then. Or invited a bullet, like a fallen mule.

'Okay. We're out of here.'

As they pounded away down the lane in the direction of the sea the shotgun sounded again. A dozen seconds later it was followed by the sound of automatic fire from the direction of the radar station at Hopton, which grew quickly in intensity as more flares rose into the air. Then came the roar of a violent explosion, sounding like an enormous door slamming in the bowels of the earth. It took the five men as many breathless minutes to reach the clay cliff above the beach, during which a fitful battle erupted a half mile further up the coast, tracers and flares arcing through the night sky like atomic fireflys.

By the time they reached the wire-choked gully which lead

down to the beach stray rounds were whistling and zinging above their heads. A line of thin metal poles like ski sticks marked the way across the sand to the surf, where three rubber boats were bobbing in the water. A Brandenburg feldwebel in British uniform ran forward, glancing anxiously around. Following a short, heated exchange with Wagner, the American returned and struck Johnson hard across the jaw.

'You asshole - three men dead, thanks to your big mouth. Give me one good reason why I shouldn't make it four.'

Johnson said nothing, paralysed with fear. Then a yell from the clifftop behind them signalled that the defenders were closing fast. Goodman fielded a last desperate bluff.

'Don't leave me with his corpse. Our network's been damaged enough since he fell out of the sky.'

Wagner fixed Goodman keenly, then relented. Grabbing Johnson's briefcase in one hand he shoved the frozen Englishman towards Weidenmann with the other. 'Get this sorry sack of shit in the boat.'

The feldwebel did as he was ordered. Now only Goodman and Wagner remained on the beach. Wagner nodded at the dinghy. 'You coming? Thanks to your friend there's room on the bus.'

Goodman shook his head. 'I've work to do here.'

'Like stopping a bullet? Any second now this beach will be hell with the lid off.'

'I'll take my chances.' Still clutching the rifle, Goodman turned and made to hurry away, but a moment later Wagner hailed him.

'Hey - at least help push the boat away.'

Goodman hesitated, then flung aside the rifle and waded back into the cold salt water. Pushing forward the dinghy he stumbled through the breakers until the water reached his waist.

'Stand back,' said Wagner. 'I'm starting the outboard.'

As the engine coughed into life and the boat started away, another parachute flare rose into the sky, slowing gracefully to hang directly over the beach. Goodman watched as Johnson gave him two fingers and spat over the side. For his trouble he received another punch, this time from Weidenmann. Then, as the three assault boats slipped away across the dark North Sea water, Goodman turned and waded back towards to the beach.

No sooner had he started across the sand than a fusillade of small arms fire opened up from the cliff. Almost immediately Goodman felt his head punched aside, as if by a hammer blow, and his body compressed so violently that his vision was distorted. Then, as a dense, blessed blackness overcame him, he plunged rapidly downwards into empty space.

THIRTY-SIX

Morley was sitting down on a low metal stool beside the bed, noisily consuming one of the apples he had brought for Goodman. 'You know, nobody in the know can make up their mind whether you should be marched to the scaffold, or given a gong.'

'Blessed if I know,' Goodman replied, wincing at a sudden twinge. He had woken an hour or so earlier with a bandaged head, the mother of all migraines and a throbbing pain behind his right eye. His fingertips told him there were half a dozen stitches above it.

'What happened is, you helped the King's enemies make good their escape.'

'Those were my orders, as far as I can remember.'

'Well at least there's something left in there. Frankly you're lucky to be alive. The lads from the Devon Light Infantry took several pot shots from the cliff. Of course Territorials can't shoot straight, but one of them hit a mine instead and you caught the blast.'

'Christ, not again.'

'Beg pardon?' said Morley, nonplussed.

'Nothing. Forget I spoke.'

'Ah...' rejoined Morley after a pause. 'That business in Belgium.' He laughed heartily. 'Good grief, Goodman. Getting shot by one's own side once is unlucky, but twice is downright careless.'

'I never did care much for Oscar Wilde.'

'Nor me, as a matter of fact.' Leisurely Morley produced his battered gunmetal case and retrieved a cigarette. 'Mind if I smoke?'

'Yes. But you will anyway.'

'How much do you remember?'

'Not much. I think I must be concussed.'

'So the doctor said.'

Goodman thought for a moment. 'Were we shot at from the church tower?'

'By the LDV,' Morley nodded. 'Only with rock salt, mind you, fired from a twelve-gauge shotgun.'

'Rock salt?'

'Much against my wishes, our troops were given a warning. They were told a Home Guard Auxiliary Unit would attempt to infiltrate the station. Hence your being slightly shot.'

'One of them was bloody well laughing.'

'Thank God he was awake, otherwise Hopton CHL would now be a hole in the ground.'

'CHL?'

'Chain Home Low. Some new form of this radio location business. Jerry was after a gander last night.'

'They were wearing British uniforms.'

'So I noticed. They probably wore them at Hollesley Bay too. Talk to them much?'

'A little. I can't really remember.'

'SS, were they?'

'I've no idea. We didn't get as far as swapping jerseys. One of them was...' Goodman tailed off mid sentence as another blurred instant rushed back into focus. One of them was Paul Wagner, the former lover of Sophie Gold in another life. Although he knew full well that he should reveal it to Morley, for a moment the conflict between duty and matters of the heart made him hesitate.

'Was...?' Morley encouraged.

'The officer in charge was an American. I think his name is Paul Wagner.'

Morley frowned. 'He told you that? Sounds like the pair of you got on famously.'

'Hardly. I know an old girlfriend of his.'

'Sophie Gold?'

Goodman turned towards Morley, perplexed. 'How do you know?'

'You passed me a note for her. Back when I was a dentist.'

'Look, I want her kept out of this.'

'You've already dragged her in, I'm afraid. Now, tell me more about this man Wagner.'

'If it was him. He disappeared from New York when her father broke off their affair, about two years ago. Into jazz, apparently. He seemed decent enough.'

Morley frowned. 'He shot your sergeant in cold blood.'

So far this strand had not resurfaced in Goodman's mind. Now, as the memory flooded back, the dry cough of the silenced gunshots returned to his ears, and the hard thud of the bodies of Kydd and Barnes on the ground beneath the bridge.

Goodman closed his eyes. 'Bloody hell.'

'Fortunes of war,' Morley offered blandly. 'Road accident of course, should anybody ask.'

'Did you get any of them?'

'Three sausages potted. No prisoners, more's the pity.'

From the several fragments so far revealed the whole was beginning to form in Goodman's mind. 'Were they trying for the low chain thingy?'

'Tried and failed, thankfully,' Morley confirmed, drawing heavily on his cigarette. 'Otherwise they'd have locked me in the Tower and thrown away the key. The church bells raised the alarm. After the chaps at CHL opened fire some sort of demolition charge went off prematurely. The Hun made off after that, didn't even get through the wire.'

'You'll have a job keeping this one quiet.'

'We're putting it about that an exercise went wrong, one of those new commando units Churchill wants raising. The Terriers are hardly likely to brag about killing their own side.'

'You really are a prize bastard, Morley.'

'No place for Queensbury in total war, Goodman.'

'I take it Johnson got away safely.'

Morley nodded. 'Nore Command were most put out. Could have sunk the sub a dozen times over, so they say. Mind you, Berlin are welcome to a character like Harry Johnson. File as thick as you like at the Yard.'

'He didn't want to go back.'

'I don't doubt it. Still, if Hitler doesn't pin a medal on his tit then the King might be persuaded to when all this is over. You can hold his hand at the Palace.'

'I just hope it was worth it,' Goodman said seriously. 'Charlie Kydd was a good man.'

'Time alone will tell. You're quite sure Johnson didn't suspect he was being set-up?'

'As I can be.'

'Good.' Morley ground his cigarette in an ashtray, then stood and replaced his cap. 'Well, I'd best run along. Report to me at Blenheim when you're mended. Plenty of work down our way for talented fellows like you.'

Goodman saw through the compliment. 'Meaning, I know too much to be posted anywhere else.'

'Something like that. But don't be so hard on yourself. You did damned well on Twenty.'

Morley crossed to the door, then paused with his hand on the latch. 'By the way, the service has decided to reward your valiant efforts with a visitor. Enjoy.'

As the major left, Goodman glimpsed a military police sergeant standing guard in the corridor. A moment later Sophie Gold appeared in the doorway. For a moment Goodman was lost for words.

'Hello, you,' she said uncertainly, frowning at his stitches and bandaged head.

'Sophie - how on earth...?'

'Major Morley. You sent me a letter, remember? I only got it this morning. Half an hour later a car turned up at Bawdsey and brought me here.'

'I don't even know where here is.'

'Shotley Cottage Hospital.' Sophie closed the door behind her and stepped towards the bed. 'You know, after you stood me up last week I feared the worst.'

'Something came up,' he smiled weakly.

'So I see. Something like a bomb by the look of it.'

'They say I'll live.'

She sat down on the edge of the bed and began to walk her fingers along his thigh. 'Tell me when it hurts.'

'Everything already does.'

'Poor Johnny.' Sophie took his hand in hers and squeezed his fingers. 'I've missed you. I've been humming our tune all the time, like some silly lovesick schoolgirl.'

Our tune... As the melody ran through his pounding head it seemed suddenly ugly and discordant to Goodman. For it was Paul Wagner's rendition, not Benny Goodman, that now uncoiled and wound through his aching head.

THIRTY-SEVEN

The majority of the staff officers crowded into the cramped projection room at OKW had already seen the grainy stills taken over Dumpton Gap four weeks earlier. The colour film from Wilhelmshaven was a disturbing novelty, however. Thus far, the written reports prepared by the Abwehr on the state and extent of the English defences had formed a contradictory mosaic, each one a masterpiece of discouragement. Now the images on the screen, judiciously edited, spoke volumes more. As the oil burned, a pall of dense black smoke choked the dockside and rose high into the air above the Baltic port, vicious tongues of orange flame licked fiercely at its underside.

When after two minutes the film ended, Canaris instructed the projectionist to raise the lights. Seated as if for a Saturday matinee, the joint chiefs of staff - Keitel, Jodl and Raeder, together with Halder, von Brauschitsch, Schniewind and Warlimont and their senior aides - wore uniformly grave expressions. Satisfied that he had their attention, the chief of intelligence began his pitch.

'The footage you have just seen was shot at the Chemisch-Physikalischen Versuchsanstalt. One hundred tons of a petrol-oil mixture burned for twenty minutes. A great deal of smoke and heat were produced, and certain obvious dangers demonstrated.'

'Most impressive, Herr Admiral.' The speaker was Colonel Liss, the Abwehr's unsparing critic at Foreign Armies West. 'But I've seen the CPV report with my own eyes. It concludes that such a system is useless on anything other than a millpond.'

'In that respect it shares something in common with our invasion armada.'

Liss ignored the Admiral's barbed reply. 'The Ordnance Technical Office tell me it raises insuperable difficulties. First there's the problem of obtaining a fuel mixture light enough to ignite, but sufficiently heavy to sustain a continuous blaze. Second, an effective burn off an open coast requires a prohibitive amount of fuel.'

'The English have fuel to spare. A single wide-bore pipeline linked to the Thameshaven refineries could flood an area of water of several square miles.'

'Witzell's department have already devised counter-measures.'

'Such as?' Canaris' tone betrayed irritation.

'Depth charges to break up the slicks, and fire fighting equipment mounted on tugs.'

'Meanwhile the Wehrmacht have ordered ten thousand asbestos suits from a reputable Paris tailor.' The comedian was Zwicker, intelligence adviser to Field Marshal Keitel. The quip earned him a frosty look from Liss.

'Has Witzell tested these counter-measures?' asked Canaris.

'Not as yet.'

'Then let's hope the practice is equal to the theory.'

'When did you say the trial was held at Wilhelmshaven?' asked Zwicker.

'Four days ago, August eighteenth. The next day the English ignited another barrage on the shores of the Solent, near Titchfield. This was the cause of the so-called large scale fires in the vicinity of Portsmouth, for which the Luftwaffe took care to claim credit.'

'A good game!' The speaker was a Luftwaffe officer of junior rank, sent to OKW by Goring to emphasise that, despite the setbacks of the last few days, the air force were capable of conquering England unaided.

Canaris nodded. 'Perhaps. Of course, aircrew can climb over it. Whereas the navy and infantry must charge through.'

Bartels, the naval chief-of-staff, cleared his throat. 'How can such a system work?'

'Oil is piped out to sea from bulk storage onshore. It floats to the surface, and the pools are ignited at the critical moment, probably electronically. At Wilhelmshaven the CPV used sodium flares.'

Bartels turned to Liss, two rows behind him. 'It seems simple enough.'

Canaris drove home his advantage. 'In addition, England boasts

208

many natural sea defences - tides and sandbanks, as well as intricate and difficult navigation channels. For this reason we must assume that their Admiralty already has a good idea of the beaches where we intend to land. Add to that the fact that the English have almost forty divisions, well equipped and with good morale. Take my word, not even the survivors of Dunkirk will retreat.'

In the silence that followed this solemn resume a new voice spoke up from the back of the projection room. It belonged to Walter Schellenberg.

'Operation Sealion provides fertile soil for rumours. There's been a fine crop since July. Two weeks ago we lost eighty thousand men attempting to land in the Wash.'

A ripple of mirth rose from the stalls. Even Liss allowed himself a thin smile, Canaris noted. He could only marvel at the speed with which the head of SD Amt IV had covered the distance from Berlin. A tip-off, probably, courtesy of Liss. He decided to follow the mood.

'Quite so. Half our invasion force. Hand picked troops to a man.'

'Yet you lost only three men in Suffolk last week.'

The room fell silent. Though Schellenberg's detailed knowledge of the Hopton reconnaissance came as an unpleasant surprise, the chief of intelligence remained impassive. 'Sturmbannfuhrer Schellenberg is admirably informed. Gentlemen, for some weeks a Brandenburg unit has been assisting the Luftwaffe in assessing enemy DeTe capability.'

'Three such operations so far,' added Schellenberg. 'And not once have Brandenburg been confronted by a sea of flame.'

'Meaning what? That my men should land in broad daylight, lead by dancing horses and a marching band?'

'Meaning, their deception bureaux have had the best part of a year to concoct falsehoods of this kind in order to conceal their manifest weakness.'

'You seem very sure, Walter.' Canaris kept his gaze steady, his voice even. There would be no more morning rides through the Tiergarten.

'I'll wager that not a single kilometre of the English coastline is protected in this way.'

Canaris offered no reply, and instead turned to the projectionist.

'Be so kind as to run the second film please. Gentlemen, two days ago one of our field agents returned from England with some quite remarkable footage.'

A low murmur rose from the stalls, which fell away just as quickly when Harry Johnson's film began to play on the screen. Canaris resumed his commentary.

'The location is Foulness, at the mouth of the Thames. A small local fire, no more than fifty metres in length. The film itself is rather short, but the fire was seen to burn for thirty minutes.'

Canaris paused to allow Johnson's grainy film to progress. Despite the distance and flicker, the images were chilling.

'In addition to this location, we have evidence of similar defences at Margate, Felixstowe, the Solent and Christchurch. Their entire Channel coast may be protected in this way.'

A half minute later, as the spool ended and the lights rose, Canaris congratulated himself on a torpedo well run. Even Liss had turned his eyes to the floor.

Schellenberg, however, was nowhere to be seen.

THIRTY-EIGHT

Wagner's heart sank through his boots. Doctor Froese, it seemed, was just beginning to hit his conceptual stride. 'Everyone knows that America's contribution to the music of the world consists of nothing but jazzed-up nigger music. That garbage belongs among the Hottentots, not in German dancehalls. It's nothing less than a disgusting treason against civilized Occidental culture.'

Wagner shook his head wearily. 'Jesse Owens didn't do so badly at the Olympics in 1936. For a Hottentot, that is.'

Froese waved his hand dismissively. 'So the chocolate people can run fast! Let me tell you something, leutnant. The black man can wash himself as often as he likes, but he can never become white. No amount of breeding can turn a negro into a Frisian farmer.'

Wagner closed his eyes. After eight long hours as a guest of the Sicherheitsdienst, the last two of these in the company of - God forbid - an SS jazz expert, he had become not so much cowed as short-tempered. The men who had bundled him into the black Mercedes on the Kurfurstendamm that morning had played the role of goon-squad well, but the bespectacled zealot who had spent the last hour holding forth on the supposed primitivism of the negro, as though rehearsing a script, barely passed muster even as a charlatan.

Froese continued to pace self-consciously around the table. 'Tell me, Wagner, did you contract the jazz bacillus here in Germany, or carry it with you from New York - like Typhoid Mary?'

'I think you'll find the jitterbug is a musical expression of Americanism, not a disease.'

'There's a difference? The sole purpose of nigger music is to

211

introduce obscenities into society. It's indicative of their infamous lack of sexual control. And now the Yids are getting in on the game. Jazz plays a pivotal role of their systematic plot to poison the blood of Nordic German womanhood, by seducing them through acts of musical race defilement.'

Wagner managed to laugh. 'And if they can't dance then Cubism does the job, right?'

Froese nodded enthusiastically. 'Yes! Futurism, Dadaism, bloodless intellectuality, rootless pacifism - the list is endless, each and every one of them exports from Zion. Of course, the Jew ranges above the African by dint of his superior mental powers, coupled with his strong sense of determination. The obverse of the happy-go-lucky animal state of the negro, in fact.'

'Let me get this straight in my head,' said Wagner. 'In your version, jazz is the invention of some nigger in Chicago. Now the Jews have muscled in on the act and created swing. Goodman, Gershwin and all the rest are the cadres charged with the task of corrupting German women, and undermining the stamina of the armed forces.'

'You sound incredulous. I should have thought your presence here at Wilhelmstrasse was proof enough.'

'Look, am I under arrest? Because I'd like to enjoy what's left of my leave?'

Froese was about to answer when Walter Schellenberg entered the interrogation room. Wagner took the measure of the newcomer. The SD officer was perhaps five years his senior, smart in his black uniform, and without a single feature out of place. A blue-eyed boy, in fact, whose investigative brief undoubtedly ranged far beyond nonsensical race science.

Schellenberg studied the Brandenburg officer briefly, then turned to Froese. 'That will be all for now, Herr Doctor. Leutnant Wagner and I wish to discuss matters unconnected to your research.'

Froese nodded, and after a final contemptuous glance at Wagner left the room.

Schellenberg sat down on the opposite side of the table. 'My name is Schellenberg. Bureau chief, SD Amt IV.'

'I'm impressed. Nice place you've got here. Why the invite?.'

'I was hoping you might tell me.'

'Well, we covered jazz already. I saw a couple of Chaplin films before I left the States. That a hanging offence yet?'

'A week ago you inflicted critical injuries on one of my officers behind a nightclub in Antwerp, while assisting two Belgian civilians in an act of civil disobedience. Even allowing for your Iron Cross, I can guarantee you ten years in a military prison.'

'I was drunk.'

'Not according to the barman at the Rififi Club. I understand you hold your bourbon very well.'

'Is there anything you don't know?'

'Very little. The Weintraub's home address, for instance. De Ronge 18, a most attractive villa. I can have Klaartje and her brother Willem picked up at any time. It's in your hands.'

Wagner felt his stomach begin to knot. 'They're just a couple of kids. I put them up to it, told them I was an American journalist after a story.'

'Did money exchange hands?'

'No.'

'Then it's hardly mitigation. Why did you do it?'

Wagner's eyes sank towards his lap. There seemed little point in lying. 'I took a shine to the girl.'

'You were sleeping with her?'

'No.'

Schellenberg paused, then continued. 'As I said, I can have the pair of them pulled at any time. Their parents too, even their extended family. Their property and wealth can be confiscated, quite legally, to finance resettlement in Poland. You'd never see your precious little Jewess again. Perhaps nobody would. And all of it your doing.'

The SD man raised a quizzical eyebrow. Until now Wagner had remained more or less calm. Now he felt sick to his stomach.'Okay, cut to the chase. Is there a deal here?'

'Of a sort.'

'What is it that you want from me?'

'Information. On your Abwehr superiors, your missions to England. The V-Man you brought back from Suffolk two days ago. And the film I saw at OKW not two hours ago.'

'I don't have clue one about the film. As for the V-Man, he's English, his code-name is CRACKER, and Section II trained him at Wiesbaden. That's all I know, I swear. The rest I can quote you chapter and verse. Will that call off the dogs from the Weintraub family?'

'For now,' nodded Schellenberg.

'What guarantee can you offer?'

'Come come, leutnant. Absolutely none.'

Paul Wagner held Schellenberg's cold stare, and sensed that he was already dead. Was it Napoleon who had described Antwerp as a pistol pointed at the heart of England?

Now he felt its cold steel hard against his temple.

THIRTY-NINE

'From what you tell me, Schellenberg, this man Wagner has been remarkably helpful. Does he wish to come over to our side?'

The Reichsfuhrer SS, Heinrich Himmler, was unarguably the most powerful man in Germany after Adolf Hitler. As was his custom, he was seated so as to ensure that his eyes could not be seen behind his glistening pince-nez.

'His co-operation has more to do with self-preservation,' Schellenberg replied. 'That, and the fact that he assaulted Gorl to protect a girl. She and her older brother broke curfew to daub some half-baked nonsense on a wall. I let him know that the whole family could be made to vanish without a trace.'

Himmler paused ruminatively. 'I've seen his file. The fairer sex would seem to be a weakness where our American friend is concerned.'

'The worst of it is that the Dutch girl is a damned Jew.' The voice, unnaturally high, belonged to Reinhard Heydrich. As head of the SD, Heydrich was Himmler's chief lieutenant, and a hidden pivot of the Nazi state. Schellenberg had been left with no choice but to involve his mentor in his pitch to the Reichsfuhrer. However he had not wanted the girl's Jewishness to be revealed to Himmler.

'I see.' Himmler's reply was almost inaudible, although his tone was one of infinite distaste. Carefully he folded his hands. 'So enlighten me, please, on what this touching melodrama has to do with unseating Canaris and changing the course of the war?'

Schellenberg had rehearsed his words carefully. 'Put simply, Reichsfuhrer, Canaris wants Sealion to fail, and now thanks to his famous English film OKW are wavering. An attack by a strong force of our troops would simultaneously demonstrate the combat ability of the Waffen SS, the weakness of the enemy defences, and the rank fantasy of the Abwehr's foreign intelligence.'

Himmler's puffy, undistinguished features betrayed nothing. 'Attack where?'

'There are several suitable targets. Bawdsey Manor in Suffolk, for instance. It's no longer the centre of English radio-location research, but it's still their most vulnerable DeTe station.'

'Wagner has already kicked over the hive. What are the other possibilities?'

'Porthcurno, in the south-western county of Cornwall. The transatlantic telephone lines run ashore there.'

'Tempting, but sure to be strongly defended.'

Heydrich nodded his agreement. 'The sea crossing from France would be too long.'

Himmler smiled thinly. 'I see that your time in the senior service wasn't wholly wasted.'

As an officer cadet in 1931, Heydrich had been drummed out of the service by a court of honour following a broken engagement. His then commanding officer had been an unremarkable captain named Wilhelm Canaris. Now, in his protege's audacious scheme, Heydrich discerned a new route to undermine his nemesis.

'Such a strike might be counter-productive,' declared Himmler. 'If Roosevelt's communications with Churchill are disrupted, it will bring home to him the desperate plight of England.'

Schellenberg nodded dutifully. 'Quite so, Reichsfuhrer.'

'And the third option?'

'Another DeTe station, at Worth Matravers. Apparently the configuration is unusual. It may be involved in the interception of our blind-bombing beams.'

'Worth Matravers?' scoffed Heydrich. 'It sounds like a character from John Buchan.'

'It's near Weymouth, in Dorset, about a kilometre inland.'

Himmler weighed the options. 'Which of the three do you prefer?'

Schellenberg paused. 'My instinct tells me Worth, but for practical reasons I prefer Bawdsey. It may be a second-hand target, but we already know the lie of the land. And it integrates better with Sealion.'

'How so, Sturmbannfuhrer.'

'It looks increasingly certain that Sealion will be launched on

September fifteenth, on a narrow front across the Dover Strait. It's hard to conceive that the English suspect differently, and thus the plan allows for a number of feints against the east coast, between Edinburgh and Harwich. An attack by a Waffen SS unit across the North Sea-'

'The German Ocean,' Himmler corrected primly. Despite the fact that Schellenberg had been one of his most loyal servants for six years, the Reichsfuhrer was careful not to let him forget that the head of Amt IV was his pupil.

'The German Ocean, Reichsfuhrer. Bawdsey keys in with the existing deception plan more effectively than the other targets. Plus Canaris has been dropping hints that the port of Felixstowe, immediately south of Bawdsey, is protected by the flame weapon.'

'Which according to Amt IV does not exist.'

'That is our strong suspicion, yes.'

Himmler paused. 'Surely there's an easier way? This mysterious V-Man must be able to tell you all you need to know about this infamous defence of fire.

Schellenberg shook his head. 'He's conveniently disappeared.'

Now Heydrich lent his support. 'Reichsfuhrer, you complained only last week that the Waffen SS have been sidelined in Sealion. Schellenberg's scheme could prove our mettle.'

'Or our undoing, in full view of the world. What numbers are required, in your estimation?'

'Something like company strength, between one and two hundred men. Witzig silenced Eban Emael with just eighty-six.' Schellenberg paused. 'In fact I've already identified a suitable unit.'

Himmler frowned. 'Have you indeed.'

'Das Reich are in Holland as part of the occupation forces. Attached to them is Special Purpose Battalion 200.'

The Reichsfuhrer's expression betrayed surprise. The SPB, five hundred strong, had been raised two months earlier, in direct response to the success of Brandenburg in Poland and the Low Countries. Because the unit was not yet fully trained it had not been assigned a combat role in Sealion, and was instead earmarked for the diversionary manoeuvres in the North Sea, codenamed Autumn Journey.

'The SPB is hardly kampfbereit, Sturmbannfuhrer.'

'Only the battalion is untried. Enough of its strength have seen action in previous campaigns.'

'This is hardly comparable to pursuing a defeated rabble across Poland and France.'

'True. But Wagner has detailed knowledge of the target.'

'You intend to involve him?'

'Gruppe Wagner know the ground. Posing as English troops is their forte.'

'I do not wish to see SS troops engage the enemy led by an American who consorts with Jews,' said Himmler coldly. 'Even one with an Iron Cross.'

Schellenberg steeled himself to cross an invisible line. The plan prepared by Eichner was the boldest scheme he had yet run past his superiors, and one which could hardly be allowed to crash and burn on account of some nonsensical blood law. 'Reichsfuhrer, one way or another we need to involve Brandenburg. Last week the Naval Operations Office began rounding up every fast big launch on the occupied coast - police boats, customs vessels and so forth. The flotilla is being assembled at Dordrecht.'

'With what purpose?'

'A pathfinder strike. One of the Brandenburg units attached to the 16th Army will attack Dover ahead of the main landings, to prevent the English sinking blockships in the harbour.

'A suicide squad no less, whose transport you now wish to borrow.'

'Precisely. What's more, Dordrecht lies directly opposite Bawdsey as the crow flies. In those boats, with the weather on our side, the crossing might take less than four hours.'

Heydrich leaned forward in his chair. 'How many nautical miles?'

'About one hundred and forty, each way.'

'Minefields?'

'The boats have a shallow draft.'

'So far so good, Schellenberg. But even if your force is only ashore for thirty minutes, the entire round trip could not be completed under cover of darkness.'

'The Luftwaffe can cover the tail end of the return journey. It'll give them something to do. In the last four days they've scarcely dropped a single bomb.'

Schellenberg's aside was well chosen. Himmler had harboured differences with the corpulent air force chief since wresting control of the Prussian Gestapo in 1934. Now mention of the Reichsmarschall provoked a brief and typically schoolmasterly lecture.

'Goring is misguided. He still clings to the belief that England will capitulate beneath a sustained aerial bombardment. He should listen less to Von Boetticher in Washington. That man completely misunderstands political sentiment in America.

Schellenberg pressed home his advantage. 'There's also the Russian question. If Germany moves east next year, we cannot afford to be drawn into a war on two fronts. The conquest on the British Isles has to be completed by the end of this year.'

Himmler's expression became grave. 'If, in a fit of insanity, I were to authorise this operation, when might it take place?'

'If our aim is to force OKW into crossing the Channel, no later than the first week in September. That would give all three services time to prepare fully for a full scale assault before the winter weather closes.'

Himmler made a minute adjustment to his pince-nez. 'The price of failure would be catastrophic, Schellenberg. In addition, you find yourself in competition for a scarce resource. Only yesterday an enterprising SPB officer submitted a proposal to parachute into the grounds of Buckingham Palace to seize the King and the royal household. With the Windsors under the protection of the armed SS, Hauptsturmfuhrer Bartels predicts a rapid end to the campaign.'

'I hope he finds better luck than I did in Lisbon with Wallace and Edward.'

'Indeed. King George is known to have stated that he intends to lead a British resistance movement. I have no intention of allowing such an eventuality.'

'By my timetable, Gruppe Bartels could complete both missions.'

'Not if they fail to return from the first. I don't discount your proposal, Schellenberg, but I'll need time to deliberate.'

'Forgive me, Reichsfuhrer, but we're now in the fourth week of August-'

Himmler waved an enigmatic hand. 'I know, Schellenberg - you want a decision. How long has Wagner been in custody?'

'Eighteen hours.'

'Will he be missed?'

'Not yet. He's on a three day pass.'

'Then you shall know my answer by noon tomorrow.' Himmler took up a paper from his in-tray, signalling that the meeting was at an end, but was struck by an afterthought.

'Is there a code-name I might conjure with?'

Schellenberg nodded. 'Rubikon, Reichsfuhrer.'

SEPTEMBER

FORTY

The second detainee was a short man in his mid-twenties, and quite clearly of oriental descent. Seated in the interview room of the small police station at Hythe, in his crumpled linen suit and dirty white shoes, the Eurasian spy could not have looked more incongruous.

'Charles van den Kieboom?' Morley demanded sternly.

'Is my name, yes.'

'Do you still claim to be a Dutch refugee?'

'Yes,' he answered slowly.

'Because earlier you told Major Beath that you paid a French fisherman four hundred francs to take you from the Cap Griz Nez to the English coast.'

'Yes, but-'

'And that you meant to travel to Liverpool, where you hoped to obtain a passage to Canada.'

'I was scared he would shoot me for a spy.'

'Are you a spy?'

'No! At least, I am not a real.'

That much was true. As he scribbled down the exchange in note form, Goodman found himself increasingly astonished that a man such as Kieboom could have been chosen as a field agent. Both his appearance and strong foreign accent made it plain to anyone of ordinary intelligence that he was not British, although Kieboom did at least speak more fluently than his colleague, Pons, whom Morley had finished interviewing fifteen minutes earlier, in a requisitioned seaside villa in Dymchurch. Now Goodman stifled a yawn - not because he had lately become blasé about Abwehr spies, but because of the mad sprint that morning from Norfolk to the Kent coast following Morley's dawn call.

'You don't look like a Dutchman,' continued Morley.

'Dutch subject. Born in Japan.'

'I see from your passport. You'd better tell me how you came to be here.'

'I train as clerk. Before war I was employed as a book-keeper and cashier at the YMCA in Amsterdam. Then mobilized as ambulance driver.'

'Is that where you met Sjoerd Pons?'

On learning that his colleague was known to his captors, Kieboom turned pale. 'Is Sjoerd dead?'

'No.'

'Where is he?'

'I'll ask the questions, Mr Kieboom, if you don't mind. Now, how did you meet Pons?'

Kieboom deflated visibly. 'We friends before the army, in Amsterdam.'

'Then what?'

'I was demobilised in June, after Dutch army was given up. I was without a job. No good back at YMCA.'

'Why?'

'They found out I do something with Pons.'

'That would be smuggling German currency across the border.'

Kieboom nodded.

'I see. How long were you out of work?'

'One month. Then German fellow approached me and ask whether I would be interested to do work for the German government.'

'Did he give you his name?'

'Jules Boeckel. I think him Gestapo.'

'Where did this meeting take place?'

'In a hotel bar, Amsterdam. He already knew everything about me.'

'He knew what, exactly?'

'Where I had worked. Where my army barracks, the name of my commanding officer. About my friendships.'

'Then what happened?'

'Two days later he invite me to lunch, to offer me translation work, and listen radio messages.'

'Did you accept?'

223

Kieboom hesitated. 'Yes. I needed money, you understand.'

'Did you introduce Pons to this man?'

'No. Pons had told him about me.'

Another contradiction. Goodman added a star in the margin of his notes.

'According to Pons, the pair of you then went to Brussels and stayed in a grand hotel.' Morley glanced at Goodman. 'Which one was it, Captain?'

'The Metropole.'

Kieboom shook his head. 'We stayed in a family pension. They fed us and give us money. Then after a week we begin some training. They took us to house where we take lessons in morse code.'

'Where was the house?'

'Vilvoorde.'

'How long did you stay there?'

'Maybe one month.'

'Did anyone else join you?'

'No.'

'What else did you learn?

Kieboom paused. 'They give Pons a wireless set. He learned more about that than me. We keep on asking what our duties would be, but they refuse to tell us nothing.'

'When were you told you'd be sent to England?'

'After about three weeks. They said we are expected to go to England and tell all the things that are here. How the people is living, how many soldiers there are. I refuse at once.'

'Then why are we having this conversation?'

Kieboom looked away. 'They started talking about what had happened before the war. That me and Pons are caught smuggling marks. They threaten to put me in prison in Germany if I did not work for them, give me two or three days to think it over. After that I accept.'

'What about Pons?'

'The same. Listen, they find all the people who had done something wrong against Germany. I know what it means to go to Germany. They said after I had been to England they forget all things I have done before.'

Morley paused to allow Goodman time to transcribe Kieboom's

outburst. 'When did you complete your training?'

'One week since. Then we are taken away to Brest.'

Goodman marked another star. According to Pons they had travelled to Boulogne.

'Where did you stay?'

'An empty house. I don't know the address. We arrived in the middle of the night. Not allowed to go outside. They gave us our last instructions yesterday and took a photograph, like a wedding. Then we were put on fishing boat.'

'When did you sail?'

'About five o'clock. Evening time. It was dark before we began. Two navy boats escort us. When we were near England they put us in a little boat and told us row north-west.'

'What time was that?'

'About midnight. Maybe one o'clock.'

'How long did you row?'

'Hours. Hours and more hours.'

'When did you land?'

'I don't know. I suppose just before I surrendered.'

'You suppose?'

'I don't look at my watch.'

'Do you know where you landed, or where you are now?'

Like Pons, Kieboom shook his head. Four hours earlier, shortly before five in the morning, a stand-to patrol from the Somerset Light Infantry had discovered a small rowing boat on the beach near Dymchurch, its oars still in the rawlocks. Minutes later a private glimpsed the shadow of a man move across the coast road, then disappear into the grass beside the sea wall. On challenging the figure, the soldier was confronted by a diminutive man dressed in civilian clothes, with field glasses and a spare pair of shoes slung around his neck. Kieboom had claimed to be a Dutch refugee, and asked to speak to an officer in order to explain his situation. On being searched he was found to be carrying a loaded Colt automatic. A quarter-hour later another Somerset patrol discovered a sack containing provisions, and a suitcase. Ten minutes later Pons was found changing his trousers behind a clump of reeds on Romney Marsh.

'Did you bring a wireless transmitter with you?' continued Morley.

225

'No.'

'Pons says you did.'

'He had it, not me. I told you, he learns all about wireless.'

'Why didn't you surrender as soon as you landed?'

'I did,' Kieboom protested loudly, becoming animated once more.

'No. You tried to hide below the sea wall. Then you told Major Beath a pack of lies.'

'I had a gun!' Kieboom's chin began to tremble, as though he were about to break down in tears. 'Because they told us if we not do as we told, Gestapo find us later when they came to England.'

Morley paused. 'Can you tell me when they're coming to England, Charles?'

Kieboom shook his head, then let it fall into his hands. A moment later his shoulders began to heave beneath the weight of silent sobs.

'Let's get some air,' Morley announced, scraping his chair noisily across the linoleum as he rose to his feet.

Kieboom looked up expectantly, hoping perhaps that the Englishman meant him to follow. Morley crushed the forlorn hope in an instant.

'Not you. Although I don't doubt that we'll be meeting again soon.'

Outside, Morley instructed a fresh-faced lieutenant from the Somersets to arrange for both prisoners to be transferred to secure police cells, and to continue the search for the wireless set on Romney Marsh. Then he and Goodman left the station and walked around the corner to the promenade, now choked with barbed wire and anti-tank obstacles. They paused beside an empty pillbox, disguised, not wholly convincingly, as an ice cream kiosk.

'And I thought Harry Johnson was badly prepared,' observed Goodman.

'If he wasn't a Jap I'd almost feel sorry for him.' Morley retrieved and lit a cigarette. 'How do you weigh the evidence? As a lawyer, I mean.'

'Kieboom will hang, as sure as night follows day. I'm not so sure about Pons. He seems keen to tell the truth.'

'Damned unhandy, mandatory hanging for spies. A live agent, even if he cannot transmit messages, is of some use as a reference

226

source. But a dead one is no sort of use, save for worms. Not squeamish about the death penalty are you, Goodman?'

'Not for spies. Why do you ask?'

'Because you might find yourself prosecuting those two. Or defend if you prefer, so long as you make a hash of it. How did you get on at Great Yarmouth, by the way?'

'Well enough. The navy landed about eighty survivors while I was there. I think the rest are being put ashore at Immingham.'

'So, fifty or sixty dead.'

'More like three hundred.'

'Three hundred!' Morley repeated incredulously. 'From one destroyer?'

'Two, actually. Both the Esk and Ivanhoe were sunk, and a third, Express, had her bows blown off. So far, not a single man from Esk has been accounted for, including the flotilla commander.'

'Good God. E-boats, was it?'

Goodman shook his head. 'An uncharted minefield north west of the Texel. In their eagerness to intercept this so-called invasion fleet spotted by the RAF, the flotilla ran straight into it. Single worst day for the Nore Command since Dunkirk.'

'And the barges?'

'Hard to say. Most of the survivors were adamant that's what they attacked. But no-one actually saw any.'

'Sounds to me like a fool's errand. I take it you launched my Chinese whisper?'

'Just as you suggested. They ferried most of the men to Norwich. I told the ambulance drivers to tell anyone who asked they were carrying the bodies of dead Germans washed up on the beaches. It went down a treat.'

'Good. We may want to float the rumour at other locations if it sticks up in Norfolk.'

'It may grow legs of its own, like the Angel of Mons. As a matter of fact, I gave it a spin.'

'Oh yes?' said Morley warily.

'I asked some of the dockers to put it about that they're being paid to clear bodies from the shoreline. Two shillings a corpse.'

Morley nodded. 'Two shillings is a bit steep for a German. Still, I like it. I'll pass it on to the black propaganda chaps at Woburn.'

The two fell silent as a sentry passed, and stared out across the waves towards the invisible French shore. Churchill could not have been more acute in his description of the veil of the unknown.

'Our visitors scream invasion imminent,' said Goodman.

'The owl and the pussycat? Quite possibly. Hun transports have been slipping down from the North Sea towards the Channel ports for the past two days. The weathermen say the tides will be suitable between the eighth and the tenth.'

'What about the air war?'

'Oh, we're shooting them down in droves alright. But they're crippling our airfields and sector stations. There's even been a mutiny by ground crew at Manston. They've refused to come out of the shelters. And we're losing pilots faster than we can replace them.' Morley finished his cigarette and ground the butt beneath his heel. 'This Texel scare won't help any. Half the General Staff are still convinced Jerry will land on the east coast, the upshot being that we've only got five divisions between Dover and north Cornwall.'

From behind them a voice called out. They turned to find the lieutenant from the Somerset Light Infantry jogging across the promenade towards them.

'Something up?' asked Morley.

'You won't believe it, sir, but another spy has turned up.'

'Where?'

'Lydd. In a bloody pub, if you please.'

FORTY-ONE

During the first three days in September the invasion of England was captured on film for the benefit of German newsreels. Because the first wave were timed to land at dawn on S-Day proper, at an hour when there would be insufficient light to shoot the decisive event of the European war, the pleasure beach at St Anne, across the River Schelde from the vast harbour at Antwerp, had been selected as a suitable substitute for the Kent coast. Now, before the cameras of the Propagandakompagnie, barges drew into the shore to disgorge light armour and motorcycle combinations onto the sandy beach, while troops in canvas lifejackets and field grey uniforms leapt cheerfully into the shallow water from assault boats, firing - and sometimes laughing - as they went.

Wagner lowered his field glasses. 'They should work in footage of English prisoners too. Or are the massacres at Wormhoudt and Le Paradis now standing orders for the Waffen SS?'

'Thanks to Dunkirk, the PK already have an abundance of footage of Tommies with their hands in the air,' Schellenberg replied.

Wagner turned to Eichner. 'Bartels and his men are crossing the North Sea in motor boats. Even in calm weather they'll arrive in no condition to fight.'

'I've seen dozens of men throw up before going into combat,' countered Eichner. 'Did it myself outside Warsaw in September.'

'It's a question of exhaustion, not just nausea.'

'Whick makes it all the more important for your men to do their job properly,' observed Schellenberg coolly.

'The job being?'

'To secure the gully which connects the beach with the main DeTe site.'

'Then what, assuming Bartels and his men get off the beach alive.'

'The principal target is the transmitter bunker.'

'And the steel towers,' Eichner added.

'All four of them?'

Eichner nodded. 'Even with one mast standing the station can still function.'

'We'll need some big hacksaws.'

'H15 hollow charges. They weigh about twelve kilos each, and punch through seventeen centimetres of steel. Two dozen should take care of the footings, and get Bartels through the door.'

Without enthusiasm, Wagner continued to put the questions that he supposed were expected of him. 'Any secondary targets?'

'There's a receiver block to the south. The wooden towers are less important. Even if we knock them down the English can replace them in a matter of hours.'

All three became temporarily preoccupied with the progress of a waterproofed schnorkel tank, which emerged from the water on the opposite bank like a prehistoric steel amphibian.

'Fire the manor house if you get the chance,' Schellenberg continued casually. 'Kill everyone you find there.'

'Do you have a date in mind for this happy little outing?'

'Four days from now,' replied Eichner. 'Sailing on the evening of the seventh, and attacking during the early hours of the eighth. Your men will have to be in position two or three hours beforehand. Can you be ready?'

'I don't have any choice in the matter. But there is the small matter of my commanding officer.'

'Who is he?' asked Schellenberg.

'As far as this goes, Colonel Erwin Lahousen.'

'Leave him to me.'

'What about heavy support? Without that your operation begins to resemble the charge of the Light Brigade.'

'S-boats, with twenty millimetre cannon.'

'They'll be busy protecting themselves. Has the navy agreed to any of this?'

'Naturally,' Schellenberg replied shortly. He saw no reason to reveal that Himmler had authorised Rubikon only twenty-four hours earlier, as a consequence of which the detailed preparations would have to be completed in a unseemly rush. 'Now, can the plan succeed?'

Wagner rubbed his chin. 'As an excuse for another solemn decoration ceremony at the Chancellory, it scans nicely. As a military operation, it's suicidal.'

'How so?'

'It's a frontal assault against an elevated position, without adequate support.'

'According to your own report, Bawdsey is poorly defended.'

'That was two months ago. Since the air war intensified the defences will be stronger. And they surely know we've been before.'

Wagner's negative evaluation nettled Schellenberg. 'Rubikon offers you a chance for redemption. Really, leutnant, you should be more grateful.'

'For a bit part in a massacre? I don't think so.'

'Sachsenhausen,' Schellenberg replied coolly. 'I can provide confirmation within the hour. Above the signature of the Reichsführer SS.'

'Screw you.'

'As for the girl, I have Buchenwald in mind. Then of course there's your men...'

Wagner turned sharply away and looked across the river to St Anne, where the filming was now in recess. The invaders stood around in small groups, chatting and smoking, some sporting photogenic wounds, others cheering at a raft covered with engineers, which had broken loose and was drifting away down the Schelde. Laughing loudest of all were the men of Gruppe Bartels, clearly visible in the distinctive camouflage smocks of the Waffen SS.

It would be churlish, Wagner mused, to deny them a little amusement. For after all, four days from now each and every one of them would be stone dead and far from home.

FORTY-TWO

The warm sunlight which bathed the Tirpitzufer was unusually bright for September, but thankfully less intense than the withering heat of August. Behind the doors of the Fox Hole, however, the mood of the chief of intelligence was dark. For Hummer Nord, the renewed Abwehr intelligence offensive against England, had claimed its first casualty.

'How did it happen?' Canaris demanded impatiently.

Ritter was obliged to shout above the static on the line between Berlin and Hamburg. 'The four of them staged a send-off at the Lowenbrau before leaving for Stavanger. Dierks tied one on, as usual. On the way back to his apartment he took a corner too fast and rolled the car on Sierichstrasse. He died instantly.'

'The damned fool!'

'It was probably the cobblestones. There was a slight fall of rain earlier in the evening.'

Canaris appeared not to hear. 'What about the other three?'

'Cuts and bruises only. Erikson is in mild shock. She and Dierks were... close.'

'I know they were lovers,' Canaris said sharply, his tone disapproving. 'Well, press on and fix a new departure date. Erikson will just have to pull herself together.'

'Herr Admiral, with Hans dead we can hardly send the three of them to Scotland alone.'

'Nor can we call off Hummer Nord with OKW on our backs. I want Dierks' team in Scotland within ten days, understood?'

'Perfectly, sir.'

'Now, I take it the four men bound for the south coast left according to schedule?'

'Boeckel saw them off from Le Touquet. Waldberg has sent

232

back several messages already.'

'Anything useful?'

Ritter hesitated. 'They are slightly confused. Unfortunately Meier's already been captured.'

'Hardly surprising. And the two Dutchmen? I forget their names.'

'Pons and Kieboom, sir. No word yet.'

Canaris released a melodramatic sigh. Pressure of time, and Johnson's startling success, had swayed Stelle X into sending agents to their chosen operational zones by perilously direct routes. 'This is beginning to sound like Ireland all over again. How do you rate their chances?'

'Of survival, or success?'

'I know no difference.'

'They've all received adequate training. Waldberg has been with us since 1938.' Ritter paused. 'As for success, who can say? Unlike Johnson they can't fall back on the Welsh ring.'

'What about the Swede, Caroli?'

'We hope to drop him over Oxfordshire tomorrow night. As you know, the weather was against us last week.'

'Good,' replied Canaris. 'Keep me informed. And I want to see the full text of Waldberg's messages.'

'Very good, Herr Admiral.'

No sooner had Ritter rung off than the telephone rang again. Canaris cast his eyes upwards and bunched his fists, then snatched up the handset and barked: 'Yes?'

'Colonel Lahousen, sir,' announced his aide, Jencke. 'Calling from Antwerp.'

'I'm busy.'

'He said it can't wait.'

Canaris paused, then sighed wearily: 'Very well.'

A moment later Lahousen's voice came on line, more clearly than Ritter.

'Admiral?'

'What is it?'

'Can you scramble?'

Canaris grunted irritably, but punched down the button. 'Well?'

'It's Leutnant Wagner. Two weeks ago you told me to make him disappear.'

'So I did.'

'Well, Schellenberg found him. And now he's got Himmler's approval for a raid on the English coast at Bawdsey, with a force of Waffen SS troops.'

The Admiral sat bolt upright in his chair. 'When?'

'The night of the seventh. Gruppe Wagner is to land in advance of the main attack. A pathfinder force, if you will.'

'Out of the question. I trust you told Schellenberg so.'

'Unfortunately the situation is a little complicated. Schellenberg had Wagner tailed. He got himself involved with a girl in Antwerp, and ended up braining some SD goon with a bottle.'

'Unfortunate, I'm sure, but hardly a capital offence.'

'The girl is a Jew. She defaced some proclamation posters. Schellenberg has threatened to have her family resettled in the east if Wagner refuses to co-operate. He's threatened Wagner with Sachsenhausen too.'

'For assaulting some halfpenny stooge?'

'And consorting with Jews, and listening to jazz music.'

'Jazz?' Canaris repeated, his tone incredulous.

'It's blackmail. But Schellenberg has Himmler and Heydrich squarely behind him.'

'What do Amt IV hope to achieve?'

'Officially, this Operation Rubikon is intended to test the strength of the English coastal defences. The real agenda is to contradict our reports, and persuade OKW to press ahead with the invasion. Schellenberg is looking to influence the Fuhrer. And he wants the flotilla at Dordrecht.'

Canaris gave a snort of derision. 'I suppose Seppel and Sabine are commandeered too.'

'Schellenberg is interested less in dachshunds than in scapegoats.'

The admiral paused, then asked: 'Is their plan a good one?'

'At present it's more an idea. A captain on Schellenberg's staff is in the driving seat, name of Eichner.'

'I know of him.

Momentarily the conversation lapsed into silence. After several empty seconds Lahousen enquired: 'How should we proceed?'

'I can't see how we can stop it. That tyke Schellenberg has us over a barrel. You'd better place Wagner at his disposal, for the time being at least. The Dordrecht boats too.'

'Sir?' the colonel enquired uncertainly.

'Schellenberg may have succeeded famously at Venlo, Lahousen, but this Rubikon adventure is quite different to kidnapping two dozy English agents from a tea room. Only yesterday the Fuhrer postponed his decision on Sealion until the twentieth. This Rubikon business is sure to go the same way.'

'There's always hope.' Lahousen paused. 'By the way, Dierks is dead.'

'I know. I spoke to Ritter ten minutes ago.'

'Did he tell you that Meier has been captured?'

'Yes.'

'Perhaps I should return to Berlin.'

'Really, I see no need. Let me speak to Schellenberg. I'll wager ten marks to a pfennig his men never sail.'

'Very well, Herr Admiral. I'll leave it in your hands.'

'And on my head. Goodnight, colonel.'

After Lahousen rang off, Canaris sat motionless in his chair for several minutes, lost in thought. Presently he rose and crossed the floor of his office to the balcony, four storeys above the street. For the chief of intelligence the sudden turn of events was devastating. Schellenberg's plan was a declaration of war on the Abwehr, nothing less, and aptly named. For the sudden arrival of the operation code-named Rubikon now required a decision which, in his heart of hearts, Wilhelm Canaris had recognised was inevitable since the previous September.

His balcony afforded the Admiral a fine view of both the Tiergarten and the Landwehrkanal. Surveying them now in the late summer sunlight, his own past surged through his memory on a flood-tide of melancholy. In 1934 he had been marking time as the commandant of a fortress at Swinemunde on the Baltic, a posting that should have been his last before retirement with the rank of Rear-Admiral. Then, in November, quite without warning, Raeder had appointed him chief of intelligence. Not, in truth, because his superior recognised a born spy, or had any great liking for his chosen nominee, but because Raeder was prepared to pay any price to prevent the army from wresting control of the Abwehr. For Canaris, the choice between a comfortable, well-earned retirement and a new and demanding career was no choice at all. While never a Party member, he had approved of Germany's strong economy, and of the rapid rearmament programme, particularly in respect of the fleet. Not before time, his Fatherland had freed itself of the shackles imposed at Versailles, and for four years Canaris had worked assiduously in the service of a Germany which might re-assume its rightful position as a world power.

But he had misread Hitler entirely, and clung far too long to the belief that the Generals were capable of controlling the former corporal, and to oust him if necessary. Now, following the fall of Poland and France, the truth was plain for even a blind man to see. In conquering half of Europe Germany had alienated at least two-thirds of the world, and no nation in all history had succeeded in holding such intense hostility in abeyance. Italy was weak, Spain uncommitted, Japan too far removed. Already Germany had reached its industrial and military limits, and, like the Hohenzollern state, could field at best no more than two hundred and fifty divisions. The Reich was unbeatable to a point, perhaps, but nowhere near capable of sustaining a thousand-year dream of unlimited empire.

Canaris was a German and a patriot. He had performed his military duties for the Fuhrer according to the standards of the Imperial officers under whom he had trained. Lately, however, and in common with many other field commanders, he had lived each moment of victory, from Poland to the English Channel, in the certain knowledge that Germany was not capable of winning Hitler's war. The failure of Operation Sealion, hastily planned and disastrously uncoordinated, against a background of defeat in the air, was a foregone conclusion. Now, in the shape of Rubikon, it was within the power of Walter Schellenberg to bring about this calamity.

On the Tirpitzufer below a tram rattled to a halt and disgorged its human cargo, several of them Abwehr personnel. Canaris had never condoned murder or assassination, much less of his own countrymen. Surely a company of Waffen SS was an acceptable price to pay for the salvation of tens of thousands of ordinary German servicemen? Cold, dispassionate reason told him so. And yet...

And yet if thousands had to die, better that they did so fighting Bolshevism in Russia in six months' time, rather than in England

236

in less than one.

This, he told himself, as bitter salt tears whelmed in his eyes, was the law of retribution from which neither individuals or nations could escape.

And yet...

Canaris closed his eyes. To think that, in 1935, he had fondly imagined that he might reach an accommodation with the SS and Gestapo authorities. Indeed less than a month ago he had ridden with Schellenberg beneath the trees of the Tiergarten. The irony was far from sweet.

With heavy heart, Canaris returned to his desk and summoned Jencke. Arrangements would have to be made with Gisevious in Berne. For one year to the day after the outbreak of war with England, the time had come to talk with Halina.

FORTY-THREE

At the Sportpalast in Berlin on September fourth, Adolf Hitler had made an impassioned address to a rally of nurses and social workers. To the delight of his fevered audience, the Fuhrer entreated the population of England to remain calm; his armies, he promised, would be crossing the Channel soon. Very soon.

The weight of these words hung heavy on the minds of the three men gathered in a spartan London bedroom situated fifty feet below the rear of the Board of Trade building opposite St James's Park. The Prime Minister, whose private chamber it was, sat propped up on a camp bed, resplendent in a red dressing gown and silk slippers, each embroidered with the initials W.C. His box, half full of papers, stood open beside his bed, and strategically positioned by his side was a large chrome-plated cuspidor. His black cat, Nelson, temporarily transplanted from Downing Street, sprawled leisurely at the foot of the bed. In the stygian gloom of the Cabinet War Rooms this quaint scene resembled a tarnished Flemish portraiture in need of careful restoration.

It was the first full night that the Prime Minister had spent in the depths of the Hole, and already he found the pervasive smell of fresh concrete most disagreeable. Looking up from the document Menzies that had placed before him, Churchill released a low growl.

'Menzies, you shall open the meeting, with or without Harker. As soon as I've finished my whisky soda or my cigar, whichever comes sooner.'

'I'd be only too pleased, Prime Minister.'

Major-General Sir Stewart Menzies, Director of MI6, had called the meeting at immediate notice shortly before midnight. His opposite number at MI5, Brigadier Jasper Harker, was already ten minutes late. In common with others in the intelligence community, Menzies considered Harker an inadequate guardian of the security service, and was lobbying hard for a new Director-General to be appointed over his head. Harker's tardiness tonight served his cause admirably.

The third man was General Sir Hastings Ismay, assistant secretary to the War Cabinet, and the main channel of communication between Churchill and the Chiefs of Staff. Ismay, enured already to the foibles of the Prime Minister, had calculated with some certainty that the Prime Minister would pull twice more on his cigar before discarding it when a knock sounded on the door.

It was Harker, ushered inside by a Royal Marine guard, and followed by Major Morley.

'Terribly sorry,' Harker apologised, with little conviction. 'Nothing to be done. Got held up at a barricade on Horse Guards. Prize idiots, those Coldstream.'

'Menzies has promised a red box special,' Churchill declared impatiently. 'Given the lateness of the hour, a red eye special might be a more fitting appellation. I trust that what the Director has to say is sufficiently important to bypass the Joint Intelligence Committee, and keep the rest of us from our beds.' He turned to Menzies. 'Does SIS have the invasion date?'

'After a fashion, Prime Minister. What I can tell you is that the enemy are coming, and somewhat sooner than expected.'

'We've all heard the radio, Stewart,' Ismay observed drily. 'Bloody point of the Nazi spear pointing toward our shore, and all that.'

'Forget Hitler and Haw-Haw. On the night of September seventh an enemy raiding force will attack Bawdsey Manor, the RDF station on the coast near Felixstowe. As you may recall, they carried out a reconnaissance in June.'

Churchill turned to Ismay. 'Did I not say, Pug, that I should have demanded a stronger nightcap?'

'Is this Ultra?' demanded Harker abruptly.

Menzies shook his head.

'Then what is your source?'

'SIS Z network,' replied Menzies tersely. 'Better to leave it at that.'

'Beg to differ, Stewart. This is hardly chicken-feed. Dates, location - it sounds too good to be true.'

Menzies glanced at Morley and Harker, then back to Churchill: 'Prime Minister, my source is Ultra Top Secret.'

'I am sure you may trust the home service,' Churchill assured the Director.

Morley cursed inwardly. 'Very well. Our source is Admiral Wilhelm Canaris.'

'Good Lord!' gasped Ismay.

'Better late than never,' muttered Churchill.

'Do we have more detail?' ventured Morley.

'A little. The force earmarked for Bawdsey are Waffen SS. They will come by sea, in company strength. I invited Morley along tonight because the good admiral expressed a wish that they be burned alive.'

'Amen to that,' said Churchill. 'If Operation Twenty has hit the bullseye, then Major Morley is to be congratulated. Although if I remember correctly, that scheme was intended to keep the enemy at bay.'

Harker looked from the Prime Minister to Menzies in astonishment. 'Could someone please explain to me how this contact came about?'

The Director waited for Churchill's nod before replying. 'Our agent - Z51 - is Halina Szymanska, the wife of the former Polish military attache in Berlin. He was the Polish General Staff's German expert, and currently languishes in a Russian jail. Madame Halina has been close to Canaris for two years. Last December he arranged safe passage to Switzerland for her and her daughters, after which she knocked on the door of the Polish Legation in Berne, who kindly passed her on to us.'

'And they're...?'

Menzies nodded. 'They meet in Paris as and when his schedule allows. SIS have supplied her with a set of false papers in the name of a French subject.'

Harker considered this a moment, then said disparagingly: 'And we're supposed to believe that Canaris is free with his pillow talk.'

'Not at all. There exists between Madame Halina and Canaris a tacit understanding that anything he may care to disclose will be passed on to our Berne station. By avoiding direct contact, he feels that his own hands remain clean of treachery. He's a curiously moral man. Religious too. So far it's been tittle-tattle, inconsequential political manoeuvrings in Berlin. Now suddenly this.'

'If you want my opinion, the whole thing reeks of double-cross,' declared Harker.

Menzies shook his head. 'It may be our biggest break since the Oslo report. We ignored that. Let's not make the same mistake twice.'

'I simply don't understand why,' said Ismay. 'After all, Canaris is head of the Abwehr.'

'We've known for a year that he's anti-Hitler. There undoubtedly exists a resistance movement in Germany, comprising patriots and generals. It's simply that the information we received prior to Norway and France via the Vatican was so fluid as to be useless.'

Churchill swirled the last of his whisky in the bottom of his glass. 'It is only natural that Harker is sceptical, Menzies. The generals can hardly free Germany from Nazi tyranny between breakfast and dinner. But I'm troubled as to why, if the admiral has decided to betray his own cause, should he now pass us this single detail? I would have thought he might have given us rather more, and given it sooner.'

'As I said, Prime Minister, previous contacts have been indirect. Z51 has been passed information by an Abwehr middleman in Berne. I suspect Canaris lacked time, or felt he was unable to risk using an intermediary given the weight of this latest matter. It may be significant that SS troops are involved, rather than regular Wehrmacht.'

'Himmler's private army,' said Churchill contemptuously. 'I am well aware of it. Their insignia is a silver death's head.'

'Quite so. And we know there exists a deep antipathy between the SS and the Abwehr.'

Churchill re-lit his cigar and fixed the Director through an impressive cloud of grey smoke. 'Supposing this intelligence were genuine. Are we to believe that the admiral's purpose is merely to have us aid political in-fighting in Germany?'

'Would it matter? Ultimately we all desire to defeat Hitler.'

'I still say it could be a blind,' rejoined Harker.

'Canaris provided some collateral. Tonight the Luftwaffe are going to drop an agent over Oxfordshire, a Swede. If he turns up as promised, I'd say we're in business.'

'That gives our RSLO rather a lot of countryside to stake out in one night.'

'Could be the Twenty experience,' offered Morley cautiously. 'CRACKER had a close shave on landing. It may have put them off sending precise co-ordinates. Besides, it would be unreasonable to assume that each and every agent dispatched to the United Kingdom is destined for the SNOW network.'

'Or it could be a double-cross,' Harker persisted stubbornly.

'Come, come, Jasper - do you really believe that the Abwehr can afford to throw away good agents?'

'Perhaps not. But bad ones are another matter. Take those four jokers who washed up at Hythe and Dungeness.'

'It occurs to me,' pronounced Churchill, 'that if Canaris truly wishes to see the invasion defeated, and Hitler deposed, those four spies sent to Kent could have been markers.'

Harker addressed Morley. 'What about it? You've been interrogating them with Stephens at Latchmere House for the last two days.'

'It's conceivable,' allowed Morley. 'There's no denying they were poorly prepared. But the German, Waldberg, got three messages away before he was captured. These seem to relate to proposed landing zones.'

'Seem?' queried Churchill.

'They're hopelessly garbled. I brought the texts with me, as a matter of fact. Here: "Arrived safely - document destroyed - English patrol two hundred metres from coast - beach with brown nets and railway sleepers at a distance of fifty metres - three hundred metres south water reservoir painted red." That's as good as it gets. Nothing so useful as map co-ordinates.'

'Such intelligence is hardly likely to facilitate the establishment of the Nazi bridgehead,' the Prime Minister observed drily.

'Was Waldberg the chap they arrested in the pub?' asked Menzies.

'No, that was Meier, another Dutchman. Tried to order a glass of champagne cider at half past nine in the morning. To judge from Waldberg's signal, he perhaps met with greater success in a bar elsewhere.'

'A landing in Kent and Sussex ties in with the latest photo reconnaissance,' offered Ismay. 'The evidence of growing barge concentrations is unmistakable. Within the last four days more than one hundred have arrived at Flushing alone, and fifty self-propelled vessels at Cap Griz-Nez.'

'In which case, Alan Brooke might wish to re-think our dispositions,' said Menzies. 'Half the army is still tied up on the east coast.'

'I still say it could be a double-bluff,' pressed Harker. 'Think the thing through. Send four fools over to the south coast, in full knowledge that they'll be captured, but guessing we'll smell a rat, and focus on the east coast instead. Throw in this Bawdsey feint, then Jerry hops across the Channel from France anyway, and takes London inside forty-eight hours.'

'I fear the brigadier would lead us into a wilderness of mirrors,' said Churchill.

'I believe we should act,' declared Ismay. 'The very least we can do is warn every unit that seaborne raids can be expected between the sixth and the tenth.'

Morley cleared his throat. 'With respect, sir, we can do far more than place Home Forces on high alert.'

'Another grand scheme, Morley?' Harker seemed determined to kick down every statue.

'I make no apology, sir. This demands a sequel. The Abwehr sent over CRACKER to gather evidence of flame defences. We served it up on a plate, and sent him home. Now they're sending a probe. Armed with this warning we can promise them a very warm reception indeed.'

Ismay leaned forward in his chair. 'You mean fire a flame weapon at Bawdsey?'

'Precisely. Drench them with mustard too if we have to. Anything to give them such a bloody nose that they'll think twice before dispatching an army across the water. I'll wager my boots that's precisely what Canaris has in mind.'

'Lured like moths to a flame,' mused Churchill, with evident pleasure.

'If nothing else, the propaganda value could be immeasurable,' said Menzies.

'Like the French fleet at Oran,' agreed Ismay. 'If we succeed, it would do a great deal to convince the American public that Britain's no quitter.'

Churchill shook his head. 'It is better that the Americans see us as victims, not victors. As you know, six hours ago President Roosevelt finally ratified the agreement by which he will lend to us fifty destroyers in exchange for leases on naval bases in Newfoundland and the West Indies. To my mind it marks a giant step forward in American commitment to eventual war with Germany. But it's also a necessary admission that we're incapable of continuing the fight unaided. To safeguard the flow of war materials across the Atlantic an impression of weakness must be maintained.'

'Does the Petroleum Warfare Department have the necessary equipment?' enquired Menzies.

'Almost certainly. We have a date, and a location. Two dozen fuel bowsers should do it, with a heavy concentration of conventional weapons. I understand a new ignition system for the flame barrage was successfully tested on the Solent ten days ago.'

'But can these rude mechanicals be arranged in three days?' asked Churchill. 'Major Morley, I am most reluctant to allow any German within ten miles of our shores. I'd far sooner have Bomber Command blow them out of the water halfway across, and drown them in the salt sea. Might the fireship scheme not achieve your purpose.'

In war, as in peace, Churchill remained a curious amalgam of the radical and the traditionalist. Operation Lucid involved sailing tramp oil tankers into the enemy ports, in an effort to replicate Drake's success at Cadiz four centuries before. Having read the proposal, Morley recognised a suicide mission.

'Prime Minister,' he began, 'I know little of Lucid, but I do know that Agar is nowhere near ready to sail.'

Churchill rose slowly from his bunk, and for half a minute surveyed the East Anglian coastline on a huge wall-mounted map of the British Isles. His back still turned, he intoned gravely: 'At Harrow a gardener once told me that the juniper plant could be used as an abortificant. Hence its rustic sobriquet: bastard-killer.'

'Prime Minister?' asked Ismay uncertainly.

'I am devising a code-name, Pug. Canaris warns us that they will send troops of the dread SS. The same elite force I hear butchered our men on the road to Dunkirk.'

'And guard the camps in the east,' added Menzies darkly.

'There you have it!' declared the Prime Minister, turning back to face the room. 'Our objective at Bawdsey is to kill bastards. Plenty of fire and brimstone and soft-nosed bullets. Neglect no means, and make haste.'

'Thank you, Prime Minister.'

'Thank you, Major Morley,' Churchill replied with emphasis. 'But remember this. You must have no hesitation in cancelling Juniper and calling upon the services of the fleet and the air arm should you discern the slightest chance of the Nazis gaining a lodgement in Suffolk. No hesitation at all.'

FORTY-FOUR

Just as Goodman picked up the receiver at the desk Sophie walked into the lobby of the Excelsior Hotel, carrying her overnight case and looking a little self-conscious. Goodman pulled a sympathetic face, then nodded towards the lounge where a vacant window seat overlooked Felixstowe beach from the north cliff.

He watched as Sophie sat down, and noticed that she looked a little drawn. The rigors, no doubt, of the four-day watch. The next moment a too-familiar voice came on the line.

'Morley here. Sorry to disturb.'

'This had better be good,' said Goodman testily.

'You could say that. Stay where you are, though - I'll be coming up to the Manor first thing tomorrow morning.'

'I can meet you at the gatehouse. What time?'

'About eight, I should think. Business to take care of at this end. Forgive my curiosity, but I take it that you're with the charming Miss Gold.'

'Yes.'

'And you've mentioned nothing about your encounter with our American friend?'

'Not a whisper.'

'Good, because I'm lifting the embargo.'

Goodman frowned. 'I'm not really sure I want to tell her.'

'Well you're in luck, because I've taken the decision for you. There's a good chance Wagner may pay another call. Can't say any more on the blower - careless talk and all that. If I get up country earlier I'll look you up at your hotel.'

The line went dead before Goodman could protest. He felt his heart sink into his boots. Although he had been with the security service for less than a week, already Goodman understood that his

246

life was not his own. True, the mews flat off the Cromwell Road was delightful, and the south coast spies a diverting assignment. Yet now, for the first time, he experienced a sharp stab of guilty nostalgia for his irregular Field Security routine at GHQ, and sensed it would not be the last.

'I need a stiff drink,' announced Sophie as he sat down beside her. 'What's more, I deserve it.'

'Have I grown horns?'

She took his hand in hers. 'Don't be an ass. Just be aware that your lover is a real live heroine.'

'Oh?'

Sophie nodded. 'One of the riggers froze on a TX tower this afternoon. I volunteered to climb up and coax him down.'

'And did you?'

'Of course. I can persuade any man to do anything.'

'I hope you didn't go too far.'

'Oh, all the way. Three hundred and sixty feet.'

Goodman smiled. 'You'll get a reputation.'

'I already have,' she laughed. 'Everyone's taken to calling me Tarzan.'

'Let me get you that drink. Jungle juice, is it?'

'I'll settle for a brandy.'

When Goodman returned from the bar with the glasses Sophie took a generous swallow, their reached into her pocket and handed him a plain buff envelope.

'Actually, there's something else,' she said quietly.

The gum was already unsealed. Inside Goodman found a one-way rail warrant to Ashington in Northumberland, and felt his spirits sink once more. 'You're being posted?

'It's called rotation. To a CH called Ottercops Moss, bang in the middle of nowhere, where there's nothing to do but count the crows. It's just not fair. They warned us when we joined that we'd be moved every three months, but there are girls who've been at Bawdsey for at least six.'

'When do you go?'

'The date's on the warrant, silly.'

Goodman looked down as the slip. Twelve days hence. She shifted closer to him.

'The RAF don't like you being happy for too long.'

He paused. 'You may be needed here.'

'By who - MI5?'

'Maybe.'

Sophie took up her glass and drained it. 'I'm sorry, John, but I'm not really in the mood for jokes tonight.'

'I'm serious. That was Morley on the line. He's coming up here tomorrow.'

'Why?'

'Not exactly sure.'

'I'm not sure I want to play at Mata Hari, if that's what all this is leading to. I like being a CH operator.'

'That's not what I meant.' Goodman paused, summoning courage and wondering how much to reveal. 'The thing is, when you came to see me at Shotley, I told you I'd been injured in a training accident.'

'Which was a big fat lie.'

Goodman dropped his voice to a whisper. 'Truth is, I got tangled up with a German landing party.'

'It was the CHL at Hopton, wasn't it?'

'Yes. How did you know?'

'The grapevine's been alive with rumours. They put it about that some troops from the VP Wing flipped their lids, but no-one believed it for a minute. Then there was all that hoo-hah about ambulances convoys and dead Germans.'

Goodman hesitated. 'Look Sophie, there's no easy way of telling you this. I think the man in charge of the landing party was Paul Wagner.'

Sophie set down her glass on the table.

'Oh.'

'I would have told you before, but Morley blue-pencilled it.'

Still Sophie offered no real reply. Although Goodman had scarcely dared second guess her reaction, he had expected something more than quiet resignation.

'You don't seem very surprised.'

She shrugged her shoulders. 'Ever since the war broke out I've wondered if he went back to Germany, if he's fighting. Can you be sure it was him?'

'How many Americans are serving in the Germany army, and hum It Had to Be You?'

'Not many, I suppose. What did he look like?'

'My height and build, a few years younger. Probably better looking. Then again, it was dark.'

'Perhaps the Nazis have forced him.'

Goodman steeled himself and leaned towards her. 'He's an officer, Sophie, in a special purpose unit. They operate in British uniforms, and his men killed Sergeant Kydd in cold blood. What's more, we're probably the only two people in the country who can recognise him. And now Morley thinks he may be coming back.'

Sophie tensed visibly. 'To Bawdsey?'

Goodman nodded.

Sophie stared out through the window, towards the beach strewn with scaffold, wire and mines. 'You know, Northumberland seems suddenly very appealing. Funny how quickly things change.'

'If I could, I'd have told you before.'

'It's not that,' she sighed. 'It's not even him. Once I leave all we've got to look forward to are letters, and a few seven-day passes that never coincide. I love you, John, but I'm scared that it won't be enough to keep our love alive.'

'It can if we try,' he reassured her softly.

They sat in silence, and watched as an elderly man began to erect the first of several black-out screens mounted in stout wooden frames.

Darkness falling down.

FORTY-FIVE

In the closing hours of September fifth a force of eighty-two Bomber Command aircraft took off from bases in Yorkshire, Lincolnshire and East Anglia, and set course for assorted targets from Turin to Stettin. Among them were four Handley-Page Hampden medium bombers of Number 22 Operational Training Unit, operating from its home base at Waddington near Lincoln. The Hampden had entered service in 1938, but by 1940 was already outclassed, boasting a meagre bomb load of two thousand pounds and a maximum airspeed of two hundred and fifty miles per hour. Of the four OTU crews, only one could be called experienced, the others having completed between them no more than a dozen uneventful sea sweeps, and even fewer night operations. It was anticipated, however, that attacks on the invasion ports would be a relatively safe exercise for novice crews, since such 'barge-bashing' runs entailed little more than a quick dash over the enemy coast, rather than hours of stooging over blacked-out territory, high on altitude and low on fuel.

In an effort to avoid interception by German radar the bombers flew in low across the North Sea, then swung overland around Vlissingen at the mouth of the Schelde to avoid the fierce anti-aircraft barrage already in progress. The moon made it easy to follow the broad western course of the river directly to Antwerp, where, in accordance with 5 Group standing instructions, each aircraft had been assigned a specific target. The lead Hampden, S-Sugar, would attack the giant Kattendijkdok, in which photo reconnaissance had revealed two large steamers and at least fifty densely-packed landing barges.

Unbeknownst to the British airmen, the northern end of the long basin also contained the motor torpedo boat which was due to carry Paul Wagner and his men across the North Sea to the Suffolk coast. Lahousen had joined Wagner on the bridge of the S-boat only a short time earlier, a flat tyre outside Turnhout having delayed his journey considerably. Besides Wagner, two other men made up the Brandenburg component of Operation Rubikon. Schrek was a seasoned veteran of all three previous landings, while Dorper was a new arrival, a radio operator who had spent two years at the Slade art school in London.

As yet, none of them had changed into British uniforms. Lahousen handed the overprinted Ordnance Survey map back to Wagner. 'What unit will you be impersonating?'

'Signals Corps. The ordinary army units in the area will have changed since we paid our last visit.'

'I assumed Bartels would be here.'

'On his way back from the Baltic. His men have been attacking the Halligen Islands for a solid week.'

'I assume you'll guide them in with the short wave.'

'Too risky, sir,' said Dorper.

Wagner nodded. 'I plan to send up a flare as they start their final run-in. Green for go, red for danger. Bartels can aim for the point below the flare.'

'The defile?'

'If all goes well.'

Now the attention of each man on the bridge was distracted by the deadly activity in the night sky three thousand feet above. Although Antwerp was not yet protected by night fighters or heavy anti-aircraft cannon, the hailstorm of light flak from the guns lining both sides of the river had been successful in breaking up the small formation of Hampdens from 22 OTU. The result, as intended, was disastrous. Within seconds one of the four bombers sat naked and defenceless atop a cone of blinding white light from several searchlight beams, and surrounded instantly by vari-coloured tracer rounds. Only after a shell had exploded directly inside the bomb bay did the numbed pilot take evasive action, but by then the aircraft was already on fire. With both the port and starboard fuel tanks pierced, and with the first of thousands of rounds of ammunition on board beginning to explode, the bomber came to resemble the hot end of a rocket. Searing heat quickly melted the aluminium floor, leaving a gaping hole through which the rear-gunner had no option but to bale out.

The bridge of the S-boat afforded the Abwehr men a grandstand view of the raid as it unfurled. All gazed up in horrified awe as the stricken aircraft limped north-east for half a minute like a slow motion comet, then detonated above the suburbs in a lurid ball of flame.

Wagner watched as the gunner's parachute drifted down through the arcing tracer towards the waters of the Schelde. 'Let's hope they swim better than they fly.'

'Is it like this every night?' asked Lahousen.

The skipper of the S-boat lowered his binoculars. 'Getting worse day by day. Take a look around. There's transports everywhere, and the docksides are piled high with equipment. A blind man could see what's going on.'

'Are there men on the ferries?'

'Just horses and mules.'

From the vicinity of the Asiadok came a blinding white flash, followed by the dull crump of high explosive.

'Someone hit something, at least,' Wagner observed.

'Hardly a patriotic sentiment, leutnant,' Lahousen said wryly.

'What with all these costume changes you can get confused. Maybe I should send up a flare and thumb a ride.'

Lahousen raised his arm and pointed toward the far end of the Kattendijkdok. 'I fear you've tempted fate.'

Wagner turned to look. S-Sugar, the lead Hampden, flew in straight and level over the Willemdok at two hundred feet. The pilot took his time, keen to ensure that every bomb hit the spot. The run-in triggered a sudden surge in the volume of fire from the flak batteries, with tracer now spraying up almost indiscriminately in all directions. Multicoloured strings of orange, red and green hosed upwards towards the lone aircraft, some forming a curious s-shaped bend as the gunners swung their barrels around.

'Coming straight for us,' the skipper croaked, his mouth suddenly dry. As one, the men on the bridge of the S-boat ducked low behind the armour.

With bombs gone just seconds away, S-Sugar detonated in mid-air, the brilliant explosion hurling a shockwave of hellish, acrid air across the basin, showering the surrounding area with fragments of debris no bigger than a cricket ball.

Even more alarming was the sight of the port engine, its airscrew still spinning like an enormous scythe, as it began to bounce across the still waters of the basin towards the S-boat like a pebble. To his left, Lahousen was aware of a blur as the chief petty officer dived overboard. But as more than a ton of Bristol Pegasus aero-engine careered towards him at three hundred miles an hour, the colonel found himself quite unable to move. He waited for his life to flash before his eyes. Then mercifully, as if in slow motion, the engine slowed, faltered, and sank with barely twenty-five metres to spare.

'Scheisse!' swore the captain as they regained their feet, straightening his cap as though he had swerved a punch.

'Captain,' began Wagner, 'could we get under way? Even at forty knots we've got a four hour crossing ahead of us. If we don't leave soon we won't make Suffolk before daybreak.'

'Give me five minutes to check over the boat. That Tommy bomber spat out more junk than Vesuvius.'

Wagner nodded his assent, then turned to Schrek and Dorper. 'You two might as well go below and get changed.'

The pair obeyed, pausing only to assist in hauling the chief petty officer back on board.

Wagner glanced around, and lowered his voice to a whisper. 'One favour, colonel.'

'Name it.'

'The girl, Klara Weintraub. If Rubikon dies like a dog I want her protected.'

Lahousen shook his head. 'Schellenberg has the entire family under constant watch. And they're Jewish. You know full well that our hands are tied.'

'If the Abwehr can spirit that idiot CRACKER in and out of England, it can get a family to Lisbon or Berne.'

The colonel paused. 'I'll speak to Canaris again. But I can't promise more.'

'So give me one good reason not to throw this mission.'

'Your men, leutnant. Blame her brother, if it helps. Sooner or later they were bound to get caught. Is that enough?'

Wagner held his stare, but gave no reply. Beneath the rear of the slender grey boat the twin diesel engines roared into life. A moment later the skipper returned to the bridge and announced. 'All clear.'

'My cue to leave,' announced Lahousen. 'Goodbye Wagner.'

'Goodbye, colonel.'

Lahousen gave Wagner a military salute, then offered his hand. Both shook in full knowledge that neither would see the other man again.

FORTY-SIX

From the topmost platform on the steel transmitter tower the spectacular view along the Suffolk coastline extended a distance of almost thirty miles, from Aldeburgh to the north to Walton-on-the-Naze in the south. Breathless after the long climb, his bad leg aching, Goodman clung to the nearest cross-beam as if to life itself. On his honeymoon four years earlier, Goodman had ascended the Eiffel Tower, at the summit of which he had fancied that he was standing on the roof of the world. At three hundred and sixty feet, the four TX towers at Bawdsey were little more than a third of its height. Far from feeling exhilarated, however, Goodman found himself almost frozen by acute vertigo.

Beside him, Morley was unconcerned, sweeping his field glasses back and forth across the flat East Anglian landscape, and casting a satisfied eye over the martial preparations below. Although it was not yet ten in the morning, the last of the two dozen fuel tankers was already in place behind the brow of the low cliff, their crews waiting for a corridor of beach mines to be lifted in order to lay the fuel hoses down to the tideline. All across the sixty hectare estate soldiers moved purposefully like khaki ants, positioning weapons, reinforcing defences and clearing fields of fire. With more than a thousand regular troops concentrated along a two mile stretch of coast, the defence of Britain looked viable for the first time since Dunkirk.

'What if they let the side down?' asked Goodman.

'In what way?'

'By refusing to land on top of your flame barrage.'

'Simple - we'll slaughter them by more conventional means. 'But I'll bet my shirt on them landing exactly where we want.'

'Oh?'

'It stands to reason,' Morley replied matter-of-factly. 'They can't aim straight for the Manor because of the cliff, which leaves only the defile.'

By a supreme effort of will Goodman forced himself to look downward. Close by the buried reserve transmitter a gap had been opened in the low earthen cliff, which in pre-war years had given sunbathers ready access to the beach. Now the defile was choked with wire and anti-tank blocks.

'Easy as shooting fish in a barrel,' Morley continued with relish.

Gritting his teeth, Goodman raised his arm and pointed south towards the mouth of the Orwell. 'What about the estuary foreshore? The ground over there is flat as a pancake.'

Morley shook his head. 'Too far. We're only expecting one hundred for dinner.'

Goodman was momentarily distracted by the labours of a team on the adjacent tower, struggling to manhandle a heavy Vickers machine gun and tripod up the narrow, flimsy ladders. Again he felt dizzy and nauseous, and fixed his eyes on a distant minesweeper, inching across the grey surface of the North Sea. Not for the first time, Goodman harboured an uncomfortable hunch that Morley was planning much of Operation Juniper as he went along.

'The whole thing could be a feint, you know.'

'So what if it is? At eight o'clock this evening GHQ will issue Alert Number One to Eastern and Southern commands. Brooke was insistent.'

'CROMWELL? But that's the codeword for invasion.'

'Not quite. It means invasion imminent, and probable within twelve hours. Sort of Stand To with bells on.'

'You're not kidding. By half past eight tonight there'll be bells ringing from Perth to Penzance.'

'Oh, come come.'

'Every local commander who receives that signal will think Hitler's already halfway across the Channel.'

Morley considered this. 'Well, it's too late now. Besides, a spot of practise for the real thing won't do any harm.'

'Not if you discount the wholesale demolition of jetties, bridges, tunnels and railway stations.' Sensing he was wasting his breath, Goodman changed tack. 'I wonder if Wagner's already here?'

'I'd put money on it. The coastguard post at Orford logged engine noise last night, probably an E-boat. I'll wager he crept ashore north of Shingle Street and is heading south.'

'Shouldn't we be searching for him?'

'And ruin the party for everyone?'

'I thought that was the reason I'm here.'

'Wagner's job will be to observe and report until nightfall, nothing more. If we sweep him up too quickly, rats will be smelled across the water. They won't run the risk that he's talked.'

'If he is watching, he won't miss the preparations downstairs.'

'No way round that, I'm afraid. Besides if there's no attack tonight, we'll round him up tomorrow.'

'If that's the case, couldn't Sophie push off until she's needed, along with the rest of the spare air force bods.'

Morley shook his head. 'Worried she'll fall back into his arms?'

'Don't be absurd.'

'Miss Gold must stay put, I'm afraid. I need the two of you on the ground to pick out Wagner if he moves in.'

'Which he will, if he intends to hitch a lift home.'

'Well, you've made my point for me.'

For a fleeting, delicious moment, Goodman conjured an image of the major toppling off the platform, propelled by the toe of his boot. Then he felt sick and dizzy again. 'Look, I'm heading back down to the ground floor. You coming?'

Morley shook his head. 'Not just yet. D'you know, we could drag a cine camera up here and capture the whole shebang on film. It might liven up the newsreels.'

'Capitol idea,' Goodman offered mockingly, gritting his teeth and starting gingerly down the ladder. 'I'll give Mr Korda a ring. You might win an academy award to go with your VC.'

FORTY-SEVEN

From the cover of a ditch seven hundred metres away, Paul Wagner dropped his field glasses from the khaki figure slowly descending the furthest tower, and focused again on the row of fuel tankers lined up behind the cliff.

'Well?' asked Schreck beside him.

'It has to be a trap. The whole place is crawling with infantry.'

'How could they know?'

'Christ only knows. But they do.'

'Could be gas. Liquid mustard.'

'I'd say not. With gas there's always the danger it'll blow inland and choke the home team. My money's on burning oil.' Wagner lowered the glasses and turned to Dorper. 'Will that short-wave set reach Holland?'

Dorper nodded. 'I'll need some height. What's the message?'

'To scrub the mission. Bartels will be slaughtered if he lands.'

'What a pity,' muttered Schreck.

'And our ride home?' asked Dorper carefully.

'Can't lose what we never head. Let's get that message out and see what tonight brings.'

Dorper looked set to protest, then thought better of it and cast around for a tree.

Thirty minutes later, as his message flashed through the ether, Schellenberg kicked at a jagged chunk of shrapnel on the quayside at Vlissingen. It was an unwelcome reminder of the violent air raid the night before, which had damaged half a dozen barges and fired two warehouses on the far side of the basin, and kept the fast launches commandeered for Gruppe Bartels at Dordrecht until this morning. Both men were in buoyant mood, however: in eight hours the men of Gruppe Bartels would sail for Suffolk, and change history.

258

'One can only admire the creative energy behind the English propaganda machine,' Schellenberg observed. 'These latest falsehoods about the Vichy government have seduced every neutral editor in the western hemisphere.'

'You mean this nonsense about violent repression of the church?' replied Bartels.

'That, and the fiction our coastal batteries are lobbing French shells across the Pas de Calais. Still, the reviews are better than in 1914.'

'Meaning, we're not crucifying priests, and spitting babies on bayonets.'

'Or rendering down corpses for glycerine.'

'You've heard the latest rumours about Sealion?'

Schellenberg nodded. 'Wave upon wave of mutinies, entire regiments sent back to Germany in manacles and chains. Troops on exercise being forced to jump into the sea in full equipment a mile offshore, thousands drowned.'

'Leaving their corpses to float north in quantities so vast that Swedish fishermen have been forced to abandon trawling for herring.'

'Really, unless Stockholm stops printing this garbage we'll have to stop buying their iron ore.'

Bartels uttered a wry laugh. 'Next London will announce that man-eating sharks have been released into the Channel.'

'Now that would make even Himmler laugh.'

The joke was drowned by an unholy roar as a Siebel ferry began testing its engines. Makeshift and cumbersome in appearance, the Siebel was a pontoon large enough to carry a complete anti-aircraft unit, comprising three heavy canon and their tractors, and loaded to enable the guns to fire while the ferry was still at sea. Strangest of all were the two large aircraft engines mounted on the stern, each fitted with a three-bladed propeller to enable the unlikely contraption to run in to the beach at high speed. The ear-splitting roar caused the two SS officers to cover their ears with the hands, then turn quickly away as a stinging shower of spray hit the quay at more than one hundred kilometres an hour.

As Schellenberg and Bartels struggled to recover their poise a grey kubelwagen jeep hove into view. The car sped along the quayside for fifty metres before braking sharply to disgorge

Hauptsturmfuhrer Eichner. Bartels doubled forward, hurdling one of the thick, rusted mooring chains that criss-crossed the cluttered quayside.

'Have the launches arrived?'

'Soon. The traffic's still heavy on the Schelde.' He turned to Schellenberg as he approached. 'Sir, we've received a signal from Wagner.'

'He broke radio silence?'

Eichner nodded. 'He says it's a trap. Bawdsey is crawling with troops, and there's a flame weapon in place.'

'Show me.' Schellenberg snatched the square of yellow paper from his hand.

'What does he say?' asked Bartels, after several silent moments.

Schellenberg read aloud. '"Target prepared for attack. Heavy weapons and many troops. Fuel tankers positioned beneath tallest towers. Abort Rubikon. Confirm pick-up co-ordinates".' He rolled the slip of paper into a tight ball and let it drop to the ground. Immediately Eicher stooped to retrieve it.

'How could the Tommies know?' asked Bartels.

Schellenberg did not answer. 'Was the signal security coded?'

'The check digit was present and correct.'

'They could have been captured.'

'It's possible.'

'Perhaps the American threw in the towel to save his own skin,' offered Bartels. 'Brandenburg men know full well that capture means execution. Certain death is a powerful persuader.'

Eichner shook his head. 'If that were the case they'd be encouraging us to come.'

'We could stand here all day floating double-bluffs and be no nearer the truth,' Schellenberg said irritably.

'Which leaves Rubikon where?'

'Dead in the water,' replied Eichner. 'If the signal is genuine, Bartels can hardly proceed. If Wagner's been captured, the enemy still have twelve hours to perfect their defences. We lose either way.'

Schellenberg considered these unpalatable facts. Three days earlier, pending the outcome of Rubikon, the Fuhrer himself had postponed giving the executive order for Sealion. If the raid was cancelled, the invasion of England was certain to be set back until the following spring, and cancelled in the fullness of time. Much as the Abwehr and the navy might thank him for such service rendered, Heydrich and Himmler would hang him high. Schellenberg knew Rubikon had always been a gamble; now even its architect was of the opinion that Bartels would have to roll a thirteen to succeed.

'Get on to the Luftwaffe,' he told Eichner. 'Send something fast over the target at low level to see what's going on.'

'That will confirm their suspicions,' protested Eichner. 'Besides, there's a fighter station ten miles away at Martlesham Heath.'

'Eichner, it has evidently escaped your attention that Goring is sending three hundred bombers to London this afternoon. The RAF are likely to be busy elsewhere.'

'The London raid is not timed to begin until four, sir.'

Schellenberg suppressed his anger only with difficulty. 'Thus leaving plenty of time for Luftflotte 2 to nominate the right crew for the job, clear?'

Eichner saluted, then turned on his heel.

'One last thing, Hauptsturmfuhrer.'

Eichner turned back and found Schellenberg smiling.

'Fetch me that little Jewess.'

FORTY-EIGHT

In his office at the Fox Hole Canaris sat alone in semi-darkness. Two weeks earlier the first RAF bombers had reached Berlin, and succeeded in destroying a garden chalet in the suburb of Rosenthal. Since then the so-called terrorflieger had returned several times more, and although the damage inflicted by these pin-prick raids was negligible, their effect on morale had been salutary. Worse still, the wailing sirens much alarmed his cherished dachshunds, Seppel and Sabine.

Not that the bombing was without its compensations. Only twelve months earlier, Fat Hermann himself had rashly declared that if a single enemy aircraft reached even the Ruhr, his name was not Goring but Meier. Today, to return the compliment, more than six hundred Luftwaffe bombers were laying waste to the docks and warehouses of Woolwich and Silvertown for the first time. By night, Canaris knew, London was as good as defenceless, and powerless to resist. And now thanks to Wagner's signal he too was impotent. With Rubikon certain to be called off, his best hope for drowning Sealion was a change in the weather in the Channel, and - perhaps - a fresh attempt to foster a false conviction in the Fuhrer that Franco might soon be persuaded to join the war on the Axis side. Not that the signal from England had crushed his spirits entirely; indeed it had come in some way as a relief. Since his tryst with Halina Szymanska three days earlier, the chief of intelligence had barely slept a wink. He was, he knew, at bottom a traitor. And gnawing at the back of his mind was the fear that the blood on his hands would somehow become visible to all.

The black telephone rang. As was his habit, Canaris let it ring twice before lifting the handset.

'Yes?'

'Colonel Lahousen on line from Antwerp, Admiral,' announced Jencke.

'Thank you. Put him through. Lahousen?'

'You told me to call through any material developments, Herr Admiral.'

'Go on,' Canaris said cautiously.

'Schellenberg has arranged for an air strike on Bawdsey.'

'With what object?' Canaris demanded, unsure whether the news was good or bad.

'To destroy whatever apparatus has been positioned beneath the towers ahead of the assault.'

'You mean they still intend to proceed?'

'If the air strike is successful. It's timed for two in the morning. Bartels and his flotilla will be waiting offshore.'

'Schellenberg has lost his reason. The Luftwaffe will be lucky to even find the target at night, much less hit it.'

'The unit selected has attacked Bawdsey before. It's a Ju 88 wing operating from Schiphol. Even Himmler couldn't persuade Kesselring or Sperrle to send anything over in daylight.'

Canaris fell silent. On the one hand, he could hardly complain if Bartels pressed ahead with a suicidal attack. That, after all, was the very result he had forsaken his honour as a soldier to bring about. On the other was the chance that by some fluke the bombers might succeed.

He glanced up at the clock on the wall, an unofficial trophy from the bridge of his last ship, and still accurate to the minute after a quarter-century. It was seven o'clock, and now completely dark outside. In great haste the capital had been forced to adopt improvised black-out measures, but this evening the man who fixed the heavy drapes across the windows of his office was nowhere to be found. Perhaps, Canaris mused, he too had been co-opted by Walter Schellenberg.

'Thank you, Lahousen.'

'Should I do anything, Admiral?

'My dear colonel, I fear there's nothing to be done.'

FORTY-NINE

Although the Nazis detained by the sentries at the East Lodge guardroom did not include Wagner, they seemed oddly familiar to Goodman. It was the youngest that jogged his memory first. The last time they had met was at an improvised roadblock on a country lane in June, when the youth had been armed with a sickle and a bag of pepper. In their ill-fitting denim battledress and precarious cheese-cutter caps, the Home Guard trio looked scarcely more martial now. Recalling the shotgun waved in his face, Goodman was tempted to have them detained anyway, and might have done so had an RAF sergeant not appeared at his shoulder.

'Captain Goodman?'

'Yes.'

'Major Morley wishes to speak to you in the transmitter bunker.'

As he turned, for a moment Goodman fancied that the sergeant was accompanied by a boy soldier. Just as suddenly he recognised the figure in the oversize khaki fitters overalls as Sophie Gold.

'Good Lord!' he exclaimed.

'It was Morley's idea,' Sophie explained, as they fell in behind the sergeant and began up the gentle slope towards the TX block. 'Less chance of being recognised by Paul.'

'You look most awfully well,' Goodman chided gently.

'Ha-bloody-ha.'

Goodman craned his neck at the towering masts silhouetted against the night sky. 'Is the mad major still up in the clouds?'

'He was an hour ago.' She paused for a long moment. 'They started on London today.'

'You mean mass bombing?'

She nodded. 'The East End. I heard it in RX. Apparently the first formation that came over this afternoon covered eight hundred square miles of sky.'

Goodman released a low whistle. He recalled the estimates he had heard at GHQ: three thousand dead and twelve thousand wounded each night in the capital alone. The way Sophie described it, the figures seemed if anything conservative.

'Honestly, some of the girls are such fools,' she continued. 'There could be thousands of people being blown to pieces in town, my father among them, and all they can do is complain that the south coast stations will see all the action.'

'I'm sure he's safe. Barnes is a long way from the Whitechapel Road.'

Sophie flashed him an uncertain smile, but her voice was anxious and brittle. 'I say, weren't you being a little hard on those poor Home Guards back there?'

'Probably,' Goodman conceded. 'Fact is, on the day we first met that same happy band jammed a shotgun up my nose.'

'At least they're keen.'

'Too bloody keen. This is none of their business.'

She touched his arm in the darkness. 'I'm glad he didn't blow your head off your shoulders, darling.'

'You say the sweetest things.'

They reached the transmitter block, a squat, rectangular bunker surrounded by a blast wall of reinforced concrete and banked earth. Beside the armoured steel door a stout spanner hung suspended on a length of twine. The sergeant took hold of it and hammered on the door with evident relish. A few seconds later a judas latch snapped open, and a voice from within demanded the password.

'Lyceum.'

'That was last night.'

'Then you tell me, chum. I've got the officer and Tarzan Gold.'

'The correct password is Astoria,' offered Sophie.

'That'll do nicely,' the voice replied.

A moment later the heavy door swung open. After a brief struggle with the black-out drape, Goodman found himself inside what looked, and sounded, like the control room of a power station. Two giant transmitter units dominated the low, square

265

space, each adorned with countless dials and meters, and large enough for a mechanic to clamber inside. The light thrown out by the overhead bulbs was dim, and scarcely brighter than a theatre auditorium. A corporal sat hunched before the control desk of the live transmitter, glued to the blue cathode ray tube which monitored the shape, size and condition of the pulse being radiated from the aerial array. On one of the sickly green walls a row of sand buckets and fire extinguishers stood at action stations, and on another, beside the meteorological chalkboard, a rifle rack half-filled with Lee Enfields. Suffusing everything was the low humming of the air conditioning equipment, and three hundred and fifty unshielded kilowatts of electrical current.

The watch supervisor, a pilot officer, directed Goodman through to the centre of the block. There Morley had wired a field telephone into the line which served the workshop. Goodman cranked the handle, then waited for Morley to pick up in his crow's nest three hundred feet above.

'Jane?'

'No, it's me, Goodman.'

'Ah. You'll have to do.'

'Is it Wagner?'

'No, some of his friends. Keep this under your hat, but in the next half an hour we can expect to be bombed.'

'Have we picked up an echo?'

'Something like that,' Morley offered vaguely. In fact the intelligence had come from Bletchley Park, who six hours earlier had decrypted a routine Enigma signal from Luftflotte 2 to Schiphol airfield detailing time and target. 'The thing is, I didn't want you and Miss Gold to get caught in the open. Is she with you?'

'Yes.' Goodman lowered his voice as a figure passed in the passageway outside. 'What about the poor bloody infantry?'

'They stay where they are. Good grief man, we're expecting several boatloads of Hitler's worst. Now listen carefully. If the plotting wallahs see it coming with their magic eye, make sure they keep schtumm. We don't want to be caught on the hop if the Hun runs his boats ashore at the same time.'

'Understood,' replied Goodman. 'Is there any news from London?'

'They've been pounding the docks since late afternoon. I can see the glow on the horizon from up here.'

'What about Barnes?'

'My eyesight isn't that good.'

'I meant, have you heard anything on the wire. Sophie's father lives in SW13.'

'According to Jane, they're concentrating on the docks. Any sign of Wagner down there?'

'Not yet.'

'Never mind. Perhaps he'll break cover when the bombs start falling. Give me a ring when the dust has settled, if you're still alive.'

As he replaced the receiver, Goodman drew comfort from the fact that Morley was somewhat closer to heaven than he was. Returning to the transmitter hall, he took Sophie to one side and squeezed her hand.

'Morley says the docks are copping the worst of it. I'm sure your father will be fine.'

She nodded gravely, little convinced.

'At least Elizabeth will get to experience total war before she flits off to California.'

'You really are in a bloody mood tonight.'

'I feel bloody.' Goodman glanced upwards. 'How thick is this ceiling?'

'About eight or nine feet.'

'Bomb proof?'

'So they say. Why?'

Goodman glanced quickly about. 'According to Morley we're going to be bombed in the next half hour. That's why he called us inside.'

'Should we sound the alarm?'

'Far from it. We're not to breathe a word.'

'Oh,' she said quietly.

A telephone rang. The watch supervisor picked it up and listened briefly, his brow furrowed. 'That was the filter room,' he told the corporal on the console. 'Stoke Holy Cross report hostiles coming in towards Yarmouth.'

'Large formation?'

The supervisor shook his head. 'They reckon half a dozen, fifty miles out at two thousand feet.'

The corporal laughed. 'So, fifty crates six miles out.'

Goodman felt the beginnings of a knot form in his stomach. He looked at Sophie. 'Is that us?'

'I think so,' she answered calmly.

A moment later the telephone rang again. The supervisor listened, nodded, and hung up once more. 'They've altered course. Throw the switch up fifty kilowatts so that RX bring them in ahead of Darsham.'

The corporal frowned. 'I'll give it five seconds, no more.'

Goodman watched as the corporal eased around the dial on the console. For a half dozen seconds the humming grew louder, then subsided as the power was reduced. Suddenly from somewhere behind the transmitter there was a loud report, like a gunshot, which caused Goodman to start violently.

'It's alright, sir,' the supervisor said reassuringly. 'Only a valve.'

'I'll power up the reserve,' said the corporal, rising to his feet and crossing to the console which controlled the second transmitter unit.

'Right you are.'

The pilot officer walked through to the store room, and returned with a valve the size of a large jam jar. One by one he pulled down a row of circuit breakers on the first transmitter, then opened a door and reached inside the panel to remove the debris of the shattered valve.

A moment later there was a blinding white flash, which fused half the overhead lights and knocked the supervisor ten feet across the room. By the time Goodman's vision returned in the stygian gloom, Sophie was already kneeling beside the supervisor, who lay twitching on the floor, mumbling incomprehensibly.

'Oh dear God,' she muttered softly.

The corporal stood halfway between his console and the prone figure of the supervisor, dumbstruck and frozen. A mechanic ran through from the generator room, almost slipping on the linoleum.

'Is he bad?' he asked.

Sophie looked up, her face very pale. 'It's his hand.'

Stepping closer, Goodman saw that the fingers on the supervisor's right hand had been entirely stripped of flesh, leaving

268

little more than stumps of blackened bone. The rest of his hand looked and smelled like a char-grilled steak.

Sophie turned to the corporal. 'Fetch the first aid box. There should be a bottle of gentian violet.'

The corporal merely shuffled backwards, and half fell onto his chair as his legs gave way. Sophie glanced back to the mechanic, who nodded, and hurried away. A few seconds later the bulbs flickered back into life.

'What can I do?' Goodman asked.

'I need to call the medical post,' she replied. 'He's in shock. Hold him down and keep him still, and don't let him see the damage.'

Goodman did as he was told, and was still doing so ten minutes later when the floor beneath his feet, and the lights above his head, began to shiver and quake from the detonation of high explosive.

FIFTY

As the distant drone of aero engines grew louder in the darkness, Morley wondered whether the bombers would pass above or below his vantage point on top of the north-east tower. Not that it would much matter, he reflected, if the attack brought down the mast. Now the major found himself seized by a sudden irresistible shiver of anticipation. Rising to his feet on the narrow wooden platform, he drew his revolver and set his jaw as the humming intensified into a full-throttle roar.

The first Junkers 88 became visible later than he anticipated, a dark twin-engined shadow streaking across Hollesley Bay from the north at three hundred miles an hour. Morley had barely levelled his weapon before the sleek bomber released its bombload and flashed across the target, flying too low and banking to late to avoid clipping the top of the tower with the tip of its wing. The sound was as a colossal hammer striking an anvil, and clearly audible above the deafening roar of the radial engines.

A second split. Within it Morley ducked, lost his balance, and plunged forward into space, hands outstretched as if to catch the invisible stick of bombs. For a long, ridiculous instant he fancied he were a goalkeeper in a cup tie. Then the length of rope which served as his safety line played out to its limit, dashing Morley against the steel superstructure and snapping his right arm like a twig.

Three hundred and fifty feet below the detonation of the bombs rocked the mast with terrifying violence. Dangling face down, Morley closed his eyes against the stinging shower of earth and debris propelled skyward by the blast wave. Then the pain in his shattered arm broke across his consciousness, causing him to release an agonised, expletive scream.

As the crash of the explosions died away the approach of a second aircraft could be heard, competing with an air raid siren mounted on the roof of the manor. Ten seconds later the next Ju 88 missed the tankers by a good hundred yards, its payload instead triggering the sympathetic detonation of most of the mines on the beach, which in turn produced a result comparable to armageddon. The third found its target, the last of the stick of four 250 kilogram bombs falling between the two bowsers parked directly beneath the tower.

The result, Morley mused, looked like hell with the lid off, as an acrid orange fireball engulfed the Vickers crew on the lowest platform, then rose steadily through the night air towards him.

FIFTY-ONE

The fuel oil was still burning in patches on the ground around the transmitter block when Walter Schellenberg's voice came over the short-wave. Dorper tugged off the headset and passed it to Wagner.

'It's Schellenberg, sir.'

'Must be important if he's advertising our location,' said Schrek.

'That, or he wants us killed.' Wagner clamped the headset to his ear and depressed the button on the microphone. 'This is Wagner.'

'Well?' demanded Schellenberg impatiently.

'I could ask you the same question.'

'Don't waste time. Bartels is ready and waiting. What is your position?'

'Sitting pretty. Your first bomber went down.'

'Flak?'

'Enthusiasm.'

Schellenberg was unmoved. 'And the others?'

'One direct hit. A couple of the oil tankers went up. They're moving the others back to stop the fire spreading.'

'Are the troops still in place?'

'Hard to tell with all this smoke, but I think so.'

'Bartels wants to move in.'

'They'll be slaughtered. I told you before to abort.'

Schellenberg allowed the pause to stretch. 'There's someone here I think you should talk to.'

Lahousen, Wagner assumed. 'Put him on.'

'Hello, Mr Wagner.'

The voice was female, the language English.

God, no...

'Klara?'

272

'Klaartje. You've lost the right to call me Klara. In fact you never had it.'

Behind the bravado her voice sounded small and frightened. Wagner closed his eyes and punched the ground with his fist.

'Are you... Has anyone hurt you?'

'Not yet. But your SS friend has promised to shoot Willem if I don't co-operate.'

'I'm sorry, Klara,' Wagner said quietly.

'Me too, but not for you.'

'Where are you?'

'I can't say.'

'Well, wherever you are, I hope you die there.'

'That makes two of us.'

She gave no answer. The presence of an SS major-general of police at her shoulder was scarcely conducive to conversation.

'Enjoying this, Schellenberg?'

'It's almost as touching as the death scene in Romeo and Juliet. Now, I suggest you follow your orders. Are you ready to receive Gruppe Bartels?'

Wagner hesitated. He understood all too clearly now that Schellenberg would never release the Weintraub family, that no-one, not even Canaris, could deliver them from evil. He could offer Klara precisely nothing. Probably Schellenberg would deny him even that.

He said: 'I'll send up the flare.'

'How soon?'

'Fifteen minutes.'

'You have ten. Are you inside the perimeter?'

'Yes,' Wagner lied.

'And the flame weapon is out of action?'

'For at least twenty minutes, I'd say.'

'Are you certain?'

'My best guess.'

'Excellent. I'll signal Bartels immediately. Bring this off, leutnant, and I'll release the girl to you on the dockside. Good hunting.'

Good hunting. There could be no-one on earth less like a sporting gentleman than Walter Schellenberg. Wagner returned the headset to Dorper and turned to Schrek. 'I take it you pieced that together?'

'Just about. Sir, even without flame there are still enough Tommies over there to cut Bartels to pieces in half a minute.'

'I know that.'

'So you can't fire the flare.'

'On the contrary, nothing would give me more pleasure. If you want to stop me, shoot me now.'

Schrek shook his head. 'Do what you have to do. Just don't expect me to follow.'

'Take Dorper and get as far away as you can. Turn yourselves in, or try to get back - it's your choice. But lose those uniforms first.'

Schrek rose to his feet and stripped off his khaki battledress blouse to reveal a field-grey tunic, then motioned for Dorper to follow his lead. 'Better get moving, sir. Only nine minutes left. If the Tommies were listening they'll be on us in no time.'

'Pleasure serving with you, corporal.'

'Likewise, leutnant.'

Schrek raised his hand uncertainly, as if to salute, then abandoned the gesture as Wagner stood and offered his hand. As the two men shook the silver wire of Schrek's elegant Brandenburg cuff-title caught in the glow of the distant fire. Wagner sensed that he should be gripped by some profound emotion, but found himself cauterised of all feeling.

FIFTY-TWO

As he swerved to avoid a patch of burning fuel, his field of vision much restricted by his gas-mask, Goodman stumbled over something that might have been a body. Seconds later, less than five feet in front of him, a fuel bowser reversed past through smoke-choked night air at high speed, its burning tyres spinning like catherine wheels. To his right, towards the cliff-edge, someone was screaming above the snap of exploding small arms ammunition.

Emerging from the chaos moments later Goodman collided with a lieutenant from the Royal Engineers. The other man was squatting on the ground, hunched forward and choking violently into a handkerchief. As Goodman tugged his mask clear of his face the acrid stench of burning fuel and rubber hit him like a fist.

'Get your respirator on,' he shouted.

'No can do.'

The sapper raised his head weakly and fixed his gaze on the middle distance. Goodman saw that the right hand side of his face was blackened and blistered, and most of his hair burned away. Goodman crouched down beside him and smelled burnt flesh.

'Are you in pain?'

'Not yet. There's plenty worse off than me in the foxholes. They copped it rotten when the bowsers went up.'

'Is the barrage still serviceable?'

'No idea. There's no way of knowing how badly the pipes across the beach were damaged until we open the valves. I suppose the Fougasse drums might still be intact. You'd best ask the colonel.'

Goodman felt a twinge of panic. No mines, perhaps no barrage, and an enemy assault due any moment now. Was Morley still watching from the top of the tower? Or was the architect of the unfolding fiasco as dead as his telephone line? Goodman glanced upwards, but could see nothing through the darkness and smoke besides the still-burning corpses of the Vickers crew on the first gantry.

The operation had spiralled out of control. Now the realisation dawned on Goodman that he could do nothing more useful than seek out reinforcements, and quickly.

'Can you find your way over to the transmitter block? They can help you there.'

'I'm blinded,' the lieutenant replied calmly. 'But you go ahead.'

Goodman paused, then rose to his feet and glanced quickly about. On the fringes of the smoke directly ahead a human form was visible, like a ghost.

'You! Over here!'

The figure stopped dead, then changed direction towards him. Without waiting to observe the niceties of rank or service, Goodman stabbed his arm toward the TX block. 'Get this officer inside the bunker. Password Astoria. Then round up any other walking wounded you can find and get the poor buggers out of harm's way.'

The soldier hesitated. But Goodman was gone before Wagner could remove his own respirator, and explain himself, or where he had met the limping Welsh spy before. Who clearly was not in the pay of the Abwehr at all.

FIFTY-THREE

As Wagner guided the blind officer towards the nearest vacant chair, he glanced again at the corporal who had admitted him into this, the most secret inner sanctum. Wagner took in the distinctive insignia on the Englishman's shoulder, a trio of lighting rods gripped in a clenched fist. The technician was no doubt the prize Walter Schellenberg hoped might be delivered on the quayside at Den Helder. Or would that be the officer slumped in the far corner, staring vacantly at what little was left of his hand? Not that the question was anything other than academic now.

'Who's in charge here?' he demanded.

Without raising his eyes from the luminous blue tube the corporal yelled loudly: 'Tarzan!'

Was it mockery? Wagner had no idea. When, after a dozen seconds, no-one appeared, he glanced at the clock on the wall. Four minutes, more or less: if he was lucky Bartels would wait another five. For want of any better distraction he scanned the curious litany chalked on the meteorological board below the timepiece:

wind speed
temperature
bar pressure
icing level
sunrise/set
moonrise/set
moon phase...

The minute hand of the clock sprang forward, the soft click audible above the monotone background hum. Three minutes remaining. Time running out.

Wagner stepped towards the corporal. 'Dammit, I need to speak to your commanding officer right now!'

'You'll be lucky' the corporal muttered. Again he raised his voice to a yell. 'Tarzan! Through here, when you're ready.'

A moment later, as Sophie Gold emerged from the gloom of the passageway, Wagner turned to stone. And to think, after his encounter with the limping spy outside, he had imagined that tonight nothing else could surprise him.

'Sophie,' he said quietly.

'Hello, Paul.'

'It... had to be you.'

'Don't try to charm me. I know you're fighting for Hitler.'

'Bloody hell!' the corporal spluttered, rising to his feet and upsetting his chair.

The sudden movement returned Wagner to his senses. In an instant he had drawn his own automatic and trained it on the other man. 'Let's not get too excited. Look, Sophie, in a couple minutes a bunch of real deal Nazis are going to land in your lap. Trust me. I can help you can kill 'em all.'

'Trust you?' she replied scathingly, nodding at the cowed-looking corporal, and beginning to edge towards the rifle rack.

'Listen,' Wagner tried quickly. 'I got two minutes to send up a flare. Over one hundred stormtroopers are waiting to hit the beach directly beneath it. Get it right, and your infantry can pick them off like rats in a barrel.'

Now Sophie had reached the rack and wrenched free a Lee Enfield. As she swung round the weapon and grappled inexpertly with the bolt, Wagner tried again. Pleaded, really.

'Listen to me, Sophie. These guys are SS - the murdering bastards who're rounding up Jews into camps and ghettoes. Don't shoot the messenger.'

'Why should I believe a word you say?'

'Because, I could've already killed every person in this room twice over if I'd wanted. Look, I'm on your side.'

'Two weeks ago you killed a friend of mine. Who's side were you on then?'

Sophie brought the rifle to her shoulder and drew a bead on Wagner's head. Unable to support its weight, however, she lowered it to her waist. Wagner sensed he was fighting a losing battle. To try to explain about Klara seemed ludicrous in the circumstances - especially now that Sophie had succeeded in coaxing a round into the breach.

He tried a desperate joke. 'You know something? I still blame your old man.'

Sophie opened her mouth as if to speak, then shut her eyes and squeezed the trigger. The recoil sent the shot high, so that the bullet ricochetted off the ceiling and slammed noisily into a transmitter panel. As one, the corporal and the blind lieutenant dived for the floor.

Wagner made his choice and raised his hand. 'Okay, here's all the proof you need. I never stopped loving you, Sophie. Not for one minute. Remember now - send up a single red flare.'

Before she could fire again, Wagner raised his pistol to his temple and pulled the trigger.

A single flare, blood-red.

Less than two minutes remaining.

FIFTY-FOUR

The motor launches were still grouped a mile offshore when the red flare arced gracefully into the air. Bartels missed seeing the signal with his own eyes, having just ducked inside the wheelhouse to instruct the Kreigsmarine skipper to scratch the mission. By the time he managed to scramble back to the prow of the boat, a requisitioned police launch from Rotterdam, the flare had dropped below the treeline and was lost to view.

With little real operational experience, Bartels wrestled with the question of whether to return to Dordrecht. There had, after all, been any number of false alarms in the last quarter hour, what with the onshore holocaust triggered by the Luftwaffe raid, and the fitful firework display caused by exploding ammunition and fuel. His gut feeling was to slip swiftly back across the North Sea. But then Bartels remembered that Walter Schellenberg was waiting, and that Schellenberg would accept nothing less than a famous victory. So Bartels uttered a silent prayer and gave the order for his unit to attack.

The eight launches took little more than two minutes to cover the distance to the beach - towards a point two hundred yards wide of the target defile, and backed by a sheer cliff rising thirty feet above the shingle. Only five of the boats grounded, after one was blown apart on the approach by a fortuitous hit from a three-inch mortar, and a second was enveloped in a pool of burning oil which flared just as the lead boats reached the shore.

The destruction of what remained of Gruppe Bartels lasted less than four minutes. Of the sixty or so men who managed to drop from the boats into the cold, dark water, few made it more than halfway across the shingle beach, searching in vain for the absent exit defile. Many were vaporized as the fuel from the ruptured fuel lines flared and spread to create a firestorm, turning night into day, while the rest with cut down in a hurricane of mortar shells, grenades and withering automatic fire.

However Bartels survived, after a five second burst from a pair of twinned Lewis machine guns reduced the wheelhouse of the police launch to matchwood, and those within it to pulp. In the chaos that followed the boat sheered out of control, performing an erratic figure of eight before heading back out into the North Sea, far away from the charred remains of Operation Rubikon.

FIFTY-FIVE

For those who cared to look, the grim aftermath of the attack was visible from the turrets of the manor house. Between the breakers and the high-water mark the wreckage of the half-dozen motor launches formed a jagged line across the shingle beach, three of them burned out, one still releasing a thin trail of black smoke into the chill morning air. From the stern of another a large swastika flag fluttered in the breeze, oblivious to the recent annihilation of its servants. A broad stripe of shingle in front of the boats was stained darker than the rest of the beach, as if in the shadow of a small cloud. It was here that most of Gruppe Bartels had evaporated in a maelstrom of fuel oil, aviation spirit and small-arms fire.

The remains of the dead had been cleared from the pebbles ahead of the advancing tide, and were heaped in a black line at the base of the cliff. An hour earlier Goodman had seen some of the corpses at close quarters. Some had shrunk down to the size of children, frozen in the oddly aggressive, pugilistic postures caused by contraction of the muscles in extreme heat. One or two unlucky enough to have clung on to life through the hours of darkness had been dispatched with a pistol round, like fallen horses.

They were the enemy, of course. But Goodman knew that nothing in the world could ever be quite the same again.

'Did any of them get off the beach?' Sophie asked dispassionately.

Goodman shook his head. 'A few tried to swim clear. Most of them drowned.'

'Was it awful?'

'Very.'

'I could hear screaming from inside the block.'

She fell silent, and stared out across the vast blue-green expanse of the North Sea.

'So Paul was telling the truth after all?' she said at length. 'About the flare?'

'So it would seem.'

'Which makes it wrong of me to try to shoot him.'

'You gave him a choice. Put in his shoes, I'd like to think I'd do the same thing.'

'But not in mine.'

'Stop blaming yourself, Sophie. If he'd been captured alive he'd hang.'

'Even though he helped us?'

'There was Hopton before that. Other places too.'

She turned away now. 'I'd like to leave here today. Can you arrange it?'

'I'll speak to Morley.'

'So he's alive,' she said, without obvious pleasure. 'What with everything else I'd forgotten about him.'

'You and me both. Actually he was raving about putting you up for a gong.'

'The transfer will do fine.'

Again Goodman looked towards the scattered wreckage three-quarters of a mile further along the beach. A figure was busy trophying the swastika flag.

'None of this ever happened, you know.'

Sophie sighed heavily. 'What wouldn't I give for that to be true.'

FIFTY-SIX

The quayside had been cleared by a squad of field police a full hour before the battered grey S-boat put in. Of the dozen or so Waffen SS men who filed up the gangplank and shuffled towards the waiting ambulances, none had escaped injury. Most had suffered wounds from bullets and shrapnel, or were burned, or blackened and choked with oil. One man, wrapped in coarse blankets, was shaking uncontrollably, his teeth chattering loudly like the keys of a typewriter. The head of another, who walked only with the support of two naval ratings, was swathed completely in dressings, as if in some ghoulish parody of the invisible man.

None of the survivors troubled to salute Schellenberg and Eichner, who watched from a respectable distance. The expression on the faces of both the SD men betrayed a mixture of pity and disbelief.

Otto Bartels was last ashore, behind a stretcher on which a corpse lay beneath a blanket. In his borrowed oilskin trousers and dufflecoat, his face caked in blood and filth, neither of them recognised Bartels for several moments.

Eichner was first to step forward. 'Welcome home, hauptsturmfuhrer,' he offered awkwardly.

Bartels gestured at the stretcher, his eyes darting back and forth with alarming speed. 'That man might still be alive if we'd put in at Flushing.'

The angry swell in his voice left Schellenberg glad that Bartels had lost his weapon. 'I agree. But then news of this regrettable set-back would already have reached Berlin.'

'We were caught like fish in a frying pan.'

'I'm sorry, Bartels. Truly I am.'

'I swear, before I die I'll have that bastard Wagner's balls on the end of a shovel.'

'Oh, I think we can do better than that.'

In a single movement, Schellenberg freed his automatic from the holster on his belt and shot Eichner through the temple. The SD captain pirouetted violent around, and fell heavily to the ground. All activity on the quay ceased abruptly, as soldiers, sailors, orderlies and military police turning to gape as one.

Bartels looked down at Eichner's still body, then back to his executioner. 'He betrayed us too?'

'After a fashion. And he allowed a certain little Jewess to escape from custody.'

Despite his state of advanced exhaustion, Bartels knew full well that Schellenberg was lying through his teeth. But he knew better than to speak his mind. Even now, it was possible that the ambulances would convey his men not to a hospital, but to a forest and a firing squad. Moreover Schellenberg had not yet sheathed his pistol.

Saluting smartly, Bartels stepped over Eichner's still body, and walked quickly away.